DESCENT INTO HORROR!

The spider rushed at him across the shadowed sands, scrabbling wildly on its stalklike legs. Its body was a giant, glossy egg that trembled blackly as it charged across the windless mounds, its wake a score of sand-trickling scratches . . . the spider was gaining on him, its pulsing egg of a body perched on running legs—an egg whose yolk swam with killing poisons.

He raced on, breathless, terror in his veins. . . .

"The author who influenced me the most as a writer was Richard Matheson."

—STEPHEN KING

**Books by Richard Matheson
from Tom Doherty Associates**

The
Incredible
Shrinking Man
• •

Richard Matheson

TOR®

A TOM DOHERTY ASSOCIATES BOOK
NEW YORK

THE INCREDIBLE SHRINKING MAN

Copyright © 1994 by RXR, Inc.

A Tor Book
Published by Tom Doherty Associates, LLC
175 Fifth Avenue
New York, NY 10010

www.tor-forge.com

Tor® is a registered trademark of Tom Doherty Associates, LLC.

ISBN-13: 978-0-7653-6116-5
ISBN-10: 0-7653-6116-7

First Tor Edition: April 1995
Second Tor Edition: May 2008

Printed in the United States of America

0 9 8 7 6 5 4 3 2 1

Contents
• • • • • • • • • • •

The Incredible Shrinking Man

● ● ● ● ● ● ● ● ● ● ● ● ● ●

CHAPTER ONE

●●●●●●●●●●

First he thought it was a tidal wave. Then he saw that the sky and ocean were visible through it and it was a curtain of spray rushing at the boat.

He'd been sunbathing on top of the cabin. It was just coincidence that he pushed up on his elbow and saw it coming.

"Marty!" he yelled. There was no answer. He scuttled across the hot wood and slid down the deck. "Hey, Marty!"

The spray didn't look menacing, but for some reason he wanted to avoid it. He ran around the cabin, wincing at the hot planks underfoot. It would be a race.

Which he lost. One moment he was in sunlight. The next he was being soaked by the warm, glittering spray.

Then it was past. He stood there watching it sweep across the water, sun-glowing drops of it covering him. Suddenly he twitched and looked down. There was a curious tingling on his skin.

He grabbed for a towel and dried himself. It wasn't so much pain as a pleasant stinging, like that of lotion on newly shaven cheeks.

Then he was dry and the feeling was almost gone. He went below and woke up his brother and told him about the curtain of spray that had run across the boat.

It was the beginning.

CHAPTER
TWO

• • • • • • • • • •

The spider rushed at him across the shadowed sands, scrabbling wildly on its stalklike legs. Its body was a giant, glossy egg that trembled blackly as it charged across the windless mounds, its wake a score of sand-trickling scratches.

Paralysis locked the man. He saw the poisonous glitter of the spider eyes. He watched it scramble across a loglike stick, body mounted high on its motion-blurred legs, as high as the man's shoulders.

Behind him, suddenly, the steel-encased flame flared into life with a thunder that shook the air. It jarred the man loose. With a sucking gasp, he spun around and ran, the damp sand crunching beneath his racing sandals.

He fled through lakes of light and into darkness again, his face a mask of terror. Beams of sunlight speared across his panic-driven path, cold shadows enveloped it. Behind, the giant spider scoured sand in its pursuit.

Suddenly the man slipped. A cry tore back his lips. He skidded to a knee, then pitched forward onto outstretched palms. He felt the cold sands shaking with the vibration of the roaring flame. He pushed himself up desperately, palms flaking sand, and started running again.

Fleeing, he glanced back across his shoulder and saw that the spider was gaining on him, its pulsing egg of a body perched on running legs—an egg whose yolk swam with killing poisons. He raced on, breathless, terror in his veins.

Suddenly the cliff edge was before him, shearing off abruptly to a gray, perpendicular face. He raced along the edge, not looking down into the vast canyon below. The giant spider scuttled after him, the sound of its running a delicate scraping on the stone. It was closer still.

The man dashed between two giant cans that loomed like tanks above him. He threaded, racing, in between the silent bulks of all the clustered cans, past green and red and yellow sides all caked with livid smears. The spider had to climb above them, unable to move its swollen body rapidly enough between them. It slithered up the side of one, then sped across their metal tops, bridging the gaps between them with sudden, jerking hops.

As the man started out into the open again, he heard a scratching sound above. Recoiling and jerking back his head, he saw the spider just about to leap on him, two legs slipping down a metal side, the rest clutching at the top.

With a terrified gasp, the man dived again into the space between the giant cans, half running, half stumbling back along the winding route. Behind him, the spider drew itself back up to the top and, backing around in a twitching semicircle, started after him again.

The move gained seconds for the man, lunging out into the shadow-swept sands again, he raced around the great stone pillar and through another stack of tanlike structures. The spider leaped down on the sand and scurried in pursuit.

The great orange mass loomed over the man now as he headed once more for the edge of the cliff. There was no time for hesitation. With an extra springing of his legs, he flung himself across the gulf and clutched with spastic fingers at the roughened ledge.

Wincing, he drew himself onto the splintered orange surface just as the spider reached the cliff's edge. Jumping up, the man began running along the narrow ledge, not looking back. If the spider jumped that gap, it was over.

The spider did not jump it. Glancing back, the man saw that and, stopping, stood there looking at the spider. Was he safe now that he was out of the spider's territory?

His pale cheek twitched as he saw thread-twined cable pour like shimmering vapor from the spider's tubes.

Twisting around, he began running again, knowing that, as

soon as the cable was long enough, air currents would lift it, it would cling to the orange ledge, and the black spider would clamber up it.

He tried to run faster, but he couldn't. His legs ached, breath was a hot burning in his throat, a stitch drove dagger points into his side. He ran and skidded down the orange slope, jumping the gaps with desperate, weakening lunges.

Another edge. The man knelt quickly, tremblingly, and, holding tight, let himself over. It was a long drop to the next level. The man waited until his body was swinging inward, then let go. Just before he fell, he saw the great spider scrabbling down the orange slope at him.

He landed on his feet and toppled forward on the hard wood. Pain drove needles up his right ankle. He struggled to his feet; he couldn't stop. Overhead, he heard the spider's scratching. Running to the edge, he hesitated, then jumped into space again. The arm-thick curve of the metal wicket flashed up at him. He grabbed for it.

He fell with a fluttering of arms and legs. The canyon floor rushed up at him. He *had* to miss the flower-patched softness.

And yet he didn't. Almost at the edge of it, he landed feet first and bounced over backward in a neck-snapping somersault.

He lay on his stomach and chest, breathing in short, strangled bursts. There was a smell of dusty cloth in his nostrils, and fabric was rough against his cheek.

Alertness returned then and, with a spasmodic wrenching of muscles, the man looked up and saw another ghostlike cable being spun into the air. In a few moments, he knew, the spider would ride it down.

Pushing up with a groan, he stood a moment on trembling legs. The ankle still hurt, breathing was a strain, but there were no broken bones. He started off.

Hobbling quickly across the flower-splotched softness, the man lowered himself across the edge. As he did so, he saw the spider swinging down, a terrible, wriggling pendulum.

He was on the floor of the canyon now. He ran, limping across the wide plain of it, his sandals flopping on the leveled hardness. To his right loomed the vast brown tower in which the flame still burned, the very canyon trembling with its roar.

He glanced behind. The spider was dropping to the flower-covered softness now, then rushing for the edge. The man raced on toward the great log pile, which was half as high as the tower itself. He ran by what looked like a giant, coiled serpent, red and still and open-jawed at either end.

The spider hit the canyon floor and ran at the man.

But the man had reached the gigantic logs now, and, falling forward on his chest, he wriggled into a narrow space between two of them. It was so narrow he could hardly move; dark, damp, cold, and smelling of moldy wood. He crawled and twisted in as far as he could, then stopped and looked back.

The black, shiny-cased spider was trying to follow him.

For a horrible moment, the man thought it was succeeding. Then he saw that it was stuck and had to pull back. It could not follow.

Closing his eyes, the man lay there on the canyon floor, feeling the chill of it through his clothes, panting through his opened mouth, wondering how many more times he would have to flee the spider.

The flame in the steel tower went out then, and there was silence except for the spider's scratching at the rock floor as it moved about restlessly. He could hear it scraping on the logs as it clambered over them, searching for a way to get at him.

When at last the scratching sounds had gone, the man backed himself cautiously out from the narrow, splinter-edged passage between the logs. Out on the floor again, he stood with wary haste and looked in all directions to see where the spider was.

High up on the sheer wall he saw it climbing toward the cliff edge, its dark legs drawing its great egg of a body up the perpendicular face. A shaking breath trickled from the man's nostrils. He was safe for another while. Lowering his gaze, he started toward his sleeping place.

He limped slowly past the silent steel tower, which was an oil burner; past the huge red serpent, which was a nozzleless garden hose clumsily coiled on the floor, past the wide cushion whose case was covered with flower designs; past the immense orange structure, which was a stack of two wooden lawn chairs; past the great croquet mallets hanging in their racks. One of the wickets from the croquet set had been stuck in a groove on the top lawn chair. It was what the man, in his flight, had grabbed for and missed. And the tanklike cans were used paint cans, and the spider was a black widow.

He lived in a cellar.

Now he walked past the towering clothes tree toward his sleeping place, which was underneath a water heater. Just before he reached it, he twitched sharply as, in its concrete cave, the water pump lurched into spinning motion. He listened to its labored wheezing and sighing, which sounded like the breathing of a dying dragon.

Then he clambered up the cement block on which the looming, enamel-faced heater rested and crawled under its protective warmth.

For a long time, motionless, he lay on his bed, which was a rectangular sponge around which a torn handkerchief was wrapped. His chest rose and fell with shallow movements, his hands lay limp and curled at his sides. Without blinking, he stared up at the rust-caked bottom of the heater.

The last week.

Three words and a concept. A concept that had begun in a flash of incomprehensive shock and become the intensely intimate moment-by-moment horror it now was. The last week. No, not even that now, because Monday was already half over. His eyes strayed briefly to the row of charcoal strokes on the wood scrap that was his calendar. Monday, March the tenth.

In six days he would be gone.

Across the vast reaches of the cellar, the oil-burner flame roared up again, and he felt the bed vibrate under him. That meant the temperature had fallen in the house above and that the thermostat had kicked a switch and now heat was flowing again through the floor grilles.

He thought of them up there, the woman and the little girl. His wife and daughter. Were they still that to him? Or had the element of size removed him from their sphere? Could he still be considered a part of their world when he was the size of a bug to them, when even Beth could crush him underfoot and never know it?

In six days he would be gone.

He'd thought about it a thousand times in the past year and a half, trying to visualize it. He'd never been able to. Invariably, his mind had rebelled against it, rationalizing: the injections would start to work now, the process would end by itself, *something* would happen. It was impossible that he could ever be so small that . . .

Yet he was; so small that in six days he would be gone.

When it came on him, this cruel despair, he would lie for hours on his makeshift bed, not caring whether he lived or died. The despair had never really gone. How could it? For no matter what adjustment he thought he was making, it was obviously impossible to adjust, because there had never been a tapering or a leveling off. The process had gone on and on, ceaseless.

He twisted on the bed in restless agony. Why did he run from the spider? Why not let it catch him? The thing would be out of his hands then. It would be a hideous death, but it would be quick; despair would be ended. And yet he kept fleeing from it, and improvising and struggling and existing.

Why?

68"

When he told her, the first thing she did was laugh.

It was not a long laugh. Almost instantly it had been choked off and she stood mutely before him, staring. Because he wasn't smiling, because his face was a taut blankness.

"Shrinking?" The word was spoken in a trembling whisper.

"Yes." It was all he could manage to say.

"But that's—"

She'd been about to say that was impossible. But it wasn't impossible, because now that the word had been spoken, it crystallized all the unspoken dread she'd felt since this had begun, a month before; since Scott's first visit to Dr. Branson, when he'd been checked for possible bowing of the legs or dropping of the arches, and the doctor's first diagnosis of loss of weight due to the trip and the new environment and his pushing aside of the possibility that Scott was losing height as well.

The dread had grown through the passing days of tense, frightened suspicion while Scott kept growing shorter; through the second visit to Branson and the third; through the X-rays and the blood tests; through the entire bone survey, the search for signs of bone-mass decrease, the search for a pituitary tumor; through the long days of more X-raying and the grim search for cancer. Through today and this moment.

"But that's impossible."

She had to say it. They were the only words her mind and lips would form.

He shook his head slowly, dazedly.

"It's what he said," he answered. "He said my height's decreased more than half an inch in the last four days." He swallowed. "But it's not just my height I'm losing. Every part of me seems to be shrinking. Proportionately."

"No." There was adamant refusal in her voice. It was the only reaction she could make to such an idea. "That's *all*?" she asked, almost angrily. "That's all he can *say*?"

"Honey, it's what's *happening*," he said. "He showed me X rays—the ones he took four days ago and the ones he took today. It's true. I'm shrinking." He spoke as though he'd been kicked violently in the stomach, half dazed, half breathless with shock.

"No." This time she sounded more frightened then resolute. "We'll go to a specialist," she said.

"He wants me to," Scott said. "He said I should go to the Columbia Presbyterian Medical Center in New York. But—"

"Then you will," she said before he could go on.

"Honey, the *cost*," he said painfully. "We already owe—"

"What has that got to do with it? Do you think for one moment—"

A nervous tremor broke her words off. She stood trembling, arms crossed, her hands clutched at her loose-fleshed upper arms. It was the first time since it had started that she'd let him see how afraid she was.

"Lou." He put his arms around her. "It's all right, honey, it's all right."

"It isn't. You have to go to that center. You *have* to."

"All right, all right," he murmured. "I will."

"What did he say they'd do?" she asked, and he could hear the desperate need for hope in her voice.

"He . . ." He licked his lips, trying to remember. "Oh, he said they'd check my endocrine glands; my thyroid, pituitary—my sex glands. He said they'd give me a basal metabolism. Some other tests."

Her lips pressed in.

"If he knows that," she said, "why did he have to say what he did about—about shrinking? That's not good doctoring. It's thoughtless."

"Honey, I asked him," he said. "I established it when I started all the tests. I told him I didn't want any secrets. What else could he—"

"All *right*," she broke in. "But did he have to call it . . . what he did?"

"That's what it *is*, Lou," he said in anguish. "There's evidence for it. Those X rays . . ."

"He could be wrong, Scott," she said. "He's not infallible."

He didn't say anything for a long moment. Then quietly, he said, "Look at me."

When it had begun, he was a six-footer. Now he looked straight across into his wife's eyes; and his wife was five feet, eight inches tall.

Hopelessly he dropped the fork on his plate.

"How can we?" he asked. "The cost Lou, the *cost*. It'll take at least a month's hospitalization; Branson said so. A month away from work. Marty's already upset as it is. How can I expect him to go on paying me my salary when I don't even—"

"Honey, your health comes first," she said in a nerve-flaring voice. "Marty knows that. *You* know it."

He lowered his head, teeth clenched behind drawn lips. Every bill was a chain that weighed him down. He could almost feel the heavy links forged around his limbs.

"And what do we—" he began, stopping as he noticed Beth staring at him, her supper forgotten.

"Eat your food," Lou told her. Beth started a little, then dug her fork into a mound of gravy-topped potatoes.

"How do we pay for it?" Scott asked. "There's no medical insurance. I owe Marty five hundred dollars for the tests I've already taken." He exhaled heavily. "And the GI loan may not even go through."

"You're going," she said.

"Easily said," he answered.

"All right, what would you rather do?" she snapped with the temper of fear in her voice. "Forget it? Accept what the doctor said? Just sit back and—" A sob swallowed her words.

The hand he put over hers was not a comforting one. It was as cold and almost as shaky as hers.

"All right," he murmured. "All right, Lou."

Later, while she was putting Beth to bed, he stood in the darkened living room watching the cars drive by on the street below. Except for the murmuring voices in the back bedroom, there was no sound in the apartment. The cars swished and hummed past the building, their headlights probing ahead at the dark pavement.

He was thinking about his application for life insurance. It had been part of the plan in coming East. First working for his brother, then applying for a GI loan with the idea of becoming a partner in Marty's business. Acquiring life and medical insurance, a bank account, a decent car, clothes, eventually a house. Building a structure of security around himself and his family.

Now this, disrupting the plan. Threatening to destroy it altogether.

He didn't know at what precise second the question came to him. But suddenly it was terribly there and he was staring fixedly at his upheld, spread-fingered hands, his heart throbbing and swollen in an icy trap.

How long could he go on shrinking?

CHAPTER THREE

•••••••••••

Finding water to drink was not a problem for him. The tank near the electric pump had a minute leak on its bottom surface. Beneath its dripping he placed a thimble he had carried once from a sewing box in a cardboard carton underneath the fuel-oil tank. The thimble was always overflowing with crystal well water.

It was food that was the problem now. The quarter loaf of stale bread he'd been eating for the past five weeks was gone now. He'd finished the last crunchy scraps of it for his evening meal, washed it down with water. Bread and cold water had been his diet since he'd been imprisoned in the cellar.

He walked slowly across the darkening floor, moving toward the white, cobwebbed tower that stood near the steps leading up to the closed cellar doors. The last of the daylight filtered through the grime-streaked windows—the one that overlooked the sand hills of the spider's territory, the one over the fuel tank, and the one over the log pile. The pale illumination fell in wide gray bars across the concrete floor, forming a patchwork of light and darkness through which he walked. In a little while the cellar would be a cold pit of night.

He had mused for many hours on the possibility of somehow managing to reach the string that dangled over the floor and pulling down on it so the dust-specked bulb would light, driving away the terror of blackness. But there was no way of reaching the string. It hung, for him, a hundred feet above his head, completely unattainable.

Scott Carey walked around the dull white vastness of the refrigerator. It had been stored there since they'd first moved to the house—was it only months before? It seemed a century.

It was the old-fashioned type of refrigerator, one whose coils were encased in a cylindrical enclosure on its top. There was an open box of crackers beside that cylinder. As far as he knew, it was the only food remaining in the entire cellar.

He'd known the cracker box was on the refrigerator even before he'd become trapped down there. He'd left it there for himself one afternoon long before. No, not so long before, as time went. But, somehow, days seemed longer now. It was as if hours were designed for normal people. For anyone smaller, the hours were proportionately magnified.

It was an illusion, of course, but, in his tininess, he was plagued by manifold illusions; the illusion that he was not shrinking, but the world enlarging; the illusion that objects were what they were thought to be only when the person who thought of them was of normal size.

For him—he couldn't help it—the oil burner had virtually lost its role of heating apparatus. It was, almost actually, a giant tower in whose bowels there roared a magic flame. And the hose was, almost actually, a quiescent viper, sleeping in giant, scarlet coils. The three-quarter wall beside the burner *was* a cliff face, the sands a terrible desert across whose hills crawled not a spider the size of a man's thumbnail, but a venomous monster almost as tall as he was.

Reality was relative. He was more forcefully aware of it with every passing day. In six days reality would be blotted out for him—not by death, but a hideously simple act of disappearance.

For what reality could there be at zero inches?

Yet he went on. Here he was scanning the sheer face of the refrigerator, wondering how he might get up there and reach the crackers.

A sudden roar made him jump and spin around, his heart thudding.

It was only the oil burner leaping into life again, the rumble of its mechanism making the floor beneath him tremble, sending numbing vibrations up his legs. He swallowed with effort. It was a jungle life he led, each sound a warning of potential death.

It was getting too dark. The cellar was a frightening place when it was dark. He hurried across the chilled expanse of it, shivering under the tentlike robe he had made by poking a head hole in a piece of cloth, then ripping the edges into dangling strips and tying them into knots. The clothes he had been wearing when he had first tumbled into the cellar now lay in dirty heaps beside the water heater. He had worn them as long as he could, rolling up sleeves and cuffs, tightening the waistband, keeping them on until their sagging volume hampered movement. Then he had made the robe. He was always cold now except when he was under the water heater.

He broke into a nervous, hopping walk, suddenly anxious to be off the darkening floor. His gaze flew for a moment to the cliff edge high above and he twitched again, thinking he saw the spider clambering over. He'd started to run before he saw that it was only a shadow. His run slowed again to the erratic, jerky walk. Adjust? he thought. Who could adjust to this?

When he was back under the heater, he dragged a box top over his bed and lay down to rest underneath its shelter.

He was still shivering. He could smell the dry, acrid odor of the cardboard close to his face, and it seemed as if he were being smothered. It was another illusion he suffered nightly.

He struggled to attain sleep. He'd worry about the crackers tomorrow, when it was light. Or maybe he would not worry about them at all. Maybe he'd just lie there and let hunger and thirst finish what he could not finish, despite all dismays.

Nonsense! he thought furiously. If he hadn't done it before this, it wasn't likely that he could do it now.

64″

Louise guided the blue Ford around the wide, graded arc that led from Queens Boulevard to the Cross Island Parkway. There was no sound but the valve-knocking rumble of the motor. Idle conversation had faded off a quarter-mile after they'd emerged from the Midtown Tunnel. Scott had even jabbed in the shiny radio button and cut off the quiet music. Now he sat staring glumly through the windshield, vision glazed to all but thought.

The tension had begun long before Louise came to the Center to get him.

He'd been building himself up to it ever since he'd told the doctors that he was leaving. For that matter, the blocks of anger had been piling up from the moment he'd entered the Center. Dread of the financial burden had constructed the first one, a block whose core was the dragging weight of further insecurity. Each nerve-spent, fruitless day at the Center had added more blocks.

Then to have Louise not only angrily upset at his decision, but unable to hide her shock at seeing him four inches shorter than herself—it had been too much. He'd scarcely spoken from the moment she'd entered his room, and what he had said had been quiet, withdrawn, each sentence shackled by reserve.

Now they were driving past the understated richness of the Jamaica estates. Scott hardly noticed them. He was thinking about the impossible future.

"What?" he asked, starting a little.

"I said, did you have breakfast?"

"Oh. Yes. About eight, I guess."

"Are you hungry? Shall I stop?"

"No."

He glanced at her, at the tense indecision apparent on her face.

"Well, *say* it," he said. "Say it, for God's sake, and get it off your chest."

He saw the smooth flesh on her throat contract in a swallow.

"What is there to say?" she asked.

"That's right." He nodded in short, jerky movements. "That's right, make it sound like my fault. I'm an idiot who doesn't want to know what's wrong with himself. I'm—"

He was finished before he could get started. The undertow of nagging, unspoken dread in him swallowed all attempts at concentrated rage. Temper could come only in sporadic bursts to a man living with consistent horror.

"You know how I feel, Scott," she said.

"Sure I know how you feel," he said. "You don't have to pay the bills, though."

"I told you I'd be more than willing to work."

"There's no use arguing about it," he said. "Your working wouldn't help any. We'd still go under." He blew out a tired breath. "What's the difference anyway? They didn't find a thing."

"Scott, that doctor said it might take *months*! You didn't even let them finish their tests. How can you—"

"What do they think I'm going to do?" he burst out. "Go on letting them *play* with me? Oh, you haven't *been* there, you haven't *seen*. They're like kids with a new toy! A shrinking man, Godawmighty, a shrinking man! It makes their damn eyes light up. All they're interested in is my 'incredible catabolism.' "

"What difference does it make?" she asked. "They're still some of the best doctors in the country."

"And some of the most expensive," he countered. "If they're so damned fascinated, why didn't they offer to give me the tests free? I even asked one of them about it. You'd've thought I was insulting his mother's virtue."

She didn't say anything. Her chest rose and fell with disturbed breath.

"I'm tired of being tested," he went on, not wanting to sink into the comfortless isolation of silence again. "I'm tired of basal-metabolism tests and protein-bound tests; tired of drink-

ing radioactive iodine and barium-powdered water; tired of X
rays and blood cultures and Geiger counters on my throat and
having my temperature taken a million times a day. You
haven't been through it; you don't know. It's like a—an in-
quisition. And what the hell's the point? They haven't found
a thing. Not a *thing*! *And* they never will. And I can't see ow-
ing them thousands of dollars for nothing!"

He fell back against the seat and closed his eyes. Fury was
unsatisfying when it was leveled against an undeserving subject. But it would not disappear for all that. It burned like a
flame inside him.

"They weren't finished, Scott."

"The bills don't matter to you," he said.

"*You* matter to me," she answered.

"And who's the 'security' bug in this marriage, anyway?"
he asked.

"That's not fair."

"Isn't it? What brought us here from California in the first
place? Me? Because I decided I just had to go into business
with Marty? I was happy out there. I didn't—" He drew in a
shaking breath and let it empty from his lungs. "Forget it," he
said. "I'm sorry, I apologize. But I'm not going back."

"You're angry and hurt, Scott. That's why you won't go
back."

"I won't go back because it's pointless!" he shouted.

They drove in silence for a few minutes. Then she said,
"Scott, do you really believe I'd hold my own security above
your health?"

He didn't answer.

"*Do* you?"

"Why talk about it?" he said.

The next morning, Saturday, he received the sheaf of application papers from the life-insurance company and tore them
into pieces and threw the pieces into the wastebasket. Then
he went for a long, miserable walk. And while he was out he
thought about God creating heaven and earth in seven days.

He was shrinking a seventh of an inch a day.

* * *

It was quiet in the cellar. The oil burner had just shut itself off, the clanking wheeze of the water pump had been silenced for an hour. He lay under the cardboard box top listening to the silence, exhausted but unable to rest. An animal life without an animal mind did not induce the heavy, effortless sleep of an animal.

The spider came about eleven o'clock.

He didn't know it was eleven, but there was still the heavy thudding of footsteps overhead, and he knew Lou was usually in bed by midnight.

He listened to the sluggish rasping of the spider across the box top, down one side, up another, searching with terrible patience for an opening.

Black widow. Men called it that because the female destroyed and ate the male, if she got the chance, after one mating act.

Black widow. Shiny black, with the constricted rectangle of scarlet on its egg-shaped abdomen; what was called its "hourglass." A creature with a highly developed nervous system, possessing memory. A creature whose poison was twelve times as deadly as a rattlesnake's.

The black widow clambered over the box top under which he was hiding and the spider was almost as big as he. In a few days it *would* be as big; then, in another few days, bigger. The thought made him sick. How could he escape it then?

I have to get out of here! he thought desperately.

His eyes fell shut, his muscles clamping slowly in admission of his helplessness. He'd been trying to get out of the cellar for five weeks now. What chance had he now, when he was one sixth the size he'd been when he had first been trapped there?

The scratching came again, this time *under* the cardboard.

There was a slight tear in one side of the box top; enough to admit one of the spider's seven legs.

He lay there shuddering, listening to the spiny leg scratching at the cement like a razor on sandpaper. It never came closer than five inches from the bed, but it gave him nightmares. He clamped his eyes shut.

"Get out of here!" he screamed. "Get out of here, get *out* of here!"

His voice rang shrilly underneath the cardboard enclosure. It made his eardrums hurt. He lay there trembling violently while the spider scratched and jumped and clambered insanely around the box top, trying to get in.

Twisting around, he buried his face in the rough wrinkles of the handkerchief covering the sponge. If I could only kill it! his mind screamed in anguish. At least his last days would be peaceful then.

About an hour later, the scratching stopped and the spider went away. Once more he became conscious of his sweat-dewed flesh, the coldness and the twitching of his fingers. He lay drawing in convulsive breaths through his parted lips, weak from the rigid struggle against horror.

Kill him? The thought turned his blood to ice.

A little while later he sank into a troubled, mumbling sleep, and his night was filled with the torment of awful dreams.

CHAPTER FOUR

• • • • • • • • • •

His eyes fluttered open.

Instinct alone told him that the night was over. Beneath the box it was still dark. With an indrawn groan in his chest, he pushed up from the sponge bed and stood gingerly until he shouldered the cardboard surface. Then he edged to one corner and, pushing up hard, slid the box top away from his bed.

Out in the other world, it was raining. Gray light sifted through the erratic dripping across the panes, converting the shadows into slanting wavers and the patches of light into quiverings of pallid gelatine.

The first thing he did was climb down the cement block and walk over to the wooden ruler. It was the first thing he did every morning. The ruler stood against the wheels of the huge yellow lawnmover, where he'd put it.

He pressed himself against its calibrated surface and laid his right hand on top of his head. Then, leaving the hand there, he stepped back and looked.

Rulers were not divided into sevenths; he had added the markings himself. The heel of his hand obscured the line that told him he was five-sevenths of an inch tall.

The hand fell, slapping at his side. Why, what did you expect? his mind inquired. He made no reply. He just wondered why he tortured himself like this every day, persisting in this clinical masochism. Surely he didn't think that it was going to stop now; that the injections would begin working at this last point. Why, then? Was it part of his previous resolution to follow the descent to its very end? If so, it was pointless now. No one else would know of it.

He walked slowly across the cold cement. Except for the faint tapping, swishing sound of rain on the windows, it was quiet in the cellar. Somewhere far off there was a hollow drumming sound; probably the rain on the cellar doors. He walked on, his gaze moving automatically to the cliff edge, searching for the spider. It was not there.

He trudged under the jutting feet of the clothes tree and to the twelve-inch step to the floor of the vast, dark cave in which the tank and water pump were. Twelve inches, he thought, lowering himself slowly down the string ladder he'd made and fastened to the brick that stood at the top of the step. Twelve inches, and yet to him it was the equivalent of 150 feet to a normally sized man.

He let himself down the ladder carefully, his knuckles banging and scraping against the rough concrete. He should have thought of a way to keep the ladder from pressing directly against the wall. Well, it was too late for that now; he was too small. As it was, he could, even with painful stretching, barely reach the sagging rung below, the one below that . . . the one below that.

Grimacing, he splashed icy water into his face. He could just about reach the top of the thimble. In two days he would be unable to reach the top of it, probably unable, even, to get down the string ladder. What would he do then?

Trying not to think of ever-mounting problems, he drank palmfuls of the cold well water; drank until his teeth ached. Then he dried his face and hands on the robe and turned back to the ladder.

He had to stop and rest halfway up the ladder. He hung there, arms hooked over the rung, which to him was the thickness of rope.

What if the spider were to appear at the top of the ladder now? What if it were to come clambering down the ladder at him?

He shuddered. Stop it, he begged his mind. It was bad enough when he actually had to protect himself from the spider without filling the rest of the time with cruel imaginings.

He swallowed again, fearfully. It was true. His throat hurt.

"Oh, God," he muttered. It was all he needed.

He climbed up the rest of the way in grim silence, then started on the quarter-mile journey to the refrigerator. Around the hulking coils of the hose, by the tree-thick rake handle, the house-high lawn-mower wheels, the wicker table that was half as high as the refrigerator, which was, in turn, as high as a ten-story building. Already hunger was beginning to send out lines of tension in his stomach.

He stood, head pulled back, looking up at the refrigerator. If there had been clouds floating by its cylinder top, its mountain-peak remoteness could not have been more graphically apparent to him.

His gaze dropped. He started to sigh, but the sigh was cut off by a twitching grunt. The oil burner again, shaking the floor. He could never get used to it. It had no regular pattern of roaring ignition. What was worse, it seemed to be growing louder every day.

For what seemed a long time he stood indecisively, staring at the white piano legs of the refrigerator. Then he stirred himself loose from bleak apathy and drew in a quick breath. There was no point in standing there. Either he got to those crackers or he starved.

He circled the end of the wicker table, planning.

Like a mountain peak, the top of the refrigerator was attainable by numerous routes, none of them easy. He might try to scale the ladder, which, like the lawn mower, lay against the fuel-oil tank. Reaching the top of the tank (an Everest of achievement in itself), he could move to the huge cardboard boxes piled beside it, then across the wide leather face of Louise's suitcase, then up the hanging rope to the refrigerator top. Or he could try climbing the red cross-legged table, then jump across to the cartons, move across the suitcase again, and up the rope. Or he could try the wicker table which was right next to the refrigerator, achieve its summit, then climb the long perilous length of the hanging rope.

He turned away from the refrigerator and looked across the cellar at the cliff wall, the croquet set, the stacked lawn chairs, the gaudily striped beach umbrella, the olive-colored folding canvas stools. He stared at all of them with hopeless eyes.

Was there no other way? Was there nothing to eat but those crackers?

His gaze moved slowly along the cliff edge. There was the one dry slice of bread remaining up there; but he knew he couldn't go after it. Dread of the spider was too strong in him. Even hunger couldn't drive him up that cliff again.

He thought suddenly, Were spiders edible? It made his stomach rumble. He forced the thought out of his mind and turned again to face the immediate problem.

He couldn't manage the climb unaided, and that was the first hurdle.

He walked across the floor, feeling the chill of it through his almost worn sandals. Under the shadows of the fuel tank, he climbed between the ragged edges of the split carton side. What if the spider is in there waiting? he thought. He stopped, heartbeat jolting, one leg inside the box, the other leg out. He drew in a deep, courage-stiffening breath. It's only a spider, he told himself. It's not a master tactician.

Climbing the rest of the way into the musty depth of the carton, he wished he could really believe that the spider was not intelligent, but driven only by instinct.

Reaching for thread, his hand touched icy metal and jerked back. He reached again. It was only a pin. His lips twitched. Only a pin? It was the size of a knight's lance.

He found the thread and laboriously unrolled about eight inches of it. It took an entire minute of pulling, jerking, and teeth gnawing to separate it from its barrel-sized spool.

He dragged the thread out of the carton and back to the wicker table. Then he hiked over to the pile of logs and tore from one of them a piece the size of his arm from elbow to fingertips. This he carried back to the table and fastened to the thread.

He was ready.

The first throw was an easy one. Twisting vinelike around the main leg of the table were two narrower strips about the thickness of his body. At a point three inches below the first shelf of the table these two strips flared out from the leg, angling up to the shelf, then turning again and, three inches above the shelf, twining about the main leg again.

He flung the wood up at the space where one of the strips began jutting out from the leg. On his third attempt the wood sailed through the opening and he pulled it back carefully so that it was wedged between leg and strip. He then climbed up, feet braced on the leg as he ascended, body swung out at the end of the tautened thread.

Reaching the first point, he hauled up the thread, worked the wooden bar loose, and prepared for the next stage of his climb.

Another four throws and the wooden bar caught between two strips of latticework shelf. He pulled himself up.

Stretched out limply on the shelf, he lay there panting.

Then, after a few minutes, he sat up and looked down at what to him was a fifty-foot drop. Already he was tired, and the climb had barely started.

Far across the cellar the pump began its sibilant chugging again, and he listened to it while he looked up at the wide canopy of the tabletop a hundred feet above.

"Come on," he muttered hoarsely to himself then. "Come on, come on, come on, come on."

He got to his feet. Taking a deep breath, he flung the stick up at the next joining place of leg and twining strip.

He had to leap aside as the throw missed and the wood fell toward him heavily. His right leg slipped into a gap in the latticework and he had to clutch at the crosspieces to keep from plunging to the floor below.

He hung there for a long moment, one leg dangling in space. Then, groaning, he pulled and pushed himself to a standing position, wincing at the pain in the back muscles of his right leg. He must have sprained it, he thought. He clenched his teeth and hissed out a long breath. Sore throat, sprained leg, hunger, weariness. What next?

It took twelve muscle-jerking throws of the wooden bar to get it into the proper opening above. Pulling back until the thread grew taut in his grip, he dragged himself up the thirty-five foot space, teeth gritted, breath steaming out between them. He ignored each burning ache of muscle while he climbed; but when he reached the crotch, he wedged himself between the table leg and strip and half lay, half clung there, gasping for air, muscles throbbing visibly. I'll have to rest, he told himself. Can't go on. The cellar swam before his eyes.

He had gone to visit his mother the week he was five-feet-three. The last time he'd seen her, he'd been six feet tall.

Dread crawled in him, colder than the winter wind, as he walked up the Brooklyn street toward the two-family brownstone where his mother lived. Two boys were playing ball in the street. One of them missed the other's throw. The ball bounced toward Scott, and he reached down to pick it up.

The boy shouted, "Throw it here, kid!"

Something like an electric shock jolted through his system. He flung the ball violently.

The boy shouted, "Good throw, kid!"

He walked on, ashen-faced.

And the terrible hour with his mother. He remembered that.

The way she kept avoiding the obvious, talking about Marty and Therese and their son, Billy; about Louise and Beth, about the quietly enjoyable life she was able to live on Marty's monthly checks.

She had set the table in her impeccable way, each dish and cup in its proper place, each cookie and cake arranged symmetrically. He sat down with her, feeling hollowly sick, the coffee scorching his throat, the cookies tasteless in his mouth.

Then, finally, when it was too late, she had spoken of it. This thing, she said—he was being treated for it?

He knew exactly what it was she wanted to hear and he mentioned the Center and the tests. Relief pressed out the extra worry lines in the rose-petal skin of her face. Good, she said, good. The doctors would cure him. The doctors knew everything these days; everything.

And that was all.

As he went home, he felt dazedly ill, because of all the reactions she might have shown to his affliction, the one she had shown was the last one in the world he could have imagined.

Then, when he got home, Louise cornered him in the kitchen, insisting that he go back to the Center to finish the tests. She'd work, they'd put Beth in a nursery. It would work out fine. Her voice was firm in the beginning, obdurate; then it broke and all the withheld terror and unhappiness flooded from her.

He stood by her side, arm around her back, wanting to comfort her but able only to look up at her face and struggle futilely against the depleted feeling he had at being so much shorter than she. All right, he'd told her, all right, I'll go back. I will. Don't cry.

And the next morning the letter arrived from the Center, telling him that "because of the unusual nature of your disorder, the investigation of which might prove of inestimable value to medical knowledge," the doctors were willing to continue the tests free of charge.

And the return to the Center; he remembered that. And the discovery.

Scott blinked his eyes into focus.

Sighing, he pushed himself to a standing position, one supporting hand holding onto the table leg.

From that point on, the two twining strips left the leg entirely and flared up at opposing angles, paralleled by bolstering spars until they reached the bottom side of the tabletop. Along each upward sweep, three vertical rods were spaced like giant banisters. He would not need the thread any more.

He started up the seventy-degree incline, first lurching at the vertical rod and, catching hold of it, pulled himself up to it, sandals slipping and squeaking along the spar. Then he lunged up at the next spar and pulled himself to it. By concentrating on the strenuous effort he was able to blank away all thoughts and sink into a mechanical apathy for many minutes, only the gnawing of hunger tending to remind him of his plight.

At last, puffing, breath scratching hotly at his throat, he reached the end of the incline and sat there wedged between the spar and the last vertical rod, staring at the wide overhang of the tabletop.

His face tightened.

"No." The mutter was crusty, dry sound as his pain-smitten eyes looked around. There was a three-foot jump to the bottom edge of the tabletop. But there was no handhold there.

"No!"

Had he come all this way for nothing? He couldn't believe it, wouldn't let himself believe it. His eyes fell shut. I'll push myself off, he thought. I'll let myself fall to the floor. This is too much.

He opened his eyes again, the small bones under his cheeks moving as he ground his teeth together. He wasn't going to push himself off anything. If he fell, it would be in jumping for the edge of the tabletop. He wasn't going down on his own volition under any circumstances.

He clambered along the top of the horizontal spar just below the tabletop, searching. There had to be a way. There *had* to be.

Turning the corner of the spar, he saw it.

Running along the under edge of the tabletop was a strip of wood about double the thickness of his arm. It was fastened to the tabletop with nails a trifle shorter than he was.

Two of these nails had pulled out, and at that point the strip sagged about a quarter of an inch below the tabletop edge. A quarter of an inch—almost three feet to him. If he could jump to that gap he could catch hold of the strip and have a chance to pull himself up to the top of the table.

He perched there, breathing deeply, staring at the sagging strip and at the space he'd have to jump. It was at least four feet to him. Four feet of empty space.

He licked his dry lips. Outside, the rain was falling harder; he heard its heavy splattering at the windowpanes. Swirls of graying light swam on his face. He looked across the quarter-mile that separated him from the window over the log pile. The way the rain water ran twistingly over the glass panes made it appear as if great, hollow eyes were watching him.

He turned away from that. There was no use in standing here. He *had* to eat. Going back down was out of the question. He had to go on.

He braced himself for the leap. It may be now, he thought, strangely unalarmed. This may be the end of my long, fantastic journey.

His lips pressed together. "So be it," he whispered then, and sprang out into space.

His arms banged so hard on the wooden bar that they were almost numbed beyond the ability to hold. I'm falling! his mind screamed. Then his arms wrapped themselves around the wood and he hung there gasping, legs swinging back and forth over the tremendous void.

He dangled there for a long moment, catching his breath, letting feeling return to his arms. Then, carefully, with agonizing slowness, he turned himself around on the bar so that he faced the spar arrangement. That done, he dragged himself up to a sitting position on the bar, holding on overhead for support. He sat there, limbs palsied with exhaustion.

The last step to the tabletop was the hardest.

He'd have to stand up on the smooth, circular top of the bar and, lurching up, throw his arms over the end of the tabletop. As far as he knew, there would be nothing there to hang onto. It would be entirely a matter of pressing his arms and hands so tightly to the surface that friction would hold him there.

Then he'd have to climb over the edge.

For a moment the entire grotesque spectacle of it swept over him forcibly—the insanity of a world where he could be killed trying to climb to the top of a table that any normal man could lift and carry with one hand.

He let it go. Forget it, he ordered himself.

He drew in long breaths until the shaking of his arm and leg muscles slackened. Then slowly he eased himself up to a crouch on the smooth wood, balancing himself by holding onto the bottom edge of the tabletop.

The bottoms of his sandals were too smooth. He couldn't grip the wood well enough. As cold as it was, he'd have to take them off. Gingerly he shook them off one at a time and, after a moment, heard the faint slap as they struck the floor below.

He wavered for a moment, steadied himself, then drew in a long, chest-filling breath. He paused.

Now.

He lunged up into empty air and slapped his arms across the end of the tabletop. A broad vista of huge, piled-up objects met his eyes. Then he began slipping, and he clutched at the wood, digging his nails into it. He kept sliding toward the edge, his body moving into space, dragging him.

"No," he whimpered in a strangled voice.

He managed to lurch forward again, fingertips scraping at the wood surface, arms pressing down tightly, desperately.

He saw the curving metal rod.

He was hanging a quarter of an inch from his fingers. He had to reach it or he'd fall. Leaving one hand down, splinters gouging under its nails, he raised the other hand toward the rod.

Look out!

His raised hand slapped down again and clawed frantically at the wood. He began slipping back again.

With a last, frenzied lunge, he grabbed for the curving rod and his hands clamped over its icy thickness.

He dragged himself, kicking and struggling, over the edge of the tabletop. Then his hands dropped from the metal—which was the hanging handle of a pain can—and he collapsed heavily on his chest and stomach.

He lay there for a long time, unable to move, shaking with the remains of dread and exertion, sucking in lungfuls of the cold air. I made it, he thought. It was all he could think. I made it, I made it!

As exhausted as he was, it gave him a warming pride to think it.

CHAPTER FIVE

• • • • • • • • • •

After a while he got up shakily and looked around.

The tabletop's expanse was littered with massive paint cans, bottles and jars. Scott walked along their mammoth shapes, stepping over the jagged-toothed edge of a saw blade and racing across its icy surface to the tabletop again.

Orange paint. He strode past the luridly streaked can, the top of his head barely as high as the bottom edge of the can's label. He remembered painting the lawn chairs during one of

the many hours he'd spent in the cellar before his last, irrevocable snow-caked plunge into it.

Head back, he gazed up at an orange-spotted brush handle
sticking out of an elephantine jar. One day—not so long
ago—he'd held that handle in his fingers. Now it was ten
times as long as he was; a huge, knife-pointed length of
glossy yellow wood.

There was a loud clicking noise and then the ocean-like
roar of the oil burner filled the air again. His heartbeat raced,
then slowed once more. No, he'd never get used to its thundering suddenness. Well, there'd be only four more days of it,
anyway, he thought.

His feet were getting cold; there was no time to waste. Between the barren hulks of paint cans he walked until he'd
reached the body-thick rope that hung down in twisted loops
from the top of the refrigerator.

A stroke of fortune. He found a crumpled pink rag lying
next to a towering brown bottle of turpentine. Impulsively he
drew part of it around himself, tucked it under his feet, then
sank back into the rest of its wrinkled softness. The cloth
reeked of paint and turpentine, but that didn't matter. The
held-in warmth of his body began surrounding him comfort-
ingly.

Reclining there, he squinted up at the distant refrigerator
top. There was still the equivalent of a seventy-five foot
climb to make, and without footholds except for those he
could manage to find on the rope itself. He would, virtually,
have to pull himself all the way up.

His eyes closed and he lay there for a while, breathing
slowly, his body as relaxed as possible. If the hunger pangs
had not been so severe, he might have gone to sleep. But
hunger was a wavelike pressure at his stomach walls, causing
it to rumble emptily. He wondered if it could possibly be as
empty as it felt.

When he discovered himself beginning to dwell on
thoughts of food—of gravy-dripping roasts and broiled steaks
inundated with brown-edged mushrooms and onions—he

knew it was time to get up. With a last wiggle of his warmed toes, he threw off the smooth covering and stood.

That was when he recognized the cloth.

It was part of Louise's slip, an old one that she'd torn up and thrown into the rag box. He picked up a corner of it and fingered its softness, a strange, yearning pain in his chest and stomach that was not hunger.

"Lou." He whispered it, staring at the cloth that had once rested against her warm, fragrant flesh.

Angrily he flung away the cloth edge, his face a hardened mask. He kicked at it.

Shaken, he turned from the cloth, walked stiffly to the edge of the table, and grabbed hold of the rope. It was too thick to get his hands around; he'd have to use his arms. Luckily, it was hanging in such a way that he could almost crawl up the first section of it.

He pulled down on it as hard as he could to see if it was secure. It gave a trifle, then tautened. He pulled again. There was no further give. That ended any chance of dragging the cracker box off the refrigerator. The box was resting on top of the rope coils up there, and he'd thought it a vague possibility that he might pull it down.

"Well," he said.

And, taking a deep breath, he started climbing again.

He modeled his ascent on the method South Sea natives use in climbing coconut trees—knees high, body arched out, feet gripping at the rope, arms curled around it, fingers clutching. He kept himself moving upward steadily, not looking down.

He gasped and stiffened against the rope spasmodically as it slipped down a few inches—to him, a few feet. Then it stopped and he hung there trembling, the rope swinging back and forth in little arcs.

After a few moments the motion stopped and he began climbing again, this time more cautiously.

Five minutes later he reached the first loop of the hanging rope and eased himself into it. As if it were a swing, he sat there, holding on tightly, leaning back against the refrigerator.

The surface of it was cold, but his robe was thick enough to prevent the coldness from penetrating to his skin.

He looked out across the broad vista of the cellar kingdom in which he lived. Far across—almost a mile away—he saw the cliff edge, the stacked lawn chairs, the croquet set. His gaze shifted. There was the vast cavern of the water pump, there the mammoth water heater; underneath it one edge of his box-top shield was visible.

His gaze moved and he saw the magazine cover.

It was lying on a cushion on top of the cross-legged metal table that stood beside the one whose top he'd just left. He hadn't noticed the magazine before because the paint cans had blocked it from view. On the cover was the photograph of a woman. She was tall, passably beautiful, leaning over a rock, a look of pleasure on her young face. She was wearing a tight red long-sleeved sweater and a pair of clinging black shorts cut just below the hips.

He stared at the enormous figure of the woman. She was looking at him, smiling.

It was strange, he thought as he sat there, bare feet dangling in space. He hadn't been conscious of sex for a long time. His body had been something to keep alive, no more—something to feed and clothe and keep warm. His existence in the cellar, since that winter day, he been devoted to one thing—survival. All subtler gradations of desire had been lost to him. Now he had found the fragment of Louise's slip and seen the huge photograph of the woman.

His eyes ran lingeringly over the giant contours of her body—the high, swelling arches of her breasts, the gentle hill of her stomach, the long, curving taper of her legs.

He couldn't take his eyes off the woman. The sunlight was glinting on her dark auburn hair. He could almost sense the feeling of it, soft and silklike. He could almost feel the perfumed warmth of her flesh, almost feel the curved smoothness of her legs as mentally he ran his hands along them. He could almost feel the gelantinous give of her breasts, the sweet taste of her lips, her breath like warm wine trickling in his throat.

He shuddered helplessly, swaying on his loop of rope.
"Oh, God," he whispered. "Oh, God, God, God."
There were so many hungers.

49"

When he came out of the bathroom, damply warm from a
shower and shave, he found Lou sitting on the livingroom
couch, knitting. She'd turned off the television set and there
was no sound but the infrequent swish of cars passing in the
street below.

He stood in the doorway a moment, looking at her.

She was wearing a yellow robe over her nightgown. Both
garments were made of silk, clinging to the jut of her
rounded breasts, the broadness of her hips, the smooth length
of her legs. Electric pricklings coursed the lower muscles of
his stomach. It had been so long, canceled endlessly by medical tests and work and the weight of constant dread.

Lou looked up, smiling. "You look so nice and clean," she
said.

It was not the words or the look on her face; but suddenly
he was terribly conscious of his size. Lips twitching into the
semblance of a smile, he walked over to the couch and sat
down beside her, instantly sorry that he had.

She sniffed. "Mmm, you smell nice," she said. She was re-
ferring to his shaving lotion.

He grunted quietly, glancing at her clean-featured face, her
wheat-colored hair drawn back into a ribbon-tied horse's tail.

"You *look* nice," he said. "Beautiful."

"Beautiful!" she scoffed. "Not me."

He leaned over abruptly and kissed her warm throat. She
raised her left hand and stroked his cheek slowly.

"So nice and smooth," she murmured.

He swallowed. Was it just ego-flattened imagination, or
was she actually talking to him as if he were a boy? His left
hand, which had been lying across the heat of her leg, drew
back slowly, and he looked at the white, glaze-skinned band
across the bottom of its third finger. He'd been forced to take

the ring off almost two weeks before because the finger had become too thin.

He cleared his throat. "What are you making?" he asked disinterestedly.

"Sweater for Beth," she answered.

"Oh."

He sat there in silence while he watched her skillful manipulation of the long knitting needles. Then, impulsively, he laid his cheek against her shoulder. Wrong move, his mind said instantly. It made him feel even smaller, like a young boy leaning on his mother. He stayed there, though, thinking it would be too obviously awkward if he straightened up immediately. He felt that even rise and fall of her breathing as he rested there, a tense, unresolved sensation in his stomach.

"Why don't you go to sleep?" Lou asked quietly.

His lips pressed together. He felt a cold shudder move down his back.

"No," he said.

Imagination again? Or was his voice as frail as it sounded to him, as devoid of masculinity. He stared somberly at the V-neck of her robe, at the flesh-walled valley between her breasts, and his fingers twitched with his repressed desire to touch her.

"Are you tired?" she asked.

"No." It sounded too harsh. "A little," he amended.

"Why don't you finish up the ice cream?" she asked, after a pause.

He closed his eyes with a sigh. Imagination it might be, but that didn't prevent him from feeling like a boy—indecisive, withdrawn, much as though he'd conceived the ridiculous notion that he could somehow arouse the physical desire of this full-grown woman.

"Shall I get it for you?" she asked.

"No!" He lifted his head from her shoulder and fell back heavily against a pillow, staring morosely across the room. It was a cheerless room. Their furniture was still stored in Los Angeles and they were using Marty's attic castoffs. A depressing room, the walls a dark forest green, pictureless, only one window with ugly paper drapes, a pale, thread-worn rug hiding part of the scratched floor.

"What is it, darling?" she asked.

"Nothing."

"Have I done something?"

"No."

"What, then?"

"*Nothing*, I said."

"All right," she said quietly.

Was she unaware of it? Granted it was torture for her to be living with terrible anxiety, hoping each second to get that phone call from the Center, a telegram, a letter, and the message never coming. Still . . .

He looked at her full body again, feeling breath catch in him uncontrollably. It wasn't just physical desire; it was so much more. It was the dread of tomorrows without her. It was the horror of his plight, which no words could capture.

For it wasn't a sudden accident removing him from her life. It wasn't a sudden illness taking him, leaving the memory of him intact, cutting him from her love with merciful swiftness. It wasn't even a lingering sickness. At least then he'd be himself and, although she could watch him with pity and terror, at least she would be watching the man she knew.

This was worse, far worse.

Month after month would go by—almost a year of them still if the doctors didn't stop it. A year of living together day by day, while he shrank. Eating meals together, sleeping in the same bed together, talking together, while he shrank. Caring for Beth and listening to music and seeing each other every day, while he shrank. Each day a new incident, a new hideous adjustment to make. The complex pattern of their relationship altered day by day, while he shrank.

They would laugh, unable to keep a long face every single moment of every single day. There would be laughter, perhaps, at some joke—a forgetful moment of amusement. Then suddenly the horror would rush over them again like black ocean across a dike, the laughter choked, the amusement crushed. The trembling realization that he was shrinking covering them again, casting a pall over their days and nights.

"Lou."

She turned to face him. He leaned over to kiss her, but he couldn't reach her lips. With an angry, desperate motion he pushed up on one knee on the couch and thrust his right hand into the silky tangle of her hair, fingertips pressing at her skull. Pulling back her head with a tug, he jammed his lips on hers and forced her back against the pillow.

Her lips were taut with surprise. He heard her knitting thud on the floor, heard the liquid rustle of silk as she twisted slightly in his grip. He ran a shaking hand across the yielding softness of her breasts. He pulled away his parted lips and pressed them against her throat, slowly raking teeth across the warm flesh.

"Scott!" she gasped.

The way she said it seemed to drain him in an instant. A barren chill covered him. He drew back from her, feeling almost ashamed. His hands fell from her body.

"Honey, what *is* it?" she said.

"You don't know, do you?" He was shocked by the trembling sound of his own voice.

His hands went up quickly to his cheeks and he saw in her eyes that she suddenly knew.

"Oh, *sweetheart*," she said, bending forward. Her warm lips pressed at his. He sat there stiffly. The caress and the tone of voice and the kiss—they were not the passionate caress and tone and kiss of a woman who craved her husband's want. They were the sounds and touches of a woman who felt only loving pity for a poor creature who desired her.

He turned away.

"Honey, don't," she begged, taking hold of his hand. "How could I know? There hasn't been a bit of love-making between us in the last two months; not a kiss or an embrace or—"

"There wasn't exactly time for it," he said.

"But that's the whole point," she said. "How could I help but be surprised? Is it so odd?"

His throat contracted with a dry, clicking sound.

"I suppose," he said, barely audible.

"Oh, honey." She kissed his hand. "Don't make it sound as if I—turned you away."

He let breath trickle out slowly from his nostrils.

"I guess it . . . would be rather grotesque, anyway," he said, trying to sound detached. "The way I look. It'd be like—"

"Honey, please." She wouldn't let him finish. "You're making it worse than it is."

"Look at me," he said. How much worse can it get?"

"Scott. *Scott*." She pressed his small hand to her cheek. "If only I could say something to make it all right."

He stared past her, unable to meet her eyes. "It's not your fault," he said.

"Oh, why don't they *call*? Why don't they *find* it?"

He knew then that his desire was impossible. He'd been a fool even to think of it.

"Hold me, Scott," she said.

He sat motionless for a few seconds, chin down, the fixed dullness of his eyes sealing the mask of defeat that was his face. Then he drew back his right hand and slid it behind her; it seemed as if the hand would never reach her other side. His stomach muscles flexed in slowly. He wanted to get up from the couch and leave. He felt puny and absurd beside her, a ludicrous midget who had planned the seduction of a normal woman. He sat there stiffly, feeling the warmth of her body through the silk. And he'd rather have died than tell her that the weight of her arm across his shoulders was hurting him.

"We could . . . work it out," she suggested in a different voice. "We—"

His head twisted back and forth in erratic motions as though he were looking for escape. "Oh, stop it, will you? Let it go. Forget it. I was a fool to . . ."

His right hand pulled back and clamped tensely on the knuckles of his left hand. He squeezed until it hurt. "Just let it go," he said. "Let it go."

"Honey, I'm not just saying it to be nice," she protested. "Don't you think I—"

"No, I *don't*!" he answered sharply. "And you don't either."

"Scott, I know you're hurt, but . . ."

"Please, forget it." His eyes were shut, and the words came softly, warningly through clenched teeth.

She was still. He breathed as though he were suffocating. The room was a crypt of futility to him.

"All right," she whispered then.

He bit his lower lip. He said. "Have you written your parents?"

"My parents?" He knew she was staring at him curiously.

"I think it might be wise," he said, holding his voice in careful check. He shrugged ineffectually. "Find out about staying with them. You know."

"I *don't* know, Scott."

"Well . . . don't you think it's a good idea to make some recognition of the facts?"

"Scott, what are you trying to do?"

He lowered his chin to hide the quick swallowing movement in his throat. "I'm trying," he said, "to plan some disposition of you and Beth in the event—"

"Disposition! What are we—"

"Will you stop interrupting me?"

"You said disposition! What are we—bric-a-brac to be disposed of?"

"I'm trying to be realistic about this!"

"You're trying to be cruel about it! Just because I didn't know that you—"

"Oh, stop it, stop it. I can see there's no point in trying to be realistic."

"All right, we'll be realistic," she said, face tense with repressed anger. "Are you suggesting that I leave you and take Beth with me? Is that your idea of being realistic?"

His hands twitched in his lap.

"And what if they don't find it?" he said. "What if they *never* find it?"

"You think I should leave you, then," she said.

"I think it might be a good idea," he said.

"Well, I don't!"

And she was crying, hands spread across her face, tears trickling out between the fingers. He sat there feeling numbed and helpless, looking at her trembling shoulders.

"I'm sorry, Lou," he said. He didn't sound it.

She couldn't answer; her throat and chest were too tight with breath-shaking sobs.

"Lou. I . . ." He reached out a lifeless hand and put it on her leg. "Don't cry. I'm not worth that."

She shook her head as if at a great, unanswerable problem. She sniffed and brushed at her tears.

"Here," he muttered, handing her the handkerchief from his robe pocket. She took it without a word and pressed it against her wet cheeks.

"I'm sorry," she said.

"You have nothing to be sorry for," he said. "It's me. I got angry because I felt foolish and—stupid."

And now, he thought, he was inclined in the other direction—toward self-castigation, toward self-indulgent martyrdom. The mind troubled was capable of manifold inversions.

"No." She pressed his fingers briefly. "I had no right to—" She let the sentence hang. "I'll try to be more understanding."

For a moment her gaze rested on the white-skinned patch where his wedding ring had been. Then, with a sigh, she rose.

"I'll get ready for bed," she said.

He watched her walk across the room and disappear into the hallway. He heard her footsteps, then the clicking of the lock on the bathroom door. With slow-motion actions he got on his feet and went into the bedroom.

He lay there in the darkness, staring at the ceiling.

Poets and philosophers could talk all they wanted about a man's being more than fleshly form, about his essential worth, about the immeasurable stature of his soul. It was rubbish.

Had they ever tried to hold a woman with arms that couldn't reach around her? Had they ever told another man they were as good as he—and said it to his belt buckle?

She came into the bedroom, and in the darkness he heard the crisp rustle of her robe as she took it off and put it across the foot of the bed. Then the mattress gave on her side as she sat down. She drew her legs up and he heard her head thump back softly on her pillow. He lay there tensely, waiting for something.

After a moment there was a whispering of silk and he felt her reaching hand touch his chest.

"What's that?" she asked softly.

He didn't say.

She pushed up on her elbow. "Scott, it's your *ring*," she said. He felt the thin chain cutting slightly into the back of his neck as she fingered the ring. "How long have you been wearing it?" she said.

"Since I took it off," he said.

There was a moment's silence. Then her love-filled voice broke over him.

"Oh, darling!" Her arms slipped demandingly around him, and suddenly he felt the silk-filmed heat of her body pressing against him. Her lips fell searchingly on his, and her fingertips drew in like cat claws on his back, sending spicy tingles along the flesh.

And suddenly it was back, all the forced-down hunger in him exploding with a soundless, body-seizing violence. His hands fled across her burning skin, clutching and caressing. His mouth was an open shiver under hers. The darkness came alive, a sabled aura of heat crawling on their twining limbs. Words were gone; communication had become a thing of groping pressures, a thing felt in their blood, in the liquid torments rising, sweetly fierce. Words were needless. Their bodies spoke a surer language.

And when, too soon, it had ended and the night had fallen black and heavy on his mind, he slept, content, in the warm encirclement of her arms. And for the measure of a night there was peace, there was forgetfulness. For him.

CHAPTER
SIX
· · · · · · · · · · ·

He clung to the edge of the open cracker box, looking in with dazed, unbelieving eyes.

They were ruined.

He stared at the impossible sight—cobweb-gauzed, dirty, moldy, water-soaked crackers. He remembered now, too late, that the kitchen sink was directly overhead, that there was a faulty drainpipe on it, that water dripped into the cellar every time the sink was used.

He couldn't speak. There were no words terrible enough to express the mind-crazing shock he felt.

He kept staring, mouth ajar, a vacuous look immobile on his face. I'll die now, he thought. In a way, it was a peaceful outlook. But stabbing cramps of hunger crowded peace away, and thirst was starting to add an extra pain and dryness to his throat.

His head shook fitfully. No, it was impossible, impossible that he should have come so far to have it end like this.

"No," he muttered, lips drawing back in a sudden grimace as he clambered over the edge. Holding on, he stretched out one leg and kicked a cracker edge. It broke damply at his touch, jagged shards of it falling to the bottom of the box.

Reckless with an angry desperation, he let go of the edge and slid down the almost vertical glossiness of the wax paper, stopping with a neck-snapping jolt. Pushing up dizzily, he stood in the crumb-strewn box. He picked up one and it disintegrated wetly in his hands like dirt-engrained mush. He picked it apart with his hands, searching for a clean piece.

The smell of rot was thick in his nostrils. His cheek puffed out as a spasm shook his stomach.

Dropping the rest of the scraps, he moved toward a complete cracker, breathing through his mouth to avoid the odor, his bare feet squishing over the soaked, mold-fuzzed remains.

Reaching the cracker, he tore off a crumbling fragment and broke it up. Scraping green mold from one of the pieces, he bit off part of it.

He spat it out violently, gagging at the taste. Sucking in breath between his teeth, he stood shivering until the nausea had faded.

Then abruptly his fists clenched and he took a punch at the cracker. His vision was blurred by tears, and he missed. With a snarled curse he swung again and punched out a spray of white crumbs.

"Son-of-a-bitch!" he yelled, and he kicked the cracker to bits and kicked and flung the pieces in every direction like soggy rocks.

He leaned weakly against the wax-paper walls, his face against its cool, crackling surface, his chest expanding and contracting with short, jerking breaths. Temper, temper, came the whispered admonition. Shut up, he answered it. Shut up, I'm dying.

He felt a sharp-edged bulge against his forehead and shifted position irritably.

Then it hit him.

The other side of the wax paper. Any crumbs that had fallen there would have been protected.

With an excited grunt he clawed at the wax paper, trying to tear it open. His fingers slipped on the glossy smoothness and he thudded down on one knee.

He was getting up when the water hit him.

A startled cry lurched in his throat as the first drop landed on his head, exploding into spray. The second drop smashed across his face with an icy, blinding impact. The third bounced in crystalline fragments off his right shoulder.

With a gasp, he lunged backward across the box, tripping over a crumb. He pitched over onto the carpet of cold white mush, then shoved up quickly his robe coated with it, his hands caked with it. Across from him the drops kept crashing down in a torrent, filling the box with a leaping mist that covered him. He ran.

At the far end of the box he stopped and turned, looking dizzily at the huge drops splattering on the wax paper. He pressed a palm against his skull. It had been like getting hit with a cloth-wrapped sledge hammer.

"Oh, my God," he muttered hoarsely, sliding down the wax-paper wall until he was sitting in the mush, hands pressed to his head, eyes closed, tiny whimperings of pain in his throat.

He had eaten, and his sore throat felt much better. He had drunk the drops of water clinging to the wax paper. Now he was collecting a pile of crumbs.

First he had kicked an opening in the heavy wax paper, then squeezed in behind its rustling smoothness. After eating, he'd begun to carry dry crumbs out, piling them on the bottom of the box.

That done, he kicked and tore out handholds in the wax paper so he could climb back to the top. He made the ascent carrying one or two crumbs at a time, depending on their size. Up the wax-paper ladder, over the lip of the box, down the handholds he had formerly ripped in the paper wrapping of the box. He did that for an hour.

Then he squeezed his way behind the wax-paper lining, searching for any crumbs he might have missed. But he hadn't missed any except for one fragment the size of his little finger, which he picked up and chewed on as he finished his circuit of the box and emerged from the opening again.

He looked over the interior of the box once more, but there was nothing salvageable. He stood in the middle of the cracker ruins, hands on hips, shaking his head. At best, he'd got only two days' food out of all his work. Thursday he would be without any again.

He threw off the thought. He had enough concerns; he'd

worry about it when Thursday came. He climbed out of the box.

It was a lot colder outside. He shivered with a hunching up of shoulders. Though he'd wrung out as much as possible, his robe was still wet from the splattering drops.

He sat on the thick tangle of rope, one hand on his pile of hard-won cracker crumbs. They were too heavy to carry all the way down. He'd have to make a dozen trips at least, and that was out of the question. Unable to resist, he picked up a fist-thick crumb and munched on it contentedly while he thought about the problem of getting his food down.

At last, realizing there was only one way, he stood with a sigh and turned back to the box. Should use wax paper, he thought. Well, the hell with that; it was going to last only two days at the most.

With a straining of arm and back muscles, feet braced against the side of the box, he tore off a jagged piece of paper about the size of a small rug. This he dragged back to the edge of the refrigerator top and laid out flat. In the center of it he arranged his crumbs into a cone-shaped pile, then wrapped them up until he had a tight, carefully sealed package about as high as his knees.

He lay on his stomach peering over the edge of the refrigerator. He was higher off the floor now than he'd been on the distant cliff that marked the boundary of the spider's territory. A long drop for his cargo. Well, they were already crumbs; it would be no loss if they became smaller crumbs. The package wasn't likely to open during the fall; that was all that mattered.

Briefly, despite the cold, he looked out over the cellar.

It certainly made a difference, being fed. The cellar had, for the moment anyway, lost its barren menace. It was a strange, cool land shimmering with rain-blurred light, a kingdom of verticals and horizontals, of grays and blacks relieved only by the dusty colors of stored objects. A land of roars and rushings, of intermittent sounds that shook the air like many thunders. His land.

Far below he saw the giant woman looking up at him, still

leaning on her rock, frozen for all time in her posture of calculated invitation.

Sighing, he pushed back and stood. No time to waste; it was too cold. He got behind his bundle and, stooping over, pushed the dead weight of it to the edge and shoved it over the brink with a nudge of his foot.

Momentarily on his stomach again, he watched the package's heavy fall, saw it bounce once on the floor, and heard the crunching noise as it came to rest. He smiled. It had held together.

Standing once more, he started around the top of the refrigerator to see if there were anything he might use. He found the newspaper.

It was folded and propped against the cylindrical coil ease. Its lettered faces were covered with dust and part of the sink's leaking had splashed water across it, blotting the letters and eating through the cheap paper. He saw the large letters OST and knew it was a copy of the New York *Globe-Post*, the paper that had done his story—at least as much of it as he had been able to endure.

He looked at the dusty paper, remembering the day Mel Hammer had come to the apartment and made the offer.

Marty had mentioned Scott's mysterious affliction to a fellow Kiwani, and from there the news had drifted, ripple by ripple, into the city.

Scott refused the offer, despite the fact that they needed the money desperately. Although the Medical Center had completed the tests free of charge, there was still a sizable bill for the first series of examinations. There was the five hundred owed to Marty, and the other bills they'd accumulated through the long, hard winter—the complete winter wardrobe for all of them, the cost of fuel oil, the extra medical bills because none of them had been physically equipped to face an Eastern winter after living so long in Los Angeles.

But Scott had been in what he now called his period of furies—a time when he experienced an endless and continuously mounting anger at the plight he was in. He'd refused the newspaper offer with anger. No, thank you, but I don't care to be exposed to the morbid curiosity of the public. He flared up at Lou when she didn't support his decision as eagerly as he thought she should have, saying, "What would you like me to do—turn myself into a public freak to give you your security?"

Erring, off-target anger; he'd known it even as he spoke. But anger was burning in him. It drove him to depths of temper he had never plumbed before. Strengthless temper, temper based on fear alone.

Scott turned away from the newspaper and went back to the rope. Lowering himself over the edge with an angry carelessness, he began sliding down the rope, using his hands and feet. The white cliff of the refrigerator blurred before his eyes as he descended.

And the anger he felt now was only a vestigial remnant of the fury he'd lived with constantly in the past; fury that made him lash out incontinently at anyone he thought was mocking him. . . .

He remembered the day Terry had said something behind his back; something he thought he heard. He remembered how, no taller than Beth, he'd whirled on her and told her that he'd heard what she'd said.

Heard what? she asked. Heard what you said about me! I didn't say anything about you. Don't lie to me. I'm not deaf! Are you calling me a liar? Yes, I'm calling you a liar! I don't have to listen to talk like that! You do when you decide to talk about me behind my back! I think we've had just about enough of your screaming around here. Just because you're Marty's brother—Sure, sure, you're the boss's wife, you're the big cheese around here. Don't you talk to me like that!

And on and on, shrill and discordant and profitless.

Until Marty, grim, soft-spoken, called him into the office, where Scott had stood in front of the desk, glaring at his brother like a belligerent dwarf.

"Kid, I don't like to say it," Marty told him, "but maybe— till they get you fixed up—it'd be better if you stayed home. Believe me, I know what you're going through, and I don't blame you, not a bit. But ... well, you can't concentrate on work when you're ..."

"So I'm being fired."

"Oh, come on, kid," Marty said. "You're not being fired. You'll still be on salary. Not as much, of course—I can't afford that—but enough to keep you and Lou going. This'll be over soon, kid. And—well, Christ, the GI loan'll be coming through any day now anyway, and then—"

Scott's feet thudded on the top of the wicker table. Without pausing, he started across the wide expanse, lips set tightly in the thick blond wreathing of his beard.

Why did he have to see that newspaper and go off on another fruitless journey to the past? Memory was such a worthless thing, really. Nothing it dealt with was attainable. It was concerned with phantom acts and feelings, with all that was uncapturable except in thought. It was without satisfaction. Mostly it hurt. . . .

He stood at the edge of the tabletop, wondering how he was going to get down to the hanging strap. He stood indecisively, shifting from leg to leg, wriggling the toes of the lifted foot gingerly. His feet were getting cold again. The ache in his right leg was returning, too; he'd almost forgotten it while he was collecting crumbs, the constant movement loosening and warming him. And his throat was getting sore again.

He walked behind the paint can whose handle he had grabbed before and, bracing his back against it, pushed. The can didn't move. Turning around, he planted his feet firmly and pushed with all his strength. The can remained fixed. Scott walked around it, breathing hard with strain. With great effort, he was able to draw the handle out slightly so that it protruded over the edge of the table.

He rested for a moment, then swung over the space and dangled there until his searching feet found the strip and pressed down on it.

Cautiously he put one hand on the tabletop. Then, after a moment of feeling for balance, he let go of the paint-can handle and lowered himself quickly. His feet slipped off the ledge, but his convulsively thrusting arms caught hold of it and he clambered back on.

After a few seconds he leaped across to the spar arrangement.

The descent along the rod-spaced incline was simple; too simple to prevent the return of memories. As he slid and edged down the length of the incline, he thought of the afternoon he'd come home from the shop after the talk with Marty.

He remembered how still the apartment was, Lou and Beth out shopping. He remembered going into the bedroom and sitting on the edge of the bed for a long time, staring down at his dangling legs.

He didn't know how long it had been before he'd looked up and seen a suit of his old clothes hanging on the back of the door. He'd looked at it, then got up and gone over to it. He'd had to stand on a chair to reach it. For a moment he held the dragging weight of it in his arms. Then, not knowing why, he pulled the jacket off the hanger and put it on.

He stood in front of the full-length mirror, looking at himself.

That's all he did at first, just stood looking—at his hands, lost deep in the sagging hollow of the dark sleeves; at the hem of the coat, far below his calves; at the way the coat hung around him like a tent. It didn't strike him then; the disparity was too severe. He only stared at himself, his face blank.

Then it did strike him, as if for the first time.

It was his own coat he wore.

A wheezing giggle puffed out his cheeks. It disappeared. Silence while he gaped at his reflection.

He snickered hollowly at the child playing grownup. His chest began to shake with restrained laughs. They sounded like sobs.

He couldn't hold them back. They poured up his throat and pushed out between shaking lips. Sobbing laughter burst out against the mirror. He felt his body trembling with it. The room began to resound with his taut, shrill laughter.

He looked at the mirror again, tears raining down his cheeks. He did a little dance step and the coat puffed out, the sleeve ends flapping. Screeching with a deranged appreciation, he flailed spastic blows against his legs, doubled over to ease the pain in his stomach. His laughter came in short, explosive, throat-catching bursts. He could hardly stand.

I'm funny. He swung the sleeve again and flopped over suddenly on his side, laughing and kicking at the floor with his shoes, the thumping sounds making him even more hysterical. He twisted around on the floor, limbs thrashing, head rolling from side to side, the choked laughter pealing from his lips, until he was too weak to laugh. Then he lay there on his back, motionless, gasping for breath, his face wet with tears, his right foot still twitching. I'm funny.

And he thought, quite calmly it seemed, about going into the bathroom and getting his razor blade and cutting his wrists open. He really wondered why he went on lying there, looking up at the ceiling, when it would solve everything if he went into the bathroom and got a razor blade and—

He slid down the rope-thick thread to the shelf of the wicker table. He shook the thread until the stick came loose and fell. He fastened it and started down toward the floor.

It was strange; he still didn't know why he hadn't committed suicide. Surely the hopelessness of his situation warranted it. Yet, although he had often wished he could do it, something had always stopped him.

It was difficult to say whether he regretted this failure to end his life. Sometimes it seemed as if it didn't matter one way or the other, except in a vague, philosophical way; but what philosopher had ever shrunk?

His feet touched the cold floor, and quickly he gathered up his sandals and put them on—the sandals he had made of string. That was better. Now to drag the package to his sleeping place. Then he could strip off his wet robe and lie in the warmth, resting and eating. He ran to the package, anxious to get it over with.

The package was so heavy that he could move it only slowly. He pushed it a dozen yards, then stopped and rested, sitting on it. After he got his breath, he stood up and pushed it some more—past the two massive tables, past the coiled hose, past the lawn mower and the huge ladder, across the wide, light-patched plain toward the water heater.

The last twenty-five yards he moved backward, bent over at the waist, grunting as he dragged his bundle of food. Just a few more minutes and he'd be warm and comfortable on his bed, fed and sheltered. Teeth clenched in suddenly joyous effort, he jerked the bundle along to the foot of the cement block. Life was still worth struggling for. The simplest of physical pleasures could make it so. Food, water, warmth. He turned happily.

He cried out.

The giant spider was hanging across the top edge of the block, waiting for him.

For a single moment their eyes met. He stood frozen at the foot of the cement block, staring up in heart-stilled horror.

Then the long black legs stirred, and with a strangled groan Scott lunged into one of the two passages cut through the block. As he started running along the damp tunnel, he heard the spider drop heavily to the floor behind him.

It's not fair! his mind screamed in desolate fury.

There was time for no more thought than that. Everything was swallowed in the savage maw of panic. The pain in his leg was gone, his exhaustion was washed away. Only terror remained.

He leaped out through the opening on the other side of the cement block and cast back a glance at the shadowy lurching of the spider in the tunnel. Then, with a sucked-in breath, he started racing across the floor toward the fuel tank. There was no use trying to reach the log pile. The spider would overtake him long before he could make it.

He sped toward the big split carton under the tank, not knowing what he would do when he got there, only instinctively heading for shelter. There were clothes in the carton. Maybe he could burrow under them, out of the black widow's reach.

He didn't look back now; there was no need to. He knew

the great swollen body of the spider was wobbling erratically over the cement, carried by the long black legs. He knew that it was only because one of those legs was missing that he had any hope of reaching the carton first.

He ran through viscid squares of light, sandals thudding, robe flapping about his body. Air scorched rawly down his throat, his legs pumped wildly. The fuel tank loomed over him.

He darted into the vast shadow of it, the spider skimming the floor less than five yards behind. With a grunt Scott leaped off the cement and, grabbing hold of a hanging string, dragged himself up, then swung in feet first through the opening in the side of the carton.

He landed in a limb-twisting heap on the soft pile of clothes. As he started up he heard the rasping of the spider's legs up the carton's side. He shoved to his feet but lost his balance on the yielding cloth and fell. Sprawling, he saw the black, leg-fluttering bulk of the spider appear in the V-shaped opening. It lunged through.

With a sob, Scott pushed up, then fell again on the uneven hill of clothes. The hill gave twice; once under his weight, again under the impact of the spider's wriggling drop. It spurted through the shadows at him.

There was no time to struggle to his feet. He shoved desperately with his legs and sent himself flailing backward. He flopped heavily again, hands clawing for an opening between the clothes. There was none. The spider was almost on him now.

A high-pitched whining flooded in his throat. Scott flung himself back again as one of the spider's legs fell heavily across his ankle. He grunted in shock as he fell into the open sewing box, hands still groping. The huge spider jumped down and clambered over his legs. He screamed.

Then his hand closed over cold metal. The pin! With a sucking gasp, he kicked back again, dragging up the pin with both hands. As the spider leaped, he drove the pin like a spear at its belly. He felt the pin shudder in his grip under the weight of the partially impaled creature.

The spider leaped back off the point. It landed yards away on the clothes, then, after a second's hesitation, rushed at him again. Scott pushed up on his left knee, right leg back as a supporting brace, the pinhead cradled against his hip, his arms rigidly tensed for the second impact.

Again the spider hit the pinpoint. Again it sprang back, one of its flailing spiny legs raking skin off Scott's left temple.

"Die!" he heard himself scream suddenly. "Die! Die!"

It did not die. It stirred restlessly on the clothes a few yards away as if it were trying to understand why it couldn't reach its prey. Then suddenly it leaped at him again.

This time it had barely touched the pinpoint before it stopped and scuttled backward. Scott kept staring at it fixedly, his body remaining in its tense crouch, the heavy pin wavering a little in his grip, but always pointed at the spider. He could still feel the hideous clambering weight of it across his legs, the flesh-ripping slash of its leg. He squinted to distinguish its black form from the shadows.

He didn't know how long he remained in that position. The transition was unnoticeable. Suddenly, magically, there were only the shadows.

A confused sound stirred in his throat. He stood up on palsied legs and looked around. Across the cellar the oil burner roared into life and, heart pounding jaggedly, he twisted around in a panic, thinking that the spider was going to leap on him from behind.

He kept circling there for a long time, the weight of the lancelike pin dragging down his arms. Finally it dawned on him that the spider had gone away.

A great wave of relief and exhaustion broke over him. The pin seemed made of lead, and it fell from his hands and clattered down on the wooden bottom of the box. His legs gave way and he slipped down into a twisted heap, head fallen back against the pin that had saved his life.

For a while he lay there in limp, contended depletion. The spider was gone. He'd chased it away.

It was not too long, however, before the knowledge that the spider was still alive dampened all contentment. It might be waiting outside for him, ready to spring as soon as he came out. It might be back under the water heater again, waiting for him there.

He rolled over slowly on his stomach and pressed his face against his arms. What had he accomplished, after all? He was still virtually at the spider's mercy. He couldn't carry the pin everywhere he went, and in a day or so he might not be able to carry it at all.

And even if (he didn't believe it for a second) the spider would be too frightened to attack him again, there was still the food that would be gone in two days, still the increasing difficulties in getting to the water, still the constant altering of his clothes to be made, still the impossibility of escaping the cellar, still—worst of all, always there, constantly nagging— the dread of what was going to happen to him between Saturday night and Sunday morning.

He struggled to his feet and groped around until he found the hinged cover of the box. He pulled it over and lowered it into place, then sank back into the darkness. What if I smother? he thought. He didn't care.

He'd been running since it had all started. Running physically, from the man and the boys and the cat and the bird and the spider, and—a far worse kind of flight—running mentally. Running from life, from his problems and his fears; retreating, backtracking, facing nothing, yielding, giving in, surrendering.

He still lived, but was his living considered, or only an instinctive survival? Yes, he still struggled for food and water, but wasn't that inevitable if he chose to go on living. What he wanted to know was this: Was he a separate, meaningful person; was he an individual? Did he matter? Was it enough just to survive?

He didn't know; he didn't know. It might be that he was a man and trying to face reality. It might also be that he was a pathetic fraction of a shadow, living only out of habit, impulse-driven, moved but never moving, fought but never fighting.

He didn't know. He slept, curled up and shivering, no bigger than a pearl, and he didn't know.

CHAPTER
SEVEN

• • • • • • • • • • •

He stood up and listened carefully. The cellar was still. The spider must have gone. Surely, if it were still intent on killing him, it would have ventured into the carton again. He must have been asleep for hours.

He grimaced, swallowed, as he realized that his throat hurt again. He was thirsty, hungry. Did he dare go back to the water heater? He blew out a hissing breath. There was no question. It had to be done.

He felt around until his hands closed over the thick, icy shaft of the pin. He picked it up. It was heavy. Amazing that he had been able to handle it so well. Fright, probably. He lifted the pin in both hands, then shifted it to his right side and held it there. It dragged at his arm muscles as he climbed out of the sewing box and moved up the shifting hill of clothes toward the opening in the side of the carton. If the spider appeared, he could easily grab the pin with both hands and use it as he had before. It gave him the first definite sense of physical security he had had in weeks.

At the opening, he leaned out cautiously, looking up first, then sideways, and finally down. The spider was not to be seen. His breathing eased a little. He slid the pin out through the opening, then, after letting it dangle a moment, dropped it. It clanged on the floor and rolled a few feet before stopping. Hastily he slid out of the carton and let himself drop. As he landed, the water pump began its chugging wheeze, making him jump to the pin, grab it up, and hold it poised as if to ward off attack.

There was no attack. He lowered the gleaming spear and shifted it to his side again, then began walking across the floor toward the water heater.

He moved out from beneath the mountainous shadow of the fuel tank into the grayish light of late afternoon. The rain had stopped. Out beyond the filmed windows was utter stillness. He walked by the vast lawn-mower wheels, glancing up warily to see if the spider were crouching up there.

Now he was on the open floor. He began the short hike to the water heater. His eyes went to the refrigerator, and in his mind he saw the newspaper up there, and he endured again the agony of the photographer's invasion of his home. They had posed him in his old shoes, which were five sizes too large, and Berg said, "Look like ya was rememberin' when ya could wear 'em, Scotty." Then they posed him beside Beth, beside Lou, beside a hanging suit of his old clothes; standing beside the tape measure, Hammer's big, disembodied hand sticking out from the edge of the photograph, pointing at the proper mark; being examined by the doctors appointed by the *Globe-Post*. His case history had been rehashed for a million readers, while he suffered a new mental torture each day, thrashing in bed at night, telling himself that he was going to break the contract he'd signed whether they needed the money or not, whether Lou hated him for it or not.

He had gone on with it anyway.

And the offers came in. Offers for radio and television and stage and night-club appearances, for articles in all kinds of magazines except the better ones, for syndication of the *Globe-Post* series. People started to gather outside the apartment, staring at him, even asking for his autograph. Religious fanatics exhorted him, in person and by mail, to join their saving cults. Obscene letters arrived from weirdly frustrated women—and men.

His face was blank and unmoving as he reached the concrete block. He stood there a moment, still thinking of the past. Then he refocused his eyes and started, realizing that the spider might be up there waiting to spring.

Slowly he climbed the block, pin always ready for use if necessary. He peered over the edge of the block. His sleeping place was empty.

With a sigh, he slung the pin over the edge and watched it roll to a stop against his bed. Then he climbed down again for the crackers.

After three trips he had all the cracker bits in a pile beside his bed. He sat there crunching on a fist-sized piece, wishing he had some water. He didn't dare go down to the pump, though; it was getting dark, and even the pin was not enough assurance in the dark.

When he'd finished eating, he dragged the box top over his bed, then sank back on the sponge with a soft groan. He was still exhausted. The nap in the carton had done little to refresh him.

He remembered and, reaching around, he searched for the wood and charcoal. Finding them, he scratched a careless stroke. It would probably cross another stroke, but that hardly mattered. Chronology became less of a concern each day. There was Wednesday and there was Thursday, there were Friday and Saturday.

Then nothing.

He shuddered in the darkness. Like death, his fate was impossible to conceive. No, even worse than death. Death, at least, was a concept; it was a part of life, however strangely unknown. But who had ever shrunk into nothingness?

He rolled on his side and propped his head on an arm. If only he could tell someone what he felt. If only he could be with Lou; see her, touch her. Yes, even if she didn't know it, it would be a comfort. But he was alone.

He thought again of the newspaper stories, and of how sick it had made him to become a spectacle, how it had driven him into nerve-screaming wrath, making him maniacal with fury against his plight.

Until, at the peak of that fury, he had sped to the city and told the paper he was breaking his contract, and stormed away in a palsy of hatred.

42"

Two miles beyond Baldwin, a tire blew out with a crack like the blast of a shotgun.

Gasping, Scott froze to the wheel as the Ford lurched off balance, scouring wide tire marks across the pavement. It took all the strength in his arms to keep the car from ramming the center wall. The steering wheel shuddered in his grip, he guided the car off the highway.

Fifty yards farther on, he braked the car and twisted off the ignition. He sat there for a moment, wordless, glaring straight ahead with baleful eyes. His hands were white-ridged fists quivering in his lap.

At last he spoke. "Oh, you son-of-a—" Fury sent a jolting shudder down his back.

"Go ahead," he said, rage crouching behind the patience of his tone. "Go ahead, pour it on. Sure. Go ahead; why not?" His teeth clicked together. "Don't just stop with a flat tire, though," he said, words thumping at the closed gates of his teeth. "Kill the generator. Tear out the spark plugs. Split the radiator. Blow up the whole goddamn son-of-a-bitch car!" Apoplectic rage sprayed across the windshield.

He thudded back against the seat, spent, his eyes shut.

After a few minutes, he pulled up the door handle and pushed the door open. Cold air rushed over him. Drawing up the collar of his topcoat, he shifted his legs and slid down off the raised seat.

He landed on gravel, spilling forward, hands out for support. He got up quickly, cursing, and fired a stone across the highway. With my luck it'll break a car window and put out an old lady's eye! he thought furiously. With my luck.

He stood shivering, looking at his car, hunched blackly over the collapsed tire. Great, he thought, just great. How in the hell was he supposed to change it? His teeth gritted. He wasn't even strong enough for *that*. And, of course, Terry couldn't watch the children today and Lou had to stay home. It figured.

A spasm shook him beneath the topcoat. It was cold. Cold on a May night. Even that figured. Even the weather was against him. He closed his eyes. I'm ready for a padded cell, he thought.

Well, he couldn't just stand there. He had to get to a phone and call a garage.

He didn't move. He stared at the road. And after I call the garage, he thought, the mechanic will come and he'll talk to me and look at me and recognize me; and there'll be guarded stares, or maybe even open ones, the kind Berg always gave him—blunt, insulting stares that seemed to say, Jesus, you *are* a creep. And there would be talk, questions, the kind of withdrawn camaraderie a normal man offers to a freak.

His throat muscles drew in slowly as he swallowed. Even rage was preferable to this; this complete negation of spirit. Rage, at least, was struggle, it was a moving forward against something. This was defeat, static and heavy on him.

Weary breath emptied from him. Well, there was no other way. He had to get home. He might have called Marty under any other circumstances; but he felt awkward about Marty now.

He slid his hands into the slash pockets of his coat and started trudging along the roadside gravel.

I don't care, he kept telling himself as he walked. I don't care if I *did* sign a contract. I'm tired of playing guinea pig for a million readers.

He walked on quickly in his little-boy clothes.

Moments later, headlight beams bleached across him and he stepped farther away from the road and kept on walking. He certainly wasn't going to try to get a ride.

The dark car hulk rolled past him. Then there was a slowing of the tires on the pavement and, looking up, Scott saw that the car was stopping. His mouth tightened. I'd rather walk. He formed the words with his lips, getting them ready.

The door shoved open and a fedora-topped head appeared. "You alone, my boy?" the man asked huskily. The words came out from one side of his mouth. The other side was plugged with a half-smoked cigar.

Scott trudged toward the car. Maybe it was all right; the man thought he was a boy. He might have expected it. Hadn't they refused to let him in the movie one afternoon because he wasn't accompanied by an adult? Hadn't he been forced to show his identification before that bartender would serve him a drink?

"You alone, young fellow?" the man asked again.

"Just walking home," Scott said.

"Have you far to go?" An intelligent voice, somewhat thickened. Scott saw the man's head bobbing. So much the better, he thought.

"Just to the next town," he said. "Could you give me a ride, mister?" Deliberately he raised the already raised pitch of his voice.

"Certainly, my boy, certainly," the man said. "Just climb aboard and it's bon-voy-*age* for you and me and Plymouth, vintage fifty-five." His head drew in like that of a startled turtle. It disappeared into the shell of his car.

"Thanks, mister." It was a form of masochism, Scott knew, this playing the role of boy to its very hilt. He stood outside the car until the heavy-set man had pushed up awkwardly and was sitting behind the steering wheel again. Then he slid onto the seat.

"Just sit right here, my boy, just—Caution!"

Scott jumped up as he sat on the man's thick hand. The man drew it away, held it before his eyes.

"You have injured the member, my boy," he said. "Wreaked havoc to the knuckles. Eh?" the man's chuckle was liquid, as if it came up through a throatful of water.

Scott's smile was nervously automatic as he sat down again. The car reeked of whisky and cigar smoke. He coughed into his hand.

"Anchors, so be it, Od's blood, aweigh," the man declared. He tapped down the shift to drive position and the car jerked a little, then rolled forward. "*Fermez la porte,* dear boy, *fermez la* goddam *porte.*"

"I have," Scott told him.

The man looked over as if he were delighted. "You understand French, my boy. An excellent boy, a most seemly boy. Your health, sir."

Scott smiled thinly to himself. He wished he were drunk too. But a whole afternoon drinking in a darkened bar-room booth had done nothing to him at all.

"You reside in this humid land, my boy?" the heavy man asked. He began slapping himself about the chest.

"In the next town," Scott said.

"In the next town, the following city," the man said, still slapping at himself. "In the adjacent village, the juxtaposed hamlet. Ah, *Hamlet.* To be or not to be, that is the—God damn it's a match. My kingdom for a match!" He belched. It was like a drawn-out leopard growl.

"Use the dashboard lighter," Scott said, hoping to get both of the man's unsteady hands back on the wheel.

The man looked over, apparently astounded. "A brilliant boy," he said. "An analytic fellow. By God, I love an analytic fellow." His bubbly chuckle rippled in the stale-smelling car. *"Mon dieu."*

Scott tensed suddenly as the heavy man leaned over, ignoring the highway. The man knocked in the lighter, then straightened up again, his shoulder brushing Scott's.

"So you live in the next town, *mon cher,*" he said. "This is ... fascinating news." Another leopard-growl belch. "Dinner with old Vincent," said the man. "Old Vincent." The sound that came from his throat might have indicated amusement. It might, as well, have indicated the onset of strangulation. "Old Vincent," said the heavy man sadly.

The cigarette lighter popped out and he snatched it from its electric cavity. Scott glanced aside as the man relit his dark-tipped cigar.

The man's head was leonine beneath the wide-brimmed fedora. Glows of light washed his face. Scott saw bushy eyebrows like awnings over the man's darkly glittering eyes. He saw a puffy-nostriled nose, a long, thick-lipped mouth. It was the face of a sly boy peering out through rolls of dough.

Clouds of smoke obscured the face. "A most seemly boy, Od's bodkins," said the man. He missed the dashboard opening and the lighter thumped on the floor boards. "God's hooks!" The man doubled over. The car veered wildly.

"I'll get it," Scott said quickly. "Look out!"

The man put the car back in its proper lane. He patted Scott's head with a spongy palm. "A child of most excellent virtues," he slurred. "As I have always said—" He drew up phlegm, rolled down the window, and gave it to the wind. He forgot what he had always said. "You live around here?" he asked, belching conclusively.

"In the next town," Scott said.

"Vincent was a friend, I tell you," the man said remorsefully. "A *friend*. In the truest sense of that truest word. Friend, ally, companion, comrade."

Scott glanced back at the service station they had just passed. It looked closed. He'd better ride into Freeport and make sure he could get hold of someone.

"He insisted," the man said, "in donning the hair shirt of matrimony." He turned. "You *comprends*, dear boy? Do you, bless your supple bones, *comprends*?"

Scott swallowed. "Yes, sir," he said.

The man blew out a puff of smoke. Scott coughed. "And what," the man said, "was a *man*, dear boy, became, you see, a creature of degradation, a lackey, a serf, an automaton. A—in short—lost and shriveled soul." The man peered at Scott dizzily. "You see," he asked, "what I mean to say, dear boy? *Do* you?"

Scott looked out the window. I'm tired, he thought. I want to go to bed and forget who I am and what's happening to me. I just want to go to bed.

"You live around here?" asked the man.

"Next town."

"Quite so," said the man.

Silence a moment. Then the man said. "Women. Who come into man's life a breath from the sewer." He belched. "A pox on the she." He looked over at Scott. The car headed for a tree. "And dear Vincent," said the man, "lost to the eye of man. *Swallowed* in the spiritual quicksands of—"

"You're going to hit that tree!"

The man turned his head.

"There," he said. "Back on course, Cap'n. Back in the saddle again. Back where a friend is a—"

He peered at Scott again, face aslant as though he were a buyer examining merchandise. "You are—" he said, purse-lipped and estimating. He cleared his throat violently. "You are twelve," he said. "First prize?"

Scott coughed a little at the cigar smoke. "First prize," he said. "Look out."

The man repointed the car, his laugh ending in a belch.

"An age of pristine possibility, my dear," he said. "A time of untrammeled hope. Oh, dear boy." He dropped a portly hand and clamped it on Scott's leg. "Twelve, twelve. Oh, to be twelve again. Blessed be twelve years of age."

Scott pulled his leg away. The man squeezed it once more, then reached back to the steering wheel. "Yes, yes, yes, yes, yes," he said. "Still to meet your first woman." His lips curled. "That experience which is analogous to turning your first rock and finding your first bug."

"I can get off at—" Scott started, seeing an open gas station ahead.

"Ugly they are," stated the heavy man in the dark, wrinkled suit. "Ugly with an ugliness that worries the fringes of phenomena." His eyes moved, peering out at Scott over banks of crow-lined fat. "Do you intend to marry, dear boy?" he asked.

If I could laugh at anything these days, Scott thought, I could laugh at that.

"No," he said. "Say, could I get off at—"

"A wise, a noble decision," said the heavy man. "One of virtue, of seemliness. *Women.*" He stared wide-eyed through the windshield. "Append them to cancer. They destroy as secretly, as effectively, as—speak truth, O prophet—as *hideously.*" The man looked at him. "Eh, boy?" he said, chuckling, belching, hiccuping.

"Mister, I get off here."

"Take you to Freeport, my boy," said the man. "To Freeport away! Land of jollities and casual obliterations. Stronghold of suburban ax-grindings." The man looked directly at Scott. "You like girls, my boy?"

The question caught Scott off guard. He hadn't really been paying attention to the drift of the man's monologue. He looked over at the man. Suddenly the man seemed bigger; as if, with the questions, he had gained measurable bulk.

"I don't really live in Freeport," Scott said. "I—"

"He's *diffident*!" The heavy man's heretofore husky chuckle suddenly erupted into a cackle. "O diffident youth, beloved." The hand again went to Scott's leg. Scott's face tensed as he looked up at the man, the smell of whisky and cigar smoke thick in his nostrils. He saw the cigar tip glow and fade, glow, fade.

"I get off here," he said.

"Look thee, young chap," said the heavy man, watching the road and Scott at the same time, "the night hath yet a measure of youth. It's only a trifle past nine. Now," his voice fell to cajoling, "in the icebox of my rooms there squats a squamous quart of ice cream. Not a pint, mind you, but—"

"Please, I get *off* here." Scott could feel the heat of the man's hand through his trouser leg. He tried to draw away but he couldn't. His heartbeat quickened.

"Oh, come along, young dear," the man said. "Ice cream, cake, a bit of bawdy badinage—what more could two adventurers like you and me seek of an evening? Eh?" The hand tightened almost threateningly.

"Ow!" Scott said, wincing. "Get your hand off me!"

The man looked startled at the adult anger in Scott's voice, the lowering of pitch, the authority.

"Will you stop the car?" Scott asked angrily. "And look out!"

The man jerked the car back into its lane.

"Don't get so excited, boy," he said, beginning to sound agitated.

"I want to get *out*." Scott's hands were actually shaking.

"My dear boy," the man said in an abruptly pitiful voice, "if you knew loneliness as *I* know it—black solitude and—"

"Stop the car, damn it!"

The man stiffened. "Speak with respect to your superior, lout!" he snapped. His right hand drew back suddenly and smashed against the side of Scott's head, knocking him against the door.

Scott pushed up quickly, realizing with a burst of panic, that he was no stronger than a boy.

"Dear boy, I apologize," the man said instantly, hiccuping. "Did I hurt you?"

"I live down the next road," Scott said tensely. "Stop here, please."

The man plucked out his cigar and threw it on the floor.

"I offend you, boy," he said, sounding as if he were about to cry. "I offend you with distasteful words. Please. *Please*. Look behind the words, behind the peeling mask of jollity. For there is utter sadness, there utter loneliness. Can you understand that, dear boy? Can you, in your tender years, know my—"

"Mister, I want to get out," Scott said. His voice was that of a boy, half angry, half frightened. And the horror of it was that he wasn't sure if there was more of acting or of actuality in his voice.

Abruptly the man pulled over to the side of the highway.

"Leave me, leave me, then," he said bitterly. "You're no different from the rest, no, not at all."

Scott shoved open the door with trembling hands.

"Good night, sweet prince," said the heavy man, fumbling for Scott's hand. "Good night and dreams of plenteous goodness bless thy repose." A wheezy hiccup jarred his curtain speech. "I go on—empty, empty . . . empty. Will you kiss me once? For good-by, for—"

But Scott was already out of the car and running, headlong toward the service station they had just passed. The man turned his heavy head and watched youth racing away from him.

CHAPTER EIGHT

• • • • • • • • • • •

There was a thumping sound, like that of a hammer on wood; like the sound of a huge fingernail tapping, falsely patient, on a blackboard. The tapping pounded at his sleeping brain. He stirred on the bed, rolling over on his back with a fitful toss of arms. *Thump—thump—thump.* He moaned. At his sides, his hands raised up a trifle, then dropped again. *Thump. Thump.* He groaned irritably, still not fully conscious.

Then the water drop burst across his face.

Gagging and coughing, he reared up on the sponge, hearing a loud squishing noise. Another drop splashed off his shoulder.

"What!" His brain struggling to orient itself, his wide-eyed, startled gaze fled around the darkness. *Thump! Thump!* It was a giant's fist beating at a door; it was a monster gavel pounding on a rostrum.

Sleep was gone. He felt his chest jerk with staggering heartbeats. "Good God," he muttered. He threw his legs over the side of the sponge.

They landed in lukewarm water.

He jerked his legs back with a gasp. Overhead the noise seemed to be coming faster. *Thump-thump-thump!* Breath caught in his throat. What in God's name. . .

Grimacing at the brain-jolting sound, he let his legs over the side of the bed again and let them sink in the warm water. He stood hastily, rigid hands clamped over his ears. *Thump thump thump!* It was like standing inside a fiercely beaten drum. Gasping, he lurched for the edge of the box top. He slipped on the water-slick surface, crying out as his right knee banged down on the cement. He pushed up with a groan, then slipped again.

"Damn it!" he screamed. He hardly heard his voice; the noise was almost deafening. Frantic, he braced his feet and, reaching up, lifted the box-top edge and ducked out under it.

He slipped again, crashing down on an elbow. Pain knifed up his arm. He started up. A drop of water slammed across his back, sending him sprawling again. He twisted over like a fish and saw the water heater leaking.

"Oh, my God," he muttered, wincing at the pain in his knee and elbow.

He stood up, watching great drops splatter off the box top and cement. The water ran warmly across his ankles; there was a minor waterfall of it flowing over the edge of the block, splashing on the cellar floor.

For a long moment he stood there indecisively, staring at the falling water, feeling the robe cling warm and wet to his body.

Then he cried out suddenly. "The crackers."

He lunged at the box top again, sliding and struggling for balance. He lifted the top and carried it over the bed, feet almost slipping out from under him all the way. He dropped it, then flung himself across the sponge, hearing water burst out from its swollen pores.

"Oh, *no.*"

He couldn't drag the package up, it was so water-logged. Face wild with frightened anger, he tore it open, the soggy paper parting like tissue in his hands.

He stared at the water-soaked cracker bits molded together into an ashen paste. He picked up a handful and felt the sodden drag of it, like day-old porridge.

With a curse he flung the dripping mass away. It flew over the edge of the block and splattered into a hundred pale scraps on the floor.

He knelt there on the sponge, oblivious now of the water that poured around and over him. His eyes were fastened to the pile of crumbs, his lips pressed into a blood-pinched hating line.

"What's the use?" he muttered. His fists snapped shut like jaws. "What's the *use*?" A water drop fell in front of him and he took a savage punch at it, losing balance and toppling over, face first, on the sponge. Water flooded from the compressed honeycomb.

He jolted to his feet on the block, hard with fury.

"You're not going to beat me," he said, he hadn't the slightest idea to whom. His teeth jammed together and it was defiance and a challenge that he hurled. "You're not going to *beat* me!"

He grabbed up handfuls of the soggy cracker and carried it up to the dry safety of the first black metal shelf of the water heater. What good are soaked crackers? asked his brain. They'll dry he answered. They'll rot first, said his brain. Shut up! he answered.

He yelled it. "Shut up!" God! he thought. He flung a cracker snowball at the water heater and it spatted off the metal.

Suddenly he laughed. Suddenly the whole thing seemed hilarious—him four-sevenths of an inch tall, in a tentlike robe, standing ankle-deep in lukewarm water and throwing soggy cracker balls at a water heater. He threw back his head and laughed loudly. He sat down in the warm water and slapped his palms at it, splashing geysers of it across himself. He pulled off his robe and rolled around in the warm water. A bath, he thought. I'm having my goddam morning bath.

After a while he got up and dried himself on what was left of the handkerchief around the sponge. Then he squeezed the water from the robe and hung it up to dry. My throat is sore, he told himself. So what? he said. It'll have to wait its turn.

He didn't know why he felt so exhilarated and stupidly amused. He was certainly in a fix. It was just, he guessed, that when things got so bad they were absurd, you couldn't take them straight any more; you had to laugh or crack. He almost imagined that if the spider came lumbering over the edge of the block now, he'd laugh at it.

He ripped up the handkerchief with teeth, nails, and hands, and made a flimsy robe of it, tying up the sides as he had done with the other robe. He put it on hastily. He had to get over to the sewing box.

Picking up the heavy pin, he threw it to the floor, then climbed down the cement block and retrieved it. I'll have to find another sleeping place now, he thought. It was amusing. He might even have to go up the great cliff face after that slice of dry bread. That was amusing, too. He shook his head as he jogged across the floor toward the carton, sunlight streaming through the windows over him.

It was like the time after he'd broken the contract. There were all the bills, the pitiless insecurity, the problems of adjustment. He'd tried to go back to work. He'd begged Marty, and Marty had reluctantly agreed. But it hadn't worked. It had got worse and worse until one day Therese had seen him trying to climb onto a chair and had picked him up like a boy and set him on it.

He'd screamed at her and gone storming to Marty's office; but before he could say a word Marty had shoved a letter across the desk at him. It had been from the Veterans Administration. The GI loan had been turned down.

And that afternoon, driving home, when the same tire had gone flat a second time, half a block from the apartment, Scott had sat in the car shrieking with laughter, so hysterical that he'd fallen off his special seat, bounced off the regular one, and landed in a laughter-twitching heap on the floor boards.

It was the way. Self-defense; a mechanism the brain devised to protect itself from detonation; a release when things became wound up too tightly.

When he reached the carton, he climbed in, not even caring if the spider was waiting in there for him. He walked in long strides to the sewing box and found a small thimble. It took all the strength in him to push it up the hill of clothes and shove it out through the opening.

He rolled the thimble across the floor like a giant empty hogshead, the pin stuck through his handkerchief robe and scraping behind him on the cement as he moved.

At the heater he thought first of trying to lift the thimble to the top of the cement block, then realized it was much too heavy and pushed it up against the base of the block, where the torrent of water quickly filled it.

The water was a little dirty, but that didn't matter. He picked up palmfuls of it and washed his face. It was a luxury he'd not experienced for many months. He wished he could shave off his thick beard, too; that would really feel good. The pin? No, that wouldn't work.

He drank some of the water and made a face. Not too good. Well, it would cool. Now he wouldn't have to climb all the way down to the pump.

Straining, he managed to drag the thimble a little bit away from the waterfall and let the quivering surface still itself. Then, propping the pin against the side of the thimble, he shinnied up its slanting length to the lip. There, amidst the faint spray, he looked into the mirror-like water at his face.

He grunted. Truly, it was remarkable. Small, yes, a particled fraction of its former self; yet still the same, line for line. The same green eyes, the same dark-brown hair, the same broad taper of nose, the same jawline, the same ears and full lips. He grimaced. And the same teeth, though likely rotted after so long a time without being brushed. Yet they were still white; rubbing on them with a moistened finger had accomplished that. Amazing. He would be a poor testimonial for a toothpaste concern.

He stared a while longer at his face. It was unusually calm for the face of a man who lived each day with dread and peril. Perhaps jungle life, despite physical danger, was a relaxing one. Surely it was free of the petty grievances, the disparate values of society. It was simple, devoid of artifice and ulcer-burning pressures. Responsibility in the jungle world was pared to the bone of basic survival. There were no political connivings necessary, no financial arenas to struggle in, no nerve-knotting races for superior rungs on the social ladder. There was only to be or not to be.

He ruffled the water with a hand. Begone, face, he thought, you matter nothing in this cellar life. That he had once been called handsome seemed stupid. He was alone, with no one to please or cater to or like because it was expedient.

He let himself slide down the pin. Except, he thought, wiping spray from his face, that he still loved Louise. It was a final standard. To love someone when there was nothing to be got from that person; that was love.

He had just measured himself at the ruler and was walking back to the water heater when there came a loud creaking noise, a thunderous crash, and a glaring carpet of sunlight flung across the floor. A giant came clumping down the cellar steps.

Paralysis locked him.

He stood horror-rooted to the spot, staring up at the mammoth figure bearing down on him, its plunging shoes raised higher than his head, then slamming down and shaking the floor beneath him. It was double shock that froze him into heart-leaping petrifaction; seeing the mountainous being so abruptly and, at the same time, realizing despite numb terror that he had once been that very size himself. Head thrown back, he stared, open-mouthed, at the giant's approach.

Then thought and immobility were torn away by a bolt of instinct and with a gasp he sprinted toward the edge of the engulfing shadow. The floor shook harder; he heard the bat squeak of gigantic shoes about to mash him like a bug. With a sucked-in cry, he lunged another yard, then dived headlong toward the light, arms out to brace himself.

He landed hard, rolling on his shoulder to break the fall. The vast shoe, like a whale leaping, slammed down inches from his body.

The giant stopped. From the tunnel of a pocket it withdrew a screw driver as long as a seven-story building, then billowed out its black shadow like a spreading pool as it crouched before the water heater.

Scott ran, splashing, around its right shoe, the top of his head level with the lip of the sole. Standing beside the cement block, he peered up at the colossus.

Far up—so far he had to squint to see—was its face: nose

like a precipitous slope that he could ski on; nostrils and ears like caves into which he could climb; hair a forest he could lose himself in; mouth a vast, shut cavern; teeth (the giant grimaced suddenly) he could slide an arm between; eye pupils the height of him, black irises wide enough to crawl through, lashes like dark, curling sabers.

He stared mutely at the giant. That was what Lou looked like now—monstrously tall, with fingers as thick as redwood trees, feet like elephants that never were, breasts like pliant, hill-peaked pyramids.

Suddenly the vast shape wavered before the colorless gelatine of tears. It had never struck him so hard before. Not seeing her, his own physique the norm, he had imagined her as someone he could touch and hold, even knowing it wasn't so. Now he knew it completely; and the knowing was a cruel weight that crushed all memory beneath itself.

He stood there crying silently, not even caring when the giant picked up his sponge and, with a dinosaur grunt, tossed it aside. Moods had come with quicksilver indistinction that morning—panic to misery to hilarity to peacefulness to terror, now to misery again. He stood by the block watching the giant remove the skyscraper side of the water heater and set it aside to poke the screw driver into the heater's belly.

A cold wind fogged across him then and his head snapped around so quickly it sent painful twinges down his neck. The door!

"Oh, my God," he muttered, astonished at his own stupidity. To stand here in disconsolate gloom when all the time his escape route was waiting.

He almost dashed straight across the floor. Then, with a rocking lurch, he realized that the giant might see and think him an insect, being conscious only of smallness and movement.

Eyes on the looming figure, he backed along the side of the block until he reached the wall. Then, turning, he raced along its base to the great shadow of the fuel tank. Eyes still on the giant, he ran underneath the tank, past the fifty strides of the ladder, under the red metal table, the wicker table, hardly starting at all when the oil burner flared once more into sound. Behind, the giant tapped and probed at the machinery of the water heater. Scott reached the foot of the steps.

The first one loomed fifty feet above him. He paced in the chilly shadow of it, looking up its sheer face at the sunlight pouring overhead like a golden canopy. It was still early morning, then; the back of the house faced east.

Abruptly he ran along the block-long distance of the step, looking for a place to climb. But there was nothing except a narrow vertical passage at the far right end where mortar between two cement blocks had contracted, leaving a three-sided chimney about the thickness of his body. He'd have to climb it as mountaineers did—braced rigid between back and sandal bottoms, inching himself up by leg tension. It was a terribly difficult way, and there were seven steps to the back yard. Seven fifty-foot faces to climb. If he were exhausted after the first one . . .

The thread. It might help. He ran back to the wicker table and shook loose the bar from its place. He glanced over at the giant, still crouching in front of the heater, then ran back to the step, dragging the thick thread behind him. There was just a chance.

He flung the bar up. But it wouldn't reach the top of the step, and even if he could throw it that high, there wasn't likely to be any niche for it to catch in. He dragged the thread to the three-sided chimney and stood there searching its narrow height for a crevice in which he might lodge the bar. There was none.

He threw the bar down and half walking, half running, moved restlessly along the base of the steps. He turned like a trapped animal and ran back again. There had to be a way. He'd been waiting for this opportunity for months; through half a winter in the cellar, waiting for someone to open that vast door so he could climb to freedom.

But he was so *small.* "No, no." He wouldn't let himself think about that. There was a way; there always was a way. No matter how difficult, there always was a way. He had to believe that. Nervously he cast another glance back at the crouching giant. How long would he stay there? Hours? Minutes? There was no time to waste.

The broom.

Whirling again, Scott raced across the floor, shivering in the wind. He should have put on the heavier robe. But there had been no time. Besides, it was probably still wet. The thimble; he wondered whether the giant's monstrous feet had knocked it over, perhaps even crushed it.

It doesn't matter! he yelled at himself. I'm getting out of here! He skidded to a halt in front of the broom that leaned against the refrigerator.

There was a spider web across the top of the bound bristles. He knew it wasn't the black widow's work, but it reminded him that his pin was back at the water heater. Should he go back and try to get it?

He shook that off too. It doesn't *matter*! He was going to get out of there. That was all he'd let himself concentrate on. I'm going to get out, that's all; I'm going to get out.

He grabbed one of the club-thick straws and pulled at it with all his strength. It stuck. He pulled again, with the same result. He grabbed the next straw and jerked at it. It stuck fast. With an impatient curse, he grabbed the next straw and pulled and the next and the next. They all stuck fast.

He tried another. He pulled as hard as he could, carelessly, bracing his feet against the bristles. When one finally did pull out, it came loose so easily that it sent him flying over on his back on the cement floor. He cried out sharply, then had to roll out of the way quickly to keep the toppling straw from crashing down on his skull.

He struggled to his feet, wincing at the pain in his back. Squatting, he grabbed hold of the straw and dragged it slowly over to the step, laying it perpendicular to the face. Then he let it drop and stood there panting, hands on hips. The sunlight overhead was like a bolt of shimmering cloth, so thick and brilliant it seemed that he could run right up it to the yard.

He closed his eyes and drank in fast lungfuls of the cold March air. Then he ran back to the other end of the straw and lifted it. Bracing the end against the rough cement face, he kept lifting it, drawing in the far end so that the straw rose at a steeper and steeper angle against the step. Wouldn't the giant hear the scraping? No, of course not. Those vast ears could never pick up such a tiny sound.

When the straw was leaning against the step at approximately a seventy-degree angle, he dropped his arms and let them hang aching at his sides. His head fell forward, mouth open, gasping at the air. As cold as it was, he leaned against the cement. The cellar swam in shadowy ripples before his exhaustion-glazed eyes. The oil burner had stopped. In the void of silence, he could hear the clatter of the giant's tools in the water heater.

When normal sight returned and his arms had stopped throbbing so badly, he looked up at the straw. He groaned. It wasn't nearly as long as he had expected; and shorter yet because, reared, it sagged limply in the middle. Even if he reached its very top, there would still be a good eight to ten feet for him to scale before he reached the top of the step. Eight to ten feet of vertical cement with no handholds to help him up.

He ran a shaky hand through his hair. You're not going to beat me, he thought, addressing unknown powers again. His face was a tense mask of lines and ridges. He was going to get up there, that was all there was *to* it.

He looked around.

Against the wall near the log pile there was a hill of stones, leaves, and wood scraps. Long ago, in a life that seemed now more imaginary than real, he had swept them all there in a spurt of atypical neatness.

He ran to the pile. It rose above him like a hill of boulders and giant logs, some as high as houses. Could he hope to drag some of them to the base of the step, at least enough to prop the straw on and make up five of those eight to ten feet? The rest of the footage he could chance with an upward spring, as he had done in climbing to the tabletop. But you almost fell from the tabletop, he reminded himself. If it hadn't been for that paint-can handle . . .

He ignored the recollection. This was beyond argument. Every action since his plunge into the cellar had been dedicated to the hope of getting up those steps. In the beginning, he'd been up and down them a hundred times, always stopped by the closed door. When he thought of how easily he'd been able to mount the steps then, it made him sick. It was cruel that now, when the door was finally opened, the steps should no longer be walls to him, but cliffs.

The first stone he tried to move was so heavy he couldn't budge it. He stumbled over the uneven surface of the hill looking for smaller stones, his restless gaze pausing momentarily on various of the dark cave openings formed by the piled rock. What if the spider were hiding in one of them? Heart thudding in slow, heavy beats, he moved over the broken slope until he found a flat stone he could move.

This he pushed with agonizing slowness across the floor, jamming it up against the step. He straightened up and stepped back. The stone was a little higher than his knees. He'd need another one.

Returning to the hill of rocks, he continued searching until he'd found a similar stone plus a piece of bark. Added to the original stone, these two extra pieces would just about make up the needed height. Moreover, there was a groove in the bark onto which the end of the straw might fit.

Grunting with satisfaction, he pushed the dead weight of the second stone back to the step. There, teeth clamped, body shaking with taut-muscled exertion, he managed to lift it to the top of the first stone, something giving in his back as he did it. Straightening up, he felt a flare of pain in his back muscles. You're coming apart, Carey, he told himself. It was amusing.

The second stone teetered a little on the first, he discovered. He had to cram pieces of torn cardboard into the gaps between the two facing surfaces. That done, he climbed up on top of it and jumped up and down. So far, his little platform was secure.

Worriedly he looked over at the giant, still working on the water heater—but for how long? He jumped down off the top stone, gasping at the pain in his back, and limped back to the hill. Sore throat, aching back, twitching arms. What next? A cold wind blew over him and he sneezed. Pneumonia next, he thought. It was—well, almost—amusing.

The scrap of bark was easier to transport. He carried the thin end of it on his shoulder and walked, bent over, dragging the bark behind him. It was getting colder. It suddenly occurred to him that he didn't know what he was going to do when he got out in the yard. If it was so cold, wouldn't he freeze to death? He pushed the thought aside.

He slid the bark over the top of the two stones, then stood leaning against his structure, looking at it.

No, now that they were close together, he could see that the straw end was too thick to fit into the groove in the bark. He blew out a breath through gritted teeth. Troubles, troubles. Another anxious glance at the giant. How could he tell how much time there was? What if he got up two steps and the giant finished and went back up? If he weren't crushed to death by those monstrous shoes, he would be, at the very least, stranded on the high, darkened step, unable to see well enough to get down again.

But he wasn't going to think of that. That was it, the end, the finale. He got out now or—No, there was no *or*. He wouldn't let there be one.

Picking up a tiny scrap of rock, he climbed to the top of his platform and scraped at the groove, tearing away stringy fibers until the slot was wide enough to accommodate the end of the straw. He threw down the piece of rock and, lifting the hem of his robe, mopped his sweaty face dry.

He stood there for a few minutes, breathing deeply, letting his muscles unknot. There's no *time* for rest, his brain scolded. But he answered it, I'm sorry, I've got to rest or I'll never make the top. He'd have to take a chance on the length of time the giant would be working. He'd never make the summit in one all-out effort, that was clear.

That was when the thought occurred to him. What am I doing all this for?

For a moment it stopped him cold. What *was* he doing it

for? In a matter of days it would all be over. He would be gone. Why all this exertion, then? Why this pretense at continuing an existence that was already doomed?

He shook his head. It was dangerous to think like that. Dwelling on it could end him. For in the final analysis, everything he had done and was doing was illogical. Yet he couldn't stop. Was it that he didn't believe that everything would be over on Sunday? How could he doubt it? Had the process faltered once—*once*—since it had begun? It had not. A seventh of an inch a day, as precise as clockwork. He could have devised a mathematical system on the absolute constancy of his descent into inevitable nothingness.

He shuddered. Strange, thinking about it was debilitating. Already he felt weaker, more exhausted, less confident. If he pursued it long enough he would be finished.

He blinked his eyes and, deliberately ignoring his rise of hopeless weariness, moved to the straw. He wouldn't let it happen to him. He'd lose himself in work.

Lifting the straw to the top of the bark proved extremely difficult. It was one thing to lift an end of it, using the floor as a fulcrum. It was one thing to slide the straw to a leaning position against the step. It was another entirely to lift the whole weight of it from the floor and prop it on the base he had erected.

The first time he lifted the straw, it slipped from his grasp and banged down on the cement, crushing one edge of a sandal. He remained pinned until he lifted the straw again and pulled his foot away.

He leaned against the platform, chest throbbing with agitated breath. If the straw had landed on his foot . . .

He closed his eyes. Don't think about it, he warned himself. Please. Don't think about the things that *could* have happened.

The second time he tried, he managed to get the straw propped on the edge of the first stone. But while he was resting the straw fell over and almost knocked him down. Cursing with desperate anger, he dragged the straw to a leaning position, then, with a surge of energy, lifted it once more, this time making sure it was secure before letting go.

The next lift was harder yet. Leverage would be bad because he'd have to start raising the straw at waist level, and then up to the top of the second stone,which was at the level of his shoulders. His legs would be of no service. All the strength would have to come from his back, shoulders, and arms.

Drawing in breath through his mouth, he waited till his chest was swollen taut, then cut off air abruptly and lifted the heavy straw, setting it down on the second stone. It wasn't until he let go that he realized how much of a lift it had been. There was a painful tension through his back and groin that loosened very slowly, as if the muscles had been twisted like wrung-out cloths and were unraveling now. He pressed a palm against the soft area on his back.

A few moments later he climbed to the top of the platform. With one more short lift, he slid the end of the straw into the groove. He shook the straw until it was in the most advantageous position, then sat down to gather strength for the climb. The giant was still working. There would be time. Of course there would.

Then he stood and tested the straw. Good, he thought. He inhaled quickly. Now to get out of there. He felt at the coil of thread over his right shoulder. Good. He was ready.

He began inching up the straw, shinnying along it carefully to keep it from sliding over. It sagged even more under his weight. Once it began to slip a little to the side, and he had to stop and, with body jerks, shake it back into position.

After a pause, he started climbing again, legs wrapped around the straw, lips drawn back from clenched teeth, eyes looking straight ahead at the dead gray of the cement face. When he got to the top of the step, he'd lower a thread loop and pull up the straw. There would be no stones to prop it on up there, but he'd manage something. Now he was twenty feet up, now twenty-five, now thirty, now . . .

A gigantic shape slid over him, blotting the sun from view. He almost fell off the straw. Losing his grip, he spun around to the underside of the straw, arms hugging wildly at its smooth surface. He jerked himself to a halt, and found himself looking into the green lantern eyes of the cat.

Shock drained breath from him. He felt even more helplessly petrified than when the giant had come down the steps. He clung to the straw, staring at the cat as if hypnotized.

The spearlike whiskers twitched. The huge cat edged forward in wary curiosity, belly near the floor, front legs flattened, back slightly arched. Scott felt the warm wind of its breath misting over him, and he almost retched.

Unconsciously he let himself slide down a few inches. There was a liquid rumbling in the cat's throat and he stopped abruptly, hanging there motionless. The cat's whiskers twitched again. Its breath was sickening. Turning his head from side to side, he saw its protruding side teeth like giant, yellow-edged daggers that could pierce his body in an instant.

An electric shuddering ran down his back. He slid down the straw a little more. The cat hunched forward. No! his mind screamed. He froze to the quivering straw, heartbeat like a fist pounding at his chest.

If he tried to descend, the cat would attack. If he jumped, he'd break a leg and be eaten. Yet he couldn't stay there. His throat contracted with a dry clicking. He hung there impotently under the bland surveillance of the huge cat.

When it raised its right paw twitchingly, his breath stopped.

In a fascination of absolute horror, he watched the huge, gray, scythe-clawed paw rise up slowly, coming closer and closer to him. He couldn't move. Unblinking, stark-eyed he hung there waiting.

Just before the paw was going to touch him, everything shook loose at once.

"Get out!" he screamed into the cat's face. It jumped back, startled. With a lurch, he flung the straw to the side, and it began sliding raspingly along the cement face, faster and faster. Not looking at the cat, he hung on till the toppling straw was about five feet from the floor. Then he leaped.

Landing, he twisted himself in a somersault. Behind him

the cat glided forward, growling. Get *up*! his mind shrieked. He found his feet again and lurched forward, falling.

As he skidded to his knees, the cat jumped, great paws banging down on each side of him, claw ends raking sparks from the cement. The mouth yawned open, a cave of scimitars and hot winds.

Twitching back against the step, Scott felt the thread coil slip off his shoulder. Grabbing it, he flung it deep into the cat's mouth and it jumped back, spitting and gagging. Pushing off from the step, Scott raced to the hole of stones and dived into a cave.

A second after, the cat's paw raked across the spot where he had entered. A cuffed stone rattled away. Scott crawled to the back of the cave and down a side tunnel as the cat scratched wildly at the rocks.

"Hey, Puss."

Scott stopped abruptly, head cocked, as the deep voice thundered.

"Hey, what're you after?" asked the voice. Scott heard chuckling like a threat of distant thunder. "Got yourself a mouse in there?"

The floor shook as the giant's shoes thudded across it. With an indrawn cry, Scott ran down the sloping tunnel, off into another one, again into yet another, until he skidded to a halt before a blank wall.

There he crouched shivering and waiting.

"Got yourself a mouse, have you?" the voice asked. It made Scott's head hurt. He covered up his ears. He still heard the fierce meowing of the cat.

"Well, let's see if we can't find 'im, puss," the giant said.

"No," Scott didn't even know he spoke. He shrank against the wall hearing the boulders being shoved aside by the giant's hands, the sound a grating, screeching rasp that plunged like a knife into his brain. He pressed both palms against his ears as hard as he could.

Suddenly, light speared across him. With a cry, he dived headlong into a newly opened tunnel. Clawing wildly at the air, he fell seven feet to a hard rock shelf, landing on his side and raking skin off his right arm. In the darkness, a boulder slammed down beside him, tearing skin from the hell of his right hand. He cried out in terror.

The giant said, "We'll find 'im, puss, we'll find 'im."

Light again. With a rasping sob, Scott lurched up and dived into the darkness again. A stone bounced off the floor and knocked him down. He rolled over and up again, running across the floor of the collapsing cavern, mute with panic. Another bouncing rock sent him flailing across the floor to smash head-on into a rock wall.

As deeper blackness blotted out his mind, he felt blood trickling warmly down his cheek. His legs went limp, his hands uncurled like flowers dying, and falling rocks reared up a tomb around him.

CHAPTER NINE
●●●●●●●●●●●

At last he stumbled into light.

He stood at the mouth of the cave, looking around the cellar with dull, unwitting eyes.

The giant was gone. And the cat. The side of the water heater was fastened back in place. Everything was as it had been; the vast, piled objects, the heavy silence, the imprisoning remoteness of it all. His gaze moved slowly to the steps and up them. The door was shut.

He stared at it, feeling empty with desire. He had struggled in vain once more. All the pushing of boulders, the endless crawlings and climbings through inky tunnel twists had been in vain.

His eyes closed. He swayed weakly on the hill of rocks, one throbbing length of pain. It seemed to well over him; his arms, his hands and legs and trunk. Inside, too, in his throat and chest and stomach. He had a dull, eating headache. He didn't know if he were starving or nauseous. His hands shook fitfully.

He shuffled back to the heater.

The thimble had been knocked on its side. The few drops remaining in it he drank like a thirsty animal, sucking them up from the cuplike indentations. It hurt to swallow.

When he had finished the water, he climbed with slow, exhausted movements to the top of the cement block. His sleeping place was completely barren, the sponge, handkerchief, cracker bundle, the box top all gone. He stumbled to the edge of the block and saw the box top across the floor. He hadn't the strength to lift it.

He remained in the shadowy warmth for a long while, just standing, weaving a little, staring out at the darkening cellar. Another day ending. Wednesday. Three days left.

His stomach gurgled hungrily. Slowly he tilted his head back and looked up to where he put the few soggy cracker crumbs. They were still there. With a groan he moved to the leg of the water heater and climbed up to the shelf.

He sat there, legs dangling, eating the cracker pieces. They were still damp, but edible. His jaws moved with rhythmless lethargy, his eyes staring straight ahead. He was so tired he could hardly eat. He knew he should go down and get the box top to sleep under in case the spider came. It came almost every night. But he was too weary. He'd sleep up here on the shelf. If the spider came . . . Well, what did it matter? It reminded him of a time, long before, when he had been with the Infantry in Germany. He'd been so tired that he'd gone to sleep without digging a foxhole, knowing it might mean his death.

He plodded along the shelf until he came to a walled-in area, then climbed over the wall and sank down in the darkness, his head resting on a screw head.

He lay there on his back, breathing slowly, barely able to summon the strength to fill his lungs. He thought, Little man, what now?

It occurred to him then that, instead of fighting with the stones and the straw, he might simply have climbed into the giant's slack cuff and been carried from the cellar in a moment. The only indication of the self-fury he felt was a sudden bunching of skin around his closed eyes, a moist clicking sound as his lips pulled back suddenly from clenched teeth. Fool! Even the thought seemed to rise wearily.

His face relaxed again into a mask of sagging lines.

Another question. Why hadn't he tried to communicate with the giant? Oddly enough, that thought didn't anger him. It was so alien it only surprised him. Was that because he was so small, because he felt that he was in another world and there could be no communication? Or was it that, as in all decisions now, he counted on only himself for any desired accomplishment?

Surely not that, he thought bitterly. He was as helpless and ineffectual as ever, maybe a little more blundering, that was all.

In the darkness he felt experimentally around his body. He ran a hand over the long, raw-fleshed scrape on his right forearm. He touched the torn flesh on the heel of his right hand, nudged an elbow against the swelling, purplish bruise on his right side. He ran a finger over the jagged laceration across his forehead. He prodded at his sore throat. He reared up a trifle and felt the shoot of pain in his back. Finally he let the separate aches sink back again into the general, coalescent pain.

His eyes opened, the lids seeming to fall back of their own accord, and he stared sightlessly at the darkness. He remembered regaining consciousness in the sepulcher of rocks; remembered the horror that had almost driven him insane until he realized that there was air to breathe and he had to keep his mind if he wanted to get out.

But that first instant of realizing that he was sealed in a black crypt and still alive had been the lowest point.

He wondered why the phrase occurred to him. How did he know it was his lowest point? There might be others much worse waiting around the next corner—if he stayed alive.

But he couldn't think of anything else. It *was* the lowest point, the nadir of his existence in the cellar.

It made him think of another lowest point, in the other life he had once led.

35"

When they got home from Marty's he stood at the living-room window while Lou carried Beth to bed. He didn't offer to help. He knew he couldn't lift his daughter now.

When Lou came out of the bedroom he was still standing there.

"Aren't you going to take off your hat and coat?" she asked.

She went into the kitchen before he could answer. He stood in his boy's jacket and his Alpine hat with the red feather stuck in the band hearing her open the refrigerator. He stared out at the dark street and heard the nerve-twisting crunch of ice cubes being freed in their tray, the muted pop of a bottle cap being pried off, the carbonated gurgle of soda being poured.

"Want some Coke?" she called to him.

He shook his head.

"Scott?"

"No," he said. He felt a throbbing at his wrists.

She came in with the drink. "Aren't you going to take off your things?" she asked.

"I don't know," he said.

She sat down on the couch and kicked off her shoes. "Another day," she said. He didn't reply. He felt as if she were trying to make him feel like a boy for getting dramatic over something inconsequential, while she patiently humored him. He wanted to burst out angrily at her, but there wasn't any opening.

"Are you just going to stand there?" she asked.

"If I choose," he said.

She looked at him for a moment, blank-faced. He saw the reflection of her face in the window. Then she shrugged. "Go ahead," she said.

"No skin off *your* nose," he said.

"What?" There was a sad, weary smile on her lips.

"Nothing, nothing." Now he *did* feel like a boy.

Her drinking and swallowing sounded noisy to him. He grimaced irritably. Don't *slurp*, his mind rasped. You sound like a pig.

"Oh, come on, Scott. Brooding won't help." She sounded faintly bored.

He closed his eyes and shuddered. It has come to this, he thought. The horror was gone; she was inured. He had expected it, but it was still a shock to find it happening.

He was her husband. He had been over six feet tall. Now he was smaller than her five-year-old daughter. He was standing in front of her, grotesque in his little boy's clothes, and there was nothing but a faint boredom in her voice. It was a horror beyond horror.

His eyes were bleak as he stared out at the street, listening to the trees rustle in the night wind like a woman's skirts descending an endless stairway.

He heard her drink again and he stiffened angrily.

"Scott," she said. Falsely applied affection, he thought. "Sit down. Staring out the window won't help Marty's business."

He spoke without turning. "You think that's what I'm worried about?"

"Isn't it? Isn't it what we're both—"

"It *isn't*," he cut her off coldly. Coldness in a little boy's voice sounded bizarre—as if he were acting out a part in a grade-school play, unconvincing and laughable.

"What, then?" she asked.

"If you don't know by now . . ."

"Oh, come on, darling."

He picked on that. "Takes a little straining to call me darling now, doesn't it?" he said, skin tight across his small face. "Takes a little—"

"Oh, *stop* it, Scott. Aren't there enough troubles without your imagining more?"

"Imagining?" His voice grew shrill. "Sure I'm imagining

everything. Nothing has changed. Everything's just the same. It's all just my imagination!"

"You'll wake Beth up."

Too man enraged words filled his throat at once. They choked each other and he could only stand fuming impotently. He turned back to the window and stared out again.

Then, abruptly, he headed for the front door.

"Where are you going?" she asked, sounding alarmed.

"For a walk! Do you mind?"

"You mean down the street?"

He wanted to scream. "Yes," he said, his voice shaking with repressed anger, "down the street."

"You think you should?"

"Yes, I think I should!"

"Scott, I'm only thinking of you!" she burst out. "Can't you see that?"

"Sure. Sure you are." He jerked at the front door, but it stuck. Color sprouted in his cheeks and he jerked harder, a curse muffled on his lips.

"Scott, what have *I* done?" she asked. "Did I make you this way? Did I take that contract away from Marty?"

"Damn this goddam—" His voice shook. Then the door opened and banged against the wall.

"What if someone sees you?" she asked, staring up from the couch.

"Good-by," he said, slamming the door behind him. And even that was ineffective because the jamb was too warped and the door wouldn't slam, only crunch into its frame.

He didn't look back. He started down the block with quick, agitated strides, heading for the lake.

He was about twenty yards from the house when the front door opened.

"Scott?"

He wasn't going to answer at first. Then, grudgingly, he stopped and spoke over his shoulder.

"What?" he asked, and he could have wept at the thin, ineffectual sound of his voice.

She hesitated a moment, then asked, "Shall I come with you?"

"No," he said. It was spoken in neither anger nor despair.

He stood there a moment longer looking back in spite of himself, wondering if she would insist on coming. But she only stood there, a motionless outline in the doorway.

"Be careful, darling," she said.

He had to bite off the sob that tore up through him. Twisting around, he hurried quickly down the dark street. He never heard her close the door.

This is the bottom, he thought, the very bottom. There is nothing lower than for a man to become an object of pity. A man could bear hate, abuse, anger, and castigation; but pity, never. When a man became pitiable, he was lost. Pity was for helpless things.

Walking on the treadmill of the world, he tried to blank his mind. He stared at the sidewalk, walking quickly through the patches of street lights and into darkness again, trying not to think.

His mind would not cooperate; it was typical of introspective minds. What he told it not to think about it dwelt on. What he demanded it to leave alone it clung to, doglike. It was the way.

Summer nights on the lake were sometimes chilly. He drew up the collar of his jacket and walked on, looking ahead at the dark, shifting waters. Since it was a week night, the cafés and taverns along the shore were not open. Approaching the dark lake, he began to hear the slapping of water on the pebbled beach.

The sidewalk ended. He moved out across rough ground, the leaves and twigs crackling under his tread like things alive. There was a cold wind blowing off the lake. It cut through his jacket, chilling him. He didn't care.

About a hundred yards from the sidewalk, he came to an open area beside a dark, rustic building. It was a German café and tavern, next to it a few dozen tables and benches for outdoor eating and drinking. Scott threaded his way among them until he overlooked the lake. There he sank down on the rough, pocked surface of a bench.

He sat staring grimly at the lake. He tried to imagine sinking down in it forever. Was it so fantastic? The same thing was happening to him now. No, he would hit bottom and that would be the end of it.

He was drowning in another way.

They had moved to the lake six weeks before, because Scott had felt trapped in the apartment. If he went out, people stared at him. With the first week and a half of the *Globe-Post* series already in print and reprint, he had become a national celebrity. Requests still poured in for personal appearances. Reporters came endlessly to the door.

But mostly it was the ordinary people, the curious, staring people who wanted to look at the shrinking man and think, Thank God, *I'm* normal.

So they had moved to the lake, and somehow they had managed to get there without anyone's finding out.

Life there, he discovered, was no improvement.

The dragging of it was what made it so bad. The way shrinking went on day by day, never noticeable, never ceasing, an inch a week like hideous clockwork. And all the humdrum functions of the day went on along with it in inexorable monotony.

Until anger, crouching in him like a cornered animal, would spring out wildly. The subject didn't matter. It was the opening that counted.

Like the cat:

"I swear to God, if you don't get rid of that goddam cat, I'll kill it!"

Fury from a doll, his voice not manlike and authoritive, but frail and uncompelling.

"Scott, she's not hurting you."

He dragged up a sleeve. "What's that? Imagination?" He pointed to a ragged scar.

"She was frightened when she did that."

"Well, I'm frightened too! What does she have to do, rip open my throat before you get rid of her?"

And the two beds:

"What are you trying to do, humiliate me?"

"Scott, it was your idea."

"Only because you couldn't stand to touch me."

"That's not true!"

"Isn't it?"

"No! I tried everything I could to—"

"I'm not a boy! You can't treat my body like a little boy's!"

And Beth:

"Scott, can't you see she doesn't understand?"

"I'm still her father, damn it!"

All his outbursts ended alike, him rushing to the cool cellar, standing down there, leaning on the refrigerator, breath a rasping sound in him, teeth gritted, hands clenched.

Days passed, one torture on another. Clothes were taken in for him, furniture got bigger, less manageable. Beth and Lou got bigger. Financial worries got bigger.

"Scott, I hate to say it, but I don't see how we can go on much longer on fifty dollars a week. With all of us to feed and clothe and house . . ." Her voice trailed off; she shook her head in distress.

"I suppose you expect me to go back to the paper."

"I didn't say that. I merely said—"

"I know what you said."

"Well, if it offends you, I'm sorry. Fifty dollars a week isn't enough. What about when winter comes? What about winter clothes, and oil?"

He shook his head as if he were trying to shake away the need to think of it.

"Do you think Marty would—"

"I can't ask Marty for more money," he said curtly.

"Well . . ." She said no more. She didn't have to.

And if she forgot and undressed without turning out the light, perhaps thinking he was asleep, he would lie in bed staring at her naked body, listening to the liquid rustle of her nightgown as it undulated down over her large breasts and stomach and hips and legs. He'd never realized it before, but it was the most maddening sound in the world. And he'd look at her as if he were a man dying of thirst looking at unreachable waters.

Then, the last week in July, Marty's check didn't come.

First they thought it was an oversight. But two more days went by and the check still didn't come.

"We can't wait much longer, Scott," she said.

"What about the savings account?"

"There isn't more than seventy dollars in it."

"Oh. Well . . . we'll wait one more day," he said.

He spent that day in the living room, staring at the same page of the book he was supposedly reading.

He kept on telling himself he should go back to the *Globe-Post*, let them continue their series. Or accept one of the many offers for personal appearances. Or let those lurid magazines write his story. Or allow a ghost writer to grind out a book about his case. Then there would be enough money, then the insecurity that Lou feared so desperately would be ended.

But telling himself about it wasn't enough. His revulsion against placing himself before the blatant curiosity of people was too strong.

He comforted himself. The check will come tomorrow, he kept repeating, it'll come tomorrow.

But it didn't. And that night they'd driven over to Marty's and Marty had told him that he'd lost his contract with Fairchild and had to cut down operations to almost nothing. The checks would have to stop. He gave Scott a hundred dollars, but that was the end.

Cold wind blew across him. Across the lake a dog barked. He looked down and watched his shoes swinging above the ground like pendulum tips. And now no money coming in. Seventy dollars in the bank, a hundred in his wallet. When that was gone, what?

He imagined himself at the paper again. Berg taking pictures, ogling Lou, Hammer asking endless questions. Head-lines uttered across his mind like banners. SMALLER THAN TWO-YEAR-OLD! EATS IN HIGH CHAIR! WEARS BABY CLOTHES! LIVES IN SHOE BOX! SEX DESIRE STILL SAME!

His eyes shut quickly. Why wasn't it really acromicria? At least then his sex desire would be almost gone. As it was, it got worse and worse. It seemed twice as bad as when he had been normal, but that was doubtless because there was no outlet at all. He couldn't approach Louise any more. The drive went on burning in him, banking higher and higher each day, adding its own uniquely hideous pressure to every-thing else he was suffering.

And he couldn't talk to Louise about it. The night shc'd made that obvious offer, he'd felt almost offended. He knew it was over.

"Laughin' at the blues!
Laughin' till I'm crazee!"

He twitched up on the bench, his head snapping around. Squinting into the darkness, he saw three shadowy figures strolling a short distance away, their youthful voices thin as they sang.

"My life is nothin' but a stumblin' in the dark.
I lost my way when I was born."

Boys, he thought, singing, growing up and taking it for granted. He watched them with a biting envy.

"Hey, there's a kid down there," one of them said.

At first Scott didn't realize they were talking about him. Then he did and his mouth tightened.

"Wonder what he's doin' there."

"Prob'ly—"

Scott didn't hear the rest of it, but from the burst of coarse laughter he could guess what had been whispered. With a tensing of muscles, he slid off the bench and started walking back toward the sidewalk.

"Hey, he's goin'," one of the boys said.

"Let's have some fun," said another.

Scott felt a jolt of panic, but pride would not allow him to run. He kept steadily on toward the sidewalk.

Now the footsteps of the three boys grew faster.

"Hey, where ya goin', kid?" he heard one of the boys call to him.

"Yeah, kid, where ya goin'?" said another.

"Where's the fire, kid?"

There was a general snicker. Scott couldn't help it; he walked faster. The boys walked faster.

"I don't think Kiddo likes us," said one of them.

"That's ain't nice," said another.

It was a race. Scott knew it was a hanging tautness in his stomach. But he wouldn't run. Not from three boys. He'd never be small enough to run from three boys. He glanced aside as he started up the slope toward the sidewalk. They were gaining on him. He saw the glowing tips of their cigarettes moving toward him like hopping fireflies.

They caught up to him before he reached the sidewalk. One of them grabbed his arm and held him back.

"Let go of me," he said.

"Hey, kid, where ya goin'?" asked the boy who held him. His voice was insolent with pretended friendliness.

"I'm going home," he said.

The boy looked about fifteen, sixteen maybe. He had a baseball cap on. His fingers dug into Scott's arm. Scott didn't have to see his face; he could almost imagine it—thin, mean, the jawline and brow peppered with pimples, the cigarette drooping from one corner of a lean almost lipless mouth.

"The kid says he's goin' home," said the boy.

"Izzat wot the kid says?" said another.

"Yeah," said the third. "Ain't that somethin'?"

Scott tried to push by them, but the boy in the cap drew him back into their surrounding circle.

"Kid, you shouldn't do that," he said. "We don't like kids that do that, do we, fellas?"

"Naw, naw. He's a fresh kid. We don't like fresh kids."

"Let go of me," Scott said, shocked at the tremble of his voice.

The boy released his arm, but he was still penned in.

"I wantcha t'meet my pals," said the boy. No face. Just the flash of a pale cheek, the glitter of an eye in the tiny flaring glow of the cigarette. A black, shadowy figure leaning over him.

"This is Tony," he said. "Say hello to 'im."

"I have to go home," Scott said, moving forward.

The boy pushed him back. "Hey, kid, you don't unnerstand. Fellas, this kid don't unnerstand." He tried to sound gentle and reasonable.

"Kid, don't you unnerstand?" said one of the other boys. "That's funny, y'know? The kid should unnerstand."

"You're very funny," Scott said. "Now will you—"

"Hey. The kid thinks we're funny," said the boy with the baseball cap on. "D'ya hear that, fellas? He thinks we're funny." His voice lost its banter. "Maybe we oughta show 'im how funny we are," he said.

Scott felt a crawling sensation in his groin and lower stomach. He looked around at the boys, unable to keep down the fear.

"Listen, my mother expects me home," he heard himself saying.

"Awwwww," said the boy with the cap. "His mother's waitin'. Jesus, ain't that sad? Ain't that sad, fellas?"

"That makes me cry," said one of the others. "Boo-hoo-hoo. I'm cryin'." A vicious chuckle emptied from his throat. The third boy snickered and punched his friend playfully on the arm.

"Live around here, kid?" asked the boy with the cap. He blew smoke into Scott's face and Scott coughed. "Hey, the kid's croakin'," said the boy, with mock concern. "He's chokin' n croakin'. Ain't that sad?"

Scott tried to push past them again, but he was shoved back, more violently this time.

"Don't do that again," warned the boy in the cap. His

voice was friendly and amiable. "We wouldn't wanna hurt a kid. Would we, fellas?"

"Naw, we wouldn't wanna do *that*," said another.

"Hey, let's see if he has any dough on 'im," said the third.

Scott felt himself tightening with a weird mixture of adult fury and childlike dread. It was even worse than it had been with that man. He was smaller now, much weaker. There was no strength in him to match his man's anger.

"Yeah," said the boy in the cap. "Hey, ya got any dough on ya, kid?"

"No, I haven't," he said angrily.

He gasped as the boy in the cap hit him on the arm.

"Don't talk t'me like that, kid," said the boy. "I don't *like* fresh kids."

Dread overwhelmed anger again. He knew he'd have to play it different to get out of this.

"I don't have any money," he said. His neck was beginning to arch from looking up at them. "My mother doesn't give me any."

The boy in the cap turned to his friends. "The kid says his mother don't give him none."

"Cheap bitch!" said another.

"I'll give her a good cheap—" said the third, breaking off with a convulsive forward jerk of his lower frame.

The boys laughed loudly. "Ya hear that, kid?" said the boy in the cap. "Tell yer old lady that Tony'll give her a good cheap one."

"Cheap? I'll do it fer nothin'," Tony said, humor submerged in a sudden surge of angry desire. "Hey, kid, has she got a big pair on 'er?"

Their raucous laughter broke off as Scott lunged between two of them. The boy in the cap grabbed him by the arm and spun him around. The heel of his palm slammed across Scott's cheek.

"I *told* ya not t'do that," snarled the boy.

"Son-of-a—" Scott raged, spitting blood. The last word was swallowed in a grunt as he drove his small fist into the boy's stomach.

"Bitch!" snapped the boy in a fury. He shot a fist into Scott's face. Scott cried out as the blow drove a wedge of pain into his skull. He fell back against one of the other boys, blood streaming darkly from his nose.

"Hold 'im!" snarled the boy, and the two other boys grabbed Scott's arms.

"Hit me in the belly, will ya, ya little son-of-a-bitch?" the boy said. "I'll . . ." He seemed undecided as to what revenge to take. Then he made a sound of angry decision and pulled out a book of matches from his trouser pocket.

"Maybe I'll give ya a couple brands, kiddo," he said. "How d'ya like *that*?"

"Let me go!" Scott struggled wildly in the boys' grip. He kept on sniffing to keep the blood from running across his lips. "Please!" His voice cracked badly.

The match flared in the darkness and Scott saw the boy's face as he'd imagined it.

The boy leaned in close.

"Hey," he said, suddenly fascinated. "Hey!" a crooked smile lifted the corner of his mouth. "This ain't no kid." He stared into Scott's twisted face. "Ya know who this *is*?"

"Whattaya talkin' about?" asked one of the boys.

"It's that guy! That shrinkin' guy!"

"What?" they said.

"Look at 'im, *look* at 'im, for God's sake!"

"Damn it, let me go or I'll have you all in jail!" Scott stormed at them to hide the burst of agony in him.

"Shut up!" ordered the boy in the cap. His grin returned. "Yeah, don't ya see? It's—"

The match sputtered out and he lit another one. He held it so close to Scott's face that Scott could feel the heat of it.

"Ya see now? Ya *see*?"

"Yeah." The two other boys stared, open-mouthed, into Scott's face. "Yeah, it's him. I seen his picture on T.V."

"And he tried t'make us think he was a kid," the boy said. "The freakin' son-of-a-bitch."

Scott couldn't speak. Despair had toppled anger. They knew him, they could betray him. He stood drained, his chest rising and falling with convulsive breath. The second match was thrown on the ground.

"Uh!" His head snapped over as the boy in the cap back-handed him.

"That's fuh lyin', Freako," the boy said. His laugh was thin and strained. "Freako, that's ya name. What d'ya say, freako? What d'ya say?"

"What do you *want* of me?" Scott gasped.

"What do we want?" mimicked the boy. "Freako wants t'know what we want." The boys laughed.

"Hey," said the third boy, "let's pull down his pants and see if *all* of him shrunk!"

Scott surged forward in their grip like a berserk midget. The boy in the cap drove a palm stingingly across his face. The night was a spiraling blur before Scott's eyes. "Freako don't understand," said the boy. "He's a dumb freako." He was breathing quickly through clenched teeth.

Dread was the knife in Scott now. He knew there was no reasoning with these boys. They were hating angry with their world and could express it only through violence.

"If you want my money, take it," he said quickly, buying desperate time.

"Bet ya shrinkin' *butt* we'll take it," sneered the boy. He laughed at his own joke. "Hey, that's pretty good." The humor left again. "Hold 'im," he said coldly, "I'll get his wallet."

Scott tensed himself in the darkness as the boy in the cap started around one of his friends.

"Ow!" One of the boys howled as Scott's shoe tip flashed up against his shin. The restraining hands on Scott's left arm were dropped.

"Ow!" the other boy's cry echoed the first; his hands dropped. Scott lunged forward in the darkness, heartbeat like a fist driving at his chest.

"Get 'im!" cried the boy in the cap. Scott's short legs pumped faster as he darted up the broken incline. "Bastard!" the boy shouted, and then he started after him.

Scott was gasping for breath before he reached the sidewalk. He almost tripped across its edge, went flailing forward, palms out, legs racing, then, finally, caught his balance and ran on. A stitch jabbed hotly at his side. Behind him, rapid shoe falls spattered onto the cement. "Lou," he whimpered, and ran on, open-mouthed.

Fifty yards up, he saw his house. Then, suddenly he realized he couldn't go there, because they'd know then where he lived, where the shrinking man lived.

His teeth jammed together and he turned impulsively into a dark alley.

He reached out, thinking he might open a side screen door and, still running, slam it shut so they'd think he'd gone in there. But that house was too close to his own. He ran on, gasping. Behind him the boys swept into the alley, their shoes crunching on the gravel.

Scott dashed around the back edge of the darkened house and raced across the yard.

There was a fence. Panic leaped in him. He knew he couldn't stop. Running at top speed, he jumped at it, clutching wildly for the top. He began scrambling up, slipped, started up again.

"Gotcha!"

A fist of dread pounded at his temples as he felt rough hands clutching at his right foot. His head snapped around and he saw the boy in the cap dragging him down.

A half-mad sound filled his throat. His other foot flailed out and drove into the boy's face. With a cry the boy let go and went staggering back, clutching at his face. Scott dragged himself over the fence, shoe tips scraping at the wood. He dropped down on the other side.

Jagged lances of pain shot up his ankle. He couldn't stop. Pushing up with a groan, he ran on, limping. Behind, he heard the two boys join their friend.

He scuttled painfully across the uneven ground until he came to the next street. There, finding a cellar door open, he half slipped, half jumped down the high steps, turned, and pulled the heavy door shut. It landed on his head and knocked him sideways against the cold concrete wall. He clutched out for a handhold as he rolled down two steps and landed on the dirt floor of the cellar.

He sat hunched over on the first step, trying to catch his breath. The step was cold and damp. He could feel it through his trousers. But he was too dizzy and weak to get up.

Breath wouldn't come. His thin chest kept jerking spasmodically as his lungs labored for air. There was a hot burning in his throat. The stitch was razor-tipped, a knife stabbing at his side. His head throbbed and ached. The inside of his mouth felt raw and smarting, and there was blood still running across his lips. The muscles of his legs were cramping in the coldness of the cellar. He was sweaty and shivering.

He began to cry.

It was not a man's crying, not a man's despairing sobs. It was a little boy sitting there in the cold, wet darkness, hurt and frightened and crying because there was no hope for him in the world; he was beaten and lost in a strange, unloving place.

Later, when it was safe, he limped home, chilled to the bone.

A frightened, wretched Lou put him to bed. She kept asking him what had happened, but he wouldn't answer. He just kept shaking his head, face expressionless, his small head rustling slowly on the pillow, back and forth, endlessly back and forth.

CHAPTER TEN
• • • • • • • • • •

Waking was a gradual itemization of pains.

His throat felt scraped and dry, feeling like a raw, juiceless wound. His face contorted as he swallowed. Whimpering softly, he twisted on his side. The pain of rubbing his lacerated temple against the screw head stabbed him into wakefulness.

He started to sit up, then sank back with a gasp, hot barbs ripping across the muscles of his back. He lay staring up at the dust-coated insides of the water heater. He thought: It's Thursday; there are three days left.

His right leg was throbbing. The knee felt swollen. He flexed the leg experimentally and winced when the dull ache flared into needling pain. He lay there quietly a moment, letting the pain ebb. He felt his face, his fingers stroking over the blood-caked scratches and tears.

Finally, with a groan, he shoved himself up and stood shakily, holding on to the black wall for support. How could he have got so mauled in such a few days? He'd been in the cellar for almost three months and it had never been like this before. Was it his size? Was it because the smaller he got the more perilous life became for him?

He climbed over the wall slowly and he walked along the metal shelf to the leg. He kicked aside the few tiny scraps of crackers left there, then climbed down the leg with slow, careful movements until he stood dizzily on top of the cement block. Thursday. Thursday. His tongue stirred like a piece of thick dry cloth in his mouth. He needed water.

He climbed down the block and looked into the thimble. Empty. And all the water on the floor had dried up or flowed into the small holes drilled in the cement. He stood there staring dully into the thimble cave. That meant he'd have to climb down the endless thread to the other thimble under the water tank. He sighed drearily and shuffled over to the ruler.

Three-sevenths of an inch.

Stolidly, as if it were something he had planned and not sudden disgust, he pushed the ruler over, and it clattered onto its side. He was sick of measuring himself.

He started walking toward the cavern in which the water pump clanked and chugged. Then he stopped, remembering the pin. His gaze moved slowly over the floor, searching. It was not in sight. He went over to the sponge and looked under it. He looked under the box top. There was no pin. The giant must have kicked it away, or else the head of it had become embedded in the sole of those gargantuan shoes.

His gaze moved over to the hose-high carton under the fuel tank. It looked miles away. He turned from it. He wasn't going to get another one. I don't care, he thought. It doesn't matter; let it go. He started again for the water pump.

There was another point, he decided, a point below that at which a man either laughed or broke. There was one more step down to the level of absolute negation. He was there now. He didn't care about anything. Beyond the simple plane of bodily function, there was nothing.

As he moved from beneath the mammoth legs of the clothes tree, his gaze slid up the cliff wall. He wondered if the spider were up there. Probably it was, crouching seven-legged and silent in its web, perhaps sleeping, perhaps chewing up some bug it had killed.

It might have been himself.

Shuddering, he looked back at the floor. He'd never resign himself to the spider, no matter how depleted his spirit became. It was too alien a form to adjust to. Horror and revulsion toward it were too deeply grained in him. It was better not to think of it at all. Better not to think that today the spider was as tall as he was, its body three times the volume of his, its long, black legs the thickness of his legs.

He reached the edge of the cliff and looked down into the vast canyon. Was it really worth it? Maybe it would be better just to forget about water altogether.

His throat labored dryly. No, water was not something you could forget about. Shaking his head like a sorrowing old man, he got on his knees and lowered himself over the edge of the step, then began easing himself down the thread. Fifty feet, two days before. Seventy-five today, probably. Tomorrow?

What if the spider is waiting down there? he thought. It frightened him to think it, but he kept descending, too weak to stop himself. He tried not to think about climbing back up. Why hadn't he had the foresight to make knots at regular intervals in the thread? It would have made ascent so much easier.

His sandals finally touched bottom and he let go of the thread-rope. At least his fingers had not been scraped as badly, now that they were so small.

The thimble loomed over him like a giant vat, the lip of it a good six feet above his head. If it had been overflowing, he might have caught water in his palms. As it was, he would have to climb to the top.

But how? The side, even with its indentations, was smooth and slightly overhanging. He pushed at the thimble, thinking he might knock it over, but it was too heavy, filled with water. He stood staring at it.

The thread. He limped back to the wall and picked up the heavy end of it, lugging it as far as it would go. It didn't reach. He let go of it and it slid back to the wall.

He shoved at the thimble again. His arms fell. It was too heavy. No use. He started back for the thread. It's no use, he thought. I'll just forget about it. His face was martyred. I'm going to die anyway, what's the difference? I'll die. Who cares?

He stopped, biting his lip savagely. No, that was the old way. It was the childish way, the "I'll punish the world by dying" attitude. He needed water. The thimble had the only water available. Either he got it or he would die, and no one the wiser or the stupider or the worse for it.

Gritting his teeth, he walked around, looking for pebbles. Why do I go on? he asked himself for the hundredth time. Why do I try so hard? Instinct? Will? In many ways it was the most infuriating thing of all, this constant bewilderment at his own motivations.

At first he found nothing. He moved in the shadows, muttering to himself. What if there are other spiders here? What if there are. . .

It would have been so much better if his brain had lost its toxic introspections long before. Much better if he could have concluded life as a true bug instead of being fully conscious each hideous, downward step of the way. Awareness of the shrinking was the curse, not the shrinking.

Even thirsty, hungry, the thought stopped him. He stood in the cold shadows, turning it over in his mind.

It was true. He had realized it once, fleetingly, then forgotten it again. Sinking into the physical. But it was true. So long as he had his mind, he was unique. Even though spiders were larger than he, even though flies and gnats could shade him with their wings, he still had his mind. His mind could be his salvation, as it had been his damnation.

He almost left the floor when the pump began.

With a hoarse cry, he slammed back against the wall of the cavern, hands clutching up at his ears. The noise seemed to come in physically tangible waves, pinning him there. He thought his eardrums would burst. Even through his pressing palms the thunderous, shrieking clatter penetrated, hammering jagged spikes into his head. He couldn't think. Like a mindless beast, he cringed against the wall, drowning in noise, his face twisted, his eyes stark with pain.

When the pump finally shut off, he slumped down bonelessly into a heap, his eyes slitted, his mouth hanging open. His brain felt numb and swollen. His limbs still shook.

Oh, yes, his mind mocked faintly. Yes, so long as you can think, you're unique.

"Fool," he muttered weakly. "Fool, fool, fool."

After a while he stood up and looked for a pebble again. Finding one at last, he pushed it back beside the thimble, then climbed up on it. There were three feet left. He crouched down a little, braced himself, then jumped.

His fingers clawed at the edge of the thimble and caught. His feet kicked about and slipped on the smooth edge as he pulled himself up. Water, he thought, almost tasting it in his mouth. Water. He didn't notice at first that the thimble was tipping.

Panic speared through him as the thimble started to topple. Seeking lost balance, he tightened his grip spasmodically instead of loosening it. Let go! His mind cried shrilly. He released his hold and dropped heavily, landing on the edge of the pebble, losing balance a second time and falling back-ward, arms flailing. He flopped back on the cement, the breath knocked from him. The thimble kept falling. With a cry he flung an arm across his face and went rigid, waiting for the thimble to crash on him.

Only cold water poured across him, blinding and gagging him. Sucking air into his lungs, he struggled to his knees. Another wave of water dashed over him, almost knocking him on his back again. Coughing and spluttering, he stood up, rubbing at his eyes.

The thimble was rocking back and forth, water flooding across its lip and splattering on the cement. Scott stood there shivering, catching his breath, his tongue licking the cold drops from his mouth.

Finally, when the thimble was rocking less violently, he moved up to it warily and caught the spilling water in his palms. It was so cold it numbed his hands.

When he had finished drinking, he backed away and sneezed. Oh, God, now comes the pneumonia, he thought. His teeth were beginning to chatter. The cotton robe was cold and clammy on his flesh.

With jerky, impulsive movements he dragged the robe over his head. Cold air flooded over him. He had to get out of there. Throwing down the dripping robe, he ran to the thread and started climbing as rapidly as he could.

After he'd gone up ten feet he felt exhausted. Every upward movement became more difficult than the last. Pain seesawed in his muscles, a taut, drawing sharpness as he dragged himself up, a dull, throbbing ache as he hung resting.

He couldn't rest for more than a few seconds. With every pause he grew more chilled. His white body covered with goose flesh, he kept climbing, gasping at the air between clenched teeth. Half a dozen times he thought he was going to fall as exhaustion welled up in his arms and legs, every muscle seeming to go slack. His hands clutched desperately at the ropelike thread, his legs curled around it. He pressed against the cement face, panting.

Then, in a moment, he began climbing again, not looking

up because he knew that if he looked up, even once, he would never reach the top.

He stumbled across the floor, waves of heat and coldness breaking over him. He pressed a shaking hand against his forehead. It was hot and dry. I'm sick, he thought.

He found his old robe lying behind the cement block, crusted with dirt, but dry. He brushed it off and put it on. It helped a little. Shaking with weariness and anger, and still shivering with cold, he circled around the floor collecting the few damp pieces of cracker left and throwing them on top of the sponge.

It took all the strength he had remaining to drag the box over the sponge. Then he lay in the darkness, his breath a thin, rasping sound that faltered in his throat like steam. The cellar was without sound.

After a few minutes he tried to eat. But swallowing hurt too much. Already he was thirsty again. He rolled over on his stomach and pressed his burning face into the soft sponge, his hands opening and closing in weary, ceaseless movements. After a moment he felt moisture on his face, and he started squeezing hard, remembering that the sponge had been soaking wet the morning before. But the little water he got was so brackish it almost made him lose the food he'd managed to eat.

He rolled onto his back again. What do I do now? he thought despairingly. There was no food left but the pitiful scraps under the box top with him; no water except at the bottom of a cliff he'd never have the strength to climb again; no way of getting out of the cellar. And now, added to everything else, fever.

He rubbed fiercely at his hot forehead. The air felt close and heavy. Heat pressed down on him like a hand. I'm suffocating, he thought. He sat up abruptly, looking around with hot eyes, head lolling on his neck. Unaware, his right hand picked a cracker crumb to bits and flung the shreds aside.

"I'm sick," he groaned. His thin voice ballooned around him. He sobbed, digging teeth into the knuckles of his left hand until the skin broke. "I'm sick. I'm sick!"

He fell back with a groan and lay there limply, staring up through fever-slitted eyes.

Half-conscious, he thought he heard the spider walking on the box again. One, two, three, his twisting mind began to chant. Four, five, six. Seven legs my true love has.

Distortedly, he remembered the day when he had been twenty-eight inches tall, the height of a one-year-old child—a china doll that shaved real whiskers and bathed in a dishpan and used a baby's potty chair and wore made-over baby clothes.

He had stood in the kitchen yelling at Lou because he'd suggested that she put him in a sideshow to make some money and she hadn't insisted that he shouldn't say such things; she'd only shrugged.

He'd yelled and ranted, his little face red, stamped his cunning high-topped shoes, glared up at her, until suddenly she'd turned from the sink and shouted back, "Oh, stop squeaking at me!"

In a fury so complete it blinded him, he spun and lurched for the doorway, only to trip over the cat and get badly clawed.

Lou had run to him and tried to make it up. She'd cleaned the jagged scratch on his arm and apologized. But he'd known it wasn't a woman apologizing to a man, but a woman apologizing to a midget she felt sorry for.

And when she'd finished bandaging him, he'd gone down to the cellar again; the last refuge to which he always fled in those days. And he'd stood there by the steps staring through anger and hurt at the cellar.

He'd squatted down and picked up a rock that was lying on the floor and he'd rocked there on his heels, thinking of all the things that had happened to him in the past few weeks. He'd thought of the money almost gone, of Lou unable to find a job, of Beth's increasing disrespect, of the Medical Center never calling, of the endless shrinking of his body. And while he thought of them, his mind had grown angrier, his lips whitening on each other, his hand closed like a steel trap over the rock.

When he saw the spider walking on the wall across from him, he reared up suddenly and fired the rock at it with all his might. Fantastically the rock had pinned one of the spider's black legs to the wall and it had fled, leaving the leg behind. Scott had stood in front of the wall watching the leg twitch like a living hair. And, blank-faced, he'd thought, Someday my leg will be that small.

It had been impossible to believe.

But now his leg *was* that small, and the insane descent of his existence was bearing down toward inevitable conclusion.

He wondered what would happen if he died now. Would his body keep shrinking? Or would the process cease? Surely it could not go on if he were dead.

Far across the floor, the oil burner began its hurricane roar again, shaking the air with deafening vibrations. With a moan he pressed his hands over his ears and lay there shivering without control, feeling as if he were in a buried coffin while an earthquake shook the cemetery.

"Leave me alone," he muttered feebly. "Leave me alone." He drew in a whining breath. His eyes closed.

He twitched, woke.

The oil burner still roared. Was it the same roaring on which he had closed his eyes? Had seconds passed, or hours?

He sat up slowly, lightheaded and shaking. He lifted a trembling hand and touched his forehead. It was still hot. He rubbed the hand across his face, groaning deeply. Oh, God, I'm sick.

Weakly he pushed himself to the rim of the sponge and slid over the edge. His grip was so weak that it broke instantly and he thudded down on his feet, sitting down heavily with a startled grunt.

He sat on the cold cement a long moment, blinking, his torso weaving. His stomach rumbled with hunger. He tried to stand up. He had to lean against the sponge. Breath came from his nostrils in short, hot bursts. He swallowed. I need water. Tears ran down his cheeks. There was no water he could get. He hit the sponge with an impotent fist.

After a few minutes he stopped crying and, turning slowly,

stumbled through the darkness until he collided with the box-top wall. It knocked him down. Muttering, he crawled to the box-top side again and, lifting it first with his hands and then with his back, he squeezed out from under.

It was like crawling into a refrigerator. A shudder rippled down his back. He stood up and leaned back against the box top.

It was afternoon; he *had* slept. Rays of sunlight were visible through the window over the log pile, the window that faced south. Two, three o'clock, he estimated. Another day was half gone; more than half.

He spun around and drove a strengthless punch into the cardboard wall. Pain stung his knuckles. He hit again. Damn you! He leaned his head against the side and rained in enervated blows, feeling the impact of each one leap up his arms, across his shoulders, down his back.

"Pointless, pointless, pointless, point—" In a wild, croaking voice he chanted the word on one breath until no sound came from him. Then his arms flopped to his sides like lengths of wood and he fell against the cardboard, eyes closed, twitching with jerking breaths.

When he finally turned, it was with a mind blanked to everything except water. He started across the floor slowly. I can't go down to the tank, but I need water, he thought. But there isn't any water anywhere else. There's water that drips in the cracker box, but I can't climb that high. But I need water. He walked, eyes down, hardly seeing. I need water.

He almost fell in the hole.

For a frightening instant, he wavered on the very edge of it. Then he caught himself and stepped back.

He got down on his knees and peered into the dark cavity drilled through the cement floor. It was like looking down a well, except that the well broke off about fifteen feet down and there was nothing but lightless void.

He poised his tilted head over the hole, listening. At first there was only the sound of his own labored breathing. Then, holding his breath, he began to hear another sound. The sound of softly dripping water.

It was a nightmare to lie there on his stomach, racked with thirst, and listen to the drip of unreachable water. His tongue kept stirring in his mouth, seeking to escape the imprisonment of his lips. He kept swallowing endlessly, hardly noticing the jabs of pain it caused.

For one moment he almost dived headfirst into the hole. I don't care! he thought in a fury. I don't care if I die!

What kept him from it he didn't know. Whatever it was, it was below consciousness, for on the surface he was angrily determined to plunge into the well-like hole and find that water.

But he drew back from the hole and got on his knees again. He hesitated. Then he fell forward again and listened to the sound, almost inhaling it like air. He moaned. He pushed to his knees once more, stood dizzily, and then began walking away from the drainage hole. He turned and walked back to the brink of it. He swung a foot over it, staring down into its unseeable depths.

"Oh, God, why don't you . . ."

He turned and walked away from the hole on rigid legs, hands clenched into fists at his sides. There's no point! he wanted to scream. Why *shouldn't* he go down the hole? Why not, like some grotesque, latter-day Alice, plunge into yet another world?

He thought it was a red wall at first. He stopped in front of it, staring at it. He prodded it. Not stone or wood. It was the hose.

He walked around its serpentine bulk until he came to one end of it. There he stared into the long, shadowy tunnel curving away from him. He stepped up onto the metal ring and stood in a groove, thinking. Sometimes when you picked up a hose water dripped from the end of it.

With a gasp, he started running clumsily down the smooth-floored tunnel, banging into hard walls where the hose twisted abruptly, racing as fast as he could along the winding labyrinth of it. Until, curving to the right for what seemed to be the hundredth time, he found himself ankle-deep in cold liquid. With a grateful sob, he squatted down and lifted trembling palmfuls of the water to his lips. It tasted stale and it hurt his throat to swallow, but he had never gulped the finest wine so eagerly.

Thank God! he kept thinking. Thank God! All the water I need now. All I need! He grunted, almost in amusement, thinking of the many times he'd climbed down that fool thread to the water tank. What an ass he'd been! Well, it didn't matter now. He was all right now.

It wasn't until he began walking back along the tunnel that he realized it had been, at best, a reactive triumph. How different did it make the situation, how better off? His minuscule existence was preserved a little longer, yes. He would see the end of it intact; but the end would come. Was that a triumph?

Or would he see the end of it?

As he emerged into the cellar again, he realized how weak with sickness he was; worse, how weak with hunger. The sickness he might alleviate with rest and sleep, but to hunger there was only one answer.

His gaze moved to the towering cliff.

He stood there in the shadow of the hose, looking up at the place where the spider lived. One piece of food remained in the cellar; he knew that much for sure. One slice of dried-up bread; more than enough to keep him for the last two days. And it was up there.

It came upon him with annihilating simplicity. He hadn't the strength to climb up there. Even if he could, by some incredible extension of will power, make it up the cliff, there was the spider. And he hadn't the courage to face the spider again. Not a black, scuttling horror three times the size of him.

His head fell forward. Then that was it; that was the decision he must accept. He stepped away from the hose and started across the floor toward the sponge. What decision was there but that? Was there, after all, a choice? Wasn't it out of his hands, inexorable? He was three-sevenths of an inch tall. What could he hope to do?

Something made him look again at the cliff face.

The giant spider was running down the wall.

With a body-jarring gasp, Scott fled across the floor. Before the spider had reached the bottom of the cliff, he had squeezed beneath the edge of the box top and climbed onto the sponge. When the spider clambered, black and bulbous, onto the box top, he was waiting for the sound of it, his teeth jammed so hard together that his jaws ached.

There could be no hope of food, then; not with that quivering black cannibal guarding it. He closed his eyes, sobs dragging at his throat, hearing overhead the scratching, scrabbling movements of the spider.

Chapter Eleven
● ● ● ● ● ● ● ● ● ●

As in a dream, delirium-driven, he was back again at the Columbia Presbyterian Medical Center, being tested.

Voice a crispness, voice a hollow waver, Dr. Silver told him that no, he did not have acromicria, as had first been suspected. Yes, there was the bodily shrinkage, but no, his pituitary gland was not diseased. There was no loss of hair, no cyanosis of extremities, no bluish discoloration of skin, no suppressed sexual function.

There were urinary-excretion tests to establish the amounts of creatin and creatinine in his system; important tests, because they would tell much about the functioning of his testes, his adrenals, about the balance of nitrogen in his body.

Discovery: You have a negative nitrogen balance, Mr. Carey. Your body is throwing off more nitrogen than it is retaining. Since nitrogen is one of the major building blocks of the body, consequently, we have shrinkage.

An imbalance of creatinine was causing further involution.

Phosphorus and calcium were being thrown off, too, in the precise proportion in which those elements were found in his bones.

ACTH was administered, possibly to check the catabolic breakdown of tissue.

ACTH was ineffective.

There was much discussion about a possible dosage of pituitary extract. "It might enable his body to retain nitrogen and cause the disposition of new protein," they murmured.

It seemed there was danger, though. The response of the human body to administered growth hormone is not ascertainable; even the best extracts are poorly tolerated and often give abberant results.

"I don't care. I want it. Can I be worse off?" he said.

Dosage administered.

Negative.

Something was combating the extract.

At last the paper chromatography; the capillary trailing of body elements across paper, the specific gravity of each one causing it to stain a different part of the paper.

And a new element was found in his system. A new toxin.

Tell us something, they said. Were you ever exposed to any kind of germ spray? No, not bacterial warfare. Have you, for instance, ever been accidentally sprayed with a great deal of insecticide?

No remembrance at first; just a fluttering amorphous terror. Then sudden recollection. Los Angeles, a Saturday afternoon in July. He had come out of the house, heading for the store. He had walked through a tree-lined alley, between rows of houses. A city truck had turned in suddenly, spraying the trees. The spray misted over him, burning on his skin, stinging his eyes, blinding him momentarily. He yelled at the driver.

Could *that* possibly be the cause of all this?

No, not that. They told him so. That was only the beginning of it. Something happened to that spray, something fantastic and unheard of; something that converted a mildly virulent insecticide into a deadly growth-destroying poison.

And so they searched for that something, asking endless questions, constantly-probing into his past.

Until, in a second, it came. He remembered the afternoon on the boat, the mist washing over him, the acid sting on his body.

A spray impregnated with radiation.

And that was it; the search was over at last. An insect spray hideously altered by radiation. A one-in-a-million chance. Just that amount of insecticide coupled with just that amount of radiation, received by his system in just that sequence and with just that timing; the radiation dissipating quickly, becoming unnoticeable.

Only the poison left.

A poison that, without destroying the pituitary gland, destroyed, little by little, its ability to maintain growth. A poison that day by day forced his system to convert nitrogen into excess waste matter; a poison that affected creatinine and phosphorus and calcium and left them as waste to be thrown off. A poison that decalcified his bones so that, soft and pliant, they could shrink, little by little. A poison that nullified any administered hormone extract by causing antihormone action in direct opposition.

A poison that made him, little by little, the shrinking man.

The search over at last? Not really. Because there was only one way to fight a toxin, and that was with an anti-toxin.

So they'd sent him home. And while he waited there, they sought the antitoxin that might save him.

At his sides, hands folded into gnarled fists. Why, asleep or waking, did he have to think about those days of waiting? Those days when his very body was continuously tensed for the sound of a knock on the door, the sudden stridency of the telephone ringing. It had been a free fall of the mind, taut consciousness never finding a base to settle on, but hanging in constant suspense, waiting.

The countless trips to the post office, where he'd rented a box so he could get two and three deliveries a day, instead of only one. That cruel walk from the apartment to the post office, wanting to run and still walking, his body twitching with his desperate desire to run. Entering the post office, hands numb, heart pounding. Crossing the marble floor, stooping and looking into the box. And, when there were letters, his hands shaking so badly that he could barely slide the key into the lock. Jerking out the letters, gaze stabbing at the return addresses. No letter from the Center. The sudden feeling that life was gone from him, his feet and legs were running into the floor like candle wax.

And when they'd moved to the lake the suffering was even worse, because then he had to wait for Lou to go to the post office—standing at the front window, hands shaking when he saw her come walking back down the street. He would know she had no letter because she walked so slowly, and yet he would be unable, until she actually said so, to believe that no letter had come.

He pitched over on his stomach and bit into the sponge savagely. It was so horribly true that thought was his undoing. To be unaware; dear God, to be joyously unaware. To be able to rip the tissues of his brain away and let them drip like clouded paste from his fingertips. Why couldn't—

His breath stopped. He reared up sharply, ignoring the sudden throb of pain in his head.

Music.

"Music?" He murmured faintly. How could there be music in the cellar?

Then he knew; it wasn't in the cellar, but upstairs. Louise was playing music on the radio: Brahms' First Symphony. He leaned on his elbows, lips parted, holding his breath and listening to the sturdy beat of the symphony's opening phrase. It was barely audible, as though he stood in the lobby of a concert hall hearing the orchestra through closed doors.

Breath escaped finally, but he did not move. His face was still, eyes unblinking. It was still the same world, then, and he was still a part of it. The connecting sound of music told him so. Upstairs, gigantically remote, Louise was listening to that music. Below, incredibly minute, he was listening too. And it was music to both of them, and it was beauty.

He remembered how, toward the end of his stay in the house, he had been incapable of listening to music unless it was played so low that Lou couldn't even hear it. Otherwise the music was magnified into a clubbing noise at his ears, giving him a headache. The clatter of a dish was a knife jab at his brain. The sudden cry or laughter of Beth assailed him like a gun fired beside his ear, making his face contort, making him cover his ears.

Brahms. To lie like a mote, an insignificance in a cellar, listening to Brahms. If life itself were not fantastic, that moment could be labeled so.

The music stopped. His gaze jerked up as if he might see, in the darkness, the reason for its stopping.

He lay there, silent, listening to the muffled voice of the woman who had been his wife. His heart seemed to stop. For a moment he was really part of that old world again.

His lips formed the name Lou.

21"

Because the summer ended, the teen-aged girl who had worked at the lake grocery store had to return to school. The opening had been given to Lou, who had applied for it a month before.

Vaguely she'd thought that Scott would take care of Beth when she got a job. But now it was painfully clear that, barely reaching the height of Beth's chest, he couldn't take care of her at all. Moreover, he refused to try. So she made arrangements with a neighborhood girl who had left high school. The girl agreed to take care of Beth while Lou was working.

"Lord knows, we won't have much money left after paying her," Lou had said, "but I guess there's no alternative."

He'd said nothing. Not even when she told him that, as much as she hated to say it, he'd have to stay in the cellar during the day unless he wanted the girl to know who he was; for, obviously, he couldn't pass for a child. He'd only shrugged his dainty shoulders and left the room without a word.

Before Lou left for work the first morning, she prepared sandwiches and two thermos bottles—one of coffee, one of water—for Scott. He sat at the kitchen table, propped up on two thick pillows, his pencil-thin fingers partially curled around a mug of steaming coffee, his face giving no indication that he heard a word she was saying to him.

"This should last you easily," she was saying. "Take a book with you; read. Take naps. It won't be so bad. I'll be home early."

He stared at the circles of cream floating like oil drops on the coffee. He twisted the cup very slowly on its saucer. It made a squeaking sound that he knew irritated Lou.

"Now remember what I told you, Beth," Lou said. "Don't say a word about Daddy. Not a *word*. Do you understand?"

"Yes." Beth nodded.

"What did I say?" Lou demanded.

"I don't say a word about Daddy."

"About the freako," Scott mumbled.

"What?" Lou asked, looking at him. He stared into the coffee. She didn't pursue it; he had fallen into the habit of muttering to himself since they'd moved to the lake.

After breakfast, Lou went down to the cellar with him, carrying one of the lawn chairs for him to sit on. She pulled down her suitcase from a pile of boxes between the fuel tank and the refrigerator and set it on the floor. She put two chair cushions in it.

"There, you can take a nice nap there," she said.

"Like a dog," he muttered.

"What?"

He looked at her like a bellicose doll.

"I don't think the girl will try to come down," she went on. "Then again, she might be nosy. Maybe I'd better put the lock on the door."

"No."

"But what if the girl comes down?"

"I don't want the door locked!"

"But, Scott, what if—"

"I don't want the door locked!"

"All right, all right," she said, "I won't put the lock on. We'll just have to hope the girl doesn't decide she wants to see the cellar."

He didn't speak.

While she made sure he had everything he needed, bent far over to give him a dutiful peck on the forehead, went back up the steps and lowered the door into place, Scott stood motionless in the middle of the floor. He watched her walk past the window, the skirt of her dress windblown around her shapely legs.

Then she was gone, but he remained unmoving, staring out the window at the spot where she had passed. His small hands kept flexing slowly against his legs. His eyes were motionless. He seemed engrossed in somber thought, as if he might be contemplating the relative merits of life and death.

At last the expression slipped from his features. He drew in a long breath and looked around. He lifted his palms briefly in a gesture of wry surrender, then let them slap down on his thighs.

"Swell," he said.

He climbed up on the chair, taking his book with him. He opened the book to the fringe-bottomed leather marker that read, "This Is Where I Fell Asleep," and started to read.

He read the passage twice. Then the book fell forward in his lap and he thought about Louise, about the impossibility of his touching her in any way. He reached her kneecaps and a little more. Somewhat short of manliness, he thought, teeth gritted. His expression did not change. Casually he shoved the book off the chair arm and heard it slap down loudly on the cement.

Upstairs he heard Lou's footsteps moving toward the front of the house, then fading. When they returned they were accompanied by another set of footsteps and he heard the voice of the girl, typically adolescent, thin, fluttery, and superficially confident.

Ten minutes later Lou was gone. In front of the house he'd heard the sputtering cough, the sudden gas-fed roar of the Ford being warmed up. Then, after a few minutes, the gun-ning sound had gradually disappeared. Now there were only the voices of the girl Catherine and Beth. He listened to the rise and fall of Catherine's voice, wondering what she was saying and what she looked like.

Bemused, he put the indistinct voice to distinct form. She was five feet six, slim-waisted and long-legged, with young, uptilted breasts nudging out her blouse. Fresh young face, reddish-blonde hair, white teeth. He watched her moving lightly as a bird, her blue eyes bright as polished berries.

He picked up the book and tried to read, but he couldn't. Sentences ran together like muddy rivulets of prose. The page was obscured with commingling words. He sighed and stirred uncomfortably on the chair. The girl stretched to the urging of his fancy, and her breasts, like firm-skinned oranges, forced out their silken sheathing.

He blew away the picture with an angry breath. Not that, he ordered.

He drew his legs up and wrapped both arms around them, resting his chin on his knees. He sat there like a child musing on the case for Santa Claus.

The girl had half taken off her blouse before he shut the curtain on her forcibly imposed indelicacy. The taut look was on his face again, the look of a man who has found effort unrewarding and has decided on impassivity instead. But, far beneath, like lava threatening in volcanic bellies, the bubbling of desire went on.

When the screen door of the back porch slapped shut and the voices of Beth and the girl floated into the yard, he slid off the chair with sudden excitement and ran to the pile of boxes beside the fuel tank. He stood there for a moment, his heart jolting. Then, when his mind came up with no authoritative resistance, he clambered up the pile and peered through a corner of the cobweb-streaked window.

Lines of pain shriveled in around his eyes.

Five feet six had become five feet three. The slim waist and legs had become chunky muscle and fat; the young, uptilted breasts had vanished in the loose folds of a long-sleeved sweat shirt. The fresh young face lurked behind grossness and blemishes, the reddish-blonde hair had been dyed to a lackluster chestnut. There were, feebly remaining, white teeth and movements like a bird's; a rather heavy bird's. The color of her eyes he couldn't see.

He watched Catherine move around the yard, her broad buttocks cased in faded dungarees, her bare feet stuck in loafers. He listened to her voice.

"Oh, you have a cellar," she said.

He saw the look on Beth's face change obviously and felt his muscles tightening.

"Yes, but it's just empty," Beth said hastily. "Nobody lives there."

Catherine laughed unsuspiciously.

"Well, I hope not," she said, looking toward the window. He shrank back, then realized that the cellar could not be seen through any of the windows because of the glare of light on them.

He watched them until they disappeared around the back end of the house. His eyes caught the fleeting sight of them as they moved past the window over the log pile. Then they were gone. Grunting, he climbed back down the pile of boxes and went back to the chair. He put one of the thermos bottles on the arm of the chair and retrieved the book. Then, sitting down, he poured smoking coffee into the red plastic cap and sat there, the book open and unread on his lap, sipping slowly.

I wonder how old she is, he thought.

He started up on the chair cushion, eyes jerking open.

Someone was lifting the cellar door.

With a gasp, he flung his legs over the edge of the suitcase just as the person's hold slipped and the door crashed down. He struggled to his feet, looking frantically toward the steps. The door started to rise again; a spear of light shot across the floor, widening.

With two distinct lunges, Scott grabbed the coffee thermos and the book and almost dived under the fuel tank. As the opened door slammed down, he slid himself behind the big carton of clothes. He clutched the book and thermos bottle to his chest, feeling sick. Why did he have to be so vitriolically stubborn about having the lock put on the door? Yes, it was the idea of being imprisoned that he hadn't liked. But at least in prison, others could not come in.

He heard the cautious descent on the stairs, the clicking of loafers, and he tried to stop breathing. As the girl entered he shrank back into the shadows.

"Hmm," the girl said. She moved around the floor. He heard her kick the chair experimentally. Would she wonder why it was there? Wasn't it an odd place for a chair, right in the middle of a cellar floor? He swallowed dryly. And what about the suitcase with the pillows in it? Well, that might be where the cat slept.

"Jesus, what a mess," said the girl, her shoes scuffing over the cement. For a moment he saw her thick calves as she stood by the water heater. He heard her fingernails tapping on the enameled metal.

"Water heater," she said to herself. "Uh-huh."

She yawned. He heard the straining sound in her throat that accompanied tense stretching. It broke off with a loud grunt. "Boop-dee-doodle-oodle," said the girl.

She moved around some more. Oh, my God, the sandwiches and the other thermos, he thought. Damn nosy bitch! his mind snapped. Catherine said, "Hmm. Croquet."

Then, in a few minutes, she said, "Oh, well," and went back up the steps and the cellar shook with the crash of the dropped door. If Beth were taking a nap, that would end it.

As Scott crawled out from under the fuel tank, he heard the back screen door slam shut and Catherine's footsteps overhead. He got up and put the thermos bottle back on the chair arm. Now he'd have to let Lou put the lock on the door.

"Damn the stupid little . . ."

He paced the floor like a caged animal. Nosy bitch! You couldn't trust one of them. First damn day and she had to see the whole house. She'd probably gone through every bureau, cabinet, and closet in the house.

What had she thought about seeing male clothing? What

lie might Lou have to tell—or already told? He knew that she'd given Catherine a false last name. Since no mail was delivered to the house, there was not too much danger of the girl's discovering the lie.

The only danger was that Catherine might have read those articles in the *Globe-Post* and seen the pictures. Yet if that were so, surely she already suspected that he must be hiding in the cellar and would have searched more carefully. Or *had* she been searching?

It was ten minutes later when he decided to have a second sandwich and discovered that the girl had taken them.

"Oh, *Christ*!" He slammed an infuriated fist on the arm of the chair and almost wished she'd hear him and would come down so he could berate her for a stupid pryer.

He sank back on the chair and shoved the book off the arm again. It slapped loudly on the floor. The hell with it, he thought.

He drank all the coffee and sat there, sweating, glaring straight ahead. Upstairs, the girl walked around and around. Fat slob, he called her in the jaded smallness of his head.

"Sure, go ahead," he said. "Lock me in."

"Oh, Scott, *please*," she begged. "It was your decision. Do you want to take a chance on her finding you?"

He didn't answer.

"She may come down again if the door's open," Lou said. "I don't think she thought anything one way or the other about finding that bag of sandwiches here yesterday. But if she finds another one . . ."

"Good-by," he said, turning away.

She looked down at him for a moment. Then she said quietly, "Good-by, Scott," and she kissed him on the top of the head. He drew away.

While she went up the steps he stood on the floor, rhythmically slapping the folded newspapers against the calf of his right leg. Every day it's going to be the same, he thought; sandwiches and coffee in the cellar, a good-by peck on the head, exit, door lowering, lock snapping shut.

When he heard it, a great suction of terror pulled the breath from him and he almost screamed. He saw Lou's moving-legs, and suddenly he shut his eyes, pressing his lips together to block the cry wavering in his vein-ridged throat. Oh, God, dear God, a *prisoner* now. A monster that good and decent people lock into their cellars so the world may not know the awful secret.

After a while the tension ran out of him and passive withdrawal came back again. He climbed up on the chair and lit a cigarette, drank coffee, and thumbed carelessly through the previous evening's *Globe-Post* that Lou had brought home.

The short article was on page three. Head: WHERE IS THE SHRINKING MAN? Subhead: *No Word Since Disappearance Three Months Ago*.

"New York: Three months ago Scott Carey, the 'Shrinking Man,' so called because of the strange disease he had contracted, disappeared. Since then, no word about him has been received from any quarter."

What's the matter, you want more pictures? he thought.

"Authorities at the Columbia Presbyterian Medical Center, where Carey was being treated, said they could make no comment as to his present whereabouts."

They also can't make antitoxin, he thought. One of the top medical centers in the country, and here I sit, shriveling away while they fumble.

He was going to shove the thermos bottle off the chair, but then he realized it would only be hurting himself. Compulsively he gripped one hand with the other and squeezed until the fingernails went bloodless, until his wrists began to ache. Then he let his hands flop on the arms of the chair and stared morosely at the orange wood between his spread fingers. Stupid color to paint lawn chairs, he thought. What an idiot the landlord must have been!

He wriggled off the chair and began pacing. He had to do something besides sit and stare. He didn't feel like reading. His eyes moved restlessly about the cellar. Something to do, something to do. . . .

Impulsively he stepped over to a brush leaning against the

wall and, grabbing it, began to sweep. The floor needed sweeping; there was dirt all over, stones, scraps of wood. He cleared all of them from the floor with quick, savage motions; he swept them into a pile beside the steps, and flung the brush against the refrigerator.

Now what?

He sat down and had another cup of coffee, kicking nervously at the chair leg.

While he was drinking, the back screen door opened and closed, and he heard Beth and Catherine. He didn't get up, but his gaze moved to the window, and in a moment he saw their bare legs move past.

He couldn't help it. He got up and went to the pile of boxes and climbed up.

They were standing by the cellar door in bathing suits, Beth's red and frilly, Catherine's pale blue and glossy, in two pieces. He looked at the round swell of her breasts in the tight, pulled-up halter.

"Oh, your mother locked the door," she said. "Why did she do that, Beth?"

"I don't think I know," Beth answered.

"I thought maybe we could play croquet," said Catherine.

Beth shrugged ineffectually. "I don't know," she said.

"Is the key in the house?" asked Catherine.

Another shrug. "I don't know," said Beth.

"Oh," said Catherine. "Well . . . let's have a catch, then."

Scott crouched on top of the boxes, watching Catherine as she caught the red ball and threw it back to Beth. It wasn't until he'd been there five minutes that he realized he was rigidly tensed, waiting for Catherine to drop the ball and bend over to pick it up. When he realized that, he slid off the boxes with a disturbed clumsiness and went back to the chair.

He sat there breathing harshly, trying not to think about it. What in God's name was happening to him? The girl was fourteen, maybe fifteen, short and chubby, and yet he'd been staring at her almost hungrily.

Well, is it my fault? he suddenly flared, letting fury take over. What am I supposed to do—become a monk?

He watched his hand shake as he poured water. He watched the water spill over the sides of the red plastic cup and dribble down his wrist. He felt the water like a trickling of ice down his hot, hot throat.

How old *was* she? he wondered.

Flesh pulsed over his jaws as he kept biting. He stared through the grimy window at Catherine, who was lying on her stomach, reading a magazine.

She lay sideways to him, stretched out on a blanket, her chin propped up by one hand, the other hand idly turning the pages.

His throat was dry but he didn't notice it; not even when it tickled and he had to clear it. His small fingers pressed for balance against the rough surface of the wall.

No, she couldn't be less than eighteen, he commented to himself. Her body was too well developed. That bulge of breast as she lay there, the breadth of her hips. Maybe she was only fifteen, but if so she was an awfully advanced fifteen.

His nostrils flared angrily and he shuddered. What the hell difference did it make? She was nothing to him. He took a deep breath and prepared to return to the floor but just then Catherine bent her right knee and the leg wavered lazily in the air.

His eyes were moving, endlessly moving over Catherine's body—down her leg and across the hill of her buttock, up the slope of her back and around her white shoulder, down to the ground-pressing breast, back along the stomach to her leg, up her leg, down her—

He closed his eyes. He climbed down rigidly and went back to the chair. He sank back in it, ran a finger over his forehead, and drew it away dripping. His head fell back against the wooden chair.

He got up and went back to the boxes. He climbed up without a thought. Yes, that's it, have another look at the back yard, mocked his alien mind.

At first, he thought she had gone into the house. A betraying groan began in his throat. Then he saw that she was standing by the cellar door, lips pursed estimatingly, looking at the lock.

He swallowed. Does she know? he thought. For one wild instant he thought he would run to the door and scream, "Come down, come down here, pretty girl!" His lips shook as he fought the desire.

The girl walked past the window. His eyes drank her in thirstily, as if it were the final view of all time. Then she was gone and he sat down on the top of the boxes, back to the wall. He stared at his ankles, the thickness of a policeman's club. He heard the back door shut and then the footsteps of the girl moving around overhead.

He felt drained. He felt that if he relaxed an iota more, his body would run down over the boxes like sirup on a hill of ice cream.

He didn't know how long he'd been there when the back door whined open and slammed shut again. He twitched, startled, and rose up again.

Catherine walked past the window, a key chain dangling from her fingers. His breath caught. She'd been in the bureau drawers and found the extra keys!

He half slid, half jumped down the stacked boxes, wincing as he landed on his right ankle. He grabbed the sandwich bag and shoved the thermos bottles into it. He tossed the half-finished box of crackers on top of the refrigerator.

His eyes fled around. The paper! He darted to it and snatched it up, as he heard the girl experimenting with the keys at the door. He stuck the folded newspaper on the shelf of the wicker table, then grabbed his book and the bag and ran for the dark, sunken room where the tank and water pump were. He'd decided beforehand that if Catherine ever came down again, that was where he'd hide.

He jumped down the step to the damp cement floor. At the door, the lock clicked open and was pulled out of the metal loop. He stepped gingerly over the network of pipes and slid in behind the high, cold-walled tank. He set down the bag and book and stood there panting as the door was pulled up and Catherine came down in the cellar.

"Locking the cellar," he heard her say in slow disgust. "Think I was gonna steal somethin' or somethin'."

His lips drew back in a teeth-clenched, soundless snarl. Stupid bitch, he thought.

"Hmmmph," said Catherine. He heard her loafers clicking over the floor. She kicked the chair again. She kicked the oil burner and it resounded hollowly. Keep your goddam feet to yourself! his brain exploded.

"Croquet," she said. He heard a mallet being slid out of the rack. "Hmmph," she said again, a little more amusedly. "Fore!" The mallet clicked loudly on the cement.

Scott edged cautiously to the right. His shirt back scratched over the rough cement wall and he froze. The girl hadn't heard. "Uh-huh," she was saying. "Hoops, clubs, balls, stakes. Yowza."

He stood looking at her.

She was bending over the croquet rack. She'd loosened her halter while she'd been lying in the sun, and it hung down almost off her breasts as she leaned over. Even in the dim light, he could see the distinct line of demarcation where tanned flesh became milk-white.

No, he heard someone begging in his mind. No, get back. She'll see you.

Catherine leaned over a little more, reaching for a ball, and the halter slipped.

"Oops," said Catherine, putting things to order. Scott's head fell back against the wall. It was damply cool in there, but wings of heat were buffeting his cheeks.

When Catherine had gone and locked the door behind her, Scott came out. He put the bag and book on the chair and stood there feeling as if every joint and muscle were swollen and hot.

"I can't," he muttered, shaking his head slowly. "I can't. I *can't.*" He didn't know what he meant exactly, but he knew it was something important.

"How old's that girl?" he asked that evening, not even glancing up from his book, as though the question had just, idly and unimportantly, occurred to him.

"Sixteen, I think," Lou answered.

"Oh," he said, as if he had already forgotten why he asked.

Sixteen. Age of pristine possibility. Where had he heard that phrase?

He shook it off, crouching on the boxes, a delicately limbed dwarf in corduroy rompers, looking out bleakly at the rain, watching the drops spatter on the ground, splashing freckles of mud on the windowpanes. His face was a mask of expressionless defeat. It shouldn't have precipitated, thought his mind. Oh, it shouldn't have.

He hiccuped. Then, with a tired sigh, he climbed down the pile and walked unsteadily to the chair. He jolted back in it and—whoops!—he caught the whisky bottle as it almost toppled off the arm. O bottle of booze beloved! He snickered.

The cellar was a haze of gelatine around his bobbing head. He tilted back the bottle and let the whisky trickle hot in his throat, burning in his stomach.

His eyes watered. I am drinking Catherine! his mind cried fiercely. I have distilled her, synthesizing loins and breasts and stomach and sixteen years of them into a conflagrating liquor, which I drink—*so*. His throat moved convulsively as the whisky gurgled down. Drink, drink! And it shall make thy belly bitter, but it shall be in thy mouth sweet as honey.

Drunk I am and drunk I mean to stay, he thought. He wondered why it had never occurred to him before. This bottle that he held before him now had stood in the cupboard for three months and, before that, two months in the old apartment. Five months of suffering neglect. He patted the brown glass bottle; he kissed it fervently. I kiss thee, Catherine liquefied. I buss the distillation of thy warm, sugared lips.

Simple, came the thought, because she is so much smaller than Lou, that's why I feel like this.

He sighed. He swung the empty bottle over his lap. Catherine gone. Down the hatch with Catherine. Sweet girl, you swim now in my veins, a dizzying potion.

He jumped up suddenly and flung the bottle with all his might against the wall. It exploded sharply and a hundred whisky-fragrant scraps of glass danced across the cool cement. Good-by, Catherine.

He stared at the window. Why'd it have to rain? he thought. Oh, why'd it? Why couldn't it be sunny so the pretty girl could lie outside in her bathing suit and he could stare at her and lust in secret, sick vicariousness?

No, it had to rain; it was in the stars.

He sat on the edge of the chair swinging his legs. Upstairs there were no footsteps. What was she doing? What was the pretty girl doing? Not pretty—*ugly*. What was the ugly girl doing? Who cared whether she was pretty or ugly? What was the girl doing.

He watched his feet swinging in the air. He kicked out. Take that, air; and *that*.

He groaned. He got up and paced around. He stared at the rain and the mud-spattered windows. What time was it? Couldn't be more than noon. He couldn't take this much longer.

He went up the steps and pushed at the door. It was locked, of course, and Louise had taken all the keys with her this time. "Fire her!" he'd yelled that morning. "She's dishonest!" and Lou had answered, "We can't, Scott. We simply can't. I'll take the keys. It'll be all right."

He braced his back against the door and reared up. It hurt his back. He gasped angrily at the air and butted his head against the door. He fell down on the step, dizziness clouding his brain.

He sat there mumbling, hands pressing at his skull. He knew why he wanted the girl discharged. It was because he couldn't stand to look at her, and it was far beyond his ability to tell Lou about it. The most she could do would be to make one more insulting offer. He wouldn't take that.

He straightened up, smiling in the shadows.

Well, I fooled her, he said. I fooled her and sneaked a whisky bottle down, and she never knew.

He sat there, breathing heavily, thinking about Catherine leaning over the croquet rack, about her halter slipping.

He stood abruptly, banging his head again. He jumped down the steps, ignoring the pain. And I'll fool her again!

He managed to feel grimly justified as he climbed the box pile clumsily. A drunken, crooked grin on his face, he knocked up the hook on the window and shoved at the bottom of its frame. It stuck. His face got red as he pushed at it. Get out, goddam your stupid bones!

"Son-of-a—"

The window flew out and he flopped across the ledge. The window flew back in and banged the top of his head. The hell with it! His teeth were gritted. *Now*, he dizzily told the world. Now we'll see. He crawled out into the rain, not fighting at all against the vicious dredging of heat in him.

He stood up and shivered. His eyes fled up to the dining-room window and the rain drizzled in his eyes and ran across his face and spattered on his cheeks. What now? he thought. The cold air and rain were cooling off the surface of impulsion.

Deliberately he walked around the house, staying close to the brick base until he'd reached the porch. Then he ran to the steps and up them. What are you *doing*? he asked. He didn't know. His mind was not conducting the tour.

He stood on tiptoe and cautiously looked into the dining room. No one was there. He listened but didn't hear anything. The door to Beth's room was shut; she must be taking a nap. His gaze moved to the bathroom door. It was shut.

He sank back on his heels and sighed. He licked raindrops from his lips. Now what? he asked again.

Inside the house, the bathroom door opened.

With a start, Scott backed away from the window, hearing footsteps pad across the kitchen floor, then fade. He thought she'd gone into the living room and edged to the window again, pushed up on his toes.

His breath stopped. She was standing at the window looking out at the yard. She was holding a yellow bath towel in front of her.

He couldn't feel the rain spattering off him, crisscrossing like cold, unrolling ribbons across his face. His mouth hung open. His gaze moved slowly down the smooth concavity of her back, the indentation of her spine a thin shadow that ran down and was lost between the muscular half-moons of her white buttocks.

He couldn't take his eyes from her. His hands shook at his sides. She stirred and he saw the glitter of water drops on her, quivering like tiny blobs of gelatine. He sucked in a ragged, rain-wet breath.

Catherine dropped the towel.

She put her hands behind her head and drank in a heavy breath. Scott saw her left breast swing up and stand out tautly, the nipple like a dark spear point. Her arms moved out. She stretched and writhed.

When she turned he was still in the same tense, muscle-quivering pose. He shrank back, but she didn't see him because the top of his head was barely higher than the window sill. He saw her bend over and pick up the towel, her breasts hanging down, white and heavy. She stood up and walked out of the room.

He sank down on his heels and had to clutch at the railing to keep his legs from going limp beneath him. He half hung there, shaking in the rain, a stark look on his face.

After a minute he stumbled weakly down the steps and around the house to the cellar window. He crawled through and locked the window behind him. He climbed down the hill of boxes, still shuddering.

He sat on the lawn chair, an old sweater wrapped around himself. His teeth were chattering, and he shivered uncontrollably.

Later he took his clothes off and hung them on the oil burner to dry. He stood by the fuel tank in his brown, high-topped shoes, holding the sweater around his shoulders, staring up at the window. And finally, when he couldn't bear the stillness or the pressure or the thoughts a second longer, he began to kick the cardboard carton. He kicked it until his leg ached and the cardboard side was split almost to the floor.

"But how did you get a cold?" Lou asked, her voice carrying a note of exasperation.

His voice was nasal and thick. "What do you expect when I'm stuck in that damn cellar all day!"

"I'm sorry, darling, but . . . well, shall I stay home tomorrow so you can stay in bed all day?"

"Don't bother," he said.

She didn't mention that she'd noticed that the whisky bottle was gone from the kitchen cupboard.

If Lou had been able to lock the windows, too, it would have been all right. But knowing he could get out any time he wanted; knowing that he could spy on Catherine, made it an impossible situation.

Hours dragged in the cellar. He might manage to absorb himself in a book for an hour or two, but ultimately the vision of Catherine would flit across his mind and he would put down the book.

If Catherine had come out in the yard more often, it would have been all right. Then, at least, he could look at her through the window. But days were getting colder as September waned, and Catherine and Beth stayed in the house most of the time.

He had taken to bringing a small clock to the cellar. He'd told Lou he wanted to be able to keep track of the time, but what he really wanted was to be able to know when Beth was napping. Then he could go out and peer through the windows at Catherine.

One day she might be on the couch reading a magazine, and there would be no satisfaction. But the next day she might be ironing, and, for some reason, when she ironed she always took off part of her clothes. Another time she might take a shower and, afterward, stand naked at the back window. And once she had lain naked in the bedroom under the skin-purpling glare of Lou's portable sun lamp. That had been one cloudy afternoon and she hadn't drawn the shades all the way down. He'd stood outside for thirty minutes and never budged.

Days kept passing. Reading was almost forgotten. Life had become one unending morbid adventure. Almost every afternoon at two o'clock, after having sat in shaking excitement for an hour or more, he would crawl out into the yard and walk secretively around the house, climbing up and peering over the sills of every window, looking for Catherine.

If she were partly or completely nude, he counted the day a success. If she was, as was most often the case, dressed and engaged in some dull occupation, he would return angrily to the cellar to sulk out the afternoon and snap at Louise all evening.

Whatever happened, though, he would lie awake at night, waiting for the morning to come, hating and despising himself for being so impatient, but still impatient. Sleep grew turgid with dreams of Catherine; dreams in which she grew progressively more alluring. Finally he even gave up scoffing at the dreams.

In the mornings he would eat hastily and go down to the cellar for the long wait until two o'clock, when, heart pounding, he would crawl out through the window again to spy.

The end of it came with shocking suddenness.

He was on the porch. In the kitchen, Catherine was standing naked under Lou's open bathrobe, ironing some clothes.

He shifted his feet, slipped, and thumped down on the boards. Inside, he heard Catherine call out, "Who's there?"

Gasping, he jumped down the step and started running around the house, looking over his shoulder in fright, to see a frozen-faced Catherine standing at the kitchen window, gaping at his fleeing childlike form.

All that afternoon he stood shivering behind the water tank, unable to come out because, even though she hadn't seen him go into the cellar, he was sure she was looking in through the window. And he cursed himself and felt sickly wretched thinking about what Lou would say to him and how she would look at him when she knew.

* * *

He lay still under the box top, listening to the scratching clamber of the spider over the cardboard.

He moistened his lips with a sluggish tongue and thought of the pool of cold water in the hose. He felt around with his hand until it closed over a fragment of damp cracker; then he decided he was too thirsty to eat and his hand drew back again.

For some reason the sound of the spider's crawling didn't bother him too much. He sensed that he was beyond stark disruption, lying in the shallows of emotion, spent and quiescent. Even memory failed to hurt. Yes, even the memory of the month they'd discovered the antitoxin and injected him three times with it—to no avail. All past laments were undone by the drag of present illness and exhaustion.

I'll wait, he told himself, until the spider is gone, and then I'll go through the cool darkness and walk over the cliff and that will be the end of it. Yes, that's what I'll do. I'll wait until the spider's gone and then I'll go over the cliff and that will be the end of it.

He slept, heavily, motionlessly. And, in his dream, he and Lou were walking in September rain, talking as they went. And he said, "Lou, I had an awful dream last night. I dreamed I was as small as a pin."

And she smiled and kissed his cheek and said, "Now, wasn't that a foolish dream?"

CHAPTER TWELVE

• • • • • • • • • • •

Thunder woke him. His fingers shriveled in abruptly, his eyes jerked open. There was an instant of blank suspension, consciousness hanging submerged beneath the shock of sudden awakening. His eyes stared mindlessly; his face was a pale, unmarked tautness, mouth a dash embedded in beard.

Then he remembered; and the scars of worry and defeat gouged across his brow and around his eyes and mouth again. Staring became sightlessness behind fallen lids, his hands uncurled. Only the faint murmur in his throat acknowledged the pain it was to lie in thunder.

In five minutes the oil burner clicked off, and the cellar became a vast, heavy silence.

With a grunt he sat up slowly on the sponge. The headache was almost gone. Only when he grimaced did it flare minutely. His throat still hurt, his body felt encrusted with aches and twinges, but at least the headache was gone and—he felt his forehead—the fever had abated somewhat. The able ministrations of sleep, he thought.

He sat weaving a little, licking his dry lips. Why did I sleep? he wondered. What had drugged him when he'd decided to end it all?

He wormed his way across the sponge and, holding on to the edge, dropped to the floor. Pain shot up his legs, faded. If only he could believe there had been purpose in his helpless sleep; that it might have been the act of a watching benevolence. He could not. More than likely it had been cowardice that had sent him off to sleep instead of to the cliff's edge. Even wanting to, he could not honor it with the title "will to live." He had no will to live. It was simply that he had no will to die.

At first he couldn't lift the box top, it had become so heavy. That told him what he'd meant to verify at the ruler; that overnight he had shrunk another fraction and was now only two-sevenths of an inch tall.

The cardboard edge scraped across his side as he dragged himself out from beneath it. It pinned his ankle so that he had to bend over and work at it with his hands. Free at last, he sat on the cold cement, letting the waves of dizziness settle. His stomach was a flagon of air.

He didn't measure himself; there was no point in it. He walked slowly across the floor looking to neither one side nor the other. On unsteady legs he headed for the hose. Why had he slept?

"No reason." He framed the words with his cracked lips.

It was cold. Gray, cheerless light filtered through the windows. March fourteenth. It was another day.

After the half-mile walk, he clambered over the metal lip of the hose and trudged along the black tunnel, listening to the echo of his scuffing sandals. His feet kept coming loose from the strings, and the robe dragged heavily along the rubber floor.

Ten minutes of walking through the twisting, lightless maze brought him to the water. He crouched in its shallow coldness and drank. It hurt to swallow, but he was too grateful there was water to care.

As he drank, there crossed his mind a brief vision of himself holding a hose much like this one, carrying it outside, connecting it to the faucet, playing a glittering stream of water across the lawn. Now, in a similar hose, he crouched, less than one fifth of its width, a mote man sipping dribblets of water from a hand no bigger than a grain of salt.

The vision passed. His size was too common now, too much a reality. It was no longer a phenomenon.

When he had finished drinking, he walked back out of the hose, shaking his feet to get the water off his sandals. March forth, he thought, march forth to nothingness. March fourteenth, he thought. In a week the first day of spring would come upon the island.

He would never see it.

Out on the floor again, he walked back to the box top and stood beside it, one palm braced against it. His gaze moved slowly over the cellar. Well? he thought. What happened now? Did he crawl under the box top, lie down again and sleep once more, a surrendering sleep? His teeth raked slowly across his lower lip as he looked at the cliff that went up to the spider's land.

Avoid it.

He started walking around the cement block, searching for cracker crumbs. He found a dirty one, scraped off its surface, and kept walking, chewing ruminatively. Well, what was he going to do? Go back to his bed, or—

He stopped and stood motionless on the floor. Something in his eyes caught minor fire. His lips drew back from his teeth as he grimaced.

All right. He had a brain. He'd use it. After all, wasn't this his universe? Couldn't he determine its values and its meanings? Didn't the logic of a cellar life belong to him, who lived alone in that cellar?

Very well, then. He had planned suicide, but something had kept him from it. Call it what you will, he thought—fear, subconscious desire to survive, action of outside intelligence maintaining him. Whatever it was, it had happened. He lived still, his existence unbroken. Positive function was still possible; decision was still his.

"All right," he muttered. He may as well act alive.

It was like the clearing of a mist in his brain, like a rush of cool wind across a parched desert of intentions. It made—absurdly, perhaps—his shoulders draw back, made him move with more certainty, ignoring the pain of his body. And, as if in instant reward, he found a large chunk of cracker behind the cement block. He cleaned it off and ate it. It tasted horrible. He didn't care. It was nourishment.

He walked back across the floor. What did his decision mean? He knew, really, but he was afraid to dwell on it. Rather, he let himself drift surely toward the giant carton under the fuel tank, knowing what had to be done; knowing that he would do it or perish.

He stopped before the looming mass of the carton. Once, he thought, he had kicked open its side himself. At the time, it had been an act of rage, of frustration turned to acid fury. How odd that an ancient fury was making it easier for him now; that it had, indeed, saved his life more than once.

For hadn't he got two thimbles from that carton, one that he'd put under the water tank, and another that he'd put under the dripping water heater? Hadn't he got the material for his robe from the carton? Hadn't he got there the thread that enabled him to reach the top of the wicker table and get the crackers? Finally, hadn't he actually fought off the spider in there, discovering in a flash of astonishment that he did have some efficacy against its horrible seven-legged blackness?

Yes, all these. And all because, one day long ago, he had burned with a terrible, angry desire and kicked open the side of the carton.

He hesitated for a moment, thinking he should search for the needle he'd taken from the carton before and lost. Then he decided he might not find it and the fruitless search would waste not only time, but valuable, needed energy.

He jumped up the carton side and dragged himself through the opening. It was difficult to get in. The difficulty pointed up, disconcertingly, how hard it was going to be to get up to the cliff, much less fight the——

No. He wasn't going to let himself think about that. If anything could stop him, it was thoughts about the spider. He blanked his mind to them. Only far behind the conscious barrier did they move.

He slid down the hill of clothes until he went over the edge and fell down into the sewing box. For a moment panic jarred him as he thought that he might not be able to get out of the box. Then he remembered the rubber cork into which the pins and needles were inserted. He could push that to the edge of the box and then be able to climb out.

He found a cool needle lying on the bottom of the box and picked it up.

"God," he muttered. It was like a harpoon made of lead. He let it fall and it clanked loudly. He stood there a moment, lines of distress around his eyes. Was he to be defeated already? He couldn't possibly carry that needle up the face of the cliff.

Simple, said his mind. Take a pin.

He closed his eyes and smiled at himself. Yes, yes, he thought. He searched around in the shadows for a pin, but there were none loose. He'd have to get one from the rubber cork.

First he had to knock the cork over. It was four times as

high as he was. Gritting his teeth, he shoved at the rubber
cork until it toppled. Then he moved around it and jerked out
a pin, hefted it in his hands. That was better. Still heavy, but
manageable.

How could he carry it, though? Sticking it into his robe
was no good; it would dangle, bang against surfaces, impede
his climb, maybe cut him. He'd fasten a thread sling on the
pin and carry it across his back. He looked around for thread.
No point in going after the thread he'd flung into the cat's
mouth; it was probably lost.

He cut himself a short length of rope-heavy thread by dragging the sharp pin point across it until the fibers were weakened enough to be torn apart. Panting in the dark, shadowy
cavern, he tied one end of the thread around the pinhead, then
tied the other end near the point. The second loop slid a little,
but it would hold well enough. With a grunt he slung the pin
across his back, then flexed on his toes to test the weight.
Good enough.

Now. Was that all he needed? He stood indecisively, brow
lined, but not with worry. He didn't actually acknowledge it,
but it gave him a good feeling to be calculating positively.
Maybe there was something to the theory that true satisfaction was based on struggle. This moment was certainly the
antithesis of the hopeless, listless hours of the night before.
Now he was working toward a goal. True, it might be self-
induced emotion, but it gave him the first definite pleasure he
could remember experiencing for a long time.

All right, then, what was needed? The climb was too difficult to be attempted unaided. He was simply too small; he
needed apparatus. Very well, then. Since it was a cliff, that
made him a mountaineer. What did mountaineers use?
Cleated shoes. He couldn't manage that. Alpenstocks. Nor
that. Grappling hooks. Nor—

Yes, he could! What if he got another pin and managed
somehow to bend it into a semicircle? Then if he attached it
to a long thread, he would fling it at openings in the lawn
chairs, hook it in, and climb the thread. It would be perfect
equipment.

Excited he pulled another pin from the rubber cork, then unrolled about twenty feet—to him—of thread. He threw the pins and thread out of the box, climbed out by using the cork, and dragged his prizes up the hill, throwing them out onto the floor.

He slid out of the carton and dropped down. He started toward the cement block, dragging the pins and thread behind. Now, he thought, if only I could take a little food and water with me ...

He stopped, squinting at the box top. Suddenly he remembered, there were still pieces of cracker on the sponge! He could put them inside his robe somehow and take them with him.

And water? On his face there was a look of concentration bordering on exultation. The sponge itself! Why couldn't he tear off a small piece of it, soak it with water from the hose, and carry it with him? Certainly it would drip, it would run, but some of the water would stay in it, enough to see him through.

He didn't let himself think about the spider. He didn't let himself think about the fact that there were only two days left to him, no matter what he did. He was too absorbed, in the small triumphs of conquered detail and in the large triumph of conquered despair to let himself be dragged down again by crushing ultimates.

That was it, then. The pin spear slung across his back, the cracker crumbs and water-soaked sponge in his robe, the pin hook for climbing.

In half an hour he was ready. Although he already felt tired from the tremendous effort required to bend the pin (which he had done by shoving the point under the cement block and lifting at the head), hacking and tearing off a fragment of sponge, getting the water and the crackers and carrying everything to the foot of the cliff, he was too pleased to care. He was alive, he was trying. Suicide was a distant impossibility. He wondered how he could ever have considered it.

Excitement faded, almost died when he tilted back his head and looked up toward the soaring top of the lawn chairs as they leaned against the Everest heights of the wall. Could he possibly climb that high?

He lowered his eyes angrily. Don't look, he ordered himself. To look at the entire journey all at once was stupidity. You thought of it in segments; that was the only way. First segment, the shelf. Second, the seat of the first chair. Third, the arm of the second chair. Fourth—

He stood at the very bottom of the cliff. Never mind anything else, he told himself. He had the resolve to get up there; that was what mattered.

He remembered another time in the past when resolution had come. Thoughts of it ran through his mind as he flung up the hook and began to climb.

18″

It was a giant's toy; a glowing, moving, incredible toy. The Ferris wheel, like a vast white-and-orange gear, turned slowly against the black October sky. Scarlet-lit Loop-the-Loop cages blurred across the night like shooting stars. The merry-go-round was a bright, cacophonous music box that turned and turned, the grimacing, wild-eyed horses rising and falling, endlessly rising and falling, frozen in their galloping postures. Tiny cars and trains and trolleys, like merry bugs, raced around in their imprisoning circles, overflowing red-faced children who waved and screamed. Aisles were sluggish currents of doll people who clustered like filings around the magnetism of barker stands, food concessions, and booths where balloons could be exploded with broken-feathered darts, wooden milk bottles toppled with scratched and grimy baseballs, and pennies tossed upon mosaics of colored squares. The air pulsed with a many-tongued clamor and spotlights cast livid ribbons across the sky.

As they drove up, another car pulled away from the curb and Lou eased the Ford into the opening, pulling out the hand brake, and turned off the engine.

"Mamma, can I go to the merry-go-round, *can* I?" Beth asked excitedly.

"Yes, dear." Lou spoke distractedly, her gaze moving to

where Scott was sitting, dwarfed in a shadowy corner of the back seat, the carnival glare splashed across his pale cheek, his eye like a tiny, dark berry, his mouth a pencil gash.

"You *will* stay in the car," she said worriedly.

"What else can I do?"

"It's for your own good," she said.

It was a phrase she used all the time now; spoken with a hopeless patience, as if she could think of nothing better to say.

"Sure," he said.

"Mother, let's *go*," Beth said with determined anxiety. "We'll *miss* it."

"All right." Lou pushed open the door. "Push down your button," she said, and Beth punched down the knob-topped rod that locked the door on her side, then scrambled across the seat.

"Maybe you'd better lock yourself in," Lou said.

Scott didn't speak. His baby shoes thudded down slowly on the seat. Lou managed a smile.

"We won't be long," she said, and she closed the door. He stared at her shadowy figure as she twisted the key in the lock; he heard the button clicking down.

Lou and Beth moved across the street, Beth tugging eagerly at her mother's hand, and entered the crowded carnival grounds.

He sat for a while, wondering why he'd been so insistent on coming when he'd known all along he couldn't go into the carnival with them. The reason was obvious, but he wouldn't admit it to himself. He'd yelled at Lou to hide the shame he felt at forcing her to give up her job at the lake store; the shame he felt because she had to stay home, because she didn't dare get another sitter, because she'd had to write her parents and borrow money. That's why he'd yelled and insisted on going with them.

After a few minutes he stood up on the seat and walked over to the window. Dragging a pillow over, he stepped on its yielding surface and pressed his nose against the cold window. He stared at the carnival with hard, unenjoying eyes, looking for Lou and Beth; they had been ingested by the slowly moving crowd.

He watched the Ferris wheel revolving, the little pivoted seats rocking back and forth, passengers holding on tight to the safety bars. His gaze shifted to the Loop-the-Loop. He wathced it flip over, the two cage-tipped arms flashing past each other like clock hands gone berserk. He watched the merry-go-round's rhythmic turn and heard faintly the clash-grind-thump of its machinelike music. It was another world.

Once, long ago, a boy named Scott Carey had sat on another Ferris-wheel seat, transfixed with delicious terror, white-knuckled hands clutched over the bar. He had ridden other toy cars, twisting the steering wheel like a chauffeur. He had, in a perfect agony of delight, flipped over and over in another Loop-the-Loop, feeling the frankfurters and popcorn and cotton candy and soda and ice cream homogenized in his stomach. He had walked through the glittering unreality of another carnival, overjoyed with a life that built such wonders overnight on empty lots.

Why *should* I stay in the car? The question came minutes later, belligerently, demanding satisfaction. So what if people saw him? They'd think he was a lost baby. And even if they knew who he was, what difference did it make? He wasn't going to stay in the car, that's all there was to it.

The only trouble was that he couldn't open the door. It was hard enough to push one of the front seats forward and clamber over it. It was impossible for him to get the door handles up. He kept jerking at them, angrier and angrier, until he kicked the gray-lined door and butted it with his shoulder.

"Well, the *hell* . . ." he muttered then, and impulse-driven, rolled down the window.

He sat on the thin ledge a few moments, legs kicking restlessly. The cold wind blew up his legs. His shoes drummed on the door. I'm going, I don't care. Abruptly he turned, lowered himself over the window edge, and hung suspended above the ground. Carefully he reached down one hand and caught hold of the outside door handle. After a moment he swung down.

"Oh!" His fingers slipped off the smooth chrome and he fell in a heap on the ground, banging against the side of the car. Momentary fear nibbled coldly at his insides when he realized he couldn't get back; but it passed quickly. Louise would return soon enough. He walked to the end of the car, jumped down the steep curb, and moved into the street.

He flinched back as a car roared by. It passed at least eight feet away from him, but the noise of the motor was almost deafening. Even the crisp sound of its tires on the pavement was inordinately loud in his ears. When it was past he darted across the street, leaped up the knee-high curb, and raced around to a deserted area behind a tent. He walked beside the dark, wind-stirred canvas wall, listening to the din of the carnival.

A man came around the corner of the tent and started toward him. Scott froze into immobility and the man walked by without noticing him. It was a thing about people. They did not look down expecting to see anything but dogs and cats.

When the man was out on the sidewalk, Scott moved on again, ducking through the triangles the ropes made with the ground and the tent side.

He stopped before a pale bar of light that poked out from beneath the tent, blocking his path. He looked at the loosened canvas, delicate excitement mounting in him. Impulsively he got on his knees, then fell forward on his chest on the cold ground, lifted the flap, and, wriggling forward a little, peered in.

He found himself looking at the hind end of a two-headed cow. It was standing in a hay-strewn, rope-enclosed square, staring at the people with four glossy eyes. It was dead.

The first smile Scott had managed in more than a month eased his tight little face. If he had jotted down a list of all the things in the world he might have seen in this tent, somewhere near the bottom of the list he might conceivably have put a dead two-headed cow pointed the wrong way.

His gaze moved around the tent. He couldn't see what was on the other side of the aisle; clustering people hid the view. On his side, he saw a six-legged dog; (two of the legs atrophied stumps), a cow with skin like a human being's, a goat with three legs and four horns, a pink horse, and a fat pig that had adopted a thin chicken. He looked over the assemblage, the faint smile wavering on his lips. Monster show, he thought.

And then the smile faded. Because it had occurred to him how remarkable an exhibit he would make, posed, say, between the chicken-mothering pig and the dead two-headed cow. Scott Carey, *Homo reductus.*

He drew back into the night and stood up, brushing automatically at his corduroy rompers and jacket. He should have stayed in the car; it had been stupid to leave.

Yet he didn't start back; he couldn't make himself start back. He trudged past the end of the tent and saw people walking, heard the clatter of wooden bottles being struck by flying baseballs, the pop of rifles, and the tiny explosions of burst balloons. He heard the dirgelike grind of the merry-go-round music.

A man came out through the back doorway of one of the booths. He glanced at Scott. Scott kept walking, moving quickly behind the next tent.

"Hey, kid," he heard the man call.

He broke into a run, looking for a place to hide. There was a trailer parked behind the tent. He raced to it and crouched behind a thick-tired wheel, peering around the edge.

Fifteen yeards away he saw the man appear at the corner of the tent and, fists poked on hips, look around. Then, after a few seconds, the man grunted and went away. Scott stood up and started to leave the shadow of the trailer, then stopped. Someone was singing overhead.

Scott's face grew taut-browed with attention. "If I loved you," sang the voice, "time and again I would try to say . . ."

He moved from under the trailer and looked up at the white-curtained window glowing with light. He could still hear the singing, faint and sweet. He stared at the window, feeling a strange restlessness.

The happy screams of a girl in the Loop-the-Loop shook him loose from his reverie. He started away from the trailer, then turned and went back. He stood beside it until the song was ended. Then he walked slowly around the trailer, looking up first at one window, then at the other and wondering why he felt so drawn to that voice.

Then he became fully conscious of the steps that led up to the windowed door of the trailer, and convulsively he jumped up on the first one.

It was just the right height.

His heart began to throb suddenly, his hand clamped rigidly on the waist-high railing. Breath shook in his shallow chest. It couldn't be!

He moved slowly up the steps until he stood just below the door that was only a little higher than he was. There were some words painted under its window, but he couldn't read them. He felt his skin alive with strange, electric pricklings. He couldn't help himself; he moved up the last two steps and stood before the door.

Breath stopped. It was his world, his very own world—chairs and a couch that he could sit on without being engulfed; tables he could stand beside and reach across instead of walk under; lamps he could switch on and off, not stand futilely beneath as if they were trees.

She came into the little room and saw him standing there.

His stomach muscles jerked in suddenly. He wavered there, staring blankly at the woman, sounds of disbelief hovering in his throat.

The woman stood rooted to the floor, one hand pressed against her cheek, her eyes round and still with shock. Time stood stricken and apart while she stared at him. It's a dream, his mind insisted. It *is* a dream.

Then the woman slowly, stiffly started for the door.

He shrank away. He almost slipped off the step edge. He flailed out at the railing and jerked himself rigidly upright as the woman opened the tiny door.

"Who are you?" she asked in a frightened whisper.

He couldn't take his eyes from her fragile face; her doll-like nose and lips, her irises like pale-green beads, her ears like faded rose petals barely seen through hair of fine-spun gold.

"Please," she said, holding the bodice of her robe together with tiny alabaster hands.

"I'm Scott Carey," he said, his voice thin with shock.

"Scott Carey," she said. She didn't know the name. "Are you . . ." She faltered. "Are you . . . like me?"

He was shivering now. "Yes," he said. "*Yes.*"

"Oh." It was as if she breathed the word.

They stared at each other.

"I . . . heard you singing," he said.

"Yes, I—" A nervous smile twitched her pale lips. "Please," she said, "Will you . . . come in?"

He stepped into the trailer without hesitation. It was as though he'd known her all his life and had come back from a long journey. He saw the words that were on the door: "Mrs. Tom Thumb." He stood there staring at her with a strange, black hunger.

She closed the door and turned to face him.

"I'm . . . I was surprised," she said. She shook her head and once more drew together the bodice of her yellow robe. "It's such a surprise," she said.

"I know," he said. He bit his lower lip. "I'm the shrinking man," he blurted, wanting her to know.

She didn't speak for a long moment. Then she said, "Oh," and he didn't know what it was he heard in her voice, whether it was disappointment or pity or emptiness. Their eyes still clung.

"My name is Clarice," the woman said.

Their small hands clasped and did not let go. He couldn't breathe right; air faltered in his lungs.

"What are you doing here?" she asked, drawing back her hand.

He swallowed dryly. "I . . . came," was all he could say. He kept staring at her with stark eyes that would not believe. Then he saw a darkening flush creep into her cheeks and he sucked in a calming breath. "I'm—I'm so sorry," he said. "It's just that I haven't—" he gestured helplessly—"haven't seen anyone like *me*. It's ..." He shook his head in little twitching movements. "I can't tell you what it's like."

"I know, I know," she answered quickly, looking intently at him. "When—" She cleared her throat. "When I saw you at the door, I didn't know what to think." Her laugh was faint and trembling. "I thought maybe I was losing my mind."

"You're alone?" he asked suddenly.

She stared at him blankly. "Alone?" she asked, not understanding.

"I mean your—your name. On the door," he said, not even realizing that he had alarmed her.

Her face relaxed into its natural soft lines. She smiled a sad smile. "Oh," she said, "it's what I'm called." She shrugged her small round shoulders. "It's just what they call me," she said.

"Oh." He nodded. "I see." He kept trying to swallow the hard, dry lump in his throat. He felt dizzy. His fingertips tingled like frozen fingers being thawed. "I see," he said again.

They kept staring at each other as if they just couldn't believe it was true.

"I guess you read about me," he said.

"Yes, I did," she answered. "I'm sorry that . . ."

He shook his head. "It's not important." A shudder ran down his back. "It's so good to—" He stood motionless, looking into her gentle eyes. "Clarice," he murmured. "So good to . . ." His hands twitched as he repressed the desire to reach out and touch her. "It was such a surprise seeing the— the room here," he said hastily. "I'm so used to—" he shrugged nervously—"*vast* things. When I saw those steps leading up here . . ."

"I'm glad you came up," Clarice said.

"So am I," he answered. Her gaze dropped from his, then rose instantly as if she feared he might disappear if she looked away too long.

"It's really an accident I'm here," she said. "I don't usually work the off seasons. But the owner of this carnival is an old friend who's feeling the pinch a little. And—well, I'm glad I'm here."

They looked at each other steadily.

"It's a lonely life," he said.

"Yes," she answered softly, "it can be lonely."

They were silent again, looking. She smiled restively.

"If I'd stayed home," he said, "I wouldn't have seen you."

"I know."

Another shudder rippled down his arms.

"Clarice," he said.

"Yes?"

"You have a pretty name," he said. The hunger was tearing at him now, shaking him.

"Thank you—Scott," she said.

He bit his lips. "Clarice, I wish . . ."

She looked back at him a long moment. Then, without a word, she stepped close to him and laid her cheek against his. She stood quietly as he put his arms around her.

"Oh," he whispered, "Oh, God. To—"

She sobbed and pressed against him suddenly, her small hands catching at his back. Wordlessly they clung to each other in the quiet room, their tear-wet cheeks together.

"My dear," she murmured, "my dear, my dear."

He drew back his head and looked into her glistening eyes.

"If you knew," he said brokenly. "If you—"

"I *do* know," she said, running a trembling hand across his cheek.

"Yes. Of course you do."

He leaned forward and felt her warm lips change under his from soft acceptance to a harsh, demanding hunger.

He held her tensely. "Oh, God, to be a man again," he whispered. "Just to be a man again. To hold you like this."

"Yes. *Do* hold me. It's been so long."

After a few minutes, Clarice led him to the couch and they sat there holding tightly to each other's hands, smiling at each other.

"It's strange," she said, "I feel so close to you. And yet I never saw you in my life before."

"It's because we're the same," he said. "Because we share the pity of our lives."

"Pity?" she murmured.

He looked up from his shoes. "My feet are touching the floor," he said wonderingly. His chuckle was melancholy. "Such a little thing," he said, "but it's the first time in so long that my feet have touched the floor when I've sat down. Do you—" He squeezed her hand. "You do know; you *do*," he said.

"You said pity," she said.

He looked a moment at her concerned face. "Isn't it pity?" he asked. "Aren't we pitiful?"

"I don't . . ." Distress flickered in her eyes. "I never thought of myself as pitiful."

"Oh, I'm sorry, I'm *sorry*," he said. "I didn't mean to—" His face was contrite. "It's just that I've become so bitter. I've been alone, Clarice. All alone. Once I was past a certain height, I was absolutely alone." He stroked her hand without consciousness. "It's why I feel so—so strongly toward you. Why I . . ."

"Scott!"

They pressed against each other and he could feel her heartbeat hitting at his chest like a little hand.

"Yes, you *have* been alone," she said. "So alone. I've had others like me—like us. I was even married once." Her voice faded to a whisper. "I almost had a child."

"Oh, I—"

"No, no, don't say anything," she begged. "It's been easier for me. I've been like this all my life. I've had time to adjust."

A shuddering breath bellowed his lungs. He said—he couldn't help saying it—"Someday even you'll be a giant to me."

"Oh, my dear." She pressed his face to her breasts, still stroking his hair. "How terrible it's been for you; to see your wife and child magnifying every day—leaving you behind."

Her body had a clean, sweet smell. He drank in the perfume of it, trying to forget everything except her presence and her soothing voice, the blessing of each moment as it was.

"How did you get here?" she asked him, and he told her. "Oh," she said, "won't she be frightened if—"

His urgent whisper cut her off. "Don't make me go."

She drew him more securely against the yielding swell of her breasts. "No, no," she said quickly. "No, stay as long as—"

She stopped. He heard her swallowing again and he asked, "What is it?"

She hesitated before answering. "Just that I have to give another show in—" she twisted slightly, looking at the clock across the room—"ten minutes."

"No!" He clung to her desperately.

Her breathing grew heavier. "If only you could stay with me a little while. Just a *little* while."

He didn't know what to say. He straightened up and looked at her tense face. He drew in a shaky breath.

"I can't," he said. "She'll be waiting. She'll—" His hands stirred fitfully in his lap, grew immobile once again. "It's no use," he said.

She bent forward and pressed both palms gently to his cheeks. She put her lips on his. He ran shaking hands over her arms, his fingertips scratching delicately at the silk robe. Her arms slid around his neck.

"Would she be so frightened if—" she began, breaking off as she kissed his cheek. He still couldn't answer. She drew back and he stared at her flushed face. Her eyes fell.

"You mustn't, please, you mustn't think I'm just an—an *awful* person," she said. "I've always lived—decently. I just . . ." Nervously she ran smoothing fingers over the lap of her robe. "I just feel, as you said, so *strongly* toward you. After all, it's not as if we were just two people in a world of people all alike. We're—we're only *two* of us. If we went a thousand miles we wouldn't find another. It just doesn't seem the same as if—"

She stopped abruptly as a heavy shoe sounded on the trailer steps and there was a single knock on the door. A deep voice said, "Ten minutes, Clar."

She started to answer, but the man was already gone. She

sat there shivering, looking toward the door. Finally she turned to him. "Yes, she would be frightened," she said.

Suddenly his hands tightened on her arms, his face grew hard. "I'm going to tell her," he said. "I won't leave you. I *won't*."

She threw herself against him, her breath hot on his cheek. "Yes, tell her, *tell* her," she begged. "I don't want her to be hurt. I don't want her to be frightened, but tell her. Tell her what it's like, how we feel. She couldn't say no. Not when . . ."

She pulled away and stood, breathing harshly. Her trembling fingers ran down the front of her robe, undoing buttons. The robe slid, hissing, from her ivory shoulders, catching in the crook of her bent arms. She wore pale underthings that clung to the contours of her body.

"Tell her!" she said almost angrily. Then she turned and rushed into the next room.

He stood up, staring at the half-open door that led to the room she had entered. He could hear the quick rustle of clothes as she dressed for her performance. He stood there motionless until she came out.

She stood apart from him, her face pale now.

"I was unfair," she said. "Very unfair to you." Her eyes fell. "I shouldn't have done what I did. I—"

"But you'll wait," he interrupted. He grabbed her hand and squeezed it until she winced. "Clarice, you'll wait for me."

At first she wouldn't look at him. Then suddenly her head jerked up, her eyes burned into his. "I'll wait for you," she said.

He listened to the faint clacking of her high heels as she ran down the trailer steps. Then he turned and walked around the small room, looking at the furniture, touching it.

Finally he went into the other room and, after a hesitant moment, sat down on her bed and picked up the yellow silk robe. It was smooth and yielding in his fingers; it still smelled of her flesh.

Suddenly he plunged his face into its folds, gasping in the perfume of it. Why did he have to ask? There was nothing left between Lou and him; nothing. Why couldn't he just stay with Clarice? It wouldn't matter to Lou. She'd be glad to get rid of him. She'd . . .

. . . be frightened, be concerned.

With a weary sigh, he put aside the robe and pushed to his feet. He walked through the trailer, opened the door, moved down the steps, and started back across the cold, night-shrouded earth. I'll tell her, he thought. I'll just tell her and come back.

But when he reached the sidewalk and saw her standing by the car, a heavy despair fell over him. How could he possibly tell her? He stood hesitantly; then, as some teen-aged boys started out of the carnival grounds, he darted into the street.

"Hey, ain't that a midget?" he heard one of the boys say.

"Scott!"

Lou ran to him and, without another word, snatched him up, her face both angry and concerned. She walked back to the car and pulled opened the door with her free hand.

"Where have you *been*?" she asked.

"Walking," he said. No! cried his mind. Tell her, *tell* her. The vision flitted across his mind; Clarice unrobed, saying it to him. Tell her!

"I think you might have considered how I'd feel when I got back and found you gone," Lou said, pushing forward the front seat so he could get in the back of the car.

He didn't move. "Well, get in," she said.

He sucked in a fast breath. *"No,"* he said.

"What?"

He swallowed. "I'm not going," he said. He tried not to be so conscious of Beth staring at him.

"What are you talking about?" Lou asked.

"I—" He glanced at Beth, then back again. "I want to talk to you," he said.

"Can't it wait till we get home? Beth has to go to bed."

"No, it can't wait." He wanted to scream out in fury. The old feeling was coming back—the feeling of being useless, grotesque, a freak. He should have known it would return the moment he left Clarice.

"Well, I don't see—"

"Then leave me here!" He yelled at her. There was no strength, no resolution now. He was the stringless marionette again, pulling for inconsequential succor.

"What's the matter with you?" she asked angrily.

He choked on a sob, cut it off. Abruptly he turned and started across the pavement.

"Scott!"

A mind-jarring flurry of sights and sounds; the roar of an oncoming car, a blinding glare of headlights, the crunch of Lou's running heels, the bruising of her fingers on his body, the head-snapping jerk as she pulled him out of the car's path and around to the back of the Ford, the screeching of the other's car's tires as it lurched across the center line, then back into the proper lane.

"What in God's name!" Her voice was furiously agitated. "Have you lost your mind?"

"I wish it had hit me!" Everything flooded out in his voice, all the anguish, the fury, and the shattered hopes.

"Scott!" She crouched down so she could speak to him. "Scott, what is it?"

"Nothing," he said. Then, almost immediately, "I want to stay. I'm *going* to stay."

"Stay where, Scott?" she asked.

He swallowed quickly, angrily. Why did he have to feel like a fool, like an unimportant fool? It had seemed so vital before; now it seemed absurd and trashy.

"Stay *where*, Scott?" she asked in failing patience.

He looked up, stiff-faced, going on with it willessly.

"I want to stay with . . . her," he said.

"With—" She stared at him and his gaze fell. He looked along the broad length of her slack-covered leg. He gritted his teeth and pain flared along his jawline.

"There's a woman," he said, not looking up at her.

She was silent. He glanced up at her. In the light of a distant street lamp he could see the glow of her eyes.

"You mean that midget in the sideshow?"

He shuddered. The way she said it, the sound in her voice,

made his desire seem vile. He dragged his teeth across his upper lip. "She's a very kind and understanding woman," he said. "I want to stay with her for a while."

"You mean overnight."

His head jerked back. "Oh, God, how you can—!" His eyes burned. "You can make it sound so—"

He caught himself. He stared down at her shoes. He spoke as distinctly as possible.

"I'm going to stay with her," he said. "If you'd rather not come back for me, all right. Leave me. I'll get by somehow."

"Oh, stop being so—"

"I'm not just talking, Lou," he said. "I swear to God I'm not just talking."

When she didn't reply, he looked up and saw her staring down at him. He didn't know what the expression on her face meant.

"You don't know, you just don't know any more," he said. "You think this is something ... disgusting, something animal. Well, it isn't. It's more—much more. Don't you understand? We're not the same any more, you and I. We're apart now. But you can have companionship if you want. I can't. We've never spoken of it, but I expect you to remarry when this is done—as it *will* be done.

"Lou, there's nothing for me now, can't you see that? Nothing. All I have to look forward to is dissolution. Going on like this, day after day, getting smaller and smaller and—lonelier. There's nobody in the world who can understand now. Even this woman will one day be as ... be beyond me. But now—for *now*, Lou—she's companionship and—and affection and love. All right, and love! I don't deny it, I can't help it. I may be a freak but I still need love and I still need—" He drew in a quick, rasping breath. "One night," he said. "It's all I ask. One night. If it were you and you had a chance for one night of peace, I'd tell you to take it. I would."

His eyes fell. "She has a trailer," he said. "It has furniture I can sit on. It's my size."

He looked up a little. "Just to sit on a chair as if I were a man and not ..." He sighed. "Just that, Lou. Just *that*."

He looked up at her face finally, but it wasn't until a car drove by and the headlights flared across her face that he saw the tears.

"Lou!"

She couldn't speak. She stood biting at a fist, her body shaking with noiseless sobs. She struggled against them. She took a deep breath and brushed away the tears while he stood beside her, staring at her even though it hurt his neck muscles to look up so high.

"All right, Scott," she said then. "It would be pointless and—and cruel of me to stop you. You're right. There's nothing I can do."

She breathed in laboredly. "I'll come back in the morning," she blurted then, and ran to the car door.

He stood in the wind-swept street until the red taillights had faded out of sight. Then he ran across the street, feeling ill and miserable. He shouldn't have done it. It wasn't the same now.

But when he saw the trailer again, and the light in the window, and the little easy steps that led up to her, it all returned. It was like stepping into another world and leaving behind all the sorrows in the old one.

"Clarice," he whispered.

And he ran to her.

CHAPTER
THIRTEEN
• • • • • • • • • •

He was sitting on one of the broad slats that formed the seat of the lower lawn chair, leaning against a tree-thick arm support, and chewing on a piece of cracker. He hadn't touched the sponge except to squeeze a few drops from it halfway up the first stage of the climb. By his side lay the coils of thread, the pin hook attached to them, and the long, shiny pin spear.

Weariness eased slowly from his relaxing muscles. Slowly he reached down and rubbed at his knee. It was a little swollen again. While he was climbing the thread, he'd banged the knee against the chair leg. A wince drew back his lips as he rubbed. He hoped it wouldn't get worse.

It was quiet in the cellar. The oil burner hadn't roared on once in the past hour. It must be warm out, he thought. He glanced far across at the window over the fuel tank. It was a shimmering square of light. He closed his eyes. He wondered why Beth wasn't out in the yard playing. The water pump hadn't started lately, either. Lou and Beth probably weren't home. He wondered where they might be.

Warned by the stirring of uneasiness in his chest, he blanked his mind to thoughts of sunlight and outdoors, of his wife and child. They were not a part of his life now, and it was a senseless man who dwelt on things that were not a part of his life.

Yes, he was still a man. Two-sevenths of an inch tall and still a man.

He remembered the night he'd been with Clarice, and how, then too, it had come to him that he was still a man.

"You aren't pitiful," she whispered to him. "You're a man." She'd dragged tense fingers across his chest.

It had been a moment of decisive alteration.

Almost all night, lying beside her, feeling the warm flutter of her breath against his shoulder, he had lain awake, thinking of what she'd said.

It was true; he *was* still a man. Living beneath the degrading weight of his affliction, he had forgotten it. Looking at his marriage and his inadequacy in it, he had forgotten it. Looking at his life and the barrenness of that life's achievements, he had forgotten it. The diminishing effect that the size of his body had had on the size of his thoughts had made him forget it. It had not been just introspection. All he'd had to do was look into a mirror to know that it was so.

And yet it was not so. A man's self-estimation was, in the end, a matter of relativity. Here he lay in a bed in which he was full size and there was a woman held in his arms. It made all the difference. He could see again.

And he saw that size had changed nothing essential; he still had his mind, he was still unique.

In the morning, lying in the warm bed with her, bars of butter-colored sunlight across their legs, he'd told her of his thoughts and the change in his thoughts.

"I'm not going to fight it any more," he said. "No, I don't mean I'm giving up," he'd added hastily, seeing the look on her face. "I mean I'm going to stop struggling against the part of it I can't beat. I know I'm incurable now. I can say it; even that's an accomplishment. I've never really admitted it before. I was so afraid I'd find out I was incurable that I even left the doctors once. I said it was because of money, but it wasn't; I know that now. It was because I was terrified of finding out."

He'd lain there, staring at the ceiling, feeling Clarice's small hand on his chest, her eyes watching him.

"Well, I accept it," he'd finally said. "I accept it and I'm not going to scream at fate any more. I'm not going to go down hating." He'd turned to her suddenly. "You know what I'm going to do?" he asked, almost excitedly.

"What, dear?"

His smile had been quick, almost boyish. "I'm going to write about it," he said. "I'm going to follow myself as far as I can. I'm going to tell about everything that happened to me, and everything that's *going* to happen to me. This is a rare thing; I'm going to look at it as rare—as a thing of potential value, not just as a curse. I'm going to study it," he said. "I'm going to tear it apart, see what there is to see. I'm going to live with it and beat it. And I'm not going to be afraid. *I'm not going to be afraid.*"

* * *

He finished the bit of cracker and opened his eyes. Reaching into his robe, he drew out the piece of sponge and squeezed a few drops of water into his mouth. They were warm and brackish, but they felt good in his dry throat. He put the sponge back. There was still a long climb ahead.

He looked at the pin hook. It had been spread apart a little by the dragging weight of his body. He ran a hand over its smoothness. Well, he could probably rebend it somehow if it became necessary.

He thought he heard a noise overhead and his head jerked back.

There was nothing. But that didn't make his heartbeat any slower. It was a grim reminder of what was waiting up there for him.

He shuddered and a mirthless smile moved his lips. *I'm not going to be afraid.* The words mocked him. If I'd known, he thought. If he'd known the moments of rank terror he was still to experience, he'd never have made it. Only the blessing of an unknown future enabled him to keep the promise he had made to himself.

For he *had* kept it. Without telling Lou, he had gone to the cellar every day, armed with stubby pencil and thick school notebook. He'd sat there in the damp coolness, writing until his wrist ached so much that he couldn't hold the pencil.

Desperate, he would knead at his wrist and hand, trying to press strength back into them so he could go on. Because, more and more, his mind was becoming an uncontrollable powerhouse of memories and thoughts, generating them endlessly. If they were not written down, they would flow from his brain and be lost. He wrote so persistently that in a matter of weeks he had brought himself up to date on his life as the shrinking man. Then he'd begun to type it up, picking slowly and laboriously at the keys as the days fled by. When it had reached the typing stage, he hadn't been able to keep it a secret from Lou any longer. The typewriter had to be rented. At first he'd planned to tell her he just wanted the typewriter to pass the time. But the rental fee was high and he knew there wasn't enough money to pay for it if it were just a whim. So he'd told her what he'd done. She had been unexcited, but she had got the typewriter and paper.

When he wrote the letters to the magazines and book publishers, she said nothing, but he sensed a rising interest in her.

And, when, almost immediately, he'd received a flood of interested offers, she suddenly had to realize that, despite everything, he was giving her the security she'd already given up hoping for.

One glorious afternoon he'd received the first check for his manuscript along with a congratulatory letter, and Lou had sat with him in the living room and told him how sorry she was for having fallen into a state of withdrawal. It was protective, she said, but she regretted even that. She'd told him how proud she was of him. She'd held his tiny hand and said, "You're still the man I married, Scott."

He stood up. Enough of the past. He had to get on; there was still a long way to go.

Picking up the pin spear, he slung it across his back again. The added weight stirred up hot pressures in his knee, and he grimaced. Never mind, he told himself. Teeth gritted he bent over and picked up the pin hook. He looked around.

Now if he stayed where he was, he would have approximately fifty feet to climb to the level of the chair arm. The only trouble was that there were no places to catch the hook there. He'd have to do as he'd done before; go up the back of the chair.

The shelf below ran in a downward slope parallel to the seat. This shelf almost touched the floor. He'd had to throw up the hook only a short way to make it catch onto one of the shelf's bottom slats. Ascending the shelf itself had been no more difficult than walking up a moderately steep incline, using the hook and thread to bridge the gaps between the slats. The only hard part had been the vertical climb to the seat where he was now.

No help for it, then; in order to get up higher, he had to descend again a short distance.

He started walking down the slope toward the back of the chair. The openings between slats were somewhat wider here than they had been on the shelf. All in all though, it looked simple enough.

He reached the first opening. Pulling in the ropelike thread, he coiled it and tossed it across the gap. It landed heavily and he heard the metallic ring as the hook struck the wood.

The thundering of the oil burner caught him by surprise. He staggered with shock, his lips jerking back from his teeth. He jammed rigid hands over his ears and stood there trembling, eyes almost closed, feeling the thunderous shudder running through his frame.

When it finally stopped, he stood limply for a long while, staring ahead. Then, shaking his head, he took a running start and leaped across the opening between the slats.

It wasn't as easy as he'd imagined. He barely made the other side, and the pain of landing sharply on the leg with the swollen knee made him gasp. He sat down quickly, face contorted.

"Good God," he muttered. He'd better not do that again.

After a minute, he pushed up and limped down across the next wide slat, dragging the thread behind him.

At the next gap he tossed the rope thread across. Carefully he unslung the spear. He'd toss that across too, then follow without its dragging weight on him. He'd try to land on his good leg, too.

He threw the spear across the opening. Its point dug into the orange wood, then the pin flew over, the weight of it tearing the point loose. Scott was backing up to get his running start when he saw the pin start rolling down the slope.

It would fall through the next opening!

Thoughtlessly he ran to the edge of the slat and jumped into space. He landed on the bad leg again, lines of pain gashing across his face. He couldn't stop; the pin was gaining momentum, heading for the gap. He lunged after it, loose sandals flapping on the wood. One of the sandals came off and the bottom of his lurching foot dragged up a splinter from the wood. He still kept running, trying to gain on the pin.

Frantic, he dived forward to catch it as it started over the edge of the slat. Pain exploded in his knee. He almost went over the edge himself. He missed the pin.

But the pin was not going over parallel to the opening, and its spinning movement was suddenly checked as its point stuck into the slat on the far side and the head held it up on the side where Scott sprawled.

Gasping, he pulled the pin back and dug its point into the wood, standing it like a spear in sand. Then he twisted his foot around and, teeth clenched, picked at the brown leathery-skinned sole until he'd drawn out the long wood sliver. Drops of blood followed it. He pressed them out angrily. Not going to be afraid, not going to be afraid, he thought. Oh, sure.

He started to rub his knee, then jerked back his hand with a gasp. In falling, he'd scraped his hand. He blew out a short heavy breath as he looked at it. He felt water trickling down his chest and across the creases of his stomach. In falling he'd also pressed water from the sponge.

He closed his eyes again. Never mind, he thought, it's all right.

He tore a strip of cloth from the hem of his robe and tied it around his hand. Better. He rubbed determinedly at the knee, biting down hard to fight the pain. There. That was better; much better.

Limping cautiously, he retrieved his sandal and tied extra knots in the strings to keep the sandal from slipping off again. Then he turned to the thread coil and carried it to the edge of the slat. This time he'd fasten the end of the thread to the spear. Then when he threw the spear over it would not only carry over the thread, but it would be prevented from rolling again.

It worked that way. He jumped over after the spear, landing on his good leg, then pulled in the thread and hook. Yes, that was much better. A little thought is all it takes, he told himself.

In this fashion he maneuvered across the sloping seat of the orange chair until he reached its back. There he rested, looking up the almost sheer back of the chair. Far up, he saw the croquet wicket sticking out in space. He could use that wicket now.

After he'd caught his breath and squeezed a couple more water drops into his mouth, he stood up and prepared to complete the next stage of the climb, to the arm of the top lawn chair.

It would not be too difficult. Spaced across the three boards that made up the back of the chair were bracing slats. He had only to throw up the hook, catch it over the first of these slats, climb up to it, throw the hook over the second slat, climb up to it, and so on.

He began throwing up the hook. On the fourth try it caught and, slinging the spear over his back, he climbed up to the first slat.

An hour later, when he reached the top slat, the pin hook was almost unbent. He tossed it up on the arm of the upside-down chair, climbed up beside it, and lay down, breathing heavily. God, I'm tired, he thought, rolling over. He looked down the vast face he had just climbed, and he couldn't help remembering that once his back could have covered that area completely. Once he could have carried this chair. He rolled on his back again. At least being exhausted cut down on thoughts. Ordinarily, he might have been thinking about the spider, about the past, about a good many purposeless things. Instead, he lay there almost stupefied, and that was good. . . .

He stood up on shaky legs and looked around. He must have fallen asleep for a while; a black, peaceful sleep, unmarred by dreams.

He put the spear across his back, picked up the hook, and hiked across the long orange plain of the chair arm, the thread trailing behind him like a lazy serpent.

For some reason he found himself able to think about the spider. It disturbed him vaguely that he hadn't seen any sign of it since he'd got up that morning. It was usually somewhere around when he was moving about. Night and day, it was never absent for long.

Was it possible it was dead?

For a second, an exultant feeling flooded through him. Maybe it had been killed somehow!

The excitement faded almost instantly. He just couldn't believe it was dead. That spider was immortal. It was more than a spider. It was every unknown terror in the world fused into wriggling, poison-jawed horror. It was every anxiety, insecurity, and fear in his life given a hideous, night-black form.

Before he started up on the next stage of the climb, he'd have to bend that pin again. He didn't like the way it was opening under his weight. What if it did that while he was hanging in space?

It *won't*, he told himself, jamming the point of it under the joining place of chair arm and leg and bending it around again. There.

He flung the hook up and it caught over the croquet wicket. He tested it, then began the swaying climb up to the wicket. In two minutes he was clinging to the smooth metal surface.

It took a long time for him to climb its cool, curving length. The weight of thread, hook, and spear made it difficult; it was too far to throw those things without risking their loss.

Time and again he lost balance and spun around to the underside of the sapling-thick wicket and hung there desperately, heart pounding. Each time it took him longer to get back. Finally, toward the end of the climb, he stayed under, pulling himself up with legs and arms, the thread hanging down from his body and swinging wildly beneath him.

By the time he'd reached the shelf of the upper chair, his muscles were starting to cramp. He crawled onto the shelf and lay there gasping, his forehead pressed against the wood. It hurt to have the scraped skin of his forehead against the rough wood, but he was too tired to move. His feet stuck out over the seven-hundred-foot drop.

It was twenty minutes later when he pulled himself around and looked across the edge. The cellar world lay beneath him. Far below, the red hose was a serpent once again, still asleep, still open-mouthed and motionless. The cushion was a flower-strewn plain again. He saw the well-like hole in the floor, the one he'd almost fallen into, then almost dived into when he'd heard the sound of water running deep in it. The hole was only a black dot now. The box top he slept under was only a small gray square, like a faded stamp.

He crawled over the wide leg of the chair and leaned against it, discarding the hook, thread, and spear. Pulling the sponge and the last piece of cracker from his robe, he sat there eating and drinking, legs stretched out limply before him. He emptied about half the sponge. It didn't matter. He'd be at the top soon. And if he got the bread without any trouble, he could climb down very quickly. If he was barred from reaching the bread, he would no longer be in any position to eat it, anyway.

His sandal bottoms touched the clifftop. He shook the hook loose from the lawn chair, dodged its cartwheeling fall, picked it up hastily, and dashed behind the glass base of a giant, bell-shaped fuse. There he stood, panting, peering around its edge at the wide, shadowy desert.

In the pale shaft of light that transfixed the dust-filmed window he could see nearby details: the vast pipes and ropy wires fastened under the overhead supports, the great scraps of wood, stone, and cardboard strewn across the sands; to his left, the towering hulks of paint cans and jars; in front of him, the rolling desert wastes, as far as his eye could see.

Two hundred yards off stood the slice of bread.

He licked his lips. He almost started out immediately across the sand. Then he twitched back sharply, head jerking from side to side as he looked in all directions, even behind. Where was it? He was beginning to get nervous wondering where it was.

Stillness, only stillness. The light shaft angled down like a shimmering bar leaning on the window, a bar alive with moving dust. The huge wood scraps, the stones, the concrete pillar, the hanging wires and pipes, the cans and jars and sand hills—all were motionless and still, as if they waited. He shuddered and unslung his spear. He felt a little better holding it in his hand, its head resting on the cement, its razor tip wavering high overhead.

"Well . . ." he muttered, and, swallowing dread, he started across the sand.

The hook dragged in the sand. He dropped it. I won't need it, he thought; I'll leave it here. He walked a few paces, stopped. He didn't like the idea of leaving it. Nothing could happen to it, and yet—what if something did? He'd be trapped, helpless.

Carefully he backed toward the hook, casting nervous glances over his shoulder to make sure nothing was behind him. He reached the hook and, hastily crouching, picked it up. If it came at him, he could drop the hook fast and grab the spear with both hands. Take it easy, he told himself. Nothing's happened yet.

He started across the sand again, walking slowly and warily, eyes always moving and searching. There was no help for it, of course, but it didn't help things much that the thread knots dragging in the sand behind him made a swishing, uneven sound that reminded him of—

He stopped and looked behind him in fright. There was nothing. Stop worrying, he ordered himself.

He looked around slowly, heartbeat still punching slowly at the walls of his chest. No, nothing. Just shadows and silence and waiting objects.

Maybe that was it. Maybe it was because none of the objects were straight up and down or straight across. Everything tilted, angled, leaned, sagged, beetled. Every line was restless and fluid. Something was going to happen. He knew it. The very silence seemed to whisper it.

Something was going to happen.

He drove the spear point into the sand and began drawing in the thread, looping it so he could carry it over his shoulder and do away with that dragging, whispering sound behind him. As he pulled in the dark, sand-dripping thread he kept looking around, searching.

At a breath of sound the coil thumped down and he snatched the spear from its place again, throwing it out before him. His arm and shoulder muscles shook, his legs stood tensely arched, his eyes were wide and staring.

Breath shook from his lips. He stood listening carefully. Maybe it was the settling of the house he heard. Maybe . . .

A cracking sound, a thud, a roaring wave of sound.

With a flat cry, he jerked around, terror-stricken eyes searching; but, in the very same instant, he realized that it was the oil burner. Dropping the spear, he covered his ears with shaking hands.

Two minutes later the burner clicked off and silence fell across the shadow-pooled desert again.

Scott finished coiling the thread, picked up the heavy loops and the spear and started walking again, eyes still searching. Where was it. Where was it?

When he came to the first piece of wood he stopped. He dropped the coil and thread and extended the spear. It might be hiding behind that piece of wood. He licked dry lips, moving in a half crouch for the wood. It was becoming darker the farther he went into the dunes. It might be behind there; what if it's behind there?

He jerked back his head suddenly as it occurred to him that it might be overhead, floating down on a gossamer cable.

He ground together his chattering teeth and looked down again. The fear was a cold, drawing knot in his stomach now. All right, God damn it! he thought. I'm not going to just stand here like a paralytic. On shaking but resolute legs, he walked to the edge of the wood scrap and looked around it. There was nothing.

Sighing, he went back to the thread and picked it up. It's so heavy, he thought. He really ought to leave it behind. What could happen to it, anyway? He stood indecisively. Then it occurred to him that he'd need the hook to drag the slice of bread back to the cliff edge. That settled, he picked up the heavy coil and slung it over his shoulder again. He was glad he'd thought of a use for the thread. Now he had a definite reason to take it. Heavy as it was, he didn't feel right about leaving it behind.

Every time he came to a scrap of wood, a boulder-high

stone, a piece of cardboard, a brick, a high mound of sand, he had to do the same nerve-clutching thing—put down the thread, approach the obstacle carefully, pin spear extended rigidly, until he'd found out that the spider was not hiding there. Then, each time, a great swell of relief that was not quite relief made his body sag, made the spear point drop, and he would return to his thread and hook and go on to the next obstacle; never really relieved because he knew that each reprieve was at best, only temporary.

By the time he reached the bread he wasn't even hungry.

He stood before the tall white square like a child standing beside a building. It hadn't occurred to him before, but how could he possibly drag that slice by himself?

Well, it didn't matter, he thought bluntly. He wouldn't need that much bread, anyway. It had to last only one day more.

He looked around carefully but saw nothing. Maybe the spider *was* dead. He couldn't believe it, but he should have seen it by now. On all other occasions it had seemed to sense his presence. Certainly it remembered him, and probably it hated him. He knew he hated it.

He drove the spear into the sand and broke off a hard piece of bread, bit off a chunk, and started to chew. It tasted good. A few moments of chewing seemed to restore appetite, and a few minutes of eating brought it to a point of voraciousness. Although he couldn't relax his tense caution, he found himself breaking off piece after piece of the bread and crunching rapidly on its crisp whiteness. He hadn't realized it before, but he'd missed that bread. The crackers hadn't been the same.

When he was filled as he hadn't been filled for days, he finished off the water. Then, after a moment's hesitation, he flung away the piece of sponge. It had served its purpose. He picked up the spear and hacked out a piece of bread about twice his size. More than enough, stated his mind. He ignored it.

He plunged the hook into the piece of bread and dragged it slowly back to the cliff, scraping out a road behind him in the sand. At the edge of the cliff he drew out the hook and, propping up the huge chunk, pushed it over the brink.

It fluttered through the air, tiny crumbs flaking off as it fell. Settling after it like snow. It hit the floor, breaking into three parts, which bounced once, rolled a little way, then flopped onto their respective sides. There. That was that. He'd made the hard climb, got the bread he was after, and it was done.

He turned to face the desert again.

Why then the tension continuing in his body? Why didn't that knot of cold distress leave his stomach? He was safe. The spider was nowhere around; not behind the pieces of wood or the stones or the cardboard scraps, not behind the paint cans or the jars. He was safe.

Then why wasn't he starting down?

He stood there motionless, staring out across the dim-lit desert wastes, his heart beating faster and faster, as if it were grinding out a truth for him, sending it up and up the neural pathways to his brain, pounding at the doors and the walls of it, telling him that he hadn't only gone up for the bread, he'd also gone to kill the spider.

The spear fell from his hand and clattered on the cement. He stood there shivering, knowing now what that tension in him was, knowing exactly what it was that was going to happen—that he was going to *make* happen.

Numbly he picked up the spear and walked into the desert. A few yards out his legs gave way and he slumped down heavily, cross-legged on the sand. The spear fell down across his lap and he sat there holding it, looking out across the silent sands, an unbelieving look on his face.

He waited.

CHAPTER FOURTEEN

• • • • • • • • • • •

"Life in a Dollhouse." It had been the title of a chapter in his book; the last chapter. After he'd finished it, he'd realized that he couldn't write any more. Even the smallest pencil was as big as a baseball bat. He decided to get a tape recorder, but before that was possible, he was beyond communication.

That was later, though. Now he was ten inches tall and Louise came in one day with a giant doll house.

He was resting on a cushion underneath the couch, where Beth couldn't accidentally step on him. He watched Lou put down the big doll house and then he crawled out from under the couch and stood up.

Lou got on her knees and leaned forward to put her ear near his mouth.

"Why did you get it?" he asked.

She answered softly so the sound of her voice wouldn't hurt his ears. "I thought you'd like it."

He was going to say that he didn't like it at all. He looked at her profile for a moment; then he said, "It's very nice."

It was a deluxe doll house; they could afford it now, with the sales and resales of his book. He walked over to it and went up on the porch. It gave him an odd feeling to stand there, his hand on the tiny wrought-iron railing; the feeling he'd had the night he'd stood on the steps of Clarice's trailer.

Pushing open the front door, he went into the house and closed the door behind him. He was standing in the large living room. Except for fluffy white curtains, it was unfurnished. There was a fireplace of false bricks, hardwood floors and a window seat, candle brackets. It was an attractive room, except for one thing: One of its walls was missing.

Now he saw Lou on that open side, peering in at him, a gentle half-smile on her face.

"Do you like it?" she asked.

He walked across the living room and stood where the missing wall should have been.

"Is there furniture?" he asked.

"It's in—" she began, then stopped seeing him wince at the loudness of her voice. "It's in the car," she said, more softly.

"Oh." He turned back to the room.

"I'll get it," she said. "You look at the house."

She was gone. He heard and felt her move across the floor of the big living room, the tremble reflected through the floor. Then the other front door thudded shut and he looked around his new house.

By noon, all the furniture was in place. He'd had Lou push the house against the wall behind the couch so he could have the privacy as well as the protection of four walls. Beth, on strict orders, did not approach him, but occasionally the cat got into the house, and then there was danger.

He'd also had Lou put an extension cord into the house so he could have a small Christmas-tree bulb for light. In her enthusiasm, Lou had forgotten that he would need light. He would have liked plumbing too, but that, of course, was impossible.

He moved into the doll house, but doll furniture was not designed for comfort. The chairs, even the living room chairs, were straight-backed and uncomfortable because they had no cushions. The bed was without springs or mattress. Lou had to sew some cotton padding into a piece of sheet so he could sleep on the hard bed.

Life in the doll house was not truly life. He might have felt inclined to fiddle on the keyboard of the glossy grand piano, but the keys were painted on and the insides were hollow. He might wander into the kitchen and yank at the refrigerator door in search of a snack, but the refrigerator was all in one piece. The knobs on the stove moved, but that was all. It would take eternity to heat a pot of water on it. He could twist the tiny sink faucets until his hands fell off, but not the smallest drop of water would ever appear. He could put clothes in the little washer, but they would remain dirty and dry. He could put wood scraps in the fireplace, but if he lit them, he'd only smoke himself out of the house because there was no chimney.

One night he took off his wedding ring.

He'd been wearing it on a string around his neck, but now it was too heavy. It was like carrying a great gold loop around. He carried it up the stairs to his bedroom. There he pulled out the bottom drawer of the little dresser and put in the ring and shut the drawer again.

Then he sat on the edge of the bed looking at the bureau, thinking about the ring; thinking that it was as if he'd been carrying the roots of his marriage all these months, but now the roots had been pulled up finally and were lying still and dead in the little dresser drawer. And the marriage, by that act, was formally ended.

Beth had brought him a doll that afternoon. She'd put it on his porch and left it there. He'd ignored it all day; but now, on an impulse, he went downstairs and got the doll, which was sitting on the top step in a blue sun suit.

"Cold?" he asked her as he picked her up. She had nothing to say.

He carried her upstairs and put her down on the bed. Her eyes fell shut.

"No, don't go to sleep," he said. He sat her up by bending her at the joining of her body and her long, hard, inflexible legs. "There," he said. She sat looking at him with stark, jewel-like eyes that never blinked.

"That's a nice sun suit," he said. He reached out and brushed back her flaxen hair. "Who does your hair?" he asked. She sat there stiffly, legs spread apart, arms half raised, as though she contemplated a possible embrace.

He poked her in her hard little chest. Her halter fell off. "What do you wear a halter for?" he asked, justifiably. She stared at him glassily, withdrawn. "Your eyelashes are celluloid," he said tactlessly. "You have no ears," he said. She stared. "You're flat-chested," he told her.

Then he apologized to her for being so rude, and he followed that by telling her the story of his life. She sat patiently in the half-lit bedroom, staring at him with blue, crystalline eyes that did not blink and a little red cupid's bow mouth that stayed perpetually half-puckered, as if anticipating a kiss that never came.

Later on, he laid her down on the bed and stretched out beside her. She was asleep instantly. He turned her on her side and her blue eyes clicked open and stared at him. He turned her on her back again and they clicked shut.

"Go to sleep," he said. He put his arm around her and snuggled close to her cool plaster leg. Her hip stuck into him. He turned her on her other side, so she was looking away from him. Then he pressed close to her and slipped his arm around her body.

In the middle of the night, he woke up with a start and stared dazedly at the smooth, naked back beside him, the yellow hair tied with a red ribbon. His heartbeats thundered.

"Who *are* you?" he whispered.

Then he touched her hard, cool flesh and remembered.

A sob broke in his chest. "Why aren't you real?" he asked her, but she wouldn't tell him. He pressed his face into her soft flaxen hair and held her tight, and after a while he went to sleep again.

He sat on the cool sand, staring blankly at the doll arm sticking up out of the huge cardboard box across the way from him. It had reminded him.

He blinked and looked around. How long ago had that been? He couldn't remember. More importantly, how long had he been daydreaming here? There was no way of telling. The shaft of sunlight still pierced the window.

He blinked, looked around. He hadn't much longer. If it started to get dark, he could never—

There; *there*—wasn't that indicative? That failure to finish the thought. In the dark he could never kill the spider; he wouldn't have a chance. That was the thought. Why hadn't his mind finished it?

Because the thought terrified him.

Why was he remaining, then? He didn't have to. He had to think about it; understand it. All right. He pressed his lips together, holding on to the spear with white-knuckled hands.

For some reason, the spider had come to symbolize something to him; something he hated, something he couldn't coexist with. And, since he was going to die anyway, he wanted to take a chance at killing that something.

No, it wasn't that simple. There was something else mixed in with it. Maybe it was that he didn't really think he was going to disappear tomorrow. But wasn't it the same way with death? What young, normal person could ever really believe he was going to die? Normal? he thought. Who's normal? He closed his eyes.

Then he stood up hastily, the blood throbbing at his temples. Tomorrow had nothing to do with it, or, if it had, he would assume it hadn't. Now was what counted. And now he decided that, even if he died for it, that black monstrosity would also die. He let it go at that. It was enough.

He found himself moving across the sand on legs that felt like wood. Where are you going? he asked himself. The answer was obvious. I'm going after the spider and—

The whisper of his sandals on the sand ceased. And *what*?

He shivered. What could he do? What could he possibly do against a seven-legged giant spider? It was four times the size of him. What good was his little pin?

He stood there motionless, staring out across the still desert. He needed a plan, and soon. Already he was thirsty again. There was no time to waste.

Very well, he thought, struggling against the rising flutter of dread; very well, then, consider it a beast to be destroyed. What did hunters do when they wanted to destroy a beast?

The answer came quickly. A pit. The spider would fall into it and—

The pin! Sticking up like a long, sharp spike!

Quickly he took the thread coil from his shoulder and flung

it down. Unslinging the spear, he began to scrape at the sand, using the pin as he would a hoe.

It took him forty-five minutes of constant digging to finish. Face and body dewed with sweat, his muscles shuddering, he stood in the bottom of the pit, looking up its sheer walls. If the thread weren't hanging down, he himself would be trapped.

After resting a while, he pushed the spear into the sand so the point stuck up at a slight angle. He pushed it in deep and packed hard, wet sand around it so it would be secure. Then he climbed up the thread, pulled it out after him, and stood by the side of the pit, looking down into it.

Almost immediately, doubts began to assail him. Would it work? Wouldn't the spider run up its sides as easily as it ran up a wall? What if it missed the pin? What if it jumped back before it touched the pin? Then he'd have nothing to fight it with. Wouldn't it be better to do as he had done in the carton that time—hold the pin out and let the spider impale itself on the point?

He knew he couldn't do it that way; not now. He was too small. The impact would knock him over. He remembered the hideous sensation of that great black leg raking over him. He couldn't face that again. Then why stay? He wouldn't answer.

One thing more. He'd have to cover up the pit after the spider was in it. Could he possibly bury it in sand? No, that would take too long.

He walked around until he found a flat piece of cardboard that was wide enough to drop over the pit. He dragged it back.

That was it, then. He'd lure the spider here, it would fall in on the pin, and he would throw the cover over it, and sit on it until he was sure the spider was dead.

He licked his lips. There was no other way.

He stood quietly for a few minutes, catching his breath. Then, although still tired and still a little breathless, he started off. He knew that if he waited any longer, his resolve would go.

He walked across the desert, searching.

The spider must be in its web. That's what he'd look for. He walked in carefully measured strides, looking around anxiously. There was a cold stone lying in his stomach. He felt defenseless without the pin. What if the spider got between him and the pit? The stone dropped, making him gasp. No, no, he argued desperately, I won't let it happen.

Sound again. He started, then realized that it *was* the settling of the house and regained his stride, muscles at a constant anticipating tension.

It was getting darker. He was going deeper and deeper into the shadows, walking farther from the window light. Frightened breath made his chest jump a little. It was the way with black widows, he knew; naturally reticent and secretive, they built their webs in the most dark, secluded corners.

He went on in the deepening gloom, and there it was. High on its web it hung, a pulsing black egg, a giant ebony pearl with legs, clinging to the ghostly cables.

There was a dry, hard lump in Scott's throat. He wanted to swallow, but the throat seemed calcified. He felt as if he were choking as he stood there staring at the giant spider. It was clear now why he hadn't seen it all day; underneath its motionless bulk, hanging slackly from the web, was a fat, partially eaten beetle.

Scott felt a nauseous foaming in his stomach. He closed his eyes and drew in a shuddering breath. The air seemed to reek of stale death.

His eyes jerked open. The spider hadn't moved. It was still immobile, its body like a glossy black berry hanging on a milky vine.

He stood shuddering, looking at it. Obviously he couldn't go up after it. Even if he had the courage for it, the web would doubtless snare him as it had the beetle.

What could he do? Immediately inclination told him to leave unobserved, as he had approached. He even backed away several yards before he stopped.

No. He *had* to do it. It was senseless, unreasonable, insane, and yet he had to do it. He crouched down, looking up blankly at the huge spider, his hands stroking unconsciously at the sand.

His hands twitched away from something hard. He almost fell back, gasping. Then, eyes fluttering up and down to see if the spider had heard his gasp and to see what it was he'd touched, he saw the fragment of stone on the sand.

He picked it up and juggled it in his palm, a knot in his stomach, tightening slowly. His chest rose and fell with quick, erratic breaths. His gaze was fixed again on the bloated body of the spider.

He stood up quickly, teeth clenched. He walked around a small area and found nine more pieces of stone like the first one. He put them all down before him on the sand.

Far across the desert, the oil burner suddenly began to roar. He braced himself against its thundering, hands over his ears. The sand trembled under him. Up on the wall, it seemed as if the spider moved, but it was only the web stirring slightly.

When the burner clicked off, Scott picked up a stone, hesitated for a long moment, then fired the stone at the spider.

It missed, whizzing over the dark round body and knocking a hole through the web. Filaments of the web stirred out from the edges of the hole like wind-blown curtains. The spider flexed its legs, then was still again.

You're still safe, his mind warned quickly. You're still safe; for Christ's sake, get out of here!

Stomach muscles boardlike, he picked up the second stone and hurled it at the spider.

He missed again. This time the stone stuck to the web, swaying a little, then sagging heavily, pulling down the spider's perch. The spider oozed darkly up the gossamer cables. It twitched its legs, then was motionless once more.

With a half-sobbed curse, Scott snatched up the third stone and flung it. It bulleted through the air in a blurring arc and bounced off the spider's glossy back.

The spider jumped. It seemed to hang suspended in the air, then it was on the web again, spurting across the silken hatching like a giant egg running loose. Scott jerked up another stone and pitched it, another stone and pitched it, half horrified, half in a demented fury. The stones plowed into the gelatinous web, one striking, the other tearing a second hole.

"Come on!" he suddenly screamed at the top of his voice. "Come on, damn you!" Then the spider was skimming down the web, body trembling on its scrabbling legs. Another cry died in Scott's throat. With a sucked-in breath, he whirled and started racing across the sand.

Ten yards from where he'd started, he glanced back hurriedly across his shoulder. The spider was on the sand now, an inky bubble floating after him. Sudden panic clouded his brain. His legs seemed without strength. I'm falling! he thought.

It was an illusion. He was still running hard, mouth open. His gaze flew on ahead, searching for the pit, but he couldn't see it. A little farther yet. He jerked his head around again. It was gaining on him.

His eyes turned back quickly. Don't look! he thought. A stitch slashed up his side. His fleeing sandals pounded on the sand. He kept on searching ahead for the pit.

He couldn't help it, he looked back. It was closer still, quivering blackly on its leg stalks, scrambling almost sideways over the sand, eyes fixed on him. He sprinted, wild-eyed, through the shadows and the light.

Where was the pit?

For now he'd gone too far—he knew it—and was almost to the paint cans and jars. No, it was impossible! He'd planned it too carefully for it to happen like this. He glanced back. Still closer; scrabbling, hopping, bogging, fluttering, a horrible blackness running at him, higher than a horse.

He had to go back again! He started running in a wide semi-circle, praying that the spider would not cut across his path. The sand seemed to hold him back more and more, his sandals plowing into it, making quick sucking sounds.

He looked back again. It was following in his wake, but it was still closer. He thought he heard the wild scratching of its legs on the sand. The spider was twelve yards behind him, it was eleven yards behind him, ten yards . . .

Still running, he sprang into the air to see if he could locate the pit. He couldn't. His body jarred down heavily. A whining fluttered in his throat. Was it going to end like this?

No, wait! Ahead, to the right! He altered direction and dashed for the parapet of sand around his pit. Nine yards behind, the huge spider raced after him.

The pit grew larger now. He ran still faster, gasping through his teeth, arms pumping at the air. He skidded to a halt at the edge of the pit and whirled. It was the vital moment; he had to stand there until the spider was almost on him.

He stood petrified, watching the black spider bear down on him, getting taller and wider with every second. He saw its black eyes now, the cruel pincer-like jaws beneath it, the hair sprouts on its legs, the great body. It rushed closer and closer; his body twitched. No, wait—wait! The spider was almost on top of him; it blotted out the world. It reared up on its back legs to cover him.

Now!

With a tremendous spring, he leaped to one side and the lurching spider toppled into the pit.

The ghastly, piercing screech almost paralyzed him. It was like the distant scream of a gutted horse. Only instinct drove him to his feet to grab the cardboard and slide it rapidly toward the pit. The screeching continued, and suddenly he found himself screaming back at it. As he shoved the cardboard across the top of the pit, he saw the great black body vibrating wildly, the thick legs scraping and clawing at the sides of the pit, raking at the sand, kicking it up in clouds.

Scott flung himself across the cover. Immediately he felt it lurch and jump beneath him as the spider's body heaved up against it. Flesh cold and crawling, he clung to the jolting cardboard scrap, waiting for the spider to die. I did it! he exulted. I *did* it!

His breath choked off. The cardboard was tilting up.

Terror drove a steel-gloved fist into his heart. He started sliding off the cardboard as it tilted more steeply.

When the black leg flailed out like the twig-spiked branch

of some living tree, he screamed. He began sliding toward the leg, sliding, sliding.

Instinct drove him to his feet. As the cardboard was flung up violently, he added the springing of his legs to the impetus and leaped high above the leg.

He landed in a heap beside his coil of thread and whirled on hands and knees, staring at the pit. The spider was crawling out, dragging the impaling pin behind.

His body was convulsed with a terrible shudder. His hands clutched at something as he struggled up and started backing away.

"No," he muttered flatly. "No. No. No."

The spider was completely out of the pit now, moving awkwardly toward him, the pin still in its body. Suddenly it leaped up, landed, then spun around in a sand-scouring circle, trying to dislodge the pin. *Do* something! screamed his mind. He stared, sickly fascinated, at the jerking spider.

Suddenly he was conscious of the pin hook in his hands, and then he was running with it, uncoiling the rest of the thread. Behind him, the spider still writhed and flung itself around, blood drops flying out from it and spattering in murky ribbons across the sand.

Abruptly the spear came loose. The spider whirled toward Scott.

He was swinging the hook around his head at the end of six feet of thread. It flashed around him like a glittering scythe, swishing at the air.

The spider ran right into it.

The point drove into its bulbous body like a needle plunged into a watermelon. It leaped back sharply, screeching again, and Scott raced around a heavy scrap of wood, looping the thread around it until it was secure. The spider rushed at him, the pin hook deep in its body. Scott turned and fled.

It almost caught him. Before the thread grew taut and jerked the spider back, one of its black legs flailed across his shoulder, almost dragging him back. He had to fall to the sand and tear away from it before he could scuttle backward to freedom.

He stood up shakily, hair dangling across his forehead, face grimy with dirt. The spider tried to leap at him, legs slashing, jaws spread wide to clamp on him. The pin jerked it back; the hideous screeching knifed into Scott's brain again.

He couldn't stand it. He fled across the sand, the spider following him as far as it could, leaping end dragging fiercely at its binding.

The pin was slick with blood. Teeth set on edge, Scott flung handfuls of sand across it, then grabbed it up and moved back quickly, spear extended and braced against his hip.

The spider leaped. Scott jabbed out quickly and the spear point pierced the black shell; another drip of blood began. The spider leaped again; the spear point tore its hide and drew blood. Again and again the spider leaped into the spear point, until its body was a mass of punctures.

By then the screeching had stopped. The spider moved in slowly, rearing shakily on its weakened legs. Scott wanted it over suddenly. He could walk away and let it die now, but he wouldn't. For some fantastic reason swimming in mists of past morality, he felt sorry for the spider now and wanted to end its suffering. Deliberately he walked inside its circle of confinement, and with a final burst of violent effort the spider leaped.

The spear point pierced its body and the spider fell into a shuddering heap, its poison-dripping jaws clamping shut inches from Scott's body. Then it was dead, its body lying still and gigantic on the bloody sands.

Scott staggered away from it and pitched across the sand, unconscious. The last sound he remembered was the slow and awful scratching of the spider's legs—dead, but not at rest.

He stirred feebly, hands drawing in slowly, clutching at the sand. A groan wavered in his chest; he rolled over onto his back. His eyes opened.

Had it been a dream? He lay breathing carefully for a minute; then, with a grunt, he sat up.

No dream. Yards away from him the spider lay, its body

like a great, dead stone, its legs like motionless spars bent in every direction. The stillness of death hung over it.

It was almost night. He had to get down the cliff before dark. Exhaling wearily, he struggled to his feet and walked across to the spider. It made him ill to stand beside its bloody hulk, but he had to have the hook.

When it was finally done, he stumbled across the desert, dragging the hook behind him so the sands would clean it.

Well, it's done, he thought. The nights of horror were ended. He could sleep without the box top now, sleep free and at peace. A tired smile eased his stark expression. Yes, it was worth it. Everything seemed worth it now.

At the cliff's edge, he flung out the hook until it bit into wood. Then slowly, wearily, he pulled himself up, drew in the thread, and started across the lawn chair's arm. A long descent yet. He smiled again. It didn't matter; he'd make it.

As he was swinging down to the lower chair, hanging in space, the hook broke.

In an instant he was plummeting through the air, turning in slow, arm-waving cartwheels. It was such an absolute shock to him that he couldn't make a sound. His brain was stricken and taut. The only emotion he felt was one of complete, dumbfounded astonishment.

Then he landed on the flower-patterned cushion, bounced once, and lay still.

After a while he stood up and felt over his body. He didn't understand it. Even if he had landed on the cushion, he'd fallen many hundreds of feet. How could he still be alive, much less unhurt?

He stood a long time, feeling ceaselessly at himself, almost unable to believe that no bones were broken, that he was only bruised a trifle.

Then it came to him: his weight. He'd been wrong all the time. He'd thought that in a fall he'd suffer the same effects as he might have when he had his full size and weight. He was wrong. It should have been obvious to him. Couldn't an ant be dropped almost any distance and still walk away from the fall?

Shaking his head wonderingly, he walked to one of the pieces of bread and carried a big hunk of it back to the sponge. Then, after he'd got a long drink from the hose, he climbed to the top of the sponge with his bread and ate supper.

That night he slept in utter peace.

Chapter Fifteen

• • • • • • • • • • •

He reared up with a cry, suddenly awake. A carpet of sunlight glared across the cement floor; there was a drum-like jarring on the steps. Breath froze in him. Cutting off the sunlight, a giant appeared.

Scott flung himself across the yielding sponge, scrambling for its edge, then toppling over it. The giant stopped and looked around, its head almost touching the ceiling, far above. Scott dropped lightly to the cement, pushing to his feet, then pitching forward, tripping on the oversized robe. He jumped up a second time, eyes staring at the giant, who stood motionless, vast arms on hips. Grabbing up handfuls of his dragging robe, Scott raced barefoot across the cold floor, his sandals left behind.

After five yards, the folds of robe slipped from his hands and he went sprawling again. The giant moved. Scott gasped, recoiling, flinging up an arm. There was no chance to flee. The floor shook with the giant's coming. Horrified, Scott saw the Gargantuan shoes crash down on the cement. His gaze leaped up. The giant's body seemed to totter over him like a falling mountain. Scott threw the other arm across his face. The end! his mind screamed.

The thunder stopped and Scott drew down his arms.

Miraculously, the giant had stopped beside the red metal table. Why hadn't it gone on to the water heater? What was it doing?

A gasp tore back his lips as the giant reached across the plateau of the table, pulled over a carton bigger than an apartment house, and tossed it to the floor. The noise it made in landing drove an aural spear through Scott's brain. He clamped both hands over his ears and, struggling to his feet, backed off hastily. What was it doing? Another vast carton was flung across the cellar, landing deafeningly. Scott's frightened gaze followed its rocking descent, then jumped back to where the giant stood.

Now it was pulling something even larger from the pile between the fuel tank and the refrigerator. Something blue. It was Lou's suitcase.

Suddenly he knew it wasn't the same giant that had been there Wednesday. His eyes fled up the cliff walls of its trousers. That blue-gray pattern of squares and lines, what was it? He stared at it. Glen plaid! The giant was a man in a glen-plaid suit, wearing black shoes that seemed a block long. Where had he seen that glen-plaid suit before?

It came to him an instant before a second, smaller giant jumped down the steps and, in a piercing voice, said, "Can I help you, Uncle Marty?"

Scott stood rigid, only his eyes moving—from the immense form of his daughter to the even more immense form of his brother, then back again.

"I don't think so, sweetheart," Marty said. "I think they're too heavy." His voice rang out in Scott's ears with such a resonant volume that he could barely make out the words.

"I could carry the small one," answered Beth.

"Well, maybe you could, at that," said Marty. Cartons still flew through the air, bounced on the floor. Now two canvas chairs went flying. "There. And there," said Marty. They crashed against the lawn chairs and were still. "And *there*," said Marty. A net pole like a two-thousand-foot tree flashed across the floor and fell against the cliff, leaning there, its bottom end braced by the moonlike metal rim to which the net was fastened.

Now Scott was back against the cement block, head back, and he was gaping at the towering shape of his brother. He watched Marty's elephantine hand close over the handle of the second suitcase and drag it raspingly across the metal table, then drop it on the floor. What was Marty taking down the suitcases for?

The answer came. They were moving.

"No," he muttered running forward impulsively. He saw Beth's gigantic form lurch across the floor in three strides, then bend over to grab the second suitcase.

"No!" His face was drawn with panic. "Marty!" He screamed, racing toward his brother. He tripped across the dragging hem of his robe again, pitched forward. He stood up, crying his brother's name again. She couldn't leave!

"Marty, it's me!" he shrieked. "Marty!"

With palsied fingers, he jerked the robe over his shoulders and head and flung it down. He ran berserkly at his brother's shoes.

"Marty!"

At the steps, he heard the sawing, teeth-setting din of Beth dragging the smaller suitcase over rough cement edges. He ignored it, still running toward his brother. He had to make him hear.

"Marty! Marty!"

With a sigh, Marty started for the steps.

"No! Don't go!" Scott yelled as loudly as he could. Like a pale white insect, he sprinted over the cold cement toward his brother's rapidly moving form.

"Marty!"

At the steps, Marty turned. Scott's eyes widened suddenly with excitement.

"Here, Marty! *Here!*" he shouted, thinking his brother had heard. He waved his thread-thin arms wildly. "I'm here, Marty! Here!"

Marty turned his giant head. "Beth?" he said.

"Yes, Uncle Marty." Her voice drifted down the steps.

"Does your mother have anything else down here?"

"Some things," Beth replied.

"Oh. Well, we'll come back, then."

By then Scott had reached the giant shoe and leaped up clawing at the high ridge of its sole. He caught at the hard leather and held on.

"Marty!" He screamed again and dragged himself up onto the shelf. Standing hurriedly, he began to beat his fists against the shoe. It was like hitting a stone wall.

"Marty, please!" he begged. "Please! Oh, Please!"

Abruptly the shelf lurched and swung around in an immense, brain-whirling circle. Scott lost his balance and fell back with a cry, arms flailing for balance.

He landed heavily on the cement and lay breathless, watching his brother move up the steps with Lou's suitcase.

Then Marty was gone and sunlight poured blindingly across him. Scott flung an arm across his eyes and twisted away. A sob tore through his chest. It wasn't fair! Why were all his triumphs undone so quickly, all his victories negated in the very next instant?

He lurched to his feet and stood trembling, his back to the blazing sunlight. She was moving; Louise was moving away. She thought he was dead and she was leaving him.

His teeth grated together. He had to let her know he was still alive.

He looked sideways, shading his eyes with a cupped hand. The door was still open. He ran to the edge of the bottom step and looked up its sheer rise. Even if he made himself another hook, he couldn't throw it that high. He walked restlessly along the base of the step, muttering to himself.

What about the cracks between the cement blocks? Could he climb them now as he'd planned to do on Wednesday? He started toward the nearest one, then stopped, realizing that he had to have some clothes and food, some water.

It was then that the impossibility of the climb fell over him like a splash of molten lead.

He fell against the cold cement of the step and stood shivering, staring with dead eyes at the floor. His head shook slowly back and forth. It was no use trying. He'd never make the top. Not now; not at one seventh of an inch.

He'd stumbled halfway back to the sponge when the idea dispersed his despair. Marty had said he was coming back down.

With a gasp, he started running for the step again, then halted once more. Wait, wait, he cautioned, you have to prepare first. He couldn't just jump at the shoe again; there was no secure hold. Somehow he had to grab Marty's trouser leg, maybe even crawl inside the cuff, and cling there until he was carried into the house. Then he could get out, climb up on a table or a chair, anything, wave a piece of cloth, catch Lou's attention. Just to have her know that he was still alive, he thought excitedly. Just to have her know that.

All right, then. Quickly, quickly. He clapped his hands together with a nervous movement. What came first?

First came eating, drinking; a good meal under his—he laughed nervously—his belt? He glanced down at his white, goose-fleshed nakedness. Yes, that was first; but what could he wear? The robe was too big and its material too strong to tear up. Maybe . . .

He ran to the sponge and, after a wild tugging and jerking and gnawing of teeth, managed to tear away a big piece of it. This he thinned as much as he could and pulled around himself, sticking his arms and then his legs through its pores. It pressed against him, rubber-like, and did not cover him very well; it kept springing open in the front. Well, it would have to do. There was no time to make anything better.

Food next. He jogged across the floor and broke a chunk of bread from one of the pieces by the cliff. He carried it quickly to the hose and sat there eating it, perched on the metal lip of the opening, legs dangling. His feet should have something on them, too; but what?

When he'd finished eating and made the long, cold trek through the black hose passage, he went back to the sponge and pulled off two small pieces for his feet. He ripped out the centers of them and jammed his feet in. The sponge didn't hold very well. He'd have to fasten them with thread.

Suddenly it occurred to him that the thread not only would fasten his improvised clothing to himself, but could also get into Marty's cuff. If he could get another pin and bend it, and tie it to a length of thread, he could hook the pin into the trousers and hang on until he was upstairs in the house.

He started to run for the carton under the fuel tank. He stopped and whirled, remembering the piece of thread he'd had when he'd fallen the night before. It must still have a piece of pin fastened to it. He ran to find it.

It did; what was more, the piece of pin was still bent enough to hook onto Marty's trouser leg.

Scott ran on the pile of stones and wood by the bottom step, waiting for his brother to come down again.

Upstairs, he could hear restless, hurried footsteps moving through the rooms, and he visualized Lou moving about, preparing to leave. His lips pressed together until they hurt. If it was the last thing he did, he'd let her know he was alive.

He looked at the cellar. It was hard to believe that, after all this time, he might be getting out. The cellar had become the world to him. Maybe he'd be like a prisoner released after long confinement, frightened and insecure. No, that couldn't be true. The cellar had been no womb of comfort to him. Life on the outside could hardly be more onerous than it had been down here.

He ran his fingers lightly over his bad knee. The swelling had gone down considerably; it ached only a little. He touched at the cuts and abrasions on his face. He unwrapped the bandage on his hand, tugged it off and dropped it to the floor. He swallowed experimentally. His throat felt sore, but that didn't matter. He was ready for the world.

Upstairs, he heard the back door shut and footsteps on the porch. He jumped from the boulder and shook loose the length of thread. Then, picking up the hook, he pressed back against the wall of the step, waiting, his chest wall thudding with heavy heartbeats. Up in the yard, he heard a crunch of shoes on the sandy ground, then a voice saying, "I'm not sure exactly what we have down there."

His face grew tautly blank, his eyes were like frozen pools. He felt as if his legs were rubber columns under him.

It was Lou.

He shrank against the cement as giant shoes stamped down the steps. "Lou," he whispered, and then the two of them blocked off the sun like dark clouds passing.

They moved around, their heads more than half a mile high. He couldn't see her face, only the great moving redness of her skirt.

"That box on the shelf is ours," she said, a voice in the sky.

"All right," said Marty, moving toward the cliff wall and pulling down the carton with the doll arm sticking from it.

Lou kicked aside the small sponge on the floor. "Let's see, now," she said. "I think . . ."

She crouched down, and abruptly Scott could see the massive features of her face as a billboard hanger might see the features of the woman's face he pasted up. There was no sense of over-all appearance; just a huge eye here, an enormous nose there, lips like a rosy-banked canyon.

"Yes," she said, "this carton under the tank."

"I'll get it," Marty said, moving up the steps with the first box.

He was alone with her.

His gaze leaped up as she stood again. She moved around slowly, giant arms crossed under the mountainous swell of her breasts. There was a twisting agony in Scott's chest and stomach. For there was no denying it; she was beyond him now. Thoughts of trying to tell her he was alive evaporated. They had disappeared the moment he saw her. He was an insect to her; he knew it now with hideous clarity. Even if he managed somehow to attract her attention, it would solve nothing, it would change nothing. He would still be gone tonight, and the only thing accomplished would be that he would have torn open an old wound that might be nearly closed by now.

He stood silent, like a tiny piece from a miniature charm bracelet, looking up at the woman who had been his wife.

Marty came down the steps again.

"I'll be glad to get out of here," Lou told him.

"I don't blame you," Marty said, walking to the fuel tank and crouching down before it.

Beth came down the steps, asking, "Can I carry something, Mamma?"

"I don't think there's anything. Oh, yes, you can take up that jar of paint brushes. I think they're ours."

"All right." Beth moved to the wicker table.

Suddenly Scott twitched out of his reverie. He didn't want to tell Lou, but he did still want to get out of the cellar. And he couldn't wait for Marty, he realized. Marty would pass by the step too quickly; there would be no time.

Pushing away from the step, he raced to the refrigerator, under its shadowing bulk, then under the wicker table. Marty was still squatting by the tank, pulling out the carton. Scott ran beneath the red metal table. Quickly! He ran faster, dragging the thread behind him. Marty stood up with the carton in his arms. He started for the steps.

There was no time. As Scott rushed out into the open, Marty's immense black shoe was already crashing down before him. With a muscle-jerking hitch, he flung the hook at the swishing trouser leg.

If he had caught a galloping horse, he couldn't have been torn off his feet more violently.

His cry choked off. Abruptly he was flying through the air, then dipping down, the floor rushing grayly at him. With a twisting of his legs, he flattened out his body, his sponge coat scratching the floor as he flashed over it. The vast leg moved again. Scott, caught in the apex of his swing, was jerked high into the air. The thread grew taut and he was snapped forward again, his arms almost wrenched from their sockets. The cellar whirled by, a flash of light and shadow blended. He wanted to scream but he couldn't. He was swinging again, rocking violently in the air, spun around, his tiny body bulleting toward the steps. A wall rushed at him, disappeared below as he was jerked above it. His feet skidded along the top of the first step, the sponge bits torn away. The violent impact tore him loose, and suddenly he was running at top speed across the cement, heading for the face of the second step. He flung out his arms to ward off the shock. He screamed.

Then he tripped over a grain of concrete and went sprawling. His legs flew up, his skull cracked against the cement. Pain exploded through his head, white and vivid, then drew in suddenly to a black core, which also exploded, splashing his brain with night. He lay there limply as the shoe of his wife slammed down an inch from his body, then was gone.

Later, while Marty was driving them to the railroad station, Beth saw the hook and thread sticking to his trouser leg, and, bending down, she plucked it out. Marty said, "I must have picked it up in the cellar," then forgot about it. Beth put it in the pocket of her overcoat, and she forgot about it too.

7"

"Put me down!" he screamed.

He could say no more. Her hand was clamped around his body, binding him from shoulder to hip, pinning his arms, squeezing out his breath. The room blurred by; he started to black out.

Then the doll-house porch was under his feet, his hand was clutching at the wrought-iron railing, and Beth was looking down at him with half-frightened eyes.

"I gave you a ride," she said.

He jerked open the front door and plunged into the house, slamming the door behind him and snapping the tiny hook into its eye. Then he slumped down weakly in the living room, breath a dry rasping in his throat.

Outside, Beth said defensively, "I didn't hurt you."

He didn't answer. He felt as if he'd just been almost crushed in a vise.

"I didn't *hurt* you," she said, and she began to cry.

He'd known that the time would come, and finally it had. He could put it off no longer. He'd have to ask Lou to keep Beth away from him. She wasn't responsible.

He got up weakly and stumbled over to the couch. He

heard Beth going outside again, the floor trembling with her exit. The crash of the front door made him start violently. She'd come in a few moments ago, seen him making the long walk to his house, and picked him up.

He fell back on the small cushions Lou had made for him. He lay there a long time, staring at the shadowy ceiling and thinking of his lost child.

She'd been born on a Thursday morning. Lou's labor had been a long one. She'd kept telling him to go home, but he wouldn't. Occasionally he'd go down to the car, curl up on the back seat, and catch a few minutes of shallow sleep, but most of the time he stayed up in the waiting room, thumbing sightlessly through magazines, the book he'd brought to read unopened on the table beside him. Oh, yes, he was going to be smart; no movie melodramatics for him, no floor pacing and mashing of butts beneath heels. For that matter, he couldn't pace the floor even though he would have liked to. The waiting room was only a small alcove at the end of the second-floor hall, and he couldn't walk in the hall because there was too much traffic there.

So he'd sat in the waiting room, feeling as if there were a bomb in his stomach, primed to explode shortly. There was one other man there, but it was his fourth baby and he was blasé. He actually read a book: *The Curse of the Conquistadores*. Scott still remembered the title. How could a man sit reading such a book when his wife was writhing and twisting in labor? Or maybe his wife was one of the easy deliverers. As a matter of fact, the man couldn't have read more than three chapters before the baby was born, about one in the morning. The man had shrugged, winked at Scott, and gone home. Scott had cursed softly after him, then sat alone in the waiting room, waiting.

At seven-one A.M., Elizabeth Louise had put in her appearance.

He remembered Dr. Arron coming out of the delivery room and starting down the hall toward him, soft-soled shoes squeaking on the tiles. A dozen different horrors had pulsed through Scott's brain. She's dead. The baby's dead. It's misshapen. It's twins. It's triplets. There was nothing in there.

Dr. Arron had said, "Well, you've got a daughter."

And he'd been led to the glass window and, inside, a nurse was holding up a blanket-wreathed child, and it had black hair and it was yawning, its red little fists twitching at the air. And he'd just managed to brush away the tears before anyone could see.

He sat up on the couch and stretched out his legs. The pain in his rib box was not so bad now. He'd had trouble breathing for a little while there. He ran exploring hands over his chest and sides. No bones broken; that was sheer luck. Beth had clutched him terribly. Doubtless she'd only meant to make sure she wouldn't drop him, but . . .

He shook his head. "Beth, Beth," he murmured. Unseen, he'd been losing her day by day ever since the shrinking began. The loss of his wife had been a clear and certain process; the divorce from his child had been something else again.

At first there had been the circumstantial separation from her. He was suffering a terrible, unknown affliction, going regularly to doctors, being examined, being installed in a hospital. He had no time for her.

Then he was home, and worry and dread and the failing of his marriage had kept him from seeing how he was losing her. Sometimes he would hold her in his lap, read her a story, or, late at night, stand beside her bed and look down at her. Mostly, though, he was too absorbed in his own state to see anything else.

Then physical size had entered into it. As he'd grown shorter and shorter, so had he grown less certain of his authority and her respect. It was not a thing to be lightly conquered. As his size affected his attitude toward Lou, so did it affect his attitude toward Beth.

The authority of fatherhood, he discovered, depended greatly on simple physical difference. A father, to his child, was big and strong; he was all-powerful. A child saw simply. It respected size and depth of voice. What physically overshadowed it, it almost always respected or at least feared. Not that Scott had gained Beth's respect by trying to make her fear him. It was simply a basic state that existed because he was six feet two and she was four feet one.

When he had sunk to her height, then gone below it, when his voice had lost depth and authority and become a high-pitched, ineffective sound, Beth's respect, had slackened. It was merely that she could not understand. God knew they had tried to explain it to her—endlessly. But it wasn't explicable, because there was nothing in Beth's mental background comparable to a shrinking father.

Consequently, when he was no longer six feet two and his voice was no longer the voice she knew, she no longer actually regarded him as her father. A father was constant. He could be depended on, he did not change. Scott was changing. Therefore, he could not be the same; he could not be treated the same.

And so it had gone, each day her respect waning more. Especially when his jaded nerves began sending him into flurries of temper. She could not understand or appreciate. She was not old enough to sympathize. She could only see him baldly. And, in the actuality of pure sight, he was nothing but a horrid midget who screamed and ranted in a funny voice. To her he had stopped being a father and had become an oddity.

And now the loss was irreparable and final. Beth had reached the stage where she was a physical menace to him. Like the cat, she had to be kept away from him.

"She didn't mean it, Scott," Lou said that night.

"I know she didn't," he answered into the small hand microphone, so that his voice came clearly through the phonograph loud-speaker. "She just doesn't understand. But she'll have to stay away from me. She doesn't realize how frail I am. She picked me up as if I were an indestructible doll. I'm not."

The next day it ended.

He was standing, stooped over, in a hay-strewn stable,

looking at the faces of Mary and Joseph and the Wise Men as they looked upon the infant Jesus. It was very quiet and, if he squinted, it seemed almost as if they were all alive and Mary's face was gently smiling and the Wise Men were wavering, awed and reverent, over the manger. The animals were stamping in their stalls and he could smell the acrid stable smells and there was the faint, beautiful sound of the infant's gurgling.

Then a cold wind blew over him, making him shudder.

He looked toward the kitchen and saw that the door had been blown open a little and the wind was blowing powdery snowflakes across the floor. He waited for Lou to close it, but she didn't. Then he heard the faint, distant drumming of water and knew she was taking a shower. He stepped out of the stable and walked across the crinkled cotton glacier under the Christmas tree, his tiny homemade shoes crunching on the artificial snow. The wind rushed over him again and he shivered fitfully.

"Beth!" he called, then remembered that she was outside playing. He muttered irritably to himself, then ran across the rug onto the wide expanse of green linoleum. Maybe he could shut it himself.

He'd barely reached the door when a throaty rumble sounded behind him.

Whirling, he saw the cat by the sink, head just lifted from a dish of milk, its furry coat wet and disheveled. There was a heavy sinking in his stomach.

"Get out of here," he said. Its ears picked up. "Get *out* of here," he said again, more loudly.

Another growl wavered liquidly in the cat's throat and it slid forward a predatory paw, claws extended.

"Get out of here!" he yelled, backing off, the icy wind across his back, snowflakes buffeting like fragile hands at his shoulders and head.

The cat moved forward as smoothly as sliding butter, mouth open, saber teeth exposed.

Then Beth came in the front door and the sudden draft

hurricaning across the floor flung the back door toward its frame, scooping Scott along with it. In an instant the door had slammed shut and he had landed in a bank of snow.

Scrambling up, his clothes feathered with snow, Scott charged back to the door and pounded his fists against it.

"Beth!" The sound was barely audible to him above the wailing of the wind. Cold snow blew across him in ghost-like clouds. A huge pile of it fell from the railing, crashing down nearby and splattering him with its freezing granules.

"Oh, my God," he muttered. Frantically he began kicking at the door. "Beth!" he howled. "Beth, let me in!" He pounded until his fists ached and throbbed, kicked until his feet felt dead, but the door remained closed.

"Oh, my God." The horror of the situation was billowing in his mind. He turned and looked out fearfully at the snow-swept yard. Everything was dazzling white. The ground was a livid desert of snow, the wind blowing powdery mists of it across the high dunes. The trees were vast white columns topped with skeleton-white branches and limbs. The fence was a leprous barricade, wind ripping off snowy flesh, exposing the bony pickets underneath.

Realization came bluntly: if he stayed out here very long, he'd freeze to death. Already his feet felt like lead, his fingers ached and tingled from the cold, his body was alive with shudders.

Indecision tore at him. Should he remain and try to get in, or should he leave the porch and seek shelter from the snow and wind? Instinct bound him to the house. Safety lay on the other side of the white, paneled door. Yet intelligent observation made it clear that to remain was to risk his life. Where could he go, though? The cellar windows were locked from the inside, the doors were much too heavy for him to lift. And it would be no warmer underneath the porch.

The front porch! If somehow he could climb the front-porch railing, he might be able to reach the bell. Then he could get in.

Still he hesitated. The snow looked deep and frightening.

What if he were swallowed in a drift? What if he got so cold he never reached the front porch?

But he knew it was his only chance, and the decision had to be made quickly. There was no guarantee that his absence would be noted soon enough. If he stayed here on the back porch, Lou might find him in time. But she might not, too.

Gritting his teeth, he moved to the edge of the porch and jumped down to the first step. Piled snow cushioned his drop. He slipped a little, regained his balance, and scuffed to the edge of the step. He jumped again.

His feet slid out from under him and he spilled forward, arms plunging into the snow to his shoulders, face slapping into its flesh-numbing chill. He jerked up, gagging, and stood with a lurching movement, brushing at his face as if it swarmed with icicle-legged spiders.

There was no time to waste. Quickly he moved to the edge of the step, putting down his feet carefully. He poised at the brink a moment, looking down, then, with a quick breath, jumped.

Again he skidded, arms striking at the air. He slid to the side edge of the step, held on for a moment, then pitched into space.

Four feet down, his body plowed into a cone of snow like a knife driven into ice cream. Frost crystals floured across his face and down his neck. He pushed up, spluttering, then fell again, legs imbedded in the icy packing. He lay there, stunned, snow clouds powdering over him.

Then cold began creeping up his limbs and he pushed to his feet. He had to keep moving.

He couldn't run. The best he could manage was a sort of lurching, staggering walk, feet torn loose from the clinging snow, then put down again, his body hitching forward as his legs sank in. As he flopped across the yard, the wind whipped his hair to lashing ribbons and tore at his clothes, cutting through the material like frozen blades. Already his feet and hands were going numb.

At last he reached the corner of the house. In the far distance he saw the covered bulk of the Ford, its tarpaulin covered with scattered peaks of snow. A groan wavered in his throat. It was so far. He sucked in a mouthful of the lip-chilling air and lurched forward again. I'll make it, he told himself. I'll make it.

An object spilled across the sky like a plummeting stone.

One moment there was only wind and cold and thigh-deep snow. The next, a weight had crushed against him suddenly, knocking him down. His face a snow-cottoned mass of shock he flung himself over just in time to see the dark sparrow diving at him again.

Gasping, he flung up an arm as the bird flashed over him, swooping up on rigid wings. It shot into the air, circled sharply, and came at him again. Before he'd reached his feet, it was hovering before him, so close that he could smell its wet feathers. Its wings beat savagely at the air; the double sabers of its beak lunged at him.

He fell back again, snatching up a handful of snow and flinging it at the sparrow's head. It rose into the air, chattering fiercely, whirled about in a tight arc, then began to circle him in narrow, blurring sweeps, dark wings beating.

Scott's stark gaze jumped to the house, and he saw the cellar window and the missing pane.

Then the bird was at him again. He flung himself forward on the snow, and the dark, wing-flashing bulk shot over him. The sparrow swooped up, circled sharply, then bulleted back. Scott ran a few feet, then was knocked over again.

He stood up, flinging more snow at the bird, seeing the snow splatter off its dark, flaring beak. The bird flapped back. Scott turned and struggled a few more strides, then the bird was on him again, wet wings pounding at his head. He slapped wildly at it and felt his hands strike the bony sides of its beak. It flew off again.

It went on like that endlessly. He would leap through the icy snow until he heard its wing-drumming approach. Then, falling to his knees, he would whirl and fling a cloud of snow into its eyes, blinding it, driving it off long enough to push on a few more inches.

Until, finally, cold and dripping, he stood with his back to the cellar window, hurling snow at the bird in the desperate hope that it would give up and he wouldn't have to jump into the imprisoning cellar.

But the bird kept coming, diving at him, hovering before him, the sound of its wings like that of wet sheets flapping in a heavy wind. Suddenly the jabbing beak was hammering at his skull, slashing skin, knocking him back against the house. He stood there dazedly, waving his arms in panic at the bird's attack. The yard swam before him, a billowing mist of white. He picked up snow and threw it, missing. The wings were still beating at his face; the beak gashed his flesh again.

With a stricken cry, Scott whirled and leaped for the open square. He crawled across it dizzily. The leaping bird knocked him through.

He fell, clawing, his screams ending with a breathless grunt as he crashed down on the sand beneath the cellar window. He tried to stand, but he had twisted his leg in falling and it refused now to bear his weight.

Ten minutes later he heard running footsteps up above. The back door opened and slammed shut. And all the while he lay there in a snarl of limbs. Lou and Beth walked around the house and through the yard, trampling down the snow, calling his name over and over until darkness fell. And they didn't stop even then.

CHAPTER SIXTEEN

• • • • • • • • • •

In the distance he could hear the thumping of the water pump. They forgot to turn it off. The thought trickled like cold honey across the fissures of his brain. He stared with vacant eyes, his face a blank. The pump clicked off, and silence draped down across the cellar. They're gone, he thought. The house is empty. I'm alone.

His tongue stirred sluggishly. Alone. His lips moved. The word began and ended in his throat.

He twisted slightly and felt a stirring of pain in the back of his skull. Alone. His right fist twitched and thumped once at the cement. Alone. After everything. After all his efforts, he was alone in the cellar.

He pushed up finally, then sank down instantly as pain seemed to tear open the back of his head. Lying there, he reached up gingerly and touched a finger to the spot. He traced the edges of the brittle lacework of dried blood; his fingertip ascended and descended the parabola of the lump. He prodded it once. He groaned and dropped his arm. He lay there on his stomach, feeling the cold, rough cement against his forehead.

Alone.

Finally he rolled over and sat up. Pain rolled sluggishly around the inside of his head. It did not stop quickly. He had to press the palms of his hands against his temples to cushion its stabbing rebound. After a long while it stopped and dragged down at the base of his skull, spikes sunk in his flesh. He wondered if his skull were fractured, then decided that, if it were, he would be in no condition to wonder about it.

He opened his eyes and looked around the cellar with pain-slitted eyes. Everything was still the same. His dismal gaze moved over the familiar landmarks. And I thought I was going to get out, he thought bitterly. He looked up over his shoulder with a wince. The door was closed again, of course. And locked too, probably. He was still trapped.

His chest shuddered with a long exhalation. He licked his dry lips. And he was thirsty again too, and hungry. It was all senseless.

Even the slight amount of tensing in his jaws sent pain

gnawing through his head. He opened his mouth and sat limply until the aching had diminished.

When he stood, it came back again. He pressed one palm against the face of the next step and leaned against it, the cellar wavering before him as though he saw it through a lens of water. It took a while for objects to appear clearly.

He shifted on his feet and hissed, discovering that his knee was swollen again. He glanced down at its puffiness, remembering that it was the leg that had been injured in his original fall into the cellar. Odd that he'd never made the connection, but that was undoubtedly why that leg always weakened first.

He remembered lying on the sand, the leg twisted under him, while outside Lou was calling him. It was night and the cellar had been dark and cold. Wind had blown snow confetti through the broken pane. It had drifted down across his face, feeling like the timid, withdrawing touches of ghostly children. And, though he answered her and answered her, she never heard him. Not even when she came down into the cellar and, unable to move, he had lain there, crying out her name.

He walked slowly to the edge of the step and looked down the hundred-foot drop to the floor. A terrible distance. Should he labor down the mortar-crack chimney or—

Abruptly, he jumped.

He landed on his feet. His knee seemed to explode and a knife-edged club smashed across his brain as he fell forward to his hands. But that was all. Shaken, he sat on the floor, smiling grimly despite the pain. It was a good thing he'd discovered that he could fall so far without being hurt. If he hadn't discovered it, he would have had to climb down the chimney and wasted time. The smile faded. He stared morosely at the floor. Time was no longer something to be wasted, because it was no longer something to be saved. It was no longer a commodity to be spent or hoarded. It had lost all value.

He got up and started walking, feet padding softly over the cold cement. Should have got the sponge shoes, he thought. Then he shrugged carelessly. What did it matter, anyway?

He got himself a drink from the hose, then returned to the sponge. He didn't feel hungry, after all. He climbed to the top of the sponge and lay back with a thin sigh.

He lay there inertly, staring up at the window over the fuel tank. There was no sunlight visible. It must be late afternoon. Soon darkness would fall. Soon the last night would begin.

He looked at the twisted latticework of a spider web that blocked off one corner of the window. Many things hung from its adhesive weave—dust, bugs, bit of dead leaf, even a stubby pencil he had thrown up there once. In all his time in the cellar he'd never seen the spider that made that web. He didn't see it now.

Silence hung over the cellar. They must have turned off the oil heater before they left. There was that faint crackling, creaking sound of warping boards, but that couldn't even scratch the surface of the silence. He could hear his own breath, uneven and slow.

Through that window, he thought, I watched that girl. Catherine; was that her name? He couldn't even recall what she'd looked like.

He'd also tried to get up to that window after he'd fallen into the cellar. It had been the only one available. The window with the broken pane was too far above the sand, only a vertical wall beneath it. The window over the log pile was even less accessible. The only one that had presented the slightest possibility had been the one over the fuel tank.

But, at seven inches, he hadn't been able to climb the boxes and suitcases. And, by the time he'd found the means, he was too small. He'd gone up there once, but, without a stone, he'd been unable to break the pane and had had to go down again.

He rolled over on his side and turned away from the window. It was unbearable to see sky and trees and know he'd never be out there again. He breathed heavily, staring at the cliff wall.

And here I am, he thought, back to morbid introspection again; all action undone. This could have ended long ago. But

he had had to fight it. Climb threads, kill spiders, look for
food. He clamped his mouth shut and stared at the long net
pole leaning against the cliff wall, the long pole leaning against
the wall. His gaze moved along the pole leaning against the
wall, the long pole leaning against the wall.

He jerked up suddenly.

With a breathless grunt, he scrambled to the edge of the
sponge and jumped down, ignoring the pain in his knee and
head. He started racing for the cliff wall, stopped. What about
water and food? Never mind, he wouldn't need it; it wasn't
going to take that long. He ran toward the pole again.

Before he reached the net, he ran into the hose and got a
drink. Then, running out again, he began to shinny up the
metal rim of the net past the body-thick cords. He climbed
until he'd reached the pole, then pulled himself up onto its
wide, curving surface.

It was better than he'd imagined. The pole was so wide
and it was leaning against the wall at such a low angle that
he wouldn't have to clamber up, hands down, for support. He
could almost run erect up the long, gradual slope. With an excited cry he started up the road to the cliff.

Was it possible, he wondered as he ran, that things had
worked out in a definite manner? Was it possible that there
was purpose to his survival? It was hard to believe, and yet,
in a greater measure, hard to disbelieve. All the coincidences
that had contributed to his survival seemed to go beyond the
limits of probability.

This, for instance; this pole thrown here in just this way by
his own brother. Was that only chance? And the spider's
death yesterday providing the final key to his escape. Was
that only chance? Most importantly, the two occurrences
combining in just this way to make possible his escape.
Could it be only coincidence?

He could hardly believe it. Yet how could he doubt the
process going on in his body, which told him clearly that he
had today and nothing more? Unless the very precision with
which he shrank indicated something. But indicated what—
beyond hopelessness?

Still he did not lose the shapeless feeling of excitement as he hurried up the broad pole. It was still rising when he passed the first lawn chair; rising when he passed the second; rising when he stopped and sat looking down at the vast gray plain of the floor; rising when, an hour later, he reached the top of the cliff and fell down, exhausted, on the sand. And it was still rising as he lay there, heart pounding, fingers clutching at the sand. Get up, he kept telling himself. Let's go. It will be dark soon. Let's get out before it's dark.

He got up and started running across the shadowy desert. After a while he passed the silent bulk of the spider. He didn't stop to look at it; it was not important now. It was only a step already taken, which provided the ground for the next step. He stopped only once, to pull loose a chunk of bread and shove it under his coat of sponge. Then he ran on again.

When he reached the spider's web, he rested a while, then began to climb. The cable was sticky. He had to pull his hands and feet loose from it before he could climb up to the next one. The web trembled and swayed beneath his weight as he climbed past the dead beetle, not looking, breathing through his mouth.

And still excitement rose. Suddenly everything seemed meaningful, as if things had to happen in just this way. He knew it might be the rationalizing of desire, but he couldn't help thinking it anyway.

He reached the top of the web and quickly climbed onto the wooden shelf that ran around the wall. He could run now, and he did, his feet pounding down with a strong rhythm. He ignored the throbbing of his knee; it didn't matter.

He ran as fast as he could. Three blocks this way along the shadow-dark path, around the corner at top speed, then a mile straight ahead. He skittered like a tiny bug along the beam, running until he could hardly breathe.

He ran into blinding light.

He stopped, chest lurching, hot breath spilling from his lips. He stood there, eyes closed, and felt the wind blowing across his face. He closed his eyes and sniffed at its sweet, clear coolness. Outside, he thought. The word ballooned in his brain until it crowded out everything else and was the only word left. Outside. Outside. Outside.

Quietly then, slowly, with a dignity befitting the moment, he pulled himself up the few inches to the open square of window, clambered over the wooden rim, and jumped down. He stepped across the cement walk on trembling legs and stopped.

He stood at the edge of the world, looking.

He lay on a soft mattress of sere, crinkly leaves, other leaves pulled over him, the vast house behind him, blocking off the night wind. He was warm and fed. He'd found a dish of water underneath the porch, and had drunk from it. Now he lay there quietly on his back, looking at the stars.

How beautiful they were; like blue-white diamonds cast across a sky of inky satin. No moonlight illuminated the sky. There was only total darkness, broken by the flaring pin points of the stars.

And the nicest thing about them was that they were still the same. He saw them as any man saw them, and that brought a deep contentment to him. Small he might be, but the earth itself was small compared to this.

Odd that after all the moments of abject terror he had suffered contemplating the end of his existence, this night—which was the very night it would end—he felt no terror at all. Hours away lay the end of his days. He knew, and still he was glad he was alive.

That was the wonderful part of this moment. That was the thick blanket of contentment that warmed his toes. To know the end was close and not to mind. This, he knew, was courage, the truest, ultimate courage, because there was no one here to sympathize or praise him for it. What he felt was felt without the hope of commendation.

Before, it had been different. He knew that now. Before he had kept on living because he had kept on hoping. That was what kept most men living.

But now, in the final hours, even hope had vanished. Yet he could smile. At a point without hope he had found contentment. He knew he had tried and there was nothing to be sorry for. And this was complete victory, because it was a victory over himself.

"I've fought a good fight," he said. It sounded funny to say it. He felt almost embarrassed. Then he shook away embarrassment. It was what was left to him. Why shouldn't he proclaim the bittersweetness of his pride?

He bellowed at the universe. "I've fought a good fight!" And under his breath he added, "God damn it to hell."

It made him laugh. His laughter was the faintest icy sprinkling of sound against the vast, dark earth.

It felt good to laugh, and good to sleep, under the stars.

CHAPTER SEVENTEEN
• • • • • • • • • •

As on any other morning, his lids fell back, his eyes opened. For a moment he stared up blankly, his mind still thick with sleep. Then he remembered and his heart seemed to stop.

With a startled grunt, he jolted up to a sitting position and looked around incredulously, his mind alive with one word:

Where?

He looked up at the sky, but there was no sky—only a ragged blueness, as if the sky had been torn and stretched and squeezed and poked full of giant holes, through which light speared.

His wide, unblinking gaze moved slowly, wonderingly. He seemed to be in a vast, endless cavern. Not far over to his right the cavern ended and there was light. He stood up hastily and found himself naked. Where was the sponge?

He looked up again at the jagged blue dome. It stretched away for hundreds of yards. It was the bit of sponge he'd worn.

He sat down heavily, looking over himself. He was the same. He touched himself. Yes, the same. But how much had he shrunk during the night?

He remembered lying on the bed of leaves the night before, and he glanced down. He was sitting on a vast plain of speckled brown and yellow. There were great paths angling out from a gigantic avenue. They went as far as he could see.

He was sitting on the leaves.

He shook his head in confusion.

How could he be less than nothing?

The idea came. Last night he'd looked up at the universe without. Then there must be a universe within, too. Maybe universes.

He stood again. Why had he never thought of it; of the microscopic and the submicroscopic worlds? That they existed he had always known. Yet never had he made the obvious connection. He'd always thought in terms of man's own world and man's own limited dimensions. He had presumed upon nature. For the inch was man's concept, not nature's. To a man, zero inches meant nothing. Zero meant nothing.

But to nature there was no zero. Existence went on in endless cycles. It seemed so simple now. He would never disappear, because there was no point of non-existence in the universe.

It frightened him at first. The idea of going on endlessly through one level of dimension after another was alien.

Then he thought: If nature existed on endless levels, so also might intelligence.

He might not have to be alone.

Suddenly he began running toward the light.

And, when he'd reached it, he stood in speechless awe looking at the new world with its vivid splashes of vegetation, its scintillant hills, its towering trees, its sky of shifting hues, as though the sunlight were being filtered through moving layers of pastel glass.

It was a wonderland.

There was much to be done and more to be thought about. His brain was teeming with questions and ideas and—yes—hope again. There was food to be found, water, clothing, shelter. And, most important, life. Who knew? It might be, it just might be there.

Scott Carey ran into his new world, searching.

Nightmare at
20,000 Feet

"Seat belt, please," said the stewardess cheerfully as she passed him.

Almost as she spoke, the sign above the archway which led to the forward compartment lit up—FASTEN SEAT BELT—with, below, its attendant caution—NO SMOKING. Drawing in a deep lungful, Wilson exhaled it in bursts, then pressed the cigarette into the armrest tray with irritable stabbing motions.

Outside, one of the engines coughed monstrously, spewing out a cloud of fume which fragmented into the night air. The fuselage began to shudder and Wilson, glancing through the window, saw the exhaust of flame jetting whitely from the engine's nacelle. The second engine coughed, then roared, its propeller instantly a blur of revolution. With a tense submissiveness, Wilson fastened the belt across his lap.

Now all the engines were running and Wilson's head throbbed in unison with the fuselage. He sat rigidly, staring at the seat ahead as the DC-7 taxied across the apron, heating the night with the thundering blast of its exhausts.

At the edge of the runway, it halted. Wilson looked out through the window at the leviathan glitter of the terminal. By late morning, he thought, showered and cleanly dressed, he would be sitting in the office of one more contact discussing one more specious deal the net result of which would not add one jot of meaning to the history of mankind. It was all so damned—

Wilson gasped as the engines began their warm-up race preparatory to takeoff. The sound, already loud, became deafening—waves of sound that crashed against Wilson's ears like club blows. He opened his mouth as if to let it drain. His eyes took on the glaze of a suffering man, his hands drew in like tensing claws.

He started, legs retracting, as he felt a touch on his arm. Jerking aside his head, he saw the stewardess who had met him at the door. She was smiling down at him.

"Are you all right?" he barely made out her words.

Wilson pressed his lips together and agitated his hand at her as if pushing her away. Her smile flared into excess brightness, then fell as she turned and moved away.

The plane began to move. At first lethargically, like some behemoth struggling to overthrow the pull of its own weight. Then with more speed, forcing off the drag of friction. Wilson, turning to the window, saw the dark runway rushing by faster and faster. On the wing edge, there was a mechanical whining as the flaps descended. Then, imperceptibly, the giant wheels lost contact with the ground, the earth began to fall away. Trees flashed underneath, buildings, the darting quicksilver of car lights. The DC-7 banked slowly to the right, pulling itself upward toward the frosty glitter of the stars.

Finally, it levelled off and the engines seemed to stop until Wilson's adjusting ear caught the murmur of their cruising speed. A moment of relief slackened his muscles, imparting a sense of well-being. Then it was gone. Wilson sat immobile, staring at the NO SMOKING sign until it winked out, then, quickly, lit a cigarette. Reaching into the seat-back pocket in front of him, he slid free his newspaper.

As usual, the world was in a state similar to his. Friction in diplomatic circles, earthquakes and gunfire, murder, rape, tornadoes and collisions, business conflicts, gangsterism. God's in his heaven, all's right with the world, thought Arthur Jeffrey Wilson.

Fifteen minutes later, he tossed the paper aside. His stomach felt awful. He glanced up at the signs beside the two lavatories. Both, illuminated, read OCCUPIED. He pressed out his third cigarette since takeoff and, turning off the overhead light, stared out through the window.

Along the cabin's length, people were already flicking out their lights and reclining their chairs for sleep. Wilson glanced at his watch. Eleven-twenty. He blew out tired breath. As he'd anticipated, the pills he'd taken before boarding hadn't done a bit of good.

He stood abruptly as the woman came out of the lavatory and, snatching up his bag, he started down the aisle.

His system, as expected, gave no cooperation. Wilson stood with a tired moan and adjusted his clothing. Having washed his hands and face, he removed the toilet kit from the bag and squeezed a filament of paste across his toothbrush.

As he brushed, one hand braced for support against the cold bulkhead, he looked out through the port. Feet away was the pale blue of the inboard propeller. Wilson visualized what would happen if it were to tear loose and, like a tri-bladed cleaver, come slicing in at him.

There was a sudden depression in his stomach. Wilson swallowed instinctively and got some paste-stained saliva down his throat. Gagging, he turned and spat into the sink, then, hastily, washed out his mouth and took a drink. Dear God, if only he could have gone by train; had his own compartment, taken a casual stroll to the club car, settled down in an easy chair with a drink and a magazine. But there was no such time or fortune in this world.

He was about to put the toilet kit away when his gaze caught on the oilskin envelope in the bag. He hesitated, then, setting the small briefcase on the sink, drew out the envelope and undid it on his lap.

He sat staring at the oil-glossed symmetry of the pistol. He'd carried it around with him for almost a year now. Originally, when he'd thought about it, it was in terms of money carried, protection from holdup, safety from teenage gangs in the cities he had to attend. Yet, far beneath, he'd always known there was no valid reason except one. A reason he thought more of every day. How simple it would be—here, now—

Wilson shut his eyes and swallowed quickly. He could still taste the toothpaste in his mouth, a faint nettling of pepper-

mint on the buds. He sat heavily in the throbbing chill of the
lavatory, the oily gun resting in his hands. Until, quite suddenly, he began to shiver without control. God, let me go! his
mind cried out abruptly.

"Let me go, *let me go.*" He barely recognized the whimpering in his ears.

Abruptly, Wilson sat erect. Lips pressed together, he
rewrapped the pistol and thrust it into his bag, putting the
briefcase on top of it, zipping the bag shut. Standing,
he opened the door and stepped outside, hurrying to his seat
and sitting down, sliding the overnight bag precisely into
place. He indented the armrest button and pushed himself
back. He was a business man and there was business to be
conducted on the morrow. It was as simple as that. The body
needed sleep, he would give it sleep.

Twenty minutes later, Wilson reached down slowly and depressed the button, sitting up with the chair, his face a mask
of vanquished acceptance. Why fight it? he thought. It was
obvious he was going to stay awake. So that was that.

He had finished half of the crossword puzzle before he let
the paper drop to his lap. His eyes were too tired. Sitting up,
he rotated his shoulders, stretching the muscles of his back.
Now what? he thought. He didn't want to read, he couldn't
sleep. And there were still—he checked his watch—seven to
eight hours left before Los Angeles was reached. How was he
to spend them? He looked along the cabin and saw that, except for a single passenger in the forward compartment, everyone was asleep.

A sudden, overwhelming fury filled him and he wanted to
scream, to throw something, to hit somebody. Teeth jammed
together so rabidly it hurt his jaws, Wilson shoved aside the
curtains with a spastic hand and stared out murderously
through the window.

Outside, he saw the wing lights blinking off and on, the lurid flashes of exhaust from the engine cowlings. Here he was,
he thought; twenty-thousand feet above the earth, trapped in
a howling shell of death, moving through polar night
toward—

Wilson twitched as lightning bleached the sky, washing its false daylight across the wing. He swallowed. Was there going to be a storm? The thought of rain and heavy winds, of the plane a chip in the sea of sky was not a pleasant one. Wilson was a bad flyer. Excess motion always made him ill. Maybe he should have taken another few Dramamines to be on the safe side. And, naturally, his seat was next to the emergency door. He thought about it opening accidentally; about himself sucked from the plane, falling, screaming.

Wilson blinked and shook his head. There was a faint tingling at the back of his neck as he pressed close to the window and stared out. He sat there motionless, squinting. He could have sworn—

Suddenly, his stomach muscles jerked in violently and he felt his eyes strain forward. There was something crawling on the wing.

Wilson felt a sudden, nauseous tremor in his stomach. Dear God, had some dog or cat crawled onto the plane before take-off and, in some way managed to hold on? It was a sickening thought. The poor animal would be deranged with terror. Yet, how, on the smooth, wind-blasted surface, could it possibly discover gripping places? Surely that was impossible. Perhaps, after all, it was only a bird or—

The lightning flared and Wilson saw that it was a man.

He couldn't move. Stupefied, he watched the black form crawling down the wing. *Impossible.* Somewhere, cased in layers of shock, a voice declared itself but Wilson did not hear. He was conscious of nothing but the titanic, almost muscle-tearing leap of his heart—and of the man outside.

Suddenly, like ice-filled water thrown across him, there was a reaction; his mind sprang for the shelter of explanation. A mechanic had, through some incredible oversight, been taken up with the ship and had managed to cling to it even though the wind had torn his clothes away, even though the air was thin and close to freezing.

Wilson gave himself no time for refutation. Jarring to his feet, he shouted: "Stewardess! Stewardess!" his voice a hollow, ringing sound in the cabin. He pushed the button for her with a jabbing finger.

"Stewardess!"

She came running down the aisle, her face tightened with alarm. When she saw the look on his face, she stiffened in her tracks.

"There's a man out there! A man!" cried Wilson.

"What?" Skin constricted on her cheeks, around her eyes.

"Look, *look*!" Hand shaking, Wilson dropped back into his seat and pointed out the window. "He's crawling on the—"

The words ended with a choking rattle in his throat. There was nothing on the wing.

Wilson sat there trembling. For a while, before he turned back, he looked at the reflection of the stewardess on the window. There was a blank expression on her face.

At last, he turned and looked up at her. He saw her red lips part as though she meant to speak but she said nothing, only placing the lips together again and swallowing. An attempted smile distended briefly at her features.

"I'm sorry," Wilson said. "It must have been a—"

He stopped as though the sentence were completed. Across the aisle a teenage girl was gaping at him with sleepy curiosity.

The stewardess cleared her throat. "Can I get you anything?" she asked.

"A glass of water," Wilson said.

The stewardess turned and moved back up the aisle.

Wilson sucked in a long breath of air and turned away from the young girl's scrutiny. He felt the same. That was the thing that shocked him most. Where were the visions, the cries, the pummelling of fists on temples, the tearing out of hair?

Abruptly he closed his eyes. There had been a man, he thought. There had, actually, been a man. That's why he felt the same. And yet, there couldn't have been. He knew that clearly.

Wilson sat with his eyes closed, wondering what Jacqueline would be doing now if she were in the seat beside him.

Would she be silent, shocked beyond speaking? Or would she, in the more accepted manner, be fluttering around him, smiling, chattering, pretending that she hadn't seen? What would his sons think? Wilson felt a dry sob threatening in his chest. Oh, God—

"Here's your water, sir."

Twitching sharply, Wilson opened his eyes.

"Would you like a blanket?" inquired the stewardess.

"No." He shook his head. "Thank you," he added, wondering why he was being so polite.

"If you need anything, just ring," she said.

Wilson nodded.

Behind him, as he sat with the untouched cup of water in his hand, he heard the muted voices of the stewardess and one of the passengers. Wilson tightened with resentment. Abruptly, he reached down and, careful not to spill the water, pulled out the overnight bag. Unzipping it, he removed the box of sleeping capsules and washed two of them down. Crumpling the empty cup, he pushed it into the seat-pocket in front of him, then, not looking, slid the curtains shut. There—it was ended. One hallucination didn't make insanity.

Wilson turned onto his right side and tried to set himself against the fitful motion of the ship. He had to forget about this, that was the most important thing. He mustn't dwell on it. Unexpectedly, he found a wry smile forming on his lips. Well, by God, no one could accuse him of mundane hallucinations anyway. When he went at it, he did a royal job. A naked man crawling down a DC-7's wing at twenty-thousand feet—there was a chimera worthy of the noblest lunatic.

The humor faded quickly. Wilson felt chilled. It had been so clear, so vivid. How could the eyes see such a thing when it did not exist? How could what was in his mind make the physical act of seeing work to its purpose so completely? He hadn't been groggy, in a daze—nor had it been a shapeless, gauzy vision. It had been sharply three-dimensional, fully a part of the things he saw which he *knew* were real. That was the frightening part of it. It had not been dreamlike in the least. He had looked at the wing and—

Impulsively, Wilson drew aside the curtain.

He did not know, immediately, if he would survive. It seemed as if all the contents of his chest and stomach were bloating horribly, the excess pushing up into his throat and head, choking away breath, pressing out his eyes. Imprisoned in this swollen mass, his heart pulsed strickenly, threatening to burst its case as Wilson sat, paralyzed.

Only inches away, separated from him by the thickness of a piece of glass, the man was staring at him.

It was a hideously malignant face, a face not human. Its skin was grimy, of a wide-pored coarseness; its nose a squat, discolored lump; its lips misshapen, cracked, forced apart by teeth of a grotesque size and crookedness; its eyes recessed and small—unblinking. All framed by shaggy, tangled hair which sprouted, too, in furry tufts from the man's ears and nose, in birdlike down across his cheeks.

Wilson sat riven to his chair, incapable of response. Time stopped and lost its meaning. Function and analysis ceased. All were frozen in an ice of shock. Only the beat of heart went on—alone, a frantic leaping in the darkness. Wilson could not so much as blink. Dull-eyed, breathless, he returned the creature's vacant stare.

Abruptly then, he closed his eyes and his mind, rid of the sight, broke free. It isn't there, he thought. He pressed his teeth together, breath quavering in his nostrils. It isn't there, *it simply is not there.*

Clutching at the armrests with pale-knuckled fingers, Wilson braced himself. There is no man out there, he told himself. It was impossible that there should be a man out there crouching on the wing looking at him.

He opened his eyes—

—to shrink against the seat back with a gagging inhalation. Not only was the man still there but he was grinning. Wilson turned his fingers in and dug the nails into his palms until pain flared. He kept it there until there was no doubt in his mind that he was fully conscious.

Then, slowly, arm quivering and numb, Wilson reached up for the button which would summon the stewardess. He would not make the same mistake again—cry out, leap to his feet, alarm the creature into flight. He kept reaching upward, a tremor of aghast excitement in his muscles now because the man was watching him, the small eyes shifting with the movement of his arm.

He pressed the button carefully once, twice. Now come, he thought. Come with your objective eyes and see what I see— but *hurry*.

In the rear of the cabin, he heard a curtain being drawn aside and, suddenly, his body stiffened. The man had turned his caliban head to look in that direction. Paralyzed, Wilson stared at him. Hurry, he thought. For God's sake, hurry!

It was over in a second. The man's eyes shifted back to Wilson, across his lips a smile of monstrous cunning. Then with a leap, he was gone.

"Yes, sir?"

For a moment, Wilson suffered the fullest anguish of madness. His gaze kept jumping from the spot where the man had stood to the stewardess's questioning face, then back again. Back to the stewardess, to the wing, to the stewardess, his breath caught, his eyes stark with dismay.

"What *is* it?" asked the stewardess.

It was the look on her face that did it. Wilson closed a vise on his emotions. She couldn't possibly believe him. He realized it in an instant.

"I'm—I'm sorry," he faltered. He swallowed so dryly that it made a clicking noise in his throat. "It's nothing. I—apologize."

The stewardess obviously didn't know what to say. She kept leaning against the erratic yawing of the ship, one hand holding on to the back of the seat beside Wilson's, the other stirring limply along the seam of her skirt. Her lips were parted slightly as if she meant to speak but could not find the words.

"Well," she said finally and cleared her throat, "if you— need anything."

"Yes, yes. Thank you. Are we—going into a storm?"

The stewardess smiled hastily. "Just a small one," she said. "Nothing to worry about."

Wilson nodded with little twitching movements. Then, as the stewardess turned away, breathed in suddenly, his nostrils flaring. He felt certain that she already thought him mad but didn't know what to do about it because, in her course of training, there had been no instruction on the handling of passengers who thought they saw small men crouching on the wing.

Thought?

Wilson turned his head abruptly and looked outside. He stared at the dark rise of the wing, the spouting flare of the exhausts, the blinking lights. He'd *seen* the man—to that he'd swear. How could he be completely aware of everything around him—be, in all ways, sane and still imagine such a thing? Was it logical that the mind, in giving way, should, instead of distorting all reality, insert, within the still intact arrangement of details, one extraneous sight?

No, not logical at all.

Suddenly, Wilson thought about war, about the newspaper stories which recounted the alleged existence of creatures in the sky who plagued the Allied pilots in their duties. They called them gremlins, he remembered. Were there, actually, such beings? Did they, truly, exist up here, never falling, riding on the wind, apparently of bulk and weight, yet impervious to gravity?

He was thinking that when the man appeared again.

One second the wing was empty. The next, with an arcing descent, the man came jumping down to it. There seemed no impact. He landed almost fragilely, short, hairy arms outstretched as if for balance. Wilson tensed. Yes, there was knowledge in his look. The man—was he to think of it as a man?—somehow understood that he had tricked Wilson into calling the stewardess in vain. Wilson felt himself tremble with alarm. How could he prove the man's existence to others? He looked around desperately. That girl across the aisle. If he spoke to her softly, woke her up, would she be able to—

No, the man would jump away before she could see. Probably to the top of the fuselage where no one could see him, not even the pilots in their cockpit. Wilson felt a sudden burst of self-condemnation that he hadn't gotten that camera Walter had asked for. Dear Lord, he thought, to be able to take a picture of the man.

He leaned in close to the window. What was the man doing?

Abruptly, darkness seemed to leap away as the wing was chalked with lightning and Wilson saw. Like an inquisitive child, the man was squatted on the hitching wing edge, stretching out his right hand toward one of the whirling propellers.

As Wilson watched, fascinatedly appalled, the man's hand drew closer and closer to the blurring gyre until, suddenly, it jerked away and the man's lips twitched back in a soundless cry. He's lost a finger! Wilson thought, sickened. But, immediately, the man reached forward again, gnarled finger extended, the picture of some monstrous infant trying to capture the spin of a fan blade.

If it had not been so hideously out of place it would have been amusing for, objectively seen, the man, at that moment, was a comic sight—a fairy tale troll somehow come to life, wind whipping at the hair across his head and body, all of his attention centered on the turn of the propeller. How could this be madness? Wilson suddenly thought. What self-revelation could this farcical little horror possibly bestow on him?

Again and again, as Wilson watched, the man reached forward. Again and again jerked back his fingers, sometimes, actually, putting them in his mouth as if to cool them. And, always, apparently checking, he kept glancing back across at his shoulder looking at Wilson. *He knows,* thought Wilson. Knows that this is a game between us. If I am able to get someone else to see him, then he loses. If I am the only witness, then he wins. The sense of faint amusement was gone now. Wilson clenched his teeth. Why in hell didn't the pilots see!

Now the man, no longer interested in the propeller, was settling himself across the engine cowling like a man astride a bucking horse. Wilson stared at him. Abruptly a shudder plaited down his back. The little man was picking at the plates that sheathed the engine, trying to get his nails beneath them.

Impulsively, Wilson reached up and pushed the button for the stewardess. In the rear of the cabin, he heard her coming and, for a second, thought he'd fooled the man, who seemed absorbed with his efforts. At the last moment, however, just before the stewardess arrived, the man glanced over at Wilson. Then, like a marionette jerked upward from its stage by wires, he was flying up into the air.

"Yes?" She looked at him apprehensively.

"Will you—sit down, please?" he asked.

She hesitated. "Well, I—"

"Please."

She sat down gingerly on the seat beside his.

"What is it, Mr. Wilson?" she asked.

He braced himself.

"That man is still outside," he said.

The stewardess stared at him.

"The reason I'm telling you this," Wilson hurried on, "is that he's starting to tamper with one of the engines."

She turned her eyes instinctively toward the window.

"No, no, don't look," he told her. "He isn't there now." He cleared his throat viscidly. "He—jumps away whenever you come here."

A sudden nausea gripped him as he realized what she must be thinking. As he realized what he, himself, would think if someone told him such a story. A wave of dizziness seemed to pass across him and he thought—I *am* going mad!

"The point is this," he said, fighting off the thought. "If I'm not imagining this thing, the ship is in danger."

"Yes," she said.

"I know," he said. "You think I've lost my mind."

"Of course not," she said.

"All I ask is this," he said, struggling against the rise of anger. "Tell the pilots what I've said. Ask them to keep an eye on the wings. If they see nothing—all right. But if they do—"

The stewardess sat there quietly, looking at him. Wilson's hands curled into fists that trembled in his lap.

"Well?" he asked.

She pushed to her feet. "I'll tell them," she said.

Turning away, she moved along the aisle with a movement that was, to Wilson, poorly contrived—too fast to be normal yet, clearly, held back as if to reassure him that she wasn't fleeing. He felt his stomach churning as he looked out at the wing again.

Abruptly, the man appeared again, landing on the wing like some grotesque ballet dancer. Wilson watched him as he set to work again, straddling the engine casing with his thick, bare legs and picking at the plates.

Well, what was he so concerned about? thought Wilson. That miserable creature couldn't pry up rivets with his fingernails. Actually, it didn't matter if the pilots saw him or not—at least as far as the safety of the plane was concerned. As for his own personal reasons—

It was at that moment that the man pried up one edge of a plate.

Wilson gasped. "Here, quickly!" he shouted, noticing, up ahead, the stewardess and the pilot coming through the cockpit doorway.

The pilot's eyes jerked up to look at Wilson, then abruptly, he was pushing past the stewardess and lurching up the aisle.

"Hurry!" Wilson cried. He glanced out the window in time to see the man go leaping upward. That didn't matter now. There would be evidence.

"What's going on?" the pilot asked, stopping breathlessly beside his seat.

"He's torn up one of the engine plates!" said Wilson in a shaking voice.

"He's what?"

"The man outside!" said Wilson. "I tell you he's—!"

"Mister Wilson, keep your voice down!" ordered the pilot. Wilson's jaw went slack.

"I don't know what's going on here," said the pilot, "but—"

"Will you look?!" shouted Wilson.

"Mister Wilson, I'm warning you."

"For God's sake!" Wilson swallowed quickly, trying to repress the blinding rage he felt. Abruptly, he pushed back against his seat and pointed at the window with a palsied hand. "Will you, for God's sake, *look*?" he asked.

Drawing in an agitated breath, the pilot bent over. In a moment, his gaze shifted coldly to Wilson's. "Well?" he asked.

Wilson jerked his head around. The plates were in their normal position.

"Oh, now wait," he said before the dread could come. "I saw him pry that plate up."

"Mister Wilson, if you don't—"

"I said I saw him pry it up," said Wilson.

The pilot stood there looking at him in the same withdrawn, almost aghast way as the stewardess had. Wilson shuddered violently.

"Listen, I *saw* him!" he cried. The sudden break in his voice appalled him.

In a second, the pilot was down beside him. "Mister Wilson, please," he said. "All right, you saw him. But remember there are other people aboard. We mustn't alarm them."

Wilson was too shaken to understand at first.

"You—mean you've *seen* him then?" he asked.

"Of course," the pilot said, "but we don't want to frighten the passengers. You can understand that."

"Of course, of course, I don't want to—"

Wilson felt a spastic coiling in his groin and lower stomach. Suddenly, he pressed his lips together and looked at the pilot with malevolent eyes.

"I understand," he said.

"The thing we have to remember—" began the pilot.

"We can stop now," Wilson said.

"Sir?"

Wilson shuddered. "Get out of here," he said.

"Mister Wilson, what—?"

"Will you stop?" Face whitening, Wilson turned from the pilot and stared out at the wing, eyes like stone.

He glared back suddenly.

"Rest assured I'll not say another word!" he snapped.

"Mr. Wilson, try to understand our—"

Wilson twisted away and stared out venomously at the engine. From a corner of his vision, he saw two passengers standing in the aisle looking at him. *Idiots!* his mind exploded. He felt his hands begin to tremble and, for a few seconds, was afraid that he was going to vomit. It's the motion, he told himself. The plane was bucking in the air now like a storm-tossed boat.

He realized that the pilot was still talking to him and, refocusing his eyes, he looked at the man's reflection in the window. Beside him, mutely somber, stood the stewardess. Blind idiots, both of them, thought Wilson. He did not indicate his notice of their departure. Reflected on the window, he saw them heading toward the rear of the cabin. They'll be discussing me now, he thought. Setting up plans in case I grow violent.

He wished now that the man would reappear, pull off the cowling plate and ruin the engine. It gave him a sense of vengeful pleasure to know that only he stood between catastrophe and the more than thirty people aboard. If he chose, he could allow that catastrophe to take place. Wilson smiled without humor. There would be a royal suicide, he thought.

The little man dropped down again and Wilson saw that what he'd thought was correct—the man had pressed the plate back into place before jumping away. For, now, he was prying it up again and it was raising easily, peeling back like skin excised by some grotesque surgeon. The motion of the wing was very broken but the man seemed to have no difficulty staying balanced.

Once more Wilson felt panic. What was he to do? No one believed him. If he tried to convince them any more they'd probably restrain him by force. If he asked the stewardess to sit by him it would be, at best, only a momentary reprieve. The second she departed or, remaining, fell asleep, the man would return. Even if she stayed awake beside him, what was to keep the man from tampering with the engines on the other wing? Wilson shuddered, a coldness of dread misting along his bones.

Dear God, there was nothing to be done.

He twitched as, across the window through which he watched the little man, the pilot's reflection passed. The insanity of the moment almost broke him—the man and the pilot within feet of each other, both seen by him yet not aware of one another. No, that was wrong. The little man had glanced across his shoulder as the pilot passed. As if he knew there was no need to leap off any more, that Wilson's capacity for interfering was at an end. Wilson suddenly trembled with mind-searing rage. I'll kill you! he thought! You filthy little animal, I'll *kill* you!

Outside, the engine faltered.

It lasted only for a second, but, in that second, it seemed to Wilson as if his heart had, also, stopped. He pressed against the window, staring. The man had bent the cowling plate far back and now was on his knees, poking a curious hand into the engine.

"Don't," Wilson heard the whimper of his own voice begging. *"Don't . . ."*

Again, the engine failed. Wilson looked around in horror. Was everyone deaf? He raised his hand to press the button for the stewardess, then jerked it back. No, they'd lock him up, restrain him somehow. And he was the only one who knew what was happening, the only one who could help.

"God . . ." Wilson bit his lower lip until the pain made him whimper. He twisted around again and jolted. The stewardess was hurrying down the rocking aisle. She'd heard it! He watched her fixedly and saw her glance at him as she passed his seat.

She stopped three seats down the aisle. Someone else had heard! Wilson watched the stewardess as she leaned over, talking to the unseen passenger. Outside, the engine coughed again. Wilson jerked his head around and looked out with horror-pinched eyes.

"Damn you!" he whined.

He turned again and saw the stewardess coming back up

the aisle. She didn't look alarmed. Wilson stared at her with unbelieving eyes. It wasn't possible. He twisted around to follow her swaying movement and saw her turn in at the kitchen.

"No." Wilson was shaking so badly now he couldn't stop. No one had heard.

No one knew.

Suddenly, Wilson bent over and slid his overnight bag out from under the seat. Unzipping it, he jerked out his briefcase and threw it on the carpeting. Then, reaching in again, he grabbed the oilskin envelope and straightened up. From the corners of his eyes, he saw the stewardess coming back and pushed the bag beneath the seat with his shoes, shoving the oilskin envelope beside himself. He sat there rigidly, breath quavering in his chest, as she went by.

Then he pulled the envelope into his lap and untied it. His movements were so feverish that he almost dropped the pistol. He caught it by the barrel, then clutched at the stock with white-knuckled fingers and pushed off the safety catch. He glanced outside and felt himself grow cold.

The man was looking at him.

Wilson pressed his shaking lips together. It was impossible that the man knew what he intended. He swallowed and tried to catch his breath. He shifted his gaze to where the stewardess was handing some pills to the passenger ahead, then looked back at the wing. The man was turning to the engine once again, reaching in. Wilson's grip tightened on the pistol. He began to raise it.

Suddenly, he lowered it. The window was too thick. The bullet might be deflected and kill one of the passengers. He shuddered and stared out at the little man. Again the engine failed and Wilson saw an eruption of sparks cast light across the man's animal features. He braced himself. There was only one answer.

He looked down at the handle of the emergency door. There was a transparent cover over it. Wilson pulled it free and dropped it. He looked outside. The man was still there, crouched and probing at the engine with his hand. Wilson sucked in trembling breath. He put his left hand on the door handle and tested. It wouldn't move downward. Upward there was play.

Abruptly, Wilson let go and put the pistol in his lap. No time for argument, he told himself. With shaking hands, he buckled the belt across his thighs. When the door was opened, there would be a tremendous rushing out of air. For the safety of the ship, he must not go with it.

Now. Wilson picked the pistol up again, his heartbeat staggering. He'd have to be sudden, accurate. If he missed, the man might jump onto the other wing—worse, onto the tail assembly where, inviolate, he could rupture wires, mangle flaps, destroy the balance of the ship. No, this was the only way. He'd fire low and try to hit the man in the chest or stomach. Wilson filled his lungs with air. Now, he thought. *Now.*

The stewardess came up the aisle as Wilson started pulling at the handle. For a moment, frozen in her steps, she couldn't speak. A look of stupefied horror distended her features and she raised one hand as if imploring him. Then, suddenly, her voice was shrilling above the noise of the engines.

"Mr. Wilson, no!"

"Get back!" cried Wilson and he wrenched the handle up.

The door seemed to disappear. One second it was by him, in his grip. The next, with a hissing roar, it was gone.

In the same instant, Wilson felt himself enveloped by a monstrous suction which tried to tear him from his seat. His head and shoulders left the cabin and, suddenly, he was breathing tenuous, freezing air. For a moment, eardrums almost bursting from the thunder of the engines, eyes blinded by the arctic winds, he forgot the man. It seemed he heard a prick of screaming in the maelstrom that surrounded him, a distant shout.

Then Wilson saw the man.

He was walking across the wing, gnarled form leaning forward, talon-twisted hands outstretched in eagerness. Wilson flung his arm up, fired. The explosion was like a popping in the roaring violence of the air. The man staggered, lashed out and Wilson felt a streak of pain across his head. He fired again at immediate range and saw the man go flailing backward—then, suddenly, disappear with no more solidity than a paper doll swept in a gale. Wilson felt a bursting numbness in his brain. He felt the pistol torn from failing fingers.

Then all was lost in winter darkness.

He stirred and mumbled. There was a warmness trickling in his veins, his limbs felt wooden. In the darkness, he could hear a shuffling sound, a delicate swirl of voices. He was lying, face up, on something—moving, joggling. A cold wind sprinkled on his face, he felt the surface tilt beneath him.

He sighed. The plane was landed and he was being carried off on a stretcher. His head wound, likely, plus an injection to quiet him.

"Nuttiest way of tryin' to commit suicide *I* ever heard of," said a voice somewhere.

Wilson felt the pleasure of amusement. Whoever spoke was wrong, of course. As would be established soon enough when the engine was examined and they checked his wound more closely. Then they'd realize that he'd saved them all.

Wilson slept without dreams.

The
Test
· · · · · · · · · · · · · · · ·

The night before the test, Les helped his father study in the dining room. Jim and Tommy were asleep upstairs and, in the living room, Terry was sewing, her face expressionless as the needle moved with a swiftly rhythmic piercing and drawing.

Tom Parker sat very straight, his lean, vein-ribbed hands clasped together on the table top, his pale blue eyes looking intently at his son's lips as though it might help him to understand better.

He was 80 and this was his fourth test.

"All right," Les said, reading from the sample test Doctor Trask had gotten them. "Repeat the following sequences of numbers."

"Sequence of numbers," Tom murmured, trying to assimilate the words as they came. But words were not quickly assimilated any more; they seemed to lie upon the tissues of his brain like insects on a sluggish carnivore. He said the words in his mind again—*sequence of . . . sequence of numbers*—there he had it. He looked at his son and waited.

"Well?" he said, impatiently, after a moment's silence.

"Dad, I've already given you the first one," Les told him.

"Well . . ." His father grasped for the proper words. "Kindly give me the—the . . . do me the kindness of . . ."

Les exhaled wearily. "Eight-five-eleven-six," he said.

The old lips stirred, the old machinery of Tom's mind began turning slowly.

"Eight . . . f—ive . . ." The pale eyes blinked slowly.

"Elevensix," Tom finished in a breath, then straightened himself proudly.

Yes, good, he thought—very good. They wouldn't fool him tomorrow; he'd beat their murderous law. His lips pressed together and his hands clasped tightly on the white table cloth.

"What?" he said then, refocusing his eyes as Les said something. "Speak up," he said, irritably. "Speak *up*."

"I gave you another sequence," Les said quietly. "Here, I'll read it again."

Tom leaned forward a little, ears straining.

"Nine-two-sixteen-seven-three," Les said.

Tom cleared his throat with effort. "Speak slower," he told his son. He hadn't quite gotten that. How did they expect anyone to retain such a ridiculously long string of numbers?

"What, *what*?" he asked angrily as Les read the numbers again.

"Dad, the examiner will be reading the questions faster than *I'm* reading them. You—"

"I'm quite aware of that," Tom interrupted stiffly. "Quite aware. Let me remind you . . . however, this is . . . not a test. It's study, it's for *study*. Foolish to go rushing through everything. *Foolish*. I have to learn this—this . . . this *test*," he finished, angry at his son and angry at the way desired words hid themselves from his mind.

Les shrugged and looked down at the test again. "Nine-two-sixteen-seven-three," he read slowly.

"Nine-two-six-seven—"

"Six*teen*-seven, Dad."

"I said that."

"You said six, Dad."

"Don't you suppose I know what I said!"

Les closed his eyes a moment. "All right, Dad," he said.

"Well, are you going to read it again or not?" Tom asked him sharply.

Les read the numbers off again and, as he listened to his father stumble through the sequence, he glanced into the living room at Terry.

She was sitting there, features motionless, sewing. She'd turned off the radio and he knew she could hear the old man faltering with the numbers.

All right, Les heard himself saying in his mind as if he spoke to her. All right, I know he's old and useless. Do you want me to tell him that to his face and drive a knife into his back? You know and I know that he won't pass the test. Allow me, at least, this brief hypocrisy. Tomorrow the sentence will be passed. Don't make me pass it tonight and break the old man's heart.

"That's correct, I believe," Les heard the dignified voice of his father say and he refocused his eyes on the gaunt, seamed face.

"Yes, that's right," he said, hastily.

He felt like a traitor when a slight smile trembled at the corners of his father's mouth. I'm cheating him, he thought.

"Let's go on to something else," he heard his father say and he looked down quickly at the sheet. What would be easy for him? he thought, despising himself for thinking it.

"Well, come on, Leslie," his father said in a restrained voice. "We have no time to waste."

Tom looked at his son thumbing through the pages and his hands closed into fists. Tomorrow, his life was in the balance and his son just browsed through the test paper as if nothing important were going to happen tomorrow.

"Come on, come on," he said peevishly.

Les picked up a pencil that had string attached to it and drew a half-inch circle on a piece of blank paper. He held out the pencil to his father.

"Suspend the pencil point over the circle for three minutes," he said, suddenly afraid he'd picked the wrong question. He'd seen his father's hands trembling at meal times or fumbling with the buttons and zippers of his clothes.

Swallowing nervously, Les picked up the stop watch, started it, and nodded to his father.

Tom took a quivering breath as he leaned over the paper and tried to hold the slightly swaying pencil above the circle.

Les saw him lean on his elbow, something he wouldn't be allowed to do on the test; but he said nothing.

He sat there looking at his father. Whatever color there had been was leaving the old man's face and Les could see clearly the tiny red lines of broken vessels under the skin of his cheeks. He looked at the dry skin, creased and brownish, dappled with liver spots. Eighty years old, he thought—how does a man feel when he's eighty years old?

He looked in at Terry again. For a moment, her gaze shifted and they were looking at each other, neither of them smiling or making any sign. Then Terry looked back to her sewing.

"I believe that's three minutes," Tom said in a taut voice.

Les looked down at the stop watch. "A minute and a half, Dad," he said, wondering if he should have lied again.

"Well, keep your eyes on the watch then," his father said, perturbedly, the pencil penduluming completely out of the circle. "This is supposed to be a test, not a—a—a *party*."

Les kept his eyes on the wavering pencil point, feeling a sense of utter futility at the realization that this was only pretense, that nothing they did could save his father's life.

At least, he thought, the examinations weren't given by the sons and daughters who had voted the law into being. At least he wouldn't have to stamp the black INADEQUATE on his father's test and thus pronounce the sentence.

The pencil wavered over the circle edge again and was returned as Tom moved his arm slightly on the table, a motion that would automatically disqualify him on that question.

"That watch is slow!" Tom said in a sudden fury.

Les caught his breath and looked down at the watch. Two and a half minutes. "Three minutes," he said, pushing in the plunger.

Tom slapped down the pencil irritably. *"There,"* he said. "Fool test anyway." His voice grew morose. "Doesn't prove a thing. Not a thing."

"You want to do some money questions, Dad?"

"Are they the next questions in the test?" Tom asked, looking over suspiciously to check for himself.

"Yes," Les lied, knowing that his father's eyes were too weak to see even though Tom always refused to admit he needed glasses. "Oh, wait a second, there's one before that," he added, thinking it would be easier for his father. "They ask you to tell time."

"That's a foolish question," Tom muttered. "What do they—"

He reached across the table irritably and picked up the watch and glanced down at its face. "Ten-fifteen," he said, scornfully.

Before Les could think to stop himself, he said, "But it's eleven-fifteen, Dad."

His father looked, for a moment, as though his face had been slapped. Then he picked up the watch again and stared down at it, lips twitching, and Les had the horrible premonition that Tom was going to insist it really was 10:15.

"Well, that's what I meant," Tom said abruptly. "Slipped out wrong. Course it's eleven-fifteen, any fool can see that. Eleven-fifteen. Watch is no good. Numbers too close. Ought to throw it away. Now—"

Tom reached into his vest pocket and pulled out his own gold watch. "Here's a *watch*," he said, proudly. "Been telling perfect time for ... sixty years! That's a watch. Not like this."

He tossed Les's watch down contemptuously and it flipped over on its face and the crystal broke.

"Look at that," Tom said quickly, to cover the jolting of embarrassment. "Watch can't take anything."

He avoided Les's eyes by looking down at his own watch. His mouth tightened as he opened the back and looked at Mary's picture; Mary when she was in her thirties, golden-haired and lovely.

Thank God, she didn't have to take these tests, he thought—at least she was spared that. Tom had never thought he could believe that Mary's accidental death at fifty-seven was fortunate, but that was before the tests.

He closed the watch and put it away.

"You just leave that watch with me, tonight," he said grumpily. "I'll see you get a decent ... uh, *crystal* tomorrow."

"That's all right, Dad. It's just an old watch."

"That's *all* right," Tom said. "That's all right. You just leave it with me. I'll get you a decent ... crystal. Get you one that won't break, one that won't break. You just leave it with me."

Tom did the money questions then, questions like *How many quarters in a five dollar bill?* and *If I took 36 cents from your dollar, how much change would you have left?*

They were written questions and Les sat there timing his father. It was quiet in the house, warm. Everything seemed very normal and ordinary with the two of them sitting there and Terry sewing in the living room.

That was the horror.

Life went on as usual. No one spoke of dying. The government sent out letters and the tests were given and those who failed were requested to appear at the government center for their injections. The law operated, the death rate was steady, the population problem was contained—all officially, impersonally, without a cry or a sensation.

But it was still loved people who were being killed.

"Never mind hanging over that watch," his father said. "I can do these questions without you ... hanging over that watch."

"Dad, the examiners will be looking at their watches."

"The examiners are the examiners," Tom snapped. "You're not an examiner."

"Dad, I'm trying to help y—"

"Well, help me then, *help* me. Don't sit there hanging over that watch."

"This is your test, Dad, not mine," Les started, a flush of anger creeping up his cheeks. "If—"

"My test, yes, my test!" his father suddenly raged. "You all saw to that, didn't you? All saw to it that—that—"

Words failed again, angry thoughts piling up in his brain.

"You don't have to yell, Dad."

"I'm not yelling!"

"Dad, the boys are sleeping!" Terry suddenly broke in.

"I don't care if—!" Tom broke off suddenly and leaned back in the chair, the pencil falling unnoticed from his fingers and rolling across he table cloth. He sat shivering, his thin chest rising and falling in jerks, his hands twitching uncontrollably on his lap.

"Do you want to go on, Dad?" Les asked, restraining his nervous anger.

"I don't ask much," Tom mumbled to himself. "Don't ask much in life."

"Dad, shall we go *on*?"

His father stiffened. *"If you can spare the time,"* he said with slow, indignant pride. *"If you can spare the time."*

Les looked at the test paper, his fingers gripping the stapled sheets rigidly. Psychological questions? No, he couldn't ask them. How did you ask your eighty-year-old father his views on sex?—your flint-surfaced father to whom the most innocuous remark was "obscene."

"Well?" his father asked in a rising voice.

"There doesn't seem to be anymore," Les said. "We've been at it almost four hours now."

"What about all those pages you just skipped?"

"Most of those are for the . . . the physical, Dad."

He saw his father's lips press together and was afraid Tom was going to say something about that again. But all his father said was, "A fine friend. Fine friend."

"Dad, you—"

Les's voice broke off. There was no point in talking about it anymore. Tom knew perfectly well that Doctor Trask couldn't make out a bill of health for this test the way he'd done for the three tests previous.

Les knew how frightened and insulted the old man was because he'd have to take off his clothes and be exposed to doctors who would probe and tap and ask offensive questions. He knew how afraid Tom was of the fact that when he redressed, he'd be watched from a peephole and someone would mark on a chart how well he dressed himself. He knew how it frightened his father to know that, when he ate in the government cafeteria at the midpoint of the day-long examination, eyes would be watching him again to see if he dropped a fork or a spoon or knocked over a glass of water or dribbled gravy on his shirt.

"They'll ask you to sign your name and address," Les said, wanting his father to forget about the physical and knowing how proud Tom was of his handwriting.

Pretending that he grudged it, the old man picked up the pencil and wrote. I'll fool them, he thought as the pencil moved across the page with strong, sure motions.

Mr. Thomas Parker, he wrote, *2719 Brighton Street, Blairtown, New York.*

"And the date," Les said.

The old man wrote, *January 17, 2003*, and something cold moved in the old man's vitals.

Tomorrow was the test.

They lay beside each other, neither of them sleeping. They had barely spoken while undressing and when Les had leaned over to kiss her goodnight she'd murmured something he didn't hear.

Now he turned over on his side with a heavy sigh and faced her. In the darkness, she opened her eyes and looked over at him.

"Asleep?" she asked softly.

"No."

He said no more. He waited for her to start.

But she didn't start and, after a few moments, he said, "Well, I guess this is ... it." He finished weakly because he didn't like the words; they sounded ridiculously melodramatic.

Terry didn't say anything right away. Then, as if thinking aloud, she said, "Do you think there's any chance that—"

Les tightened at the words because he knew what she was going to say.

"No," he said. "He'll never pass."

He heard Terry swallowing. Don't say it, he thought, pleadingly. Don't tell me I've been saying the same thing for fifteen years. I know it. I said it because I thought it was true.

Suddenly, he wished he'd signed the *Request For Removal* years before. They needed desperately to be free of Tom; for the good of their children and themselves. But how did you put that need into words without feeling like a murderer? You couldn't say: I hope the old man fails, I hope they kill him. Yet anything else you said was only a hypocritical substitute for those words because that was exactly how you felt.

Medical terms, he thought—charts about declining crops and lowered standing of living and hunger ratio and degrading health level—they'd used all those as arguments to support passage of the law. Well, they were lies—obvious, groundless lies. The law had been passed because people wanted to be left alone, because they wanted to live their own lives.

"Les, what if he passes?" Terry said.

He felt his hands tightening on the mattress.

"Les?"

"I don't know, honey," he said.

Her voice was firm in the darkness. It was a voice at the end of patience. "You have to know," it said.

He moved his head restlessly on the pillow. "Honey, don't push it," he begged. "Please."

"Les, if he passes that test it means five more years. *Five more years*, Les. Have you thought what that means?"

"Honey, he can't pass that test."

"But, what if he does?"

"Terry, he missed three-quarters of the questions I asked him tonight. His hearing is almost gone, his eyes are bad, his heart is weak, he has arthritis." His fist beat down hopelessly on the bed. "He won't even pass the *physical*," he said, feeling himself tighten in self-hatred for assuring her that Tom was doomed.

If only he could forget the past and take his father for what

he was now—a helpless, mind-jading old man who was
ruining their lives. But it was hard to forget how he'd loved
and respected his father, hard to forget the hikes in the country, the fishing trips, the long talks at night and all the many
things his father and he had shared together.

That was why he'd never had the strength to sign the request. It was a simple form to fill out, much simpler than
waiting for the five-year tests. But it had meant signing away
the life of his father, requesting the government to dispose of
him like some unwanted garbage. He could never do that.

And yet, now his father was eighty and, in spite of moral
upbringing, in spite of life-taught Christian principles, he and
Terry were horribly afraid that old Tom might pass the test
and live another five years with them—another five years of
fumbling around the house, undoing instructions they gave to
the boys, breaking things, wanting to help but only getting in
the way and making life an agony of held-in nerves.

"You'd better sleep," Terry said to him.

He tried to but he couldn't. He lay staring at the dark ceiling and trying to find an answer but finding no answer.

The alarm went off at six. Les didn't have to get up until
eight but he wanted to see his father off. He got out of bed
and dressed quietly so he wouldn't wake up Terry.

She woke up anyway and looked up at him from her pillow. After a moment, she pushed up on one elbow and looked
sleepily at him.

"I'll get up and make you some breakfast," she said.

"That's all right," Les said. "You stay in bed."

"Don't you want me to get up?"

"Don't bother, honey," he said. "I want you to rest."

She lay down again and turned away so Les wouldn't see
her face. She didn't know why she began to cry soundlessly;
whether it was because he didn't want her to see his father or
because of the test. But she couldn't stop. All she could do
was hold herself rigid until the bedroom door had closed.

Then her shoulders trembled and a sob broke the barrier
she had built in herself.

The door to his father's room was open as Les passed. He looked in and saw Tom sitting on the bed, leaning down and fastening his dark shoes. He saw the gnarled fingers shaking as they moved over the straps.

"Everything all right, Dad?" Les asked.

His father looked up in surprise. "What are you doing up this hour?" he asked.

"Thought I'd have breakfast with you," Les told him.

For a moment they looked at each other in silence. Then his father leaned over the shoes again. "That's not necessary," he heard the old man's voice telling him.

"Well, I think I'll have some breakfast anyway," he said and turned away so his father wouldn't argue.

"Oh ... *Leslie*."

Les turned.

"I trust you didn't forget to leave that watch out," his father said. "I intend to take it to the jeweler's today and have a decent ... decent crystal put on it, one that won't break."

"Dad, it's just an old watch," Les said. "It's not worth a nickel."

His father nodded slowly, one palm wavering before him as if to ward off argument. "Never-the-less," he stated slowly, "I intend to—"

"All right, Dad, all right. I'll put it on the kitchen table."

His father broke off and looked at him blankly a moment. Then, as if it were impulse and not delayed will, he bent over his shoes again.

Les stood for a moment looking down at his father's gray hair, his gaunt, trembling fingers. Then he turned away.

The watch was still on the dining room table. Les picked it up and took it in to the kitchen table. The old man must have been reminding himself about the watch all night, he thought. Otherwise he wouldn't have managed to remember it.

He put fresh water in the coffee globe and pushed the buttons for two servings of bacon and eggs. Then he poured two glasses of orange juice and sat down at the table.

About fifteen minutes later, his father came down wearing his dark blue suit, his shoes carefully polished, his nails manicured, his hair slicked down and combed and brushed. He looked very neat and very old as he walked over to the coffee globe and looked in.

"Sit down, Dad," Les said. "I'll get it for you."

"I'm not helpless," his father said. "Stay where you are."

Les managed to smile. "I put some bacon and eggs on for us," he said.

"Not hungry," his father replied.

"You'll need a good breakfast in you, Dad."

"Never did eat a big breakfast," his father said, stiffly, still facing the stove. "Don't believe in it. Not good for the stomach."

Les closed his eyes a moment and across his face moved an expression of hopeless despair. Why did I bother getting up? he asked himself defeatedly. All we do is argue.

No. He felt himself stiffening. No, he'd be cheerful if it killed him.

"Sleep all right, Dad?" he asked.

"Course I slept all right," his father answered. "Always sleep fine. Fine. Did you think I wouldn't because of a—"

He broke off suddenly and turned accusingly at Les. "Where's that watch?" he demanded.

Les exhaled wearily and held up the watch. His father moved jerkily across the linoleum, took it from him and looked at it a moment, his old lips pursed.

"Shoddy workmanship," he said. "Shoddy." He put it carefully in his side coat pocket. "Get you a decent crystal," he muttered. "One that won't break."

Les nodded. "That'll be swell, Dad."

The coffee was ready then and Tom poured them each a cup. Les got up and turned off the automatic griller. He didn't feel like having bacon and eggs either now.

He sat across the table from his stern-faced father and felt hot coffee trickling down his throat. It tasted terrible but he knew that nothing in the world would have tasted good to him that morning.

"What time do you have to be there, Dad?" he asked to break the silence.

"Nine o'clock," Tom said.

"You're sure you don't want me to drive you there?"

"Not at all, not at all," his father said as though he were talking patiently to an irritably insistent child. "The tube is good enough. Get me there in plenty of time."

"All right, Dad," Les said and sat there staring into his coffee. There must be something he could say, he thought, but he couldn't think of anything. Silence hung over them for long minutes while Tom drank his black coffee in slow, methodical sips.

Les licked his lips nervously, then hid the trembling of them behind his cup. Talking, he thought, talking and talking—of cars and tube conveyers and examination schedules—when all the time both of them knew that Tom might be sentenced to death that day.

He was sorry he'd gotten up. It would have been better to wake up and just find his father gone. He wished it could happen that way—*permanently*. He wished he could wake up some morning and find his father's room empty—the two suits gone, the dark shoes gone, the work clothes gone, the handkerchiefs, the socks, the garters, the braces, the shaving equipment—all those mute evidences of a life gone.

But it wouldn't be like that. After Tom failed the test, it would be several weeks before the letter of final appointment came and then another week or so before the appointment itself. It would be a hideously slow process of packing and disposing of and giving away of possessions, a process of meals and meals and meals together, of talking to each other, of a last dinner, of a long drive to the government center, of a ride up in a silent, humming elevator, of—

Dear God!

He found himself shivering helplessly and was afraid for a moment that he was going to cry.

Then he looked up with a shocked expression as his father stood.

"I'll be going now," Tom said.

Les's eyes fled to the wall clock. "But it's only a quarter to seven," he said tensely. "It doesn't take that long to—"

"Like to be in plenty of time," his father said firmly. "Never like to be late."

"But my God, Dad, it only takes an hour at the most to get to the city," he said, feeling a terrible sinking in his stomach.

His father shook his head and Les knew he hadn't heard. "It's early, Dad," he said, loudly, his voice shaking a little.

"Never-the-less," his father said.

"But you haven't *eaten* anything."

"Never did eat a big breakfast," Tom started. "Not good for the—"

Les didn't hear the rest of it—the words about lifetime habit and not good for the digestion and everything else his father said. He felt waves of merciless horror breaking over him and he wanted to jump and throw his arms around the old man and tell him not to worry about the test because it didn't matter, because they loved him and would take care of him.

But he couldn't. He sat rigid with sick fright, looking up at his father. He couldn't even speak when his father turned at the kitchen door and said in a voice that was calmly dispassionate because it took every bit of strength the old man had to make it so, "I'll see you tonight, Leslie."

The door swung shut and the breeze that ruffled across Les's cheeks chilled him to the heart.

Suddenly, he jumped up with a startled grunt and rushed across the linoleum. As he pushed through the doorway he saw his father almost to the front door.

"Dad!"

Tom stopped and looked back in surprise as Les walked across the dining room, hearing the steps counted in his mind—*one, two, three, four, five*.

He stopped before his father and forced a faltering smile to his lips.

"Good luck, Dad," he said. "I'll . . . see you tonight." He

had been about to say, "I'll be rooting for you;" but he couldn't.

His father nodded once, just once, a curt nod as of one gentleman acknowledging another.

"Thank you," his father said and turned away.

When the door shut, it seemed as if, suddenly, it had become an impenetrable wall through which his father could never pass again.

Les moved to the window and watched the old man walk slowly down the path and turn left onto the sidewalk. He watched his father start up the street, then straighten himself, throw back his lean shoulders and walk erect and briskly into the gray of morning.

At first Les thought it was raining. But then he saw that the shimmering moistness wasn't on the window at all.

He couldn't go to work. He phoned in sick and stayed home. Terry got the boys off to school and, after they'd eaten breakfast, Les helped her clear away the morning dishes and put them in the washer. Terry didn't say anything about his staying home. She acted as if it were normal for him to be home on a weekday.

He spent the morning and afternoon puttering in the garage shop, starting seven different projects and losing interest in them.

Around five, he went into the kitchen and had a can of beer while Terry made supper. He didn't say anything to her. He kept pacing around the living room, staring out the window at the overcast sky, then pacing again.

"I wonder where he is," he finally said, back in the kitchen again.

"He'll be back," she said and he stiffened a moment, thinking he heard disgust in her voice. Then he relaxed, knowing it was only his imagination.

When he dressed after taking a shower, it was five-forty. The boys were home from playing and they all sat down to supper. Les noticed a place set for his father and wondered if Terry had set it there for his benefit.

He couldn't eat anything. He kept cutting the meat into smaller and smaller pieces and mashing butter into his baked potato without tasting any of it.

"What is it?" he asked as Jim spoke to him.

"Dad, if Grandpa don't pass the test, he gets a month, don't he?"

Les felt his stomach muscles tightening as he stared at his older son. *Gets a month, don't he?*—the last of Jim's question muttered on in his brain.

"What are you talking about?" he asked.

"My Civics book says old people get a month to live after they don't pass their test. That's right, isn't it?"

"No, it *isn't*," Tommy broke in. "Harry Senker's grandma got her letter after only two weeks."

"How do *you* know?" Jim asked his nine-year-old brother, "Did you *see* it?"

"That's enough," Les said.

"Don't *have* t'see it!" Tommy argued. "Harry told me that—"

"That's *enough*!"

The two boys looked suddenly at their white-faced father.

"We won't talk about it," he said.

"But what—"

"*Jimmy,*" Terry said, warningly.

Jimmy looked at his mother, then, after a moment, went back to his food and they all ate in silence.

The death of their grandfather means nothing to them, Les thought bitterly—nothing at all. He swallowed and tried to relax the tightness in his body. Well, why *should* it mean anything to them? he told himself; it's not their time to worry yet. Why force it on them now? They'll have it soon enough.

When the front door opened and shut at 6:10, Les stood up so quickly, he knocked over an empty glass.

"Les, *don't*," Terry said suddenly and he knew, immediately, that she was right. His father wouldn't like him to come rushing from the kitchen with questions.

He slumped down on the chair again and stared at his

barely touched food, his heart throbbing. As he picked up his fork with tight fingers, he heard the old man cross the dining room rug and start up the stairs. He glanced at Terry and her throat moved.

He couldn't eat. He sat there breathing heavily, and picking at the food. Upstairs, he heard the door to his father's room close.

It was when Terry was putting the pie on the table that Les excused himself quickly and got up.

He was at the foot of the stairs when the kitchen door was pushed open. "Les," he heard her say, urgently.

He stood there silently as she came up to him.

"Isn't it better we leave him alone?" she asked.

"But, honey, I—"

"Les, if he'd passed the test, he would have come into the kitchen and told us."

"Honey, he wouldn't know if—"

"He'd know if he passed, you know that. He told us about it the last two times. If he'd passed, he'd have—"

Her voice broke off and she shuddered at the way he was looking at her. In the heavy silence, she heard a sudden splattering of rain on the windows.

They looked at each other a long moment. Then Les said, "I'm going up."

"Les," she murmured.

"I won't say anything to upset him," he said. "I'll ..."

A moment longer they stared at each other. Then he turned away and trudged up the steps. Terry watched him go with a bleak, hopeless look on her face.

Les stood before the closed door a minute, bracing himself. I won't upset him, he told himself; I *won't.*

He knocked softly, wondering, in that second, if he were making a mistake. Maybe he should have left the old man alone, he thought unhappily.

In the bedroom, he heard a rustling movement on the bed, then the sound of his father's feet touching the floor.

"Who is it?" he heard Tom ask.

Les caught his breath. "It's me, Dad," he said.

"What do you want?"

"May I see you?"

Silence inside. "Well . . ." he heard his father say then and his voice stopped. Les heard him get up and heard the sound of his footsteps on the floor. Then there was the sound of paper rattling and a bureau drawer being carefully shut.

Finally the door opened.

Tom was wearing his old red bathrobe over his clothes and he'd taken off his shoes and put his slippers on.

"May I come in, Dad?" Les asked quietly.

His father hesitated a moment. Then he said, "Come in," but it wasn't an invitation. It was more as if he'd said, This is your house, I can't keep you from this room.

Les was going to tell his father that he didn't want to disturb him but he couldn't. He went in and stood in the middle of the throw rug, waiting.

"Sit down," his father said and Les sat down on the upright chair that Tom hung his clothes on at night. His father waited until Les was seated and then sank down on the bed with a grunt.

For a long time they looked at each other without speaking, like total strangers, each waiting for the other one to speak. How did the test go? Les heard the words repeated in his mind. How did the test go, how did the test go? He couldn't speak the words. How did the—

"I suppose you want to know what . . . happened," his father said then, controlling himself visibly.

"Yes," Les said. "I . . ." He caught himself. "Yes," he repeated and waited.

Old Tom looked down at the floor for a moment. Then, suddenly, he raised his head and looked defiantly at his son.

"I didn't go," he said.

Les felt as if all his strength had suddenly been sucked into the floor. He sat there, motionless, staring at his father.

"Had no intention of going," his father hurried on. "No intention of going through all that foolishness. Physical tests, m-mental tests, putting b-b-*blocks* in a board and . . . Lord knows what all! Had no intention of going."

He stopped and stared at his son with angry eyes as if he were daring Les to say he had done wrong.

But Les couldn't say anything.

A long time passed. Les swallowed and managed to summon the words. "What are you . . . going to do?"

"Never mind that, never mind," his father said, almost as if he were grateful for the question. "Don't you worry about your Dad. Your Dad knows how to take care of himself."

And suddenly Les heard the bureau drawer shutting again, the rustling of a paper bag. He almost looked around at the bureau to see if the bag were still there. His head twitched as he fought down the impulse.

"W-ell," he faltered, not realizing how stricken and lost his expression was.

"Just never mind now," his father said again, quietly, almost gently. "It's not your problem to worry about. Not your problem at all."

But it is! Les heard the words cried out in his mind. But he didn't speak them. Something in the old man stopped him; a sort of fierce strength, a taut dignity he knew he mustn't touch.

"I'd like to rest now," he heard Tom say then and he felt as if he'd been struck violently in the stomach. I'd like to rest now, to rest now—the words echoed down long tunnels of the mind as he stood. Rest now, rest now . . .

He found himself being ushered to the door where he turned and looked at his father. *Goodbye.* The word stuck in him.

Then his father smiled and said, "Good night, Leslie."

"Dad."

He felt the old man's hand in his own, stronger than his, more steady; calming him, reassuring him. He felt his father's left hand grip his shoulder.

"Good night, son," his father said and, in the moment they stood close together Les saw, over the old man's shoulder, the crumpled drugstore bag lying in the corner of the room as though it had been thrown there so as not to be seen.

Then he was standing in wordless terror in the hall, listening to the latch clicking shut and knowing that, although his father wasn't locking the door, he couldn't go into his father's room.

For a long time he stood staring at the closed door, shivering without control. Then he turned away.

Terry was waiting for him at the foot of the stairs, her face drained of color. She asked the question with her eyes as he came down to her.

"He . . . didn't go," was all he said.

She made a tiny, startled sound in her throat. "But—"

"He's been to the drugstore," Les said. "I . . . saw the bag in the corner of the room. He threw it away so I wouldn't see it but I . . . saw it."

For a moment, it seemed as if she were starting for the stairs but it was only a momentary straining of her body.

"He must have shown the druggist the letter about the test," Les said. "The . . . druggist must have given him . . . pills. Like they all do."

They stood silently in the dining room while rain drummed against the windows.

"What shall we do?" she asked, almost inaudibly.

"Nothing," he murmured. His throat moved convulsively and breath shuddered through him. *"Nothing."*

Then he was walking numbly back to the kitchen and he could feel her arm tight around him as if she were trying to press her love to him because she could not speak of love.

All evening, they sat there in the kitchen. After she put the boys to bed, she came back and they sat in the kitchen drinking coffee and talking in quiet, lonely voices.

Near midnight, they left the kitchen and just before they went upstairs, Les stopped by the dining room table and found the watch with a shiny new crystal on it. He couldn't even touch it.

They went upstairs and walked past the door of Tom's bedroom. There was no sound inside. They got undressed and got in bed together and Terry set the clock the way she set it every night. In a few hours they both managed to fall asleep.

And all night there was silence in the old man's room. And the next day, silence.

The
Holiday
Man

● ● ● ● ● ● ● ● ● ● ● ● ● ●

"You'll be late," she said.

He leaned back tiredly in his chair.

"I know," he answered.

They were in the kitchen having breakfast. David hadn't eaten much. Mostly, he'd drunk black coffee and stared at the tablecloth. There were thin lines running through it that looked like intersecting highways.

"Well?" she said.

He shivered and took his eyes from the tablecloth.

"Yes," he said. "All right."

He kept sitting there.

"David," she said.

"I know, I know," he said, "I'll be late." He wasn't angry. There was no anger left in him.

"You certainly will," she said, buttering her toast. She spread on thick raspberry jam, then bit off a piece and chewed it cracklingly.

David got up and walked across the kitchen. At the door he stopped and turned. He stared at the back of her head.

"Why couldn't I?" he asked again.

"Because you can't," she said. "That's all."

"But *why*?"

"Because they need you," she said. "Because they pay you well and you couldn't do anything else. Isn't it obvious?"

"They could find someone else."

"Oh, stop it," she said. "You know they couldn't."

He closed his hands into fists. "Why should I be the one?" he asked.

She didn't answer. She sat eating her toast.

"Jean?"

"There's nothing more to say," she said, chewing. She turned around. "Now, will you go?" she said. "You shouldn't be late today."

David felt a chill in his flesh.

"No," he said, "not today."

He walked out of the kitchen and went upstairs. There, he brushed his teeth, polished his shoes and put on a tie. Before eight he was down again. He went into the kitchen.

"Goodbye," he said.

She tilted up her cheek for him and he kissed it. "Bye, dear," she said. "Have a—" She stopped abruptly.

"—nice day?" he finished for her. "Thank you." He turned away. "I'll have a lovely day."

Long ago he had stopped driving a car. Mornings he walked to the railroad station. He didn't even like to ride with someone else or take a bus.

At the station he stood outside on the platform waiting for the train. He had no newspaper. He never bought them any more. He didn't like to read the papers.

"Mornin', Garret."

He turned and saw Henry Coulter who also worked in the city. Coulter patted him on the back.

"Good morning," David said.

"How's it goin'?" Coulter asked.

"Fine. Thank you."

"Good. Lookin' forward to the Fourth?"

David swallowed. "Well . . ." he began.

"Myself, I'm takin' the family to the woods," said Coulter. "No lousy fireworks for us. Pilin' into the old bus and headin' out till the fireworks are over."

"Driving," said David.

"*Yes, sir,*" said Coulter. "Far as we can."

It began by itself. No, he thought; *not now.* He forced it back into its darkness.

"—tising business," Coulter finished.

"What?" he asked.

"Said I trust things are goin' well in the advertising business."

David cleared his throat.

"Oh, yes," he said. "Fine." He always forgot about the lie he'd told Coulter.

When the train arrived he sat in the No Smoking car, knowing that Coulter always smoked a cigar en route. He didn't want to sit with Coulter. Not now.

All the way to the city he sat looking out the window. Mostly he watched road and highway traffic; but, once, while the train rattled over a bridge, he stared down at the mirror-like surface of a lake. Once he put his head back and looked up at the sun.

He was actually to the elevator when he stopped.

"Up?" said the man in the maroon uniform. He looked at David steadily. "Up?" he said. Then he closed the rolling doors.

David stood motionless. People began to cluster around him. In a moment, he turned and shouldered by them, pushing through the revolving door. As he came out, the oven heat of July surrounded him. He moved along the sidewalk like a man asleep. On the next block he entered a bar.

Inside, it was cold and dim. There were no customers. Not even the bartender was visible. David sank down in the shadow of a booth and took his hat off. He leaned his head back and closed his eyes.

He couldn't do it. He simply could not go up to his office. No matter what Jean said, no matter what anyone said. He clasped his hands on the table edge and squeezed them until the fingers were pressed dry of blood. He just *wouldn't*.

"Help you?" asked a voice.

David opened his eyes. The bartender was standing by the booth, looking down at him.

"Yes, uh . . . beer," he said. He hated beer but he knew he had to buy something for the privilege of sitting in the chilly silence undisturbed. He wouldn't drink it.

The bartender brought the beer and David paid for it. Then, when the bartender had gone, he began to turn the glass slowly on the table top. While he was doing this it began again. With a gasp, he pushed it away. No!—he told it, savagely.

In a while he got up and left the bar. It was past ten. That didn't matter of course. They knew he was always late. They knew he always tried to break away from it and never could.

His office was at the back of the suite, a small cubicle furnished only with a rug, sofa, and a small desk on which lay pencils and white paper. It was all he needed. Once, he'd had a secretary but he hadn't liked the idea of her sitting outside the door and listening to him scream.

No one saw him enter. He let himself in from the hall through a private door. Inside, he relocked the door, then took off his suitcoat and laid it across the desk. It was stuffy in the office so he walked across the floor and pulled up the window.

Far below, the city moved. He stood watching it. How many of them? he thought.

Sighing heavily, he turned. Well, he was here. There was no point in hesitating any longer. He was committed now. The best thing was to get it over and clear out.

He drew the blinds, walked over to the couch and lay down. He fussed a little with the pillow, then stretched once and was still. Almost immediately, he felt his limbs going numb.

It began.

He did not stop it now. It trickled on his brain like melted ice. It rushed like winter wind. It spun like blizzard vapor. It leaped and ran and billowed and exploded and his mind was filled with it. He grew rigid and began to gasp, his chest twitching with breath, the beating of his heart a violent stagger. His hands drew in like white talons, clutching and scratching at the couch. He shivered and groaned and writhed. Finally he screamed. He screamed for a very long while.

When it was done, he lay limp and motionless on the couch, his eyes like balls of frozen glass. When he could, he raised his arm and looked at his wristwatch. It was almost two.

He struggled to his feet. His bones felt sheathed with lead but he managed to stumble to his desk and sit before it.

There he wrote on a sheet of paper and, when he was finished, slumped across the desk and fell into exhausted sleep.

Later, he woke up and took the sheet of paper to his superior, who, looking it over, nodded.

"Four hundred eighty-six, huh?" the superior said. "You're sure of that?"

"I'm sure," said David, quietly. "I watched every one." He didn't mention that Coulter and his family were among them.

"All right," said his superior. "Let's see now. Four hundred fifty-two from traffic accidents, eighteen from drowning, seven from sun-stroke, three from fireworks, six from miscellaneous causes."

Such as a little girl being burned to death, David thought. Such as a baby boy eating ant poison. Such as a woman being electrocuted; a man dying of snake bite.

"Well," his superior said, "let's make it—oh, four hundred and fifty. It's always impressive when more people die than we predict."

"Of course," David said.

The item was on the front page of all the newspapers that afternoon. While David was riding home the man in front of him turned to his neighbor and said, "What I'd like to know is—*how can they tell?*"

David got up and went back on the platform on the end of the car. Until he got off, he stood there listening to the train wheels and thinking about Labor Day.

Mantage

● ● ● ● ● ● ● ● ● ● ● ● ● ● ● ●

FADEOUT.

The old man had succumbed. From its movie heaven, an ethereal choir paeaned. Amid roiling pink clouds they sang: *A Moment or Forever.* It was the title of the picture. Lights blinked on. The voices stopped abruptly, the curtain was lowered, the theater boomed with p.a. resonance; a quartet singing *A Moment or Forever* on the Decca label. Eight hundred thousand copies a month.

Owen Crowley sat slumped in his seat, legs crossed, arms slackly folded. He stared at the curtain. Around him, people stood and stretched, yawned, chatted, laughed. Owen sat there, staring. Next to him, Carole rose and drew on her suede jacket. Softly, she was singing with the record, *"Your mind is the clock that ticks away a moment or forever."*

She stopped. "Honey?"

Owen grunted. "Are you coming?" she asked.

He sighed. "I suppose." He dragged up his jacket and followed her as she edged toward the aisle, shoes crunching over pale popcorn buds and candy wrappers. They reached the aisle and Carole took his arm.

"Well?" she asked. "What did you think?"

Owen had the burdening impression that she had asked him that question a million times; that their relationship consisted of an infinitude of movie-going and scant more. Was it only two years since they'd met; five months since their engagement? It seemed, momentarily, like the dreariest of eons.

"What's there to think?" he said. "It's just another movie."

"I thought you'd like it," Carole said, "being a writer yourself."

He trudged across the lobby with her. They were the last ones out. The snack counter was darkened, the soda machine stilled of technicolored bubblings. The only sound was the whisper of their shoes across the carpeting, then the click of them as they hit the outer lobby.

"What is it, Owen?" Carole asked when he'd gone a block without saying a word.

"They make me mad," he said.

"Who does?" Carole asked.

"The damn stupid people who make those damn stupid movies," he said.

"Why?" she asked.

"Because of the way they gloss over everything."

"What do you mean?"

"This writer the picture was about," said Owen. "He was a lot like I am; talented and with plenty of drive. But it took him almost ten years to get things going. *Ten years.* So what does the stupid picture do? Glosses over them in a few minutes. A couple of scenes of him sitting at his desk, looking broody, a couple of clock shots, a few trays of mashed-out butts, some empty coffee cups, a pile of manuscripts. Some bald-headed publishers with cigars shaking their heads no at him, some feet walking on the sidewalk; and that's it. Ten years of hard labor. It makes me mad."

"But they have to do that, Owen," Carole said. "That's the only way they have of showing it."

"Then life should be like that too," he said.

"Oh, you wouldn't like that," she said.

"You're wrong. I would," he said. "Why should I struggle ten years—or more—on my writing? Why not get it over with in a couple of minutes?"

"It wouldn't be the same," she said.

"That's for sure," he said.

An hour and forty minutes later, Owen sat on the cot in his furnished room staring at the table on which sat his typewriter and the half-completed manuscript of his third novel *And Now Gomorrah.*

Why not indeed? The idea had definite appeal. He knew

that, someday, he'd succeed. It had to be that way. Otherwise, what was he working so hard for? But that transition—that was the thing. That indefinite transition between struggle and success. How wonderful if that part could be condensed, abbreviated.

Glossed over.

"You know what I wish?" he asked the intent young man in the mirror.

"No, what?" asked the man.

"I wish," said Owen Crowley, "that life could be as simple as a movie. All the drudgery set aside in a few flashes of weary looks, disappointments, coffee cups and midnight oil, trays of butts, no's and walking feet. Why not?"

On the bureau, something clicked. Owen looked down at his clock. It was 2:43 a.m.

Oh, well. He shrugged and went to bed. Tomorrow, another five pages, another night's work at the toy factory.

A year and seven months went by and nothing happened. Then, one morning, Owen woke up, went down to the mail box and there it was.

We are happy to inform you that we want to publish your novel Dream Within a Dream.

"Carole! Carole!" He pounded on her apartment door, heart drumming from the half-mile sprint from the subway, the leaping ascent of the stairs. *"Carole!"*

She jerked open the door, face stricken. "Owen, what—?" she began, then cried out, startled, as he swept her from the floor and whirled her around, the hem of her nightgown whipping silkenly. "Owen, what is it?" she gasped.

"Look! Look!" He put her down on the couch and, kneeling, held out the crumpled letter to her.

"Oh, Owen!"

They clung to each other and she laughed, she cried. He felt the unbound softness of her pressing at him through the filmy silk, the moist cushioning of her lips against his cheek, her warm tears trickling down his face. "Oh, Owen. *Darling.*"

She cupped his face with trembling hands and kissed him; then whispered, "And you were worried."

"No more," he said. "No more!"

The publisher's office stood aloofly regal above the city; draped, paneled, still. "If you'll sign here, Mr. Crowley," said the editor. Owen took the pen.

"Hurray! Hurroo!" He polkaed amid a debris of cocktail glasses, red-eyed olives, squashed hors d'oeuvres and guests. Who clapped and stamped and shouted and erected monumental furies in the neighbors' hearts. Who flowed and broke apart like noisy quicksilver through the rooms and halls of Carole's apartment. Who devoured regimental rations. Who flushed away Niagaras of converted alcohol. Who nuzzled in a fog of nicotine. Who gambled on the future census in the dark and fur-coat-smelling bedroom.

Owen sprang. He howled. "An Indian I am!" He grabbed the laughing Carole by her spilling hair. "An Indian I am, I'll scalp you! No, I won't, I'll kiss you!" He did to wild applause and whistles. She clung to him, their bodies molding. The clapping was like rapid fire. "And for an encore!" he announced.

Laughter. Cheers. Music pounding. A graveyard of bottles on the sink. Sound and movement. Community singing. Bedlam. A policeman at the door. *"Come in, come in, defender of the weal!"* "Now, let's be having a little order here, there's people want to sleep."

Silence in the shambles. They sat together on the couch, watching dawn creep in across the sills, a nightgowned Carole clinging to him, half asleep; Owen pressing his lips to her warm throat and feeling, beneath the satin skin, the pulsing of her blood.

"I love you," whispered Carole. Her lips, on his, wanted, took. The electric rustle of her gown made him shudder. He brushed the straps and watched them slither from the pale curving of her shoulders. "Carole, Carole." Her hands were cat claws on his back.

The telephone rang, rang. He opened an eye. There was a heated pitchfork fastened to the lid. As the lid moved up it plunged the pitchfork into his brain. *"Ooh!"* He winced his eyes shut and the room was gone. "Go away," he muttered to the ringing, ringing; to the cleat-shoed, square-dancing goblins in his head.

Across the void, a door opened and the ringing stopped. Owen sighed.

"Hello?" said Carole. "Oh. Yes, he's here."

He heard the crackle of her gown, the nudging of her fingers on his shoulder. "Owen," she said. "Wake up, darling."

The deep fall of pink-tipped flesh against transparent silk was what he saw. He reached but she was gone. Her hand closed over his and drew him up. "The phone," she said.

"More," he said, pulling her against himself.

"The phone."

"Can wait," he said. His voice came muffled from her nape. "I'm breakfasting."

"Darling, the phone."

"Hello?" he said into the black receiver.

"This is Arthur Means, Mr. Crowley," said the voice.

"Yes!" There was an explosion in his brain but he kept on smiling anyway because it was the agent he'd called the day before.

"Can you make it for lunch?" asked Arthur Means.

Owen came back into the living room from showering. From the kitchen came the sound of Carole's slippers on linoleum, the sizzle of bacon, the dark odor of percolating coffee.

Owen stopped. He frowned at the couch where he'd been sleeping. How had he ended there? He'd been in bed with Carole.

The streets, by early morning, were a mystic lot. Manhattan after midnight was an island of intriguing silences, a vast acropolis of crouching steel and stone. He walked between the silent citadels, his footsteps like the ticking of a bomb.

"Which will explode!" he cried. *"Explode!"* cried back the streets of shadowed walls. "Which will explode and throw my shrapnel words through all the world!"

Owen Crowley stopped. He flung out his arms and held the universe. "You're mine!" he yelled.

"Mine," the echo came.

The room was silent as he shed his clothes. He settled on the cot with a happy sigh, crossed his legs and undid lace knots. What time was it? He looked over at the clock. 2:58 a.m.

Fifteen minutes since he'd made his wish.

He grunted in amusement as he dropped his shoe. Weird fancy, that. Yes, it was exactly fifteen minutes if you chose to ignore the one year, seven months and two days since he'd stood over there in his pajamas, fooling with a wish. Granted that, in thinking back, those nineteen months seemed quickly past; but not that quickly. If he wished to, he could tally up a reasonable itemization of every miserable day of them.

Owen Crowley chuckled. Weird fancy indeed. Well, it was the mind. The mind was a droll mechanism.

"Carole, let's get married!"

He might have struck her. She stood there, looking dazed. "What?" she asked.

"Married!"

She stared at him. "You mean it?"

He slid his arms around her tightly. "Try me," he said.

"Oh, Owen." She clung to him a moment, then, abruptly, drew back her head and grinned.

"This," she said, "is not so sudden."

It was a white house, lost in summer foliage. The living room was large and cool and they stood together on the walnut floor, holding hands. Outside, leaves were rustling.

"Then by the authority vested in me," said Justice of the Peace Weaver, "by the sovereign state of Connecticut, I now pronounce you man and wife." He smiled. "You may kiss the bride," he said.

Their lips parted and he saw the tears glistening in her eyes.

"How do, Miz Crowley," he whispered.

The Buick hummed along the quiet country road. Inside, Carole leaned against her husband while the radio played, *A*

Moment or Forever, arranged for strings. "Remember that?" he asked.

"Mmmm-hmmm." She kissed his cheek.

"Now where," he wondered, "is that motel the old man recommended?"

"Isn't that it up ahead?" she asked.

The tires crackled on the gravel path, then stopped. "Owen, look," she said. He laughed. *Aldo Weaver, Manager*, read the bottom line of the rust-streaked wooden sign.

"Yes, brother George, he marries all the young folks round about," said Aldo Weaver as he led them to their cabin and unlocked the door. Then Aldo crunched away and Carole leaned her back against the door until the lock clicked. In the quiet room, dim from tree shade, Carole whispered, "Now you're mine."

They were walking through the empty, echoing rooms of a little house in Northport. "Oh, *yes*," said Carole happily. They stood before the living room windows, looking out into the shadow-dark woods beyond. Her hand slipped into his. "Home," she said, "*sweet* home."

They were moving in and it was furnished. A second novel sold, a third. John was born when winds whipped powdery snow across the sloping lawn; Linda on a sultry, cricket-rasping summer night. Years cranked by, a moving backdrop on which events were painted.

He sat there in the stillness of his tiny den. He'd stayed up late correcting the galleys on his forthcoming novel *One Foot in Sea*. Now, almost nodding, he twisted together his fountain pen and set it down. "My God, my God," he murmured, stretching. He was tired.

Across the room, standing on the mantel of the tiny fireplace, the clock buzzed once. Owen looked at it. 3:15 A.M. It was well past his—

He found himself staring at the clock and, like a slow-tapped tympani, his heart was felt. Seventeen minutes later than the last time, thought persisted; thirty-two minutes in all.

Owen Crowley shivered and rubbed his hands as if at some

imaginary flame. Well, this is idiotic, he thought; idiotic to dredge up this fantasy every year or so. It was the sort of nonsense that could well become obsession.

He lowered his gaze and looked around the room. The sight of time-worn comforts and arrangements made him smile. This house, its disposition, that shelf of manuscripts at his left. These were measurable. The children alone were eighteen months of slow transition just in the making.

He clucked disgustedly at himself. This was absurd; rationalizing to himself as if the fancy merited rebuttal. Clearing his throat, he tidied up the surface of his desk with energetic movements. There. And there.

He leaned back heavily in his chair. Well, maybe it was a mistake to repress it. That the concept kept returning was proof enough it had a definite meaning. Certainly, the flimsiest of delusions fought against could disorient the reason. All men knew that.

Well, then, face it, he decided. Time was constant; that was the core. What varied was a person's outlook on it. To some it dragged by on tar-held feet, to others fled on blurring wings. It just happened he was one of those to whom time seemed overly transient. So transient that it fostered rather than dispelled the memory of that childish wish he'd made that night more than five years before.

That was it, of course. Months seemed a wink and years a breath because he viewed them so. And—

The door swung open and Carole came across the rug, holding a glass of warmed milk.

"You should be in bed," he scolded.

"So should you," she answered, "yet I see you sitting here. Do you know what time it is?"

"I know," he said.

She settled on his lap as he sipped the milk. "Galleys done?" she asked. He nodded and slid an arm around her waist. She kissed his temple. Out in the winter night, a dog barked once.

She sighed. "It seems like only yesterday, doesn't it?" she said.

He drew in faint breath. "I don't think so," he said.
"Oh, *you*." She punched him gently on the arm.

"This is Artie," said his agent. "Guess what?"
Owen gasped. *"No!"*
He found her in the laundry room, stuffing bedclothes into
the washer. "Honey!" he yelled. Sheets went flying.
"It's happened!" he cried.
"What?"
"The movies, the movies! They're buying *Nobles and Her-
alds*!"
"No!"
"Yes! And—get this now—sit down and get it—go ahead
and sit or else you'll fall!—they're paying *twelve thousand,
five hundred dollars* for it!"
"Oh!"
"And that's not all! They're giving me a ten-week guaran-
tee to do the screenplay at—*get* this—*seven hundred and fifty
dollars* a week!"
She squeaked. "We're rich."
"Not quite," he said, floor-pacing, "but it's only the begin-
ning, folks, *on*-ly the beginning!"
October winds swept in like tides over the dark field. Spot-
light ribbons wiped across the sky.
"I wish the kids were here," he said, his arm around her.
"They'd just be cold and cranky, darling," Carole said.
"Carole, don't you think—"
"Owen, you know I'd come with you if I could; but we'd
have to take Johnny out of school and, besides, it would cost
so much. It's only ten weeks, darling. Before you know it—"
"Flight twenty-seven for Chicago and Los Angeles," in-
toned the speaker, "now boarding at Gate Three."
"So soon." Suddenly, her eyes were lost, she pressed her
wind-chilled cheek to his. "Oh, darling, I'll miss you so."
The thick wheels squeaked below, the cabin walls shook.
Outside, the engines roared faster and faster. The field rushed
by. Owen looked back. Colored lights were distant now.
Somewhere among them, Carole stood, watching his plane

nose up into the blackness. He settled back and closed his eyes a moment. A dream, he thought. Flying west to write a movie from his own novel. Good God, a veritable dream.

He sat there on a corner of the leather couch. His office was capacious. A peninsula of polished desk extended from the wall, an upholstered chair parked neatly against it. Tweed drapes concealed the humming air conditioner, tasteful reproductions graced the walls and, beneath his shoes, the carpet gave like sponge. Owen sighed.

A knocking broke his reverie. "Yes?" he asked. The snugly-sweatered blonde stepped in. "I'm Cora. I'm your secretary," she said. It was Monday morning.

"Eighty-five minutes, give or take," said Morton Zuckersmith, Producer. He signed another notification. "That's a good length." He signed another letter. "You'll pick these things up as you go along." He signed another contract. "It's a world of its own." He stabbed the pen into its onyx sheath and his secretary exited, bearing off the sheaf of papers. Zuckersmith leaned back in his leather chair, hands behind his head, his polo-shirted chest broadening with air. "A world of its own, kiddy," he said. "Ah. Here's our girl."

Owen stood, his stomach muscles twitching as Linda Carson slipped across the room, one ivory hand extended. "Morton, dear," she said.

"Morning, darling." Zuckersmith engulfed her hand in his, then looked toward Owen. "Dear, I'd like you to meet your writer for *The Lady and the Herald*."

"I've been so anxious to meet you," said Linda Carson, neé Virginia Ostermeyer. "I loved your book. How can I tell you?"

He started up as Cora entered. "Don't get up," she said. "I'm just bringing you your pages. We're up to forty-five."

Owen watched her as she stretched across the desk. Her sweaters grew more skinlike every day. The tense expansion of her breathing posed threats to every fiber.

"How does it read?" he asked.

She took it for an invitation to perch across the couch arm

at his feet. "I think you're doing *wonderfully*," she said. She crossed her legs and frothy slip lace sighed across her knees. "You're very talented." She drew in chest-enhancing air. "There's just a few things here and there," she said. "I'd tell you what they were right now but—well, it's lunchtime and—"

They went to lunch; that day and others after. Cora donned a mantle of stewardship, guiding him as though he were resourceless. Bustling in with smiles and coffee every morning, telling him what foods were best prepared at dinner and, fingering his arm, leading him to the commissary every afternoon for orange juice; hinting at a p.m. continuance of their relationship; assuming a position in his life he had no desire for. Actually sniffling one afternoon after he'd gone to lunch without her; and, as he patted her shoulder in rough commiseration, pressing against him suddenly, her firm lips taking their efficient due, the taut convexities of her indenting him. He drew back, startled. *"Cora."*

She patted his cheek: "Don't think about it, darling. You have important work to do." Then she was gone and Owen was sitting at his desk, alarm diffusing to his fingertips. A week, another week.

"Hi," said Linda. "How are you?"

"Fine," he answered as Cora entered, clad in hugging gabardine, in clinging silk. "Lunch? I'd love to. Shall I meet you at the—? Oh. All right!" He hung up. Cora stared at him.

As he slipped onto the red leather seat he saw, across the street, Cora at the gate, watching him grimly.

"Hello, Owen," Linda said. The Lincoln purred into the line of traffic. This is nonsense, Owen thought. He'd have to try a second time with Cora. The first discouragement she'd taken for nobility; the gesture of a gallant husband toward his wife and children. At least she seemed to take it so. Good God, what complication.

It was lunch together on the Strip; then, later, dinner, Owen trusting that enough hours devoted to Linda would convince Cora of his lack of interest. The next night it was dinner and the Philharmonic; two nights later, dancing and a drive along the shore; the next, a preview in Encino.

At what specific juncture the plan went wrong Owen never knew. It gained irrevocable form the night when, parked beside the ocean, radio music playing softly, Linda slipped against him naturally, her world-known body pressing close, her lips a succulence at his. *"Darling."*

He lay starkly awake, thinking of the past weeks; of Cora and Linda; of Carole whose reality had faded to the tenuous form of daily letters and a weekly voice emitting from the telephone, a smiling picture on his desk.

He'd almost finished with the screenplay. Soon he'd fly back home. So much time had passed. Where were the joints, the sealing place? Where was the evidence except in circumstantial shards of memory? It was like one of those effects they'd taught him at the studio; a *montage*—a series of quickly paced scenes. That's what life seemed like; a series of quickly paced scenes that flitted across the screen of one's attention, then were gone.

Across the hotel room, his traveling clock buzzed once. He would not look at it.

He ran against the wind, the snow, but Carole wasn't there. He stood, eyes searching, in the waiting room, an island of man and luggage. Was she ill? There'd been no acknowledgment of his telegram but—

"Carole?" The booth was hot and stale.

"Yes," she said.

"My God, darling, did you *forget*?"

"No," she said.

The taxi ride to Northport was a jading travelogue of snow-cottoned trees and lawns, impeding traffic lights and tire chains rattling over slush-graveled streets. She'd been so deadly calm on the phone. No, I'm not sick. Linda has a little cold. John is fine. I couldn't get a sitter. A chill of premonitions troubled at him.

Home at last. He'd dreamed of it like this, standing silently among the skeletal trees, a mantle of snow across its roof, a rope of wood smoke spiraling from its chimney. He paid the driver with a shaking hand and turned expectantly. The door stayed shut. He waited but the door stayed shut.

He read the letter that she'd finally given him. *Dear Mrs. Crowley,* it began, *I thought you ought to know.* . . . His eyes sought out the childish signature below. *Cora Bailey.*

"Why that dirty, little—" He couldn't say it; something held him back.

"Dear God." She stood before the window, trembling. "To this very moment I've been praying it was a lie. But now . . ."

She shriveled at his touch. *"Don't."*

"You wouldn't go with me," he charged. "You *wouldn't* go."

"Is that your excuse?" she asked.

"Wha'm I gonna do?" he asked, fumbling at his fourteenth Scotch and water. *"Wha'?* I don' wanna lose 'er, Artie. I don' wanna lose 'er an' the children. Wha'm I gonna do?"

"I don't know," said Artie.

"That dirty li'l—" Owen muttered. "Hadn't been for her . . ."

"Don't blame the silly little slut for this," said Artie. "She's just the icing. You're the one who baked the cake."

"Wha'm I gonna do?"

"Well, for one thing, start working at life a little more. It isn't just a play that's taking place in front of you. You're on the stage, you have a part. Either you play it or you're a pawn. No one's going to feed you dialogue or action, Owen. You're on your own. Remember that."

"I wonder," Owen said. Then and later in the silence of his hotel room.

A week, two weeks. Listless walks through a Manhattan that was only noise and loneliness. Movies stared at, dinners at the Automat, sleepless nights, the alcoholed search for peace. Finally, the desperate phone call. "Carole, take me back, *please* take me back."

"Oh, darling. *Come home to me.*"

Another cab ride, this time joyous. The porch light burning, the door flung open, Carole running to him. Arms around each other, walking back into their home together.

The Grand Tour! A dizzying whirl of places and events. Misted England in the spring; the broad, the narrow streets of Paris; Spree-bisected Berlin and Rhone-bisected Geneva. Milan of Lombardy, the hundred crumbling-castled islands of Venice, the culture trove of Florence, Marseilles braced against the sea, the Alps-protected Riviera, Dijon the ancient. A second honeymoon; a rush of desperate renewal, half seen, half felt like flashes of uncertain heat in a great, surrounding darkness.

They lay together on the river bank. Sunlight scattered glittering coins across the water, fish stirred idly in the thermal drift. The contents of their picnic basket lay in happy decimation. Carole rested on his shoulder, her breath a warming tickle on his chest.

"Where has the time all gone to?" Owen asked; not of her or anyone but to the sky.

"Darling, you sound upset," she said, raising on an elbow to look at him.

"I am," he answered. "Don't you remember the night we saw that picture *A Moment or Forever*? Don't you remember what I said?"

"No."

He told her; of that and of his wish and of the formless dread that sometimes came upon him. "It was just the first part I wanted fast, though," he said, *"not the whole thing."*

"Darling, darling," Carole said, trying not to smile, "I guess this must be the curse of having an imagination. Owen, it's been over seven years. *Seven years.*"

He held his watch up. "Or fifty-seven minutes," he said.

Home again. Summer, fall, and winter. *Wind from the South* selling to the movies for $100,000; Owen turning down the screenplay offer. The aging mansion overlooking the Sound, the hiring of Mrs. Halsey as their housekeeper. John packed off to military academy, Linda to private school. As a result of the European trip, one blustery afternoon in March, the birth of George.

Another year. Another. Five years, ten. Books assured and flowing from his pen. *Lap of Legends Old, Crumbling Satires, Jiggery Pokery,* and *The Dragon Fly*. A decade gone, then more. The National Book Award for *No Dying and No Tomb*. The Pulitzer Prize for *Bacchus Night*.

He stood before the window of his paneled office, trying to forget at least a single item of another paneled office he'd been in—that of his publisher the day he'd signed his first contract there. But he could forget nothing; not a single detail would elude him. As if, instead of twenty-three years before, it had been yesterday. How could he recall it all so vividly unless, actually—

"Dad?" He turned and felt a frozen trap jaw clamp across his heart. John strode across the room. "I'm going now," he said.

"What? *Going?*" Owen stared at him; at this tall stranger, at this young man in military uniform who called him Dad.

"Old Dad," laughed John. He clapped his father's arm. "Are you dreaming up another book?"

Only then, as if cause followed effect, Owen knew. Europe raged with war again and John was in the army, ordered overseas. He stood there, staring at his son, speaking with a voice not his; watching the seconds rush away. Where had *this* war come from? What vast and awful machinations had brought it into being? *And where was his little boy?* Surely he was not this stranger shaking hands with him and saying his goodbyes. The trap jaw tightened. Owen whimpered.

But the room was empty. He blinked. Was it all a dream, all flashes in an ailing mind? On leaden feet, he stumbled to the window and watched the taxi swallow up his son and drive away with him. "Goodbye," he whispered. "God protect you."

No one feeds you dialogue, he thought; but was that *he* who spoke?

* * *

The bell had rung and Carole answered it. Now, the handle of his office door clicked once and she was standing there, face bloodless, staring at him, in her hand the telegram. Owen felt his breath stop.

"No," he murmured; then, gasping, started up as, soundlessly, Carole swayed and crumpled to the floor.

"At least a week in bed," the doctor told him. "Quiet; lots of rest. The shock is most severe."

He shambled on the dunes; numbed, expressionless. Razored winds cut through him, whipped his clothes and lashed his gray-streaked hair to threads. With lightless eyes, he marked the course of foam-flecked waves across the Sound. Only yesterday that John went off to war, he thought; only yesterday he came home proudly rigid in his academy uniform; only yesterday he was in shorts and grammar school; only yesterday he thundered through the house leaving his wake of breathless laughter; only yesterday that he was born when winds whipped powdery snow across—

"Dear God!" Dead. *Dead!* Not twenty-one and *dead*; all his life a moment passed, a memory already slipping from the mind.

"I take it back!" Terrified, he screamed it to the rushing sky. "I take it back, I never meant it!" He lay there, scraping at the sand, weeping for his boy yet wondering if he ever had a boy at all.

"Attendez, M'sieus, M'dames! Nice!"

"Oh my; already?" Carole said. "That was quick now, children, wasn't it?"

Owen blinked. He looked at her; at this portly, gray-haired woman across the aisle from him. She smiled. She *knew* him?

"What?" he asked.

"Oh, why do I talk to you?" she grumbled. "You're always in your thoughts, your thoughts." Hissing, she stood and drew a wicker basket from the rack. *Was this some game?*

"Gee, Dad, look at *that*!"

He gaped at the teenaged boy beside him. And who was

he? Owen Crowley shook his head a little. He looked around him. *Nice?* In France again? What about the war?

The train plunged into blackness. "Oh, *damn*!" snapped Linda. On Owen's other side she struck her match again and, in the flare, he saw, reflected in the window, the features of another middle-aged stranger and it was himself. The present flooded over him. The war over and he and his family abroad: Linda, twenty-one, divorced, bitter, slightly alcoholic; George, fifteen, chubby, flailing in the glandular limbo between women and erector sets; Carole, forty-six, newly risen from the sepulcher of menopause, pettish, somewhat bored; and he himself, forty-nine, successful, coldly handsome, still wondering if life were made of years or seconds. All this passing through his mind before Riviera sunlight flooded into their compartment again.

Out on the terrace it was darker, cooler. Owen stood there, smoking, looking at the spray of diamond pinpoints in the sky. Inside, the murmuring of gamblers was like a distant, insect hum.

"Hello, Mr. Crowley."

She was in the shadows, palely gowned; a voice, a movement.

"You know my name?" he asked.

"But you're famous," was her answer.

Awareness fluttered in him. The straining flattery of club women had turned his stomach more than once. But then she'd glided from the darkness and he saw her face and all awareness died. Moonlight creamed her arms and shoulders; it was incandescent in her eyes.

"My name is Alison," she said. "Are you glad to meet me?"

The polished cruiser swept a banking curve into the wind, its bow slashing at the waves, flinging up a rainbowed mist across them. "You little idiot!" he laughed. "You'll drown us yet!"

"You and I!" she shouted back. "Entwining under fathoms! I'd *love* that, wouldn't you?"

He smiled at her and touched her thrill-flushed cheek. She

kissed his palm and held him with her eyes. *I love you.*
Soundless; a movement of her lips. He turned his head and
looked across the sun-jeweled Mediterranean. Just keep going
on, he thought. Never turn. Keep going till the ocean swal-
lows us. *I won't go back.*

Alison put the boat on automatic drive, then came up behind him, sliding warm arms around his waist, pressing her
body to his. "You're off again," she murmured. "Where are
you, darling?"

He looked at her. "How long have we known each other?"
he asked.

"A moment, forever, it's all the same," she answered, teas-
ing at his ear lobe with her lips.

"A moment or forever," he murmured. "Yes."

"What?" she asked.

"Nothing," he said. "Just brooding on the tyranny of
clocks."

"Since time is so distressing to you, love," she said, pushing open the cabin door, "let's not waste another second of
it."

The cruiser hummed across the silent sea.

"What, *hiking*?" Carole said. "At *your* age?"

"Though it may disturb you," Owen answered, tautly, "I, at
least, am not yet prepared to surrender to the stodgy blandish-
ments of old age."

"So I'm senile now!" she cried.

"Please," he said.

"She thinks you're *old*?" said Alison. "Good God, how little that woman knows you!"

Hikes, skiing, boat rides, swimming, horseback riding,
dancing till sun dispersed the night. Him telling Carole he
was doing research for a novel; not knowing if she believed
him; not, either, caring much. Weeks and weeks of stalking
the elusive dead.

He stood on the sun-drenched balcony outside Alison's
room. Inside, ivory-limbed, she slept like some game-worn
child. Owen's body was exhausted, each inadequate muscle
pleading for surcease; but, for the moment, he was not think-

ing about that. He was wondering about something else; a clue that had occurred to him when he was lying with her.

In all his life, it seemed as if there never was a clear remembrance of physical love. Every detail of the moments leading to the act were vivid but the act itself was not. Equally so, all memory of his ever having cursed aloud was dimmed, uncertain.

And these were the very things that movies censored.

"Owen?" Inside, he heard the rustle of her body on the sheets. There was demand in her voice again; honeyed but authoritative. He turned. Then let me *remember* this, he thought. Let every second of it be with me; every detail of its fiery exaction, its flesh-born declarations, its drunken, sweet derangement. Anxiously, he stepped through the doorway.

Afternoon. He walked along the shore, staring at the mirror-flat blueness of the sea. It was true then. There was no distinct remembrance of it. From the second he'd gone through the doorway until now, all was a virtual blank. Yes, *true*! He knew it now. Interims were void; time was rushing him to his script-appointed end. He was a player, yes, as Artie said, but the play had already been written.

He sat in the dark train compartment, staring out the window. Far below slept moon-washed Nice and Alison; across the aisle slept George and Linda, grumbled Carole in a restless sleep. How angry they had been at his announcement of their immediate departure for home.

And now, he thought, and *now*. He held his watch up and marked the posture of its luminous hands. *Seventy-four minutes.*

How much left?

"You know, George," he said, "when I was young—and not so young—I nursed a fine delusion. I thought my life was being run out like a motion picture. It was never certain, mind you, only nagging doubt but it dismayed me; oh, indeed it did. Until, one day—a little while ago—it came to me that everyone has an uncontrollable aversion to the inroads of mortality. Especially old ones like myself, George. How we are inclined to think that time has, somehow, tricked us, mak-

ing us look the other way a moment while, now unguarded,
it rushes by us, bearing on its awful, tracking shoulders, our
lives."

"I can see that," said George and lit his pipe again.

Owen Crowley chuckled: "George, George," he said.
"Give full humor to your nutty sire. He'll not be with you too
much longer."

"Now stop that talk," said Carole, knitting by the fire.
"Stop that silly talk."

"Carole?" he called. "My dear?" Wind from the Sound obscured his trembling voice. He looked around. "Here, *you!
Here!*"

The nurse primped mechanically at his pillow. She chided,
"Now, now, Mr. Crowley. You musn't tire yourself."

"Where's my wife? For pity's sake go fetch her. I can't—"

"Hush now, Mr. Crowley, don't start in again."

He stared at her, at this semi-mustached gaucherie in white
who fussed and wheedled. "What?" he murmured. *"What?"*
Then something drew away the veil and he knew. Linda was
getting her fourth divorce, shuttling between her lawyer's office and the cocktail lounges; George was a correspondent in
Japan, a brace of critic-feted books to his name. And Carole,
Carole?

Dead.

"No," he said, quite calmly. "No, no, that's not true. I tell
you, fetch her. Oh, there's a pretty thing." He reached out for
the falling leaf.

The blackness parted; it filtered into unmarked grayness.
Then his room appeared, a tiny fire in the grate, his doctor
by the bed consulting with the nurse; at the foot of it, Linda
standing like a sour wraith.

Now, thought Owen. Now was just about the time. His life,
he thought, had been a brief engagement; a flow of scenes
across what cosmic retina? He thought of John, of Linda Carson, of Artie, of Morton Zuckersmith and Cora; of George
and Linda and Alison; of Carole; of the legioned people who
had passed him during his performance. They were all gone,
almost faceless now.

"What . . . time?" he asked.

The doctor drew his watch. "Four-oh-eight," he said, "a.m."

Of course. Owen smiled. He should have known it all along. A dryness in his throat thinned the laugh to a rasping whisper. They stood there, staring at him.

"Eighty-five minutes," he said. "A good length. Yes; *a good length.*"

Then, just before he closed his eyes, he saw them—letters floating in the air, imposed across their faces and the room. And they were words but words seen in a mirror, white and still.

THE END

Or was it just imagination?
Fadeout.

The
Distributor
• • • • • • • • • • • • • • • •

Time to move.

He'd found a small, furnished house on Sylmar Street. The Saturday morning he moved in, he went around the neighborhood introducing himself.

"Good morning," he said to the old man pruning ivy next door. "My name is Theodore Gordon. I just moved in."

The old man straightened up and shook Theodore's hand. "How do," he said. His name was Joseph Alston.

A dog came shuffling from the porch to sniff Theodore's cuffs. "He's making up his mind about you," said the old man.

"Isn't that cute?" said Theodore.

Across the street lived Inez Ferrel. She answered the door in a housecoat, a thin woman in her late thirties. Theodore apologized for disturbing her.

"Oh, that's all right," she said. She had lots of time to herself when her husband was selling on the road.

"I hope we'll be good neighbors," said Theodore.

"I'm sure we will," said Inez Ferrel. She watched him through the window as he left.

Next door, directly across from his own house, he knocked quietly because there was a *Nightworker Sleeping* sign. Dorothy Backus opened the door—a tiny, withdrawn woman in her middle thirties.

"I'm so glad to meet you," said Theodore.

Next door lived the Walter Mortons. As Theodore came up the walk, he heard Bianca Morton talking loudly to her son, Walter, Jr.

"You are not old enough to stay out till three o'clock in the morning!" she was saying. "Especially with a girl as young as Katherine McCann!"

Theodore knocked and Mr. Morton, fifty-two and bald, opened the door.

"I just moved in across the street," said Theodore, smiling at them.

Patty Jefferson let him in next door. As he talked to her Theodore could see, through the back window, her husband Arthur filling a rubber pool for their son and daughter.

"They just love that pool," said Patty, smiling.

"I bet they do," said Theodore. As he left, he noticed the vacant house next door.

Across the street from the Jeffersons lived the McCanns and their fourteen-year-old daughter Katherine. As Theodore approached the door he heard the voice of James McCann saying, "Aah, he's nuts. Why should I take his lawn edger? Just because I borrowed his lousy mower a couple of times."

"Darling, *please*," said Faye McCann. "I've got to finish these notes in time for the Council's next meeting."

"Just because Kathy goes out with his lousy son . . ." grumbled her husband.

Theodore knocked on the door and introduced himself. He chatted briefly with them, informing Mrs. McCann that he certainly would like to join the National Council for Christians and Jews. It was a worthy organization.

"What's your business, Gordon?" asked McCann.

"I'm in distribution," said Theodore.

Next door, two boys mowed and raked while their dog gamboled around them.

"Hello there," said Theodore. They grunted and watched him as he headed for the porch. The dog ignored him.

"I just *told* him." Henry Putnam's voice came through the living room window: "Put a coon in my department and I'm through. That's all."

"Yes, dear," said Mrs. Irma Putnam.

Theodore's knock was answered by the undershirted Mr.

Putnam. His wife was lying on the sofa. Her heart, explained Mr. Putnam. "Oh, I'm sorry," Theodore said.

In the last house lived the Gorses.

"I just moved in next door," said Theodore. He shook Eleanor Gorse's lean hand and she told him that her father was at work.

"Is that him?" asked Theodore, pointing at the portrait of a stony-faced old man that hung above a mantel crowded with religious objects.

"Yes," said Eleanor, thirty-four and ugly.

"Well, I hope we'll be good neighbors," Theodore said.

That afternoon, he went to his new office and set up the darkroom.

July 23

That morning, before he left for the office, he checked the telephone directory and jotted down four numbers. He dialed the first.

"Would you please send a cab to 12057 Sylmar Street?" he said. "Thank you."

He dialed the second number. "Would you please send a repairman to my house," he said. "I don't get any picture. I live at 12070 Sylmar Street."

He dialed the third number: "I'd like to run this ad in Sunday's edition," he said. "1957 Ford. Perfect Condition. Seven-hundred eighty-nine dollars. That's right, seven-hundred eighty-nine. The number is DA-4-7408."

He made the fourth call and set up an afternoon appointment with Mr. Jeremiah Osborne. Then he stood by the living room window until the taxicab stopped in front of the Backus house.

As he was driving off, a television repair truck passed him. He looked back and saw it stop in front of Henry Putnam's house.

Dear sirs, he typed in the office later, *Please send me ten booklets for which I enclose one hundred dollars in payment.* He put down the name and address.

The envelope dropped into the OUT box.

July 27

When Inez Ferrel left her house that evening, Theodore followed in his car. Downtown, Mrs. Ferrel got off the bus and went into a bar called the Irish Lantern. Parking, Theodore entered the bar cautiously and slipped into a shadowy booth.

Inez Ferrel was at the back of the room perched on a bar stool. She'd taken off her jacket to reveal a clinging yellow sweater. Theodore ran his gaze across the studied exposition of her bust.

At length, a man accosted her and spoke and laughed and spent a modicum of time with her. Theodore watched them exit, arm in arm. Paying for his coffee, he followed. It was a short walk; Mrs. Ferrel and the man entered a hotel on the next block.

Theodore drove home, whistling.

The next morning, when Eleanor Gorse and her father had left with Mrs. Backus, Theodore followed.

He met them in the church lobby when the service was over. Wasn't it a wonderful coincidence, he said, that he, too, was a Baptist? And he shook the indurate hand of Donald Gorse.

As they walked into the sunshine, Theodore asked them if they wouldn't share his Sunday dinner with him. Mrs. Backus smiled faintly and murmured something about her husband. Donald Gorse looked doubtful.

"Oh, please," begged Theodore. "Make a lonely widower happy."

"Widower," tasted Mr. Gorse.

Theodore hung his head. "These many years," he said. "Pneumonia."

"Been a Baptist long?" asked Mr. Gorse.

"Since birth," said Theodore with fervor. "It's been my only solace."

For dinner he served lamb chops, peas, and baked potatoes. For dessert, apple cobbler and coffee.

"I'm so pleased you'd share my humble food," he said.

"This is, truly, loving thy neighbor as thyself." He smiled at Eleanor who returned it stiffly.

That evening, as darkness fell, Theodore took a stroll. As he passed the McCann house, he heard the telephone ringing, then James McCann shouting, "It's a *mistake*, damn it! Why in the lousy hell should I sell a '57 Ford for seven-hundred eighty-nine bucks!"

The phone slammed down. "God *damn*!" howled James McCann.

"Darling, please be *tolerant*!" begged his wife.

The telephone rang again.

Theodore moved on.

August 1

At exactly two-fifteen A.M. Theodore slipped outside, pulled up one of Joseph Alston's longest ivy plants and left it on the sidewalk.

In the morning, as he left the house, he saw Walter Morton, Jr., heading for the McCann house with a blanket, a towel and a portable radio. The old man was picking up his ivy.

"Was it pulled up?" asked Theodore.

Joseph Alston grunted.

"So *that* was it," said Theodore.

"What?" the old man looked up.

"Last night," said Theodore, "I heard some noise out here. I looked out and saw a couple of boys."

"You seen their faces?" asked Alston, his face hardening.

"No, it was too dark," said Theodore. "But I'd say they were—oh, about the age of the Putnam boys. Not that it was them, of course."

Joe Alston nodded slowly, looking up the street.

Theodore drove up to the boulevard and parked. Twenty minutes later, Walter Morton, Jr., and Katherine McCann boarded a bus.

At the beach, Theodore sat a few yards behind them.

"That Mack is a character," he heard Walter Morton say. "He gets the urge, he drives to Tijuana; just for kicks."

In a while Morton and the girl ran into the ocean, laughing. Theodore stood and walked to a telephone booth.

"I'd like to have a swimming pool installed in my backyard next week," he said. He gave the details.

Back on the beach he sat patiently until Walter Morton and the girl were lying in each other's arms. Then, at specific moments, he pressed a shutter hidden in his palm. This done, he returned to his car, buttoning his shirt front over the tiny lens. On his way to the office, he stopped at a hardware store to buy a brush and a can of black paint.

He spent the afternoon printing the pictures. He made them appear as if they had been taken at night and as if the young couple had been engaged in something else.

The envelope dropped softly into the OUT box.

August 5

The street was silent and deserted. Tennis shoes soundless on the paving, Theodore moved across the street.

He found the Morton's lawn mower in the backyard. Lifting it quietly, he carried it back across the street to the McCann garage. After carefully raising the door, he slid the mower behind the work bench. The envelope of photographs he put in a drawer behind a box of nails.

Returning to his house then, he phoned James McCann and, muffledly, asked if the Ford was still for sale.

In the morning, the mailman placed a bulky envelope on the Gorses' porch. Eleanor Gorse emerged and opened it, sliding out one of the booklets. Theodore watched the furtive look she cast about, the rising of dark color in her cheeks.

As he was mowing the lawn that evening he saw Walter Morton, Sr., march across the street to where James McCann was trimming bushes. He heard them talking loudly. Finally, they went into McCann's garage from which Morton emerged pushing his lawn mower and making no reply to McCann's angry protests.

Across the street from McCann, Arthur Jefferson was just

getting home from work. The two Putnam boys were riding their bicycles, their dog racing around them.

Now, across from where Theodore stood, a door slammed. He turned his head and watched Mr. Backus, in work clothes, storming to his car, muttering disgustedly, *"A swimming pool!"* Theodore looked to the next house and saw Inez Ferrel moving in her living room.

He smiled and mowed along the side of his house, glancing into Eleanor Gorse's bedroom. She was sitting with her back to him, reading something. When she heard the clatter of his mower she stood and left the bedroom, pushing the bulky envelope into a bureau drawer.

August 15

Henry Putnam answered the door.

"Good evening," said Theodore. "I hope I'm not intruding."

"Just chatting in the den with Irma's folks," said Putnam. "They're drivin' to New York in the mornin'."

"Oh? Well, I'll only be a moment." Theodore held out a pair of BB guns. "A plant I distribute for was getting rid of these," he said. "I thought your boys might like them."

"Well, *sure*," said Putnam. He started for the den to get his sons.

While the older man was gone, Theodore picked up a couple of matchbooks whose covers read *Putnam's Wines and Liquors*. He'd slipped them into his pocket before the boys were led in to thank him.

"Mighty nice of you, Gordon," said Putnam at the door. "Sure appreciate it."

"My pleasure," said Theodore.

Walking home, he set the clock-radio for three-fifteen and lay down. When the music began, he moved outside on silent feet and tore up forty-seven ivy plants, strewing them over Alston's sidewalk.

"Oh, *no*," he said to Alston in the morning. He shook his head, appalled.

Joseph Alston didn't speak. He glanced down the block with hating eyes.

"Here, let me help you," Theodore said. The old man shook his head but Theodore insisted. Driving to the nearest nursery he brought back two sacks of peat moss; then squatted by Alston's side to help him replant.

"You hear anything last night?" the old man asked.

"You think it was those boys again?" asked Theodore, open-mouthed.

"Ain't sayin'," Alston said.

Later, Theodore drove downtown and bought a dozen postcard photographs. He took them to the office.

Dear Walt, he printed crudely on the back of one, *Got these here in Tijuana. Hot enough for you?* In addressing the envelope, he failed to add *Jr.* to *Mr. Walter Morton.*

Into the OUT box.

August 23

"Mrs. Ferrel!"

She shuddered on the bar stool. "Why, Mister—"

"Gordon," he provided, smiling. "How nice to see you again."

"Yes." She pressed together lips that trembled.

"You come here often?" Theodore asked.

"Oh, no, *never,*" Inez Ferrel blurted. "I'm—just supposed to meet a friend here tonight. A *girl* friend."

"Oh, I see," said Theodore. "Well, may a lonely widower keep you company until she comes?"

"Why . . ." Mrs. Ferrel shrugged. "I guess." Her lips were painted brightly red against the alabaster of her skin. The sweater clung adhesively to the hoisted jut of her breasts.

After a while, when Mrs. Ferrel's friend didn't show up, they slid into a darkened booth. There, Theodore used Mrs. Ferrel's powder room retreat to slip a pale and tasteless powder in her drink. On her return she swallowed this and, in minutes, grew stupefied. She smiled at Theodore.

"I like you Misser Gor'n," she confessed. The words crawled viscidly across her lolling tongue.

Shortly thereafter, he led her, stumbling and giggling, to his car and drove her to a motel. Inside the room, he helped her strip to stockings, garter belt and shoes and, while she posed with drugged complacency, Theodore took flashbulb pictures.

After she'd collapsed at two A.M. Theodore dressed her and drove her home. He stretched her fully dressed across her bed. After that he went outside and poured concentrated weed killer on Alston's replanted ivy.

Back in the house he dialed the Jefferson's number.

"Yes," said Arthur Jefferson irritably.

"Get out of this neighborhood or you'll be sorry," whispered Theodore, then hung up.

In the morning he walked to Mrs. Ferrel's house and rang the bell.

"Hello," he said politely. "Are you feeling better?"

She stared at him blankly while he explained how she'd gotten violently ill the night before and he'd taken her home from the bar. "I do hope you're feeling better," he concluded.

"Yes," she said, confusedly, "I'm—all right."

As he left her house he saw a red-faced James McCann approaching the Morton house, an envelope in his hand. Beside him walked a distraught Mrs. McCann.

"We must be *tolerant*, Jim," Theodore heard her say.

August 31

At two-fifteen a.m. Theodore took the brush and the can of paint and went outside.

Walking to the Jefferson house he set the can down and painted, jaggedly, across the door—NIGGER!

Then he moved across the street allowing an occasional drip of paint. He left the can under Henry Putnam's back porch, accidentally upsetting the dog's plate. Fortunately, the Putnams' dog slept indoors.

Later, he put more weed killer on Joseph Alston's ivy.

In the morning, when Donald Gorse had gone to work, he took a heavy envelope and went to see Eleanor Gorse. "Look at this," he said, sliding a pornographic booklet from the envelope. "I received this in the mail today. *Look* at it." He thrust it into her hands.

She held the booklet as if it were a spider.

"Isn't it hideous?" he said.

She made a face. *"Revolting,"* she said.

"I thought I'd check with you and several others before I phoned the police," said Theodore. "Have you received any of this filth?"

Eleanor Gorse bristled. "Why should I receive them?" she demanded.

Outside, Theodore found the old man squatting by his ivy. "How are they coming?" he asked.

"They're dyin'."

Theodore looked stricken. "How can this be?" he asked.

Alston shook his head.

"Oh, this is *horrible*." Theodore turned away, clucking. As he walked to his house he saw, up the street, Arthur Jefferson cleaning off his door and, across the way, Henry Putnam watching carefully.

She was waiting on his porch.

"Mrs. McCann," said Theodore, surprised, "I'm so glad to see you."

"What I came to say may not make you so glad," she said unhappily.

"Oh?" said Theodore. They went into his house.

"There have been a lot of ... *things* happening in this neighborhood since you moved in," said Mrs. McCann after they were seated in the living room.

"Things?" asked Theodore.

"I think you know what I mean," said Mrs. McCann. "However, this—this *bigotry* on Mr. Jefferson's door is too much, Mr. Gordon, too much."

Theodore gestured helplessly. "I don't understand."

"Please don't make it difficult," she said. "I may have to

call the authorities if these things don't stop, Mr. Gordon. I hate to think of doing such a thing but—"

"*Authorities?*" Theodore looked terrified.

"None of these things happened until you moved in, Mr. Gordon," she said. "Believe me, I hate what I'm saying but I simply have no choice. The fact that none of these things has happened to you—"

She broke off startledly as a sob wracked Theodore's chest. She stared at him. "Mr. Gordon—" she began uncertainly.

"I don't know what these things are you speak of," said Theodore in a shaking voice, "but I'd *kill* myself before I harmed another, Mrs. McCann."

He looked around as if to make sure they were alone.

"I'm going to tell you something I've never told a single soul," he said. He wiped away a tear. "My name isn't Gordon," he said. "It's Gottlieb. I'm a Jew. I spent a year at Dachau."

Mrs. McCann's lips moved but she said nothing. Her face was getting red.

"I came from there a broken man," said Theodore. "I haven't long to live, Mrs. McCann. My wife is dead, my three children are dead. I'm all alone. I only want to live in peace—in a little place like this—among people like you.

"To be a neighbor, a friend . . ."

"Mr.—*Gottlieb*," she said brokenly.

After she was gone, Theodore stood silent in the living room, hands clenched whitely at his sides. Then he went into the kitchen to discipline himself.

"Good morning, Mrs. Backus," he said an hour later when the little woman answered the door, "I wonder if I might ask you some questions about our church?"

"Oh. Oh, yes." She stepped back feebly. "Won't you—come in?"

"I'll be very still so as not to wake your husband," Theodore whispered. He saw her looking at his bandaged hand. "I burned myself," he said. "Now, about the church. Oh, there's someone knocking at your back door."

"There is?"

When she'd gone into the kitchen, Theodore pulled open the hall closet door and dropped some photographs behind a pile of overshoes and garden tools. The door was shut when she returned.

"There wasn't anyone," she said.

"I could have sworn ..." He smiled deprecatingly. He looked down at a circular bag on the floor. "Oh, does Mr. Backus bowl?"

"Wednesdays and Fridays when his shift is over," she said. "There's an all-night alley over on Western Avenue."

"I love to bowl," said Theodore.

He asked his questions about the church, then left. As he started down the path he heard loud voices from the Morton house.

"It wasn't bad enough about Katherine McCann and *those* awful pictures," shrieked Mrs. Morton. "Now this ... *filth!*"

"But, Mom!" cried Walter, Jr.

September 14

Theodore awoke and turned the radio off. Standing, he put a small bottle of grayish powder in his pocket and slipped from the house. Reaching his destination, he sprinkled powder into the water bowl and stirred it with a finger until it dissolved.

Back in the house he scrawled four letters reading: *Arthur Jefferson is trying to pass the color line. He is my cousin and should admit he is black like the rest of us. I am doing this for his own good.*

He signed the letter *John Thomas Jefferson* and addressed three of the envelopes to Donald Gorse, the Mortons, and Mr. Henry Putnam.

This completed, he saw Mrs. Backus walking toward the boulevard and followed. "May I walk you?" he asked.

"Oh," she said. "All right."

"I missed your husband last night," he told her.

She glanced at him.

"I thought I'd join him bowling," Theodore said, "but I guess he was sick again."

"Sick?"

"I asked the man behind the counter at the alley and he said that Mr. Backus hadn't been coming in because he was sick."

"Oh," Mrs. Backus's voice was thinly stricken.

"Well, maybe next Friday," said Theodore.

Later, when he came back, he saw a panel truck in front of Henry Putnam's house. A man came out of the alley carrying a blanket-wrapped body which he laid in the truck. The Putnam boys were crying as they watched.

Arthur Jefferson answered the door. Theodore showed the letter to Jefferson and his wife. "It came this morning," he said.

"This is *monstrous*!" said Jefferson, reading it.

"Of *course* it is," said Theodore.

While they were talking, Jefferson looked through the window at the Putnam house across the street.

September 15

Pale morning mist engulfed Sylmar Street. Theodore moved through it silently. Under the back porch of the Jeffersons' house he set fire to a box of damp papers. As it began to smolder he walked across the yard and, with a single knife stroke, slashed apart the rubber pool. He heard it pulsing water on the grass as he left. In the alley he dropped a book of matches that read *Putnam's Wines and Liquors*.

A little after six that morning he woke to the howl of sirens and felt the small house tremble at the heavy trucks passing by. Turning on his side, he yawned, and mumbled, "Goody."

September 17

It was a paste-complexioned Dorothy Backus who answered Theodore's knock.

"May I drive you to church?" asked Theodore.

"I—I don't believe I—I'm not . . . feeling too well," stumbled Mrs. Backus.

"Oh, I'm sorry," Theodore said. He saw the edges of some photographs protruding from her apron pocket.

As he left he saw the Mortons getting in their car, Bianca wordless, both Walters ill at ease. Up the street, a police car was parked in front of Arthur Jefferson's house.

Theodore went to church with Donald Gorse who said that Eleanor was feeling ill.

"I'm so sorry," Theodore said.

That afternoon, he spent a while at the Jefferson house helping clear away the charred debris of their back porch. When he saw the slashed rubber pool he drove immediately to a drug store and bought another one.

"But they love that pool," said Theodore, when Patty Jefferson protested. "You told me so yourself."

He winked at Arthur Jefferson but Jefferson was not communicative that afternoon.

September 23

Early in the evening Theodore saw Alston's dog walking in the street. He got his BB gun and, from the bedroom window, soundlessly, fired. The dog nipped fiercely at its side and spun around. Then, whimpering, it started home.

Several minutes later, Theodore went outside and started pulling up the door to the garage. He saw the old man hurrying down his alley, the dog in his arms.

"What's wrong?" asked Theodore.

"Don't know," said Alston in a breathless, frightened voice. "He's hurt."

"Quickly!" said Theodore. "Into my car!"

He rushed Alston and the dog to the nearest veterinary, passing three stop signs and groaning when the old man held his hand up, palsiedly, and whimpered, *"Blood!"*

For three hours Theodore sat in the veterinary's waiting room until the old man staggered forth, his face a grayish white.

"No," said Theodore, jumping to his feet.

He led the old man, weeping, to the car and drove him home. There, Alston said he'd rather be alone so Theodore left. Shortly afterward, the black and white police car rolled to a stop in front of Alston's house and the old man led the two officers past Theodore's house.

In a while, Theodore heard angry shouting up the street. It lasted quite a long time.

September 27

"Good evening," said Theodore. He bowed.

Eleanor Gorse nodded stiffly.

"I've brought you and your father a casserole," said Theodore, smiling, holding up a towel-wrapped dish. When she told him that her father was gone for the night, Theodore clucked and sighed as if he hadn't seen the old man drive away that afternoon.

"Well then," he said, proffering the dish, "for *you*. With my sincerest compliments."

Stepping off the porch he saw Arthur Jefferson and Henry Putnam standing under a street lamp down the block. While he watched, Arthur Jefferson struck the other man and, suddenly, they were brawling in the gutter. Theodore broke into a hurried run.

"But this is *terrible!*" he gasped, pulling the men apart.

"Stay out of this!" warned Jefferson, then, to Putnam, challenged, "You better tell me how that paint can got under your porch! The police may believe it was an accident I found that matchbook in my alley but I don't!"

"I'll tell you nothing," Putnam said, contemptuously. *"Coon."*

"Coon! Oh, of course! You'd be the first to believe that, you stupid—!"

Five times Theodore stood between them. It wasn't until Jefferson had, accidentally, struck him on the nose that tension faded. Curtly, Jefferson apologized; then, with a murderous look at Putnam, left.

"Sorry he hit you," Putnam sympathized. "Damned nigger."

"Oh, surely you're mistaken," Theodore said, daubing at his nostrils. "Mr. Jefferson told me how afraid he was of people believing this talk. Because of the value of his two houses, you know."

"Two?" asked Putnam.

"Yes, he owns the vacant house next door to his," said Theodore. "I assumed you knew."

"*No,*" said Putnam warily.

"Well, you see," said Theodore, "if people think Mr. Jefferson is a Negro, the value of his houses will go down."

"So will the values of all of them," said Putnam, glaring across the street. "That dirty, son-of-a—"

Theodore patted his shoulder. "How are your wife's parents enjoying their stay in New York?" he asked as if changing the subject.

"They're on their way back," said Putnam.

"Good," said Theodore.

He went home and read the funny papers for an hour. Then he went out.

It was a florid-faced Eleanor Gorse who opened to his knock. Her bathrobe was disarrayed, her dark eyes feverish.

"May I get my dish?" asked Theodore politely.

She grunted, stepping back jerkily. His hand, in passing, brushed on hers. She twitched away as if he'd stabbed her.

"Ah, you've eaten it all," said Theodore, noticing the tiny residue of powder on the bottom of the dish. He turned. "When will your father return?" he asked.

Her body seemed to tense. "After midnight," she muttered.

Theodore stepped to the wall switch and cut off the light. He heard her gasp in the darkness. "No," she muttered.

"Is this what you want, Eleanor?" he asked, grabbing harshly.

Her embrace was a mindless, fiery swallow. There was nothing but ovening flesh beneath her robe.

Later, when she lay snoring satedly on the kitchen floor, Theodore retrieved the camera he'd left outside the door.

Drawing down the shades, he arranged Eleanor's limbs and took twelve exposures. Then he went home and washed the dish.

Before retiring, he dialed the phone.

"Western Union," he said. "I have a message for Mrs. Irma Putnam of 12070 Sylmar Street."

"That's me," she said.

"Both parents killed in auto collision this afternoon," said Theodore. "Await word regarding disposition of bodies. Chief of Police, Tulsa, Okla—"

At the other end of the line there was a strangled gasp, a thud; then Henry Putnam's cry of "Irma!" Theodore hung up.

After the ambulance had come and gone, he went outside and tore up thirty-five of Joseph Alston's ivy plants. He left, in the debris, another matchbook reading *Putnam's Wines and Liquors*.

September 28

In the morning, when Donald Gorse had gone to work, Theodore went over. Eleanor tried to shut the door on him but he pushed in.

"I want money," he said. "These are my collateral." He threw down copies of the photographs and Eleanor recoiled, gagging. "Your father will receive a set of these tonight," he said, "unless I get two hundred dollars."

"But I—!"

"Tonight."

He left and drove downtown to the Jeremiah Osborne Realty office where he signed over, to Mr. George Jackson, the vacant house at 12069 Sylmar Street. He shook Mr. Jackson's hand.

"Don't you worry now," he comforted. "The people next door are black too."

When he returned home, there was a police car in front of the Backus house.

"What happened?" he asked Joseph Alston who was sitting quietly on his porch.

"Mrs. Backus," said the old man lifelessly. "She tried to kill Mrs. Ferrel."

"Is that right?" said Theodore.

That night, in his office, he made his entries on page 700 of the book.

Mrs. Ferrel dying of knife wounds in local hospital. Mrs. Backus in jail; suspects husband of adultery. J. Alston accused of dog poisoning, probably more. Putnam boys accused of shooting Alston's dog, ruining his lawn. Mrs. Putnam dead of heart attack. Mr. Putnam being sued for property destruction. Jeffersons thought to be black. McCanns and Mortons deadly enemies. Katherine McCann believed to have had relations with Walter Morton, Jr. Morton, Jr. being sent to school in Washington. Eleanor Gorse has hanged herself. Job completed.

Time to move.

By
Appointment
Only

• • • • • • • • • • • • • • • • •

At 11:14 that morning, Mr. Pangborn came into the barber-shop. Wiley looked up from his *Racing Form.* "Morning," he said. He glanced at his wrist watch and smiled. "You're right on time."

Mr. Pangborn did not return the smile. He removed his suitcoat wearily and hung it on the rack. He trudged across the clean-swept floor and sank down in the middle chair. Wiley put down his *Racing Form* and stood. He stretched and yawned. "You don't look so hot, Mr. Pangborn," he said.

"I don't feel so hot," Mr. Pangborn replied.

"Sorry to hear that," Wiley said. He cranked up the chair and locked it. "Usual?" he asked.

Mr. Pangborn nodded. "Okeydoke," said Wiley. He pulled a clean cloth from its shelf and shook it out. "Whatcha been doin' with yourself?" he asked.

Mr. Pangborn signed. "Not much."

"Kind o' run down, are you?" Wiley asked, wrapping tissue around his customer's neck.

"That's the word," said Mr. Pangborn. "What've *you* been doing?"

"Not a hell of a lot," Wiley answered. He pinned the cloth in place. "Drove up to Vegas last week." He made a rueful sound. "Lost a pile."

"Too bad," said Mr. Pangborn.

"Oh, well," Wiley grinned. "Easy come, easy go." He picked up the electric clipper and switched it on. "Maria!" he called.

She made an inquiring noise in the back room.

"Mr. Pangborn's here."

"Be right out," she said.

Wiley started working on the back of Mr. Pangborn's neck. Mr. Pangborn closed his eyes. "That's it," Wiley told him. "Take it easy."

Mr. Pangborn shifted on the chair uncomfortably.

"You sure don't look so hot," said Wiley.

Mr. Pangborn sighed again. "I don't know," he said. "I just don't know."

"What's the problem?" Wiley asked.

"The leg," said Mr. Pangborn. "The back. My right arm, off and on. My stomach."

"*Jesus,*" Wiley said, concerned. "You seen your doctor?"

"He doesn't know what it is," Mr. Pangborn answered scornfully. "I don't bother going to him anymore. All he ever does is send me to specialists."

Wiley clucked. "That's lousy, Mr. Pangborn."

Mr. Pangborn exhaled. "Dr. Rand's the only one who ever helps," he said.

"He *does*?" Wiley looked delighted. "Hey, I'm glad to hear that," he said. "I wasn't sure whether I should even mention him or not, him not being an MD and all. My brother swore up and down that he was something else, though."

"He is," said Mr. Pangborn. "If it weren't for him—"

"Hello, Mr. Pangborn," said Maria.

Mr. Pangborn glanced aside and managed a smile. "Maria," he said.

"How are you today?" she asked.

"Getting by," he said.

Maria set her manicuring table and chair beside the barber chair. As she sat down, her bust swelled out against the tightness of her sweater. "You look tired," she said.

Mr. Pangborn nodded. "I am," he said. "I don't sleep too well."

"That's a shame," she sympathized. She began to work on his nails.

"Well, I'm glad this Rand is working out," Wiley said. "I'll have to try him myself sometime."

"He's good," said Mr. Pangborn. "The only one who's given me relief."

"Good deal," said Wiley.

It was quiet for awhile, as Wiley cut Mr. Pangborn's hair and Maria did his nails. Then Mr. Pangborn asked, "Business slow today?"

"No," said Wiley. "I do it all by appointment now." He smiled. "It's the only way."

When Mr. Pangborn had gone, Maria carried his hair and nail clippings into the back room. Unlocking the cupboard, she took out the doll labeled PANGBORN. Wiley finished dialing the telephone and watched her as she replaced the doll's hair and nails with the fresh clippings.

"Rand?" he said when the receiver was lifted at the other end of the line. "Wiley. Pangborn was just in. When's he seeing you again?" He listened. "Okay," he said, "give him something for his back and we'll take that pin out for a couple o' weeks. All right?" He listened. "And, Rand," he said, "your check was late again this month. *Watch that.*"

He hung up and walked over to Maria. As she worked, he slid his hands up inside her sweater and cupped them over her breasts. Maria pressed back against him with a sigh, her face tightening. "When's the next appointment?" she asked.

Wiley grinned. "Not till one-thirty," he answered.

By the time he'd locked the door, hung up the OUT TO LUNCH sign and returned to the back room, Maria was waiting for him on the bed. Wiley took his clothes off, running his gaze over her brown body as it writhed on the mattress. "You little Haitian bitch," he muttered, grinning.

At twenty minutes after one, Mr. Walters came into the shop. Removing his coat, he hung it on the rack and sat down in the middle chair. Wiley put down his *Racing Form* and stood. He made a clucking sound. "Hey, you don't look so hot, Mr. Walters," he said.

"I don't feel so hot," Mr. Walters replied.

Button,
Button
• • • • • • • • • • • • • •

The package was lying by the front door—a cube-shaped carton sealed with tape, the name and address printed by hand: MR. AND MRS. ARTHUR LEWIS, 217 E. 37TH STREET, NEW YORK, NEW YORK 10016. Norma picked it up, unlocked the door, and went into the apartment. It was just getting dark.

After she put the lamb chops in the broiler, she made herself a drink and sat down to open the package.

Inside the carton was a push-button unit fastened to a small wooden box. A glass dome covered the button. Norma tried to lift it off, but it was locked in place. She turned the unit over and saw a folded piece of paper Scotch-taped to the bottom of the box. She pulled it off: "Mr. Steward will call on you at eight p.m."

Norma put the button unit beside her on the couch. She sipped the drink and reread the typed note, smiling.

A few moments later, she went back into the kitchen to make the salad.

The doorbell rang at eight o'clock. "I'll get it," Norma called from the kitchen. Arthur was in the living room, reading.

There was a small man in the hallway. He removed his hat as Norma opened the door. "Mrs. Lewis?" he inquired politely.

"Yes?"

"I'm Mr. Steward."

"Oh, yes." Norma repressed a smile. She was sure now it was a sales pitch.

"May I come in?" asked Mr. Steward.

"I'm rather busy," Norma said. "I'll get you your watchamacallit, though." She started to turn.

"Don't you want to know what it is?"

Norma turned back. Mr. Steward's tone had been offensive. "No, I don't think so," she said.

"It could prove very valuable," he told her.

"Monetarily?" she challenged.

Mr. Steward nodded. "Monetarily," he said.

Norma frowned. She didn't like his attitude. "What are you trying to sell?" she asked.

"I'm not selling anything," he answered.

Arthur came out of the living room. "Something wrong?"

Mr. Steward introduced himself.

"Oh, the . . ." Arthur pointed toward the living room and smiled. "What is that gadget, anyway?"

"It won't take long to explain," replied Mr. Steward. "May I come in?"

"If you're selling something . . ." Arthur said.

Mr. Steward shook his head. "I'm not."

Arthur looked at Norma. "Up to you," he said.

He hesitated. "Well, why not?" he said.

They went into the living room and Mr. Steward sat in Norma's chair. He reached into an inside coat pocket and withdrew a small sealed envelope. "Inside here is a key to the bell-unit dome," he said. He set the envelope on the chairside table. "The bell is connected to our office."

"What's it for?" asked Arthur.

"If you push the button," Mr. Steward told him, "somewhere in the world, someone you don't know will die. In return for which you will receive a payment of fifty thousand dollars."

Norma stared at the small man. He was smiling.

"What are you talking about?" Arthur asked him.

Mr. Steward looked surprised. "But I've just explained," he said.

"Is this a practical joke?" asked Arthur.

"Not at all. The offer is completely genuine."

"You aren't making sense," Arthur said. "You expect us to believe . . ."

"Whom do you represent?" demanded Norma.

Mr. Steward looked embarrassed. "I'm afraid I'm not at liberty to tell you that," he said. "However, I assure you the organization is of international scope."

"I think you'd better leave," Arthur said, standing.

Mr. Steward rose. "Of course."

"And take your button unit with you."

"Are you sure you wouldn't care to think about it for a day or so?"

Arthur picked up the button unit and the envelope and thrust them into Mr. Steward's hands. He walked into the hall and pulled open the door.

"I'll leave my card," said Mr. Steward. He placed it on the table by the door.

When he was gone, Arthur tore it in half and tossed the pieces onto the table. "God!" he said.

Norma was still sitting on the sofa. "What do you think it was?" she asked.

"I don't care to know," he answered.

She tried to smile but couldn't. "Aren't you curious at all?"

"No," he shook his head.

After Arthur returned to his book, Norma went back to the kitchen and finished washing the dishes.

"Why won't you talk about it?" Norma asked later.

Arthur's eyes shifted as he brushed his teeth. He looked at her reflection in the bathroom mirror.

"Doesn't it intrigue you?"

"It offends me," Arthur said.

"I know, but—" Norma rolled another curler in her hair "—doesn't it intrigue you, too?"

"You think it's a practical joke?" she asked as they went into the bedroom.

"If it is, it's a sick one."

Norma sat on the bed and took off her slippers.

"Maybe it's some kind of psychological research."

Arthur shrugged. "Could be."

"Maybe some eccentric millionaire is doing it."

"Maybe."

"Wouldn't you like to know?"

Arthur shook his head.

"Why?"

"Because it's immoral," he told her.

Norma slid beneath the covers. "Well, I think it's intriguing," she said.

Arthur turned off the lamp and leaned over to kiss her. "Good night," he said.

"Good night." She patted his back.

Norma closed her eyes. Fifty thousand dollars, she thought.

In the morning, as she left the apartment, Norma saw the card halves on the table. Impulsively, she dropped them into her purse. She locked the front door and joined Arthur in the elevator.

While she was on her coffee break, she took the card halves from her purse and held the torn edges together. Only Mr. Steward's name and telephone number were printed on the card.

After lunch, she took the card halves from her purse again and Scotch-taped the edges together. Why am I doing this? she thought.

Just before five, she dialed the number.

"Good afternoon," said Mr. Steward's voice.

Norma almost hung up but restrained herself. She cleared her throat. "This is Mrs. Lewis," she said.

"Yes, Mrs. Lewis." Mr. Steward sounded pleased.

"I'm curious."

"That's natural," Mr. Steward said.

"Not that I believe a word of what you told us."

"Oh, it's quite authentic," Mr. Steward answered.

"Well, whatever . . ." Norma swallowed. "When you said someone in the world would die, what did you mean?"

"Exactly that," he answered. "It could be anyone. All we

guarantee is that you don't know them. And, of course, that you wouldn't have to watch them die."

"For fifty thousand dollars," Norma said.

"That is correct."

She made a scoffing sound. "That's crazy."

"Nonetheless, that is the proposition," Mr. Steward said. "Would you like me to return the button unit?"

Norma stiffened. "Certainly not." She hung up angrily.

The package was lying by the front door; Norma saw it as she left the elevator. Well, of all the nerve, she thought. She glared at the carton as she unlocked the door. I just won't take it in, she thought. She went inside and started dinner.

Later, she carried her drink to the front hall. Opening the door, she picked up the package and carried it into the kitchen, leaving it on the table.

She sat in the living room, sipping her drink and looking out the window. After awhile, she went back into the kitchen to turn the cutlets in the broiler. She put the package in a bottom cabinet. She'd throw it out in the morning.

"Maybe some eccentric millionaire is playing games with people," she said.

Arthur looked up from his dinner. "I don't understand you."

"What does that mean?"

"Let it go," he told her.

Norma ate in silence. Suddenly, she put her fork down. "Suppose it's a genuine offer," she said.

Arthur stared at her.

"Suppose it's a genuine offer."

"All right, suppose it is!" He looked incredulous. "What would you like to do? Get the button back and push it? Murder someone?"

Norma looked disgusted. "Murder."

"How would *you* define it?"

"If you don't even know the person?" Norma asked.

Arthur looked astounded. "Are you saying what I think you are?"

"If it's some old Chinese peasant ten thousand miles away? Some diseased native in the Congo?"

"How about some baby boy in Pennsylvania?" Arthur countered. "Some beautiful little girl on the next block?"

"Now you're loading things."

"The point is, Norma," he continued, "that *who* you kill makes no difference. It's still murder."

"The point is," Norma broke in, "if it's someone you've never seen in your life and never will see, someone whose death you don't even have to know about, you still wouldn't push the button?"

Arthur stared at her, appalled. "You mean you would?"

"Fifty thousand dollars, Arthur."

"What has the amount . . ."

"Fifty thousand dollars, Arthur," Norma interrupted. "A chance to take that trip to Europe we've always talked about."

"Norma, no."

"A chance to buy that cottage on the Island."

"Norma, no." His face was white. "For God's sake, no!"

She shuddered. "All right, take it easy," she said. "Why are you getting so upset? It's only talk."

After dinner, Arthur went into the living room. Before he left the table, he said, "I'd rather not discuss it anymore, if you don't mind."

Norma shrugged. "Fine with me."

She got up earlier than usual to make pancakes, eggs, and bacon for Arthur's breakfast.

"What's the occasion?" he asked with a smile.

"No occasion." Norma looked offended. "I wanted to do it, that's all."

"Good," he said. "I'm glad you did."

She refilled his cup. "Wanted to show you I'm not . . ." she shrugged.

"Not what?"

"Selfish."

"Did I say you were?"

"Well—" She gestured vaguely. "—last night . . ."

Arthur didn't speak.

"All that talk about the button," Norma said. "I think you—well, misunderstood me."

"In what way?" His voice was guarded.

"I think you felt—" She gestured again. "—that I was only thinking of myself."

"Oh."

"I wasn't."

"Norma."

"Well, I wasn't. When I talked about Europe, a cottage on the Island . . ."

"Norma, why are we getting so involved in this?"

"I'm not involved at all." She drew in a shaking breath. "I'm simply trying to indicate that . . ."

"What?"

"That I'd like for us to go to Europe. Like for us to have a nicer apartment, nicer furniture, nicer clothes. Like for us to finally have a baby, for that matter."

"Norma, we will," he said.

"When?"

He stared at her in dismay. "Norma . . ."

"When?"

"Are you—" He seemed to draw back slightly. "Are you really saying . . . ?"

"I'm saying that they're probably doing it for some research project!" she cut him off. "That they want to know what average people would do under such a circumstance! That they're just saying someone would die, in order to study reactions, see if there'd be guilt, anxiety, whatever! You don't really think they'd kill somebody, do you?"

Arthur didn't answer. She saw his hands trembling. After awhile, he got up and left.

When he'd gone to work, Norma remained at the table, staring into her coffee. I'm going to be late, she thought. She shrugged. What difference did it make? She should be home anyway, not working in an office.

While she was stacking the dishes, she turned abruptly, dried her hands, and took the package from the bottom cabinet. Opening it, she set the button unit on the table. She stared at it for a long time before taking the key from its envelope and removing the glass dome. She stared at the button. How ridiculous, she thought. All this over a meaningless button.

Reaching out, she pressed it down. For us, she thought angrily.

She shuddered. Was it happening? A chill of horror swept across her.

In a moment, it had passed. She made a contemptuous noise. Ridiculous, she thought. To get so worked up over nothing.

She had just turned the supper steaks and was making herself another drink when the telephone rang. She picked it up. "Hello?"

"Mrs. Lewis?"

"Yes?"

"This is the Lenox Hill Hospital."

She felt unreal as the voice informed her of the subway accident, the shoving crowd. Arthur pushed from the platform in front of the train. She was conscious of shaking her head but couldn't stop.

As she hung up, she remembered Arthur's life insurance policy for $25,000, with double indemnity for—

"No." She couldn't seem to breathe. She struggled to her feet and walked in to the kitchen numbly. Something cold pressed at her skull as she removed the button unit from the wastebasket. There were no nails or screws visible. She couldn't see how it was put together.

Abruptly, she began to smash it on the sink edge, pounding it harder and harder, until the wood split. She pulled the sides apart, cutting her fingers without noticing. There were no transistors in the box, no wires or tubes. The box was empty.

She whirled with a gasp as the telephone rang. Stumbling into the living room, she picked up the receiver.

"Mrs. Lewis?" Mr. Steward asked.

It wasn't her voice shrieking so; it couldn't be. "You said I wouldn't know the one that died!"

"My dear lady," Mr. Steward said, "do you really think you knew your husband?"

Duel

• • • • • • • • • • • • • • • •

At 11:32 A.M., Mann passed the truck.

He was heading west, en route to San Francisco. It was Thursday and unseasonably hot for April. He had his suitcoat off, his tie removed and shirt collar opened, his sleeve cuffs folded back. There was sunlight on his left arm and on part of his lap. He could feel the heat of it through his dark trousers as he drove along the two-lane highway. For the past twenty minutes, he had not seen another vehicle going in either direction.

Then he saw the truck ahead, moving up a curving grade between two high green hills. He heard the grinding strain of its motor and saw a double shadow on the road. The truck was pulling a trailer.

He paid no attention to the details of the truck. As he drew behind it on the grade, he edged his car toward the opposite lane. The road ahead had blind curves and he didn't try to pass until the truck had crossed the ridge. He waited until it started around a left curve on the downgrade, then, seeing that the way was clear, pressed down on the accelerator pedal and steered his car into the eastbound lane. He waited until he could see the truck front in his rearview mirror before he turned back into the proper lane.

Mann looked across the countryside ahead. There were ranges of mountains as far as he could see and, all around him, rolling green hills. He whistled softly as the car sped down the winding grade, its tires making crisp sounds on the pavement.

At the bottom of the hill, he crossed a concrete bridge and, glancing to the right, saw a dry stream bed strewn with rocks and gravel. As the car moved off the bridge, he saw a trailer park set back from the highway to his right. How can anyone live out here? he thought. His shifting gaze caught sight of a pet cemetery ahead and he smiled. Maybe those people in the trailers wanted to be close to the graves of their dogs and cats.

The highway ahead was straight now. Mann drifted into a reverie, the sunlight on his arm and lap. He wondered what Ruth was doing. The kids, of course, were in school and would be for hours yet. Maybe Ruth was shopping; Thursday was the day she usually went. Mann visualized her in the supermarket, putting various items into the basket cart. He wished he were with her instead of starting on another sales trip. Hours of driving yet before he'd reach San Francisco. Three days of hotel sleeping and restaurant eating, hoped-for contacts and likely disappointments. He sighed; then, reaching out impulsively, he switched on the radio. He revolved the tuning knob until he found a station playing soft, innocuous music. He hummed along with it, eyes almost out of focus on the road ahead.

He stared as the truck roared past him on the left, causing his car to shudder slightly. He watched the truck and trailer cut in abruptly for the westbound lane and frowned as he had to brake to maintain a safe distance behind it. What's with you? he thought.

He eyed the truck with cursory disapproval. It was a huge gasoline tanker pulling a tank trailer, each of them having six pairs of wheels. He could see that it was not a new rig but was dented and in need of renovation, its tanks painted a cheap-looking silvery color. Mann wondered if the driver had done the painting himself. His gaze shifted from the word FLAMMABLE printed across the back of the trailer tank, red letters on a white background, to the parallel reflector lines painted in red across the bottom of the tank to the massive rubber flaps swaying behind the rear tires, then back up again. The reflector lines looked as though they'd been clumsily applied with a stencil. The driver must be an independent trucker, he decided, and not too affluent a one, from the looks of his outfit. He glanced at the trailer's license plate. It was a California issue.

Mann checked his speedometer. He was holding steady at 55 miles an hour, as he invariably did when he drove without thinking on the open highway. The truck driver must have done a good 70 to pass him so quickly. That seemed a little odd. Weren't truck drivers supposed to be a cautious lot?

He grimaced at the smell of the truck's exhaust and looked at the vertical pipe to the left of the cab. It was spewing smoke, which clouded darkly back across the trailer. Christ, he thought. With all the furor about air pollution, why do they keep allowing that sort of thing on the highways?

He scowled at the constant fumes. They'd make him nauseated in a little while, he knew. He couldn't lag back here like this. Either he slowed down or he passed the truck again. He didn't have the time to slow down. He'd gotten a late start. Keeping it at 55 all the way, he'd just about make his afternoon appointment. No, he'd have to pass.

Depressing the gas pedal, he eased his car toward the opposite lane. No sign of anything ahead. Traffic on this route seemed almost nonexistent today. He pushed down harder on the accelerator and steered all the way into the eastbound lane.

As he passed the truck, he glanced at it. The cab was too high for him to see into. All he caught sight of was the back of the truck driver's left hand on the steering wheel. It was darkly tanned and square-looking, with large veins knotted on its surface.

When Mann could see the truck reflected in the rearview mirror, he pulled back over to the proper lane and looked ahead again.

He glanced at the rearview mirror in surprise as the truck driver gave him an extended horn blast. What was that? he wondered; a greeting or a curse? He grunted with amusement, glancing at the mirror as he drove. The front fenders of the truck were a dingy purple color, the paint faded and chipped; another amateurish job. All he could see was the lower portion of the truck; the rest was cut off by the top of his rear window.

To Mann's right, now, was a slope of shalelike earth with patches of scrub grass growing on it. His gaze jumped to the clapboard house on top of the slope. The television aerial on its roof was sagging at an angle of less than 40 degrees. Must give great reception, he thought.

He looked to the front again, glancing aside abruptly at a sign printed in jagged block letters on a piece of plywood: NIGHT CRAWLERS—BAIT. What the hell is a night crawler? he wondered. It sounded like some monster in a low-grade Hollywood thriller.

The unexpected roar of the truck motor made his gaze jump to the rearview mirror. Instantly, his startled look jumped to the side mirror. By God, the guy was passing him *again*. Mann turned his head to scowl at the leviathan form as it drifted by. He tried to see into the cab but couldn't because of its height. What's with him, anyway? he wondered. What the hell are we having here, a contest? See which vehicle can stay ahead the longest?

He thought of speeding up to stay ahead but changed his mind. When the truck and trailer started back into the westbound lane, he let up on the pedal, voicing a newly incredulous sound as he saw that if he hadn't slowed down, he would have been prematurely cut off again. Jesus Christ, he thought. What's *with* this guy?

His scowl deepened as the odor of the truck's exhaust reached his nostrils again. Irritably, he cranked up the window on his left. Damn it, was he going to have to breathe that crap all the way to San Francisco? He couldn't afford to slow down. He had to meet Forbes at a quarter after three and that was that.

He looked ahead. At least there was no traffic complicating matters. Mann pressed down on the accelerator pedal, drawing close behind the truck. When the highway curved enough to the left to give him a completely open view of the route ahead, he jarred down on the pedal, steering out into the opposite lane.

The truck edged over, blocking his way.

For several moments, all Mann could do was stare at it in blank confusion. Then, with a startled noise, he braked, returning to the proper lane. The truck moved back in front of him.

Mann could not allow himself to accept what apparently had taken place. It had to be a coincidence. The truck driver couldn't have blocked his way on purpose. He waited for more than a minute, then flicked down the turn-indicator lever to make his intentions perfectly clear and, depressing the accelerator pedal, steered again into the eastbound lane.

Immediately, the truck shifted, barring his way.

"Jesus Christ!" Mann was astounded. This was unbelievable. He'd never seen such a thing in twenty-six years of driving. He returned to the westbound lane, shaking his head as the truck swung back in front of him.

He eased up on the gas pedal, falling back to avoid the truck's exhaust. Now what? he wondered. He still had to make San Francisco on schedule. Why in God's name hadn't he gone a little out of his way in the beginning, so he could have traveled by freeway? This damned highway was two lane all the way.

Impulsively, he sped into the eastbound lane again. To his surprise, the truck driver did not pull over. Instead, the driver stuck his left arm out and waved him on. Mann started pushing down on the accelerator. Suddenly, he let up on the pedal with a gasp and jerked the steering wheel around, raking back behind the truck so quickly that his car began to fishtail. He was fighting to control its zigzag whipping when a blue convertible shot by him in the opposite lane. Mann caught a momentary vision of the man inside it glaring at him.

The car came under his control again. Mann was sucking breath in through his mouth. His heart was pounding almost painfully. My God! he thought. *He wanted me to hit that car head on.* The realization stunned him. True, he should have seen to it himself that the road ahead was clear; that was his failure. But to wave him on. . . . Mann felt appalled and sickened. Boy, oh, boy, oh, boy, he thought. This was really one for the books. That son of a bitch had meant for not only him to be killed but a totally uninvolved passerby as well. The idea seemed beyond his comprehension. On a California highway on a Thursday morning? *Why?*

Mann tried to calm himself and rationalize the incident. Maybe it's the heat, he thought. Maybe the truck driver had a tension headache or an upset stomach; maybe both. Maybe he'd had a fight with his wife. Maybe she'd failed to put out last night. Mann tried in vain to smile. There could be any number of reasons. Reaching out, he twisted off the radio. The cheerful music irritated him.

He drove behind the truck for several minutes, his face a mask of animosity. As the exhaust fumes started putting his stomach on edge, he suddenly forced down the heel of his right hand on the horn bar and held it there. Seeing that the route ahead was clear, he pushed in the accelerator pedal all the way and steered into the opposite lane.

The movement of his car was paralleled immediately by the truck. Mann stayed in place, right hand jammed down on the horn bar. Get out of the way, you son of a bitch! he thought. He felt the muscles of his jaw hardening until they ached. There was a twisting in his stomach.

"Damn!" He pulled back quickly to the proper lane, shuddering with fury. "You miserable son of a bitch," he muttered, glaring at the truck as it was shifted back in front of him. What the hell is wrong with you? I pass your goddamn rig a couple of times and you go flying off the deep end? Are you nuts or something? Mann nodded tensely. Yes, he thought; he *is*. No other explanation.

He wondered what Ruth would think of all this, how she'd react. Probably, she'd start to honk the horn and would keep on honking it, assuming that, eventually, it would attract the attention of a policeman. He looked around with a scowl. Just where in hell *were* the policemen out here, anyway? He made a scoffing noise. What policemen? Here in the boondocks? They probably had a sheriff on horseback, for Christ's sake.

He wondered suddenly if he could fool the truck driver by passing on the right. Edging his car toward the shoulder, he peered ahead. No chance. There wasn't room enough. The truck driver could shove him through that wire fence if he wanted to. Mann shivered. And he'd want to, sure as hell, he thought.

Driving where he was, he grew conscious of the debris lying beside the highway: beer cans, candy wrappers, ice-cream containers, newspaper sections browned and rotted by the weather, a FOR SALE sign torn in half. Keep America beautiful, he thought sardonically. He passed a boulder with the name WILL JASPER painted on it in white. Who the hell is Will Jasper? he wondered. What would he think of this situation?

Unexpectedly, the car began to bounce. For several anxious moments, Mann thought that one of his tires had gone flat. Then he noticed that the paving along this section of highway consisted of pitted slabs with gaps between them. He saw the truck and trailer jolting up and down and thought: I hope it shakes your brains loose. As the truck veered into a sharp left curve, he caught a fleeting glimpse of the driver's face in the cab's side mirror. There was not enough time to establish his appearance.

"Ah," he said. A long, steep hill was looming up ahead. The truck would have to climb it slowly. There would doubtless be an opportunity to pass somewhere on the grade. Mann pressed down on the accelerator pedal, drawing as close behind the truck as safety would allow.

Halfway up the slope, Mann saw a turnout for the eastbound lane with no oncoming traffic anywhere in sight. Flooring the accelerator pedal, he shot into the opposite lane. The slow-moving truck began to angle out in front of him. Face stiffening, Mann steered his speeding car across the highway edge and curved it sharply on the turnout. Clouds of dust went billowing up behind his car, making him lose sight of the truck. His tires buzzed and crackled on the dirt, then, suddenly, were humming on the pavement once again.

He glanced at the rearview mirror and a barking laugh erupted from his throat. He'd only meant to pass. The dust had been an unexpected bonus. Let the bastard get a sniff of something rotten smelling in *his* nose for a change! he thought. He honked the horn elatedly, a mocking rhythm of bleats. Screw you, Jack!

He swept across the summit of the hill. A striking vista lay ahead: sunlit hills and flatland, a corridor of dark trees, quadrangles of cleared-off acreage and bright-green vegetable patches; far off, in the distance, a mammoth water tower. Mann felt stirred by the panoramic sight. Lovely, he thought. Reaching out, he turned the radio back on and started humming cheerfully with the music.

Seven minutes later, he passed a billboard advertising CHUCK'S CAFE. No thanks, Chuck, he thought. He glanced at a gray house nestled in a hollow. Was that a cemetery in its front yard or a group of plaster statuary for sale?

Hearing the noise behind him, Mann looked at the rearview mirror and felt himself go cold with fear. The truck was hurtling down the hill, pursuing him.

His mouth fell open and he threw a glance at the speedometer. He was doing more than 60! On a curving downgrade, that was not at all a safe speed to be driving. Yet the truck must be exceeding that by a considerable margin, it was closing the distance between them so rapidly. Mann swallowed, leaning to the right as he steered his car around a sharp curve. Is the man *insane*? he thought.

His gaze jumped forward searchingly. He saw a turnoff half a mile ahead and decided that he'd use it. In the rearview mirror, the huge square radiator grille was all he could see now. He stamped down on the gas pedal and his tires screeched unnervingly as he wheeled around another curve, thinking that, surely, the truck would have to slow down here.

He groaned as it rounded the curve with ease, only the sway of its tanks revealing the outward pressure of the turn. Mann bit trembling lips together as he whipped his car around another curve. A straight descent now. He depressed the pedal farther, glanced at the speedometer. Almost 70 miles an hour! He wasn't used to driving this fast!

In agony, he saw the turnoff shoot by on his right. He couldn't have left the highway at this speed, anyway; he'd have overturned. Goddamn it, what was wrong with that son of a bitch? Mann honked his horn in frightened rage. Cranking down the window suddenly, he shoved his left arm out to wave the truck back. *"Back!"* he yelled. He honked the horn again. "Get back, you crazy bastard!"

The truck was almost on him now. He's going to kill me! Mann thought, horrified. He honked the horn repeatedly, then had to use both hands to grip the steering wheel as he swept around another curve. He flashed a look at the rearview mirror. He could see only the bottom portion of the truck's radiator grille. He was going to lose control! He felt the rear wheels start to drift and let up on the pedal quickly. The tire treads bit in, the car leaped on, regaining its momentum.

Mann saw the bottom of the grade ahead, and in the distance there was a building with a sign that read CHUCK'S CAFE. The truck was gaining ground again. This is insane! he thought, enraged and terrified at once. The highway straightened out. He floored the pedal: 74 now—75. Mann braced himself, trying to ease the car as far to the right as possible.

Abruptly, he began to brake, then swerved to the right, raking his car into the open area in front of the cafe. He cried out as the car began to fishtail, then careened into a skid. *Steer with it!* screamed a voice in his mind. The rear of the car was lashing from side to side, tires spewing dirt and raising clouds of dust. Mann pressed harder on the brake pedal, turning further into the skid. The car began to straighten out and he braked harder yet, conscious, on the sides of his vision, of the truck and trailer roaring by on the highway. He nearly sideswiped one of the cars parked in front of the cafe, bounced and skidded by it, going almost straight now. He jammed in the brake pedal as hard as he could. The rear end broke to the right and the car spun half around, sheering sideways to a neck-wrenching halt thirty yards beyond the cafe.

Mann sat in pulsing silence, eyes closed. His heartbeats felt like club blows in his chest. He couldn't seem to catch his breath. If he were ever going to have a heart attack, it would be now. After a while, he opened his eyes and pressed his right palm against his chest. His heart was still throbbing laboredly. No wonder, he thought. It isn't every day I'm almost murdered by a truck.

He raised the handle and pushed out the door, then started forward, grunting in surprise as the safety belt held him in place. Reaching down with shaking fingers, he depressed the release button and pulled the ends of the belt apart. He glanced at the cafe. What had its patrons thought of his break-neck appearance? he wondered.

He stumbled as he walked to the front door of the cafe. TRUCKERS WELCOME, read a sign in the window. It gave Mann a queasy feeling to see it. Shivering, he pulled open the door and went inside, avoiding the sight of its customers. He felt certain they were watching him, but he didn't have the strength to face their looks. Keeping his gaze fixed straight ahead, he moved to the rear of the cafe and opened the door marked GENTS.

Moving to the sink, he twisted the right-hand faucet and leaned over to cup cold water in his palms and splash it on his face. There was a fluttering of his stomach muscles he could not control.

Straightening up. he tugged down several towels from their dispenser and patted them against his face, grimacing at the smell of the paper. Dropping the soggy towels into a wastebasket beside the sink, he regarded himself in the wall mirror. Still with us, Mann, he thought. He nodded, swallowing. Drawing out his metal comb, he neatened his hair. You never know, he thought. You just never know. You drift along, year after year, presuming certain values to be fixed; like being able to drive on a public thoroughfare without somebody trying to murder you. You come to depend on that sort of thing. Then something occurs and all bets are off. One shocking incident and all the years of logic and acceptance are displaced and, suddenly, the jungle is in front of you again. *Man, part animal, part angel.* Where had he come across that phrase? He shivered.

It was entirely an animal in that truck out there.

His breath was almost back to normal now. Mann forced a smile at his reflection. All right, boy, he told himself. It's over now. It was a goddamned nightmare, but it's over. You are on your way to San Francisco. You'll get yourself a nice hotel room, order a bottle of expensive Scotch, soak your body in a hot bath and forget. Damn right, he thought. He turned and walked out of the washroom.

He jolted to a halt, his breath cut off. Standing rooted, heartbeat hammering at his chest, he gaped through the front window of the cafe.

The truck and trailer were parked outside.

Mann stared at them in unbelieving shock. It wasn't possible. He'd seen them roaring by at top speed. The driver had won; he'd *won*! He'd had the whole damn highway to himself! *Why had he turned back?*

Mann looked around with sudden dread. There were five men eating, three along the counter, two in booths. He cursed himself for having failed to look at faces when he'd entered. Now there was no way of knowing who it was. Mann felt his legs begin to shake.

Abruptly, he walked to the nearest booth and slid in clumsily behind the table. Now wait, he told himself; just wait. Surely, he could tell which one it was. Masking his face with the menu, he glanced across its top. Was it that one in the khaki work shirt? Mann tried to see the man's hands but couldn't. His gaze flicked nervously across the room. Not that one in the suit, of course. Three remaining. That one in the front booth, square-faced, black-haired? If only he could see the man's hands, it might help. One of the two others at the counter? Mann studied them uneasily. Why hadn't he looked at faces when he'd come in?

Now *wait*, he thought. Goddamn it, *wait*! All right, the truck driver was in here. That didn't automatically signify that he meant to continue the insane duel. Chuck's Cafe might be the only place to eat for miles around. It *was* lunchtime, wasn't it? The truck driver had probably intended to eat here all the time. He'd just been moving too fast to pull into the parking lot before. So he'd slowed down, turned around and driven back, that was all. Mann forced himself to read the menu. Right, he thought. No point in getting so rattled. Perhaps a beer would help relax him.

The woman behind the counter came over and Mann ordered a ham sandwich on rye toast and a bottle of Coors. As the woman turned away, he wondered, with a sudden twinge of self-reproach, why he hadn't simply left the cafe, jumped into his car and sped away. He would have known immediately, then, if the truck driver was still out to get him. As it was, he'd have to suffer through an entire meal to find out. He almost groaned at his stupidity.

Still, what if the truck driver *had* followed him out and started after him again? He'd have been right back where he'd started. Even if he'd managed to get a good lead, the truck driver would have overtaken him eventually. It just wasn't in him to drive at 80 and 90 miles an hour in order to stay ahead. True, he might have been intercepted by a California Highway Patrol car. What if he weren't, though?

Mann repressed the plaguing thoughts. He tried to calm himself. He looked deliberately at the four men. Either of two seemed a likely possibility as the driver of the truck: the square-faced one in the front booth and the chunky one in the jumpsuit sitting at the counter. Mann had an impulse to walk over to them and ask which one it was, tell the man he was sorry he'd irritated him, tell him anything to calm him, since, obviously, he wasn't rational, was a manic-depressive, probably. Maybe buy the man a beer and sit with him awhile to try to settle things.

He couldn't move. What if the truck driver were letting the whole thing drop? Mightn't his approach rile the man all over again? Mann felt drained by indecision. He nodded weakly as the waitress set the sandwich and the bottle in front of him. He took a swallow of the beer, which made him cough. Was the truck driver amused by the sound? Mann felt a stirring of resentment deep inside himself. What right did that bastard have to impose this torment on another human being? It was a free country, wasn't it? Damn it, he had every right to pass the son of a bitch on a highway if he wanted to!

"Oh, hell," he mumbled. He tried to feel amused. He was

making entirely too much of this. Wasn't he? He glanced at the pay telephone on the front wall. What was to prevent him from calling the local police and telling them the situation? But, then, he'd have to stay here, lose time, make Forbes angry, probably lose the sale. And what if the truck driver stayed to face them? Naturally, he'd deny the whole thing. What if the police believed him and didn't do anything about it? After they'd gone, the truck driver would undoubtedly take it out on him again, only worse. *God!* Mann thought in agony.

The sandwich tasted flat, the beer unpleasantly sour. Mann stared at the table as he ate. For God's sake, why was he just *sitting* here like this? He was a grown man, wasn't he? Why didn't he settle this damn thing once and for all?

His left hand twitched so unexpectedly, he spilled beer on his trousers. The man in the jump suit had risen from the counter and was strolling toward the front of the cafe. Mann felt his heartbeat thumping as the man gave money to the waitress, took his change and a toothpick from the dispenser and went outside. Mann watched in anxious silence.

The man did not get into the cab of the tanker truck.

It had to be the one in the front booth, then. His face took form in Mann's rememberance: square, with dark eyes, dark hair; the man who'd tried to kill him.

Mann stood abruptly, letting impulse conquer fear. Eyes fixed ahead, he started toward the entrance. Anything was preferable to sitting in that booth. He stopped by the cash register, conscious of the hitching of his chest as he gulped in air. Was the man observing him? he wondered. He swallowed, pulling out the clip of dollar bills in his right-hand trouser pocket. He glanced toward the waitress. Come *on*, he thought. He looked at his check and, seeing the amount, reached shakily into his trouser pocket for change. He heard a coin fall onto the floor and roll away. Ignoring it, he dropped a dollar and a quarter onto the counter and thrust the clip of bills into his trouser pocket.

As he did, he heard the man in the front booth get up. An icy shudder spasmed up his back. Turning quickly to the door, he shoved it open, seeing, on the edges of his vision, the square-faced man approach the cash register. Lurching from the cafe, he started toward his car with long strides. His mouth was dry again. The pounding of his heart was painful in his chest.

Suddenly, he started running. He heard the cafe door bang shut and fought away the urge to look across his shoulder. Was that a sound of other running footsteps now? Reaching his car, Mann yanked open the door and jarred in awkwardly behind the steering wheel. He reached into his trouser pocket for the keys and snatched them out, almost dropping them. His hand was shaking so badly he couldn't get the ignition key into its slot. He whined with mounting dread. Come on! he thought.

The key slid in, he twisted it convulsively. The motor started and he raced it momentarily before jerking the transmission shift to drive. Depressing the accelerator pedal quickly, he raked the car around and steered it toward the highway. From the corners of his eyes, he saw the truck and trailer being backed away from the cafe.

Reaction burst inside him. "No!" he raged and slammed his foot down on the brake pedal. This was idiotic! Why the hell should he run way? His car slid sideways to a rocking halt and, shouldering out the door, he lurched to his feet and started toward the truck with angry strides. *All right, Jack,* he thought. He glared at the man inside the truck. You want to punch my nose, okay, but no more goddamn tournament on the highway.

The truck began to pick up speed. Mann raised his right arm. "Hey!" he yelled. He knew the driver saw him. *"Hey!"* He started running as the truck kept moving, engine grinding loudly. It was on the highway now. He sprinted toward it with a sense of martyred outrage. The driver shifted gears, the truck moved faster. "Stop!" Mann shouted. "Damn it, *stop!*"

He thudded to a panting halt, staring at the truck as it receded down the highway, moved around a hill and disappeared. "You son of a bitch," he muttered. "You goddamn, miserable son of a bitch."

He trudged back slowly to his car, trying to believe that the truck driver had fled the hazard of a fistfight. It was possible, of course, but, somehow he could not believe it.

He got into his car and was about to drive onto the highway when he changed his mind and switched the motor off. That crazy bastard might just be tooling along at 15 miles an hour, waiting for him to catch up. Nuts to that, he thought. So he blew his schedule; screw it. Forbes would have to wait, that was all. And if Forbes didn't care to wait, that was all right, too. He'd sit here for a while and let the nut get out of range, let him think he'd won the day. He grinned. You're the bloody Red Baron, Jack; you've shot me down. Now go to hell with my sincerest compliments. He shook his head. Beyond belief, he thought.

He really should have done this earlier, pulled over, waited. Then the truck driver would have had to let it pass. *Or picked on someone else,* the startling thought occurred to him. Jesus, maybe that was how the crazy bastard whiled away his work hours! Jesus Christ Almighty! was it possible?

He looked at the dashboard clock. It was just past 12:30. Wow, he thought. All that in less than an hour. He shifted on the seat and stretched his legs out. Leaning back against the door, he closed his eyes and mentally perused the things he had to do tomorrow and the following day. Today was shot to hell, as far as he could see.

When he opened his eyes, afraid of drifting into sleep and losing too much time, almost eleven minutes had passed. The nut must be an ample distance off by now, he thought; at least 11 miles and likely more, the way he drove. Good enough. He wasn't going to try to make San Francisco on schedule now, anyway. He'd take it real easy.

Mann adjusted his safety belt, switched on the motor, tapped the transmission pointer into drive position and pulled onto the highway, glancing back across his shoulder. Not a car in sight. Great day for driving. Everybody was staying at home. That nut must have a reputation around here. When Crazy Jack is on the highway, lock your car in the garage.

Mann chuckled at the notion as his car began to turn the curve ahead.

Mindless reflex drove his right foot down against the brake pedal. Suddenly, his car had skidded to a halt and he was staring down the highway. The truck and trailer were parked on the shoulder less than 90 yards away.

Mann couldn't seem to function. He knew his car was blocking the west-bound lane, knew that he should either make a U-turn or pull off the highway, but all he could do was gape at the truck.

He cried out, legs retracting, as a horn blast sounded behind him. Snapping up his head, he looked at the rearview mirror, gasping as he saw a yellow station wagon bearing down on him at high speed. Suddenly, it veered off toward the eastbound lane, disappearing from the mirror. Mann jerked around and saw it hurtling past his car, its rear end snapping back and forth, its back tires screeching. He saw the twisted features of the man inside, saw his lips move rapidly with cursing.

Then the station wagon had swerved back into the westbound lane and was speeding off. It gave Mann an odd sensation to see it pass the truck. The man in that station wagon could drive on, unthreatened. Only he'd been singled out. What happened was demented. Yet it was happening.

He drove his car onto the highway shoulder and braked. Putting the transmission into neutral, he leaned back, staring at the truck. His head was aching again. There was a pulsing at his temples like the ticking of a muffled clock.

What was he to do? He knew very well that if he left his car to walk to the truck, the driver would pull away and repark farther down the highway. He may as well face the fact that he was dealing with a madman. He felt the tremor in his stomach muscles starting up again. His heartbeat thudded slowly, striking at his chest wall. Now what?

With a sudden, angry impulse, Mann snapped the transmission into gear and stepped down hard on the accelerator pedal. The tires of the car spun sizzlingly before they gripped; the car shot out onto the highway. Instantly, the truck began to move. He even had the motor on! Mann thought in raging fear. He floored the pedal, then, abruptly, realized he couldn't make it, that the truck would block his way and he'd collide with its trailer. A vision flashed across his mind, a fiery explosion and a sheet of flame incinerating him. He started braking fast, trying to decelerate evenly, so he wouldn't lose control.

When he'd slowed down enough to feel that it was safe, he steered the car onto the shoulder and stopped it again, throwing the transmission into neutral.

Approximately eighty yards ahead, the truck pulled off the highway and stopped.

Mann tapped his fingers on the steering wheel. *Now* what? he thought. Turn around and head east until he reached a cutoff that would take him to San Francisco by another route? How did he know the truck driver wouldn't follow him even then? His cheeks twisted as he bit his lips together angrily. No! He wasn't going to turn around!

His expression hardened suddenly. Well, he wasn't going to *sit* here all day, that was certain. Reaching out, he tapped the gearshift into drive and steered his car onto the highway once again. He saw the massive truck and trailer start to move but made no effort to speed up. He tapped at the brakes, taking a position about 30 yards behind the trailer. He glanced at his speedometer. Forty miles an hour. The truck driver had his left arm out of the cab window and was waving him on. What did that mean? Had he changed his mind? Decided, finally, that this thing had gone too far? Mann couldn't let himself believe it.

He looked ahead. Despite the mountain ranges all around, the highway was flat as far as he could see. He tapped a fingernail against the horn bar, trying to make up his mind. Presumably, he could continue all the way to San Francisco at this speed, hanging back just far enough to avoid the worst of the exhaust fumes. It didn't seem likely that the truck driver would stop directly on the highway to block his way. And if the truck driver pulled onto the shoulder to let him pass, he

could pull off the highway, too. It would be a draining afternoon but a safe one.

On the other hand, outracing the truck might be worth just
one more try. This was obviously what that son of a bitch
wanted. Yet, surely, a vehicle of such size couldn't be driven
with the same daring as, potentially, his own. The laws of
mechanics were against it, if nothing else. Whatever advan-
tage the truck had in mass, it had to lose in stability, partic-
ularly that of its trailer. If Mann were to drive at, say, 80
miles an hour and there were a few steep grades—as he felt
sure there were—the truck would have to fall behind.

The question was, of course, whether he had the nerve to
maintain such a speed over a long distance. He'd never done
it before. Still, the more he thought about it, the more it ap-
pealed to him; far more than the alternative did.

Abruptly, he decided. *Right,* he thought. He checked ahead,
then pressed down hard on the accelerator pedal and pulled
into the eastbound lane. As he neared the truck, he tensed,
anticipating that the driver might block his way. But the truck
did not shift from the westbound lane. Mann's car moved
along its mammoth side. He glanced at the cab and saw the
name KELLER printed on its door. For a shocking instant, he
thought it read KILLER and started to slow down. Then, glancing at the name again, he saw what it really was and depressed the pedal sharply. When he saw the truck reflected in
the rearview mirror, he steered his car into the westbound
lane.

He shuddered, dread and satisfaction mixed together, as he
saw that the truck driver was speeding up. It was strangely
comforting to know the man's intentions definitely again.
That plus the knowledge of his face and name seemed, somehow, to reduce his stature. Before, he had been faceless,
nameless, an embodiment of unknown terror. Now, at least,
he was an individual. All right, Keller, said his mind, let's see
you beat me with that purple-silver relic now. He pressed
down harder on the pedal. *Here we go,* he thought.

He looked at the speedometer, scowling as he saw that he
was doing only 74 miles an hour. Deliberately, he pressed

down on the pedal, alternating his gaze between the highway ahead and the speedometer until the needle turned past 80. He felt a flickering of satisfaction with himself. All right, Keller, you son of a bitch, top that, he thought.

After several moments, he glanced into the rearview mirror again. Was the truck getting closer? Stunned, he checked the speedometer. Damn it! He was down to 76! He forced in the accelerator pedal angrily. *He mustn't go less than 80!* Mann's chest shuddered with convulsive breath.

He glanced aside as he hurtled past a beige sedan parked on the shoulder underneath a tree. A young couple sat inside it, talking. Already they were far behind, their world removed from his. Had they even glanced aside when he'd passed? He doubted it.

He started as the shadow of an overhead bridge whipped across the hood and windshield. Inhaling raggedly, he glanced at the speedometer again. He was holding at 81. He checked the rearview mirror. Was it his imagination that the truck was gaining ground? He looked forward with anxious eyes. There had to be some kind of town ahead. To hell with time; he'd stop at the police station and tell them what had happened. They'd have to believe him. Why would he stop to tell them such a story if it weren't true? For all he knew, Keller had a police record in these parts. *Oh, sure, we're on to him,* he heard a faceless officer remark. *That crazy bastard's asked for it before and now he's going to get it.*

Mann shook himself and looked at the mirror. The truck *was* getting closer. Wincing, he glanced at the speedometer. goddamn it, pay attention! raged his mind. He was down to 74 again! Whining with frustration, he depressed the pedal. Eighty!—80! he demanded of himself. There was a murderer behind him!

His car began to pass a field of flowers; lilacs, Mann saw, white and purple stretching out in endless rows. There was a small shack near the highway, the words FIELD FRESH FLOWERS painted on it. A brown-cardboard square was propped against the shack, the word FUNERALS printed crudely on it. Mann saw himself, abruptly, lying in a casket, painted like some grotesque mannequin. The overpowering smell of flowers seemed to fill his nostrils. Ruth and the children sitting in the first row, heads bowed. All his relatives—

Suddenly, the pavement roughened and the car began to bounce and shudder, driving bolts of pain into his head. He felt the steering wheel resisting him and clamped his hands around it tightly, harsh vibrations running up his arms. He didn't dare look at the mirror now. He had to force himself to keep the speed unchanged. Keller wasn't going to slow down; he was sure of that. *What if he got a flat tire, though?* All control would vanish in an instant. He visualized the somersaulting of his car, its grinding, shrieking tumble, the explosion of its gas tank, his body crushed and burned and—

The broken span of pavement ended and his gaze jumped quickly to the rearview mirror. The truck was no closer, but it hadn't lost ground, either. Mann's eyes shifted. Up ahead were hills and mountains. He tried to reassure himself that upgrades were on his side, that he could climb them at the same speed he was going now. Yet all he could imagine were the downgrades, the immense truck close behind him, slamming violently into his car and knocking it across some cliff edge. He had a horrifying vision of dozens of broken, rusted cars lying unseen in the canyons ahead, corpses in every one of them, all flung to shattering deaths by Keller.

Mann's car went rocketing into a corridor of trees. On each side of the highway was a eucalyptus windbreak, each trunk three feet from the next. It was like speeding through a high-walled canyon. Mann gasped, twitching, as a large twig bearing dusty leaves dropped down across the windshield, then slid out of sight. Dear God! he thought. He was getting near the edge himself. If he should lose his nerve at this speed, it was over. Jesus! That would be ideal for Keller! he realized suddenly. He visualized the square-faced driver laughing as he passed the burning wreckage, knowing that he'd killed his prey without so much as touching him.

Mann started as his car shot out into the open. The route ahead was not straight now but winding up into the foothills.

Mann willed himself to press down on the pedal even more. Eighty-three now, almost 84.

To his left was a broad terrain of green hills blending into mountains. He saw a black car on a dirt road, moving toward the highway. *Was its side painted white?* Mann's heartbeat lurched. Impulsively, he jammed the heel of his right hand down against the horn bar and held it there. The blast of the horn was shrill and racking to his ears. His heart began to pound. Was it a police car? *Was it?*

He let the horn bar up abruptly. *No, it wasn't.* Damn! his mind raged. Keller must have been amused by his pathetic efforts. Doubtless, he was chuckling to himself right now. He heard the truck driver's voice in his mind, coarse and sly. *You think you gonna get a cop to save you, boy? Shee-it. You gonna die.* Mann's heart contorted with savage hatred. *You son of a bitch!* he thought. Jerking his right hand into a fist, he drove it down against the seat. Goddamn you, Keller! I'm going to kill you, if it's the last thing I do!

The hills were closer now. There would be slopes directly, long steep grades. Mann felt a burst of hope within himself. He was sure to gain a lot of distance on the truck. No matter how he tried, that bastard Keller couldn't manage 80 miles an hour on a hill. But *I* can! cried his mind with fierce elation. He worked up saliva in his mouth and swallowed it. The back of his shirt was drenched. He could feel sweat trickling down his sides. A bath and a drink, first order of the day on reaching San Francisco. A long, hot bath, a long, cold drink. Cutty Sark. He'd splurge, by Christ. He rated it.

The car swept up a shallow rise. Not steep enough, goddamn it! The truck's momentum would prevent its losing speed. Mann felt mindless hatred for the landscape. Already, he had topped the rise and tilted over to a shallow downgrade. He looked at the rearview mirror. *Square,* he thought, everything about the truck was square: the radiator grille, the fender shapes, the bumper ends, the outline of the cab, even the shape of Keller's hands and face. He visualized the truck as some great entity pursuing him, insentient, brutish, chasing him with instinct only.

Mann cried out, horror-stricken, as he saw the ROAD RE-
PAIRS sign up ahead. His frantic gaze leaped down the highway. Both lanes blocked, a huge black arrow pointing toward
the alternate route! He groaned in anguish, seeing it was dirt.
His foot jumped automatically to the brake pedal and started
pumping it. He threw a dazed look at the rearview mirror.
The truck was moving as fast as ever! It *couldn't*, though!
Mann's expression froze in terror as he started turning to the
right.

He stiffened as the front wheels hit the dirt road. For an instant, he was certain that the back part of the car was going
to spin; he felt it breaking to the left. "No, don't!" he cried.
Abruptly, he was jarring down the dirt road, elbows braced
against his sides, trying to keep from losing control. His tires
battered at the ruts, almost tearing the wheel from his grip.
The windows rattled noisily. His neck snapped back and forth
with painful jerks. His jolting body surged against the binding
of the safety belt and slammed down violently on the seat. He
felt the bouncing of the car drive up his spine. His clenching
teeth slipped and he cried out hoarsely as his upper teeth
gouged deep into his lip.

He gasped as the rear end of the car began surging to the
right. He started to jerk the steering wheel to the left, then,
hissing, wrenched it in the opposite direction, crying out as
the right rear fender cracked into a fence pole, knocking it
down. He started pumping at the brakes, struggling to regain
control. The car rear yawed sharply to the left, tires shooting
out a spray of dirt. Mann felt a scream tear upward in his
throat. He twisted wildly at the steering wheel. The car began
careening to the right. He hitched the wheel around until the
car was on course again. His head was pounding like his
heart now, with gigantic, throbbing spasms. He started coughing as he gagged on dripping blood.

The dirt road ended suddenly, the car regained momentum
on the pavement and he dared to look at the rearview mirror.
The truck was slowed down but was still behind him, rocking
like a freighter on a storm-tossed sea, its huge tires scouring
up a pall of dust. Mann shoved in the accelerator pedal and

his car surged forward. A good, steep grade lay just ahead; he'd gain that distance now. He swallowed blood, grimacing at the taste, then fumbled in his trouser pocket and tugged out his handkerchief. He pressed it to his bleeding lip, eyes fixed on the slope ahead. Another fifty yards or so. He writhed his back. His undershirt was soaking wet, adhering to his skin. He glanced at the rearview mirror. The truck had just regained the highway. *Tough!* he thought with venom. Didn't get me, did you, Keller?

His car was on the first yards of the upgrade when steam began to issue from beneath its hood. Mann stiffened suddenly, eyes widening with shock. The steam increased, became a smoking mist. Mann's gaze jumped down. The red light hadn't flashed on yet but had to in a moment. How could this be happening? Just as he was set to get away! The slope ahead was long and gradual, with many curves. He knew he couldn't stop. Could he U-turn unexpectedly and go back down? the sudden thought occurred. He looked ahead. The highway was too narrow, bound by hills on both sides. There wasn't room enough to make an uninterrupted turn and there wasn't time enough to ease around. If he tried that, Keller would shift direction and hit him head on. "Oh, my God!" Mann murmured suddenly.

He was going to die.

He stared ahead with stricken eyes, his view increasingly obscured by steam. Abruptly, he recalled the afternoon he'd had the engine steam-cleaned at the local car wash. The man who'd done it had suggested he replace the water hoses, because steam-cleaning had a tendency to make them crack. He'd nodded, thinking that he'd do it when he had more time. *More time!* The phrase was like a dagger in his mind. He'd failed to change the hoses and, for that failure, he was now about to die.

He sobbed in terror as the dashboard light flashed on. He glanced at it involuntarily and read the word HOT, black on red. With a breathless gasp, he jerked the transmission into low. Why hadn't he done that right away! He looked ahead. The slope seemed endless. Already, he could hear a boiling throb inside the radiator. How much coolant was there left? Steam was clouding faster, hazing up the windshield. Reaching out, he twisted at a dashboard knob. The wipers started flicking back and forth in fan-shaped sweeps. There had to be enough coolant in the radiator to get him to the top. *Then* what? cried his mind. He couldn't drive without coolant, even downhill. He glanced at the rearview mirror. The truck was falling behind. Mann snarled with maddened fury. *If it weren't for that goddamned hose, he'd be escaping now!*

The sudden lurching of the car snatched him back to terror. If he braked now, he could jump out, run, and scrabble up that slope. Later, he might not have the time. He couldn't make himself stop the car, though. As long as it kept on running, he felt bound to it, less vulnerable. God knows what would happen if he left it.

Mann started up the slope with haunted eyes, trying not to see the red light on the edges of his vision. Yard by yard, his car was slowing down. Make it, make it, pleaded his mind, even though he thought that it was futile. The car was running more and more unevenly. The thumping percolation of its radiator filled his ears. Any moment now, the motor would be choked off and the car would shudder to a stop, leaving him a sitting target. *No,* he thought. He tried to blank his mind.

He was almost to the top, but in the mirror he could see the truck drawing up on him. He jammed down on the pedal and the motor made a grinding noise. He groaned. It had to make the top! Please, God, help me! screamed his mind. The ridge was just ahead. Closer. Closer. Make it. "Make it." The car was shuddering and clanking, slowing down—oil, smoke, and steam gushing from beneath the hood. The windshield wipers swept from side to side. Mann's head throbbed. Both his hands felt numb. His heartbeat pounded as he stared ahead. Make it, please, God, make it. Make it. *Make* it!

Over! Mann's lips opened in a cry of triumph as the car began descending. Hand shaking uncontrollably, he shoved the transmission into neutral and let the car go into a glide. The triumph strangled in his throat as he saw that there was nothing in sight but hills and more hills. Never mind! He was on a downgrade now, a long one. He passed a sign that read, TRUCKS USE LOW GEARS NEXT 12 MILES. Twelve miles! Something would come up. It had to.

The car began to pick up speed. Mann glanced at the speedometer. Forty-seven miles an hour. The red light still burned. He'd save the motor for a long time, too, though; let it cool for twelve miles, if the truck was far enough behind.

His speed increased. Fifty . . . 51. Mann watched the needle turning slowly toward the right. He glanced at the rearview mirror. The truck had not appeared yet. With a little luck, he might still get a good lead. Not as good as he might have if the motor hadn't overheated but enough to work with. There had to be some place along the way to stop. The needle edged past 55 and started toward the 60 mark.

Again, he looked at the rearview mirror, jolting as he saw that the truck had topped the ridge and was on its way down. He felt his lips begin to shake and crimped them together. His gaze jumped fitfully between the steam-obscured highway and the mirror. The truck was accelerating rapidly. Keller doubtless had the gas pedal floored. It wouldn't be long before the truck caught up to him. Mann's right hand twitched unconsciously toward the gearshift. Noticing, he jerked it back, grimacing, glanced at the speedometer. The car's velocity had just passed 60. Not enough! He had to use the motor now! He reached out desperately.

His right hand froze in mid-air as the motor stalled; then, shooting out the hand, he twisted the ignition key. The motor made a grinding noise but wouldn't start. Mann glanced up, saw that he was almost on the shoulder, jerked the steering wheel around. Again, he turned the key, but there was no response. He looked up at the rearview mirror. The truck was gaining on him swiftly. He glanced at the speedometer. The car's speed was fixed at 62. Mann felt himself crushed in a vise of panic. He stared ahead with haunted eyes.

Then he saw it, several hundred yards ahead: an escape route for trucks with burned-out brakes. There was no alternative now. Either he took the turnout or his car would be rammed from behind. The truck was frighteningly close. He heard the high-pitched wailing of its motor. Unconsciously, he started easing to the right, then jerked the wheel back suddenly. He mustn't give the move away! He had to wait until the last possible moment. Otherwise, Keller would follow him in.

Just before he reached the escape route, Mann wrenched the steering wheel around. The car rear started breaking to the left, tires shrieking on the pavement. Mann steered with the skid, braking just enough to keep from losing all control. The rear tires grabbed and, at 60 miles an hour, the car shot up the dirt trail, tires slinging up a cloud of dust. Mann began to hit the brakes. The rear wheels sideslipped and the car slammed hard against the dirt bank to the right. Mann gasped as the car bounced off and started to fishtail with violent whipping motions, angling toward the trail edge. He drove his foot down on the brake pedal with all his might. The car rear skidded to the right and slammed against the bank again. Mann heard a grinding rend of metal and felt himself heaved downward suddenly, his neck snapped, as the car plowed to a violent halt.

As in a dream, Mann turned to see the truck and trailer swerving off the highway. Paralyzed, he watched the massive vehicle hurtle toward him, staring at it with a blank detachment, knowing he was going to die but so stupefied by the sight of the looming truck that he couldn't react. The gargantuan shape roared closer, blotting out the sky. Mann felt a strange sensation in his throat, unaware that he was screaming.

Suddenly, the truck began to tilt. Mann stared at it in choked-off silence as it started tipping over like some ponderous beast toppling in slow motion. Before it reached his car, it vanished from his rear window.

Hands palsied, Mann undid the safety belt and opened the door. Struggling from the car, he stumbled to the trail edge, staring downward. He was just in time to see the truck capsize like a foundering ship. The tanker followed, huge wheels spinning as it overturned.

The storage tank on the truck exploded first, the violence of its detonation causing Mann to stagger back and sit down clumsily on the dirt. A second explosion roared below, its shock wave buffeting across him hotly, making his ears hurt. His glazed eyes saw a fiery column shoot up toward the sky in front of him, then another.

Mann crawled slowly to the trail edge and peered down at the canyon. Enormous gouts of flame were towering upward, topped by thick, black, oily smoke. He couldn't see the truck or trailer, only flames. He gaped at them in shock, all feeling drained from him.

Then, unexpectedly, emotion came. Not dread, at first, and not regret; not the nausea that followed soon. It was a primeval tumult in his mind: the cry of some ancestral beast above the body of its vanquished foe.

Shoofly

· · · · · · · · · · · · · ·

A fly descended in an arcing plummet, landing on the desk top, several inches from the edge of Pressman's right hand.

Automatically, he made a brushing movement toward it, and the fly appeared to leap up, soaring into the air.

Pressman continued reading the contract, then stopped to raise his left hand from the desk and make a thrusting motion with it, so the edge of his shirtsleeve was pulled back from his watch. Thirteen minutes after twelve. Typical of Masters. *My money, your wait.*

Pressman laid aside his pen to knead the back of his neck, wincing at the pain it caused. A headache in the offing? Maybe he should take another aspirin.

His laugh was like a cough. God forbid he nicked himself. His blood was doubtless nearing the consistency of water after all the aspirin he'd been downing in the past few weeks.

He closed his eyes and rubbed them, groaning softly. *Come on,* Masters.

Something touched the back of his right hand, and he twitched, eyes opening in time to see the fly take off and disappear again. "You little shit," he muttered.

He turned his high-backed chair to face the window. The fly was on the windowsill. At first it didn't move. Then as Pressman watched intently, it began to stroke its legs together.

Little swine, he thought, *your legs and body swarming with germs.* Unconsciously, he rubbed the fingers of his left hand on the back of his right.

He checked his watch again. Close to quarter after. *See you at noon, then,* he heard Masters' supercilious voice in his head. Sure, Ed. In a pig's patootie.

He stared at the fly, wondering if it was conscious of his observation. They didn't see the same way people did. *Compound.* The word floated up in recollection. Pressman smiled without amusement. A single strand of memory left over from Biology I. Six-sided lenses, four thousand of them in each eye. No wonder you could never sneak up on them.

There was a soft knock on the door, and Pressman turned his chair back, conscious, as he did, of the fly taking off.

Doreen was peering in. "I'm going to lunch, Mr. Pressman." He nodded, and she began to close the door, then opened it again as Pressman asked, "Did Masters call about our meeting?"

"No, sir." She shook her head.

He sighed. "I guess I won't be having lunch today."

Doreen smiled politely and closed the door. *A lot you care,* Pressman thought. He grimaced at a stabbing pain in his stomach. Much good it would do him to have lunch, anyway. His innards were, as usual, filigreed with cobwebs of gas.

Picking up his pen, he started looking at the Barker contract once again. May as well do something useful while he waited for Masters to arrive.

The fly blurred across his eyeline, then dropped to the desk. "Get out o' here," he muttered, slapping at it backhand. The fly sailed upward. "And stay away," he told it. Go find a garbage can to sit in.

He tried to concentrate on the contract, but a twinge of discomfort hit his stomach again and he straightened up, a tight expression on his face. He looked across his office toward the small refrigerator underneath the bar. *A glass of milk,* he told himself. *Coat your stomach walls with soothing primer.*

Pushing back his chair, he saw the dark form of the fly swoop down and land on the contract. "Good, *you* read it," he muttered, standing. He walked to the refrigerator, leaned over, and opened its door. Removing a half-pint container of milk, he opened the spout with difficulty, tearing it. He picked up a glass from the bar and held it over the sink, pouring milk into it, spilling some because of the torn spout. "Son of a bitch," he muttered.

Returning to the desk, he saw that the fly was still on the contract, rubbing its legs together. *Don't worry about getting shit on the contract,* he addressed it in his mind. *It's a piece of shit already.*

He sat on his chair and the fly was gone. *Jesus Christ, they move fast,* he thought. He took a sip of milk and set the glass down, looking at his watch again. *You bastard,* he thought. *What do you care if I'm stuck here, tuning up an ulcer?*

He picked up his pen and started reading the contract, then slammed his pen down, grabbed the glass of milk, and spun his chair toward the window. The throbbing in his head was getting worse. Pressman took another sip, and stared out at the city. *Gray,* he thought. *Cheerless.* "Like my life," he heard himself say.

He kneaded the back of his neck some more, teeth set against the pain.

Your neck muscles need retoning, Roy, he heard Dr. Kirby's voice. *Do some isometrics or they'll atrophy.*

"Thank you, Dr. Kirby," he muttered and then slapped down at his left leg with a look of sudden anger as the fly landed on it. Pressman groaned as pain exploded in his head.

Gradually, the pain diminished and he turned his chair back to the desk, setting down the glass. Maybe he should just forget about waiting for Masters. *Sure thing,* he told himself. *Who needs a two-hundred-thousand-dollar deal?*

The headache was expanding. Pressman closed his eyes. If only he—

He jerked his right hand as the fly came down on it. His eyes jumped open, but the fly had already gone. "Son of a *bitch,*" he muttered. *God,* he hated flies. Always had. Filthy vermin. Strolling on crap, then on our Caesar salads.

Just try to calm down, will you? he told himself. He looked at the glass of milk. Maybe he could plop two Alka-Seltzers in it, fizz it up. Combination Cocktail, Executive-style.

The fly came swooping down and lighted on his desk beside the glass of milk. He eyed it somberly. And knew.

He had to kill it.

Pressman drew in a long, slow breath. Odd that he'd been watching it with not quite idle curiosity but certainly without intent. Absorbed in more integral matters, true—Masters' insulting tardiness, the Barker contract, his afflictions. But to miss the obvious, it now seemed obvious, at least. That was odd. "Mr. Fly, you have to die," he announced.

He looked around. Weapon of choice? He grunted with amusement. Barker's contract might be good. He visualized Barker's bushy eyebrows raising as he caught sight of a dab of fly guts partially obscuring Paragraph Three, Item One. No, better not.

Carefully, he reached to his right and eased open the middle drawer of his desk. The prospectus for Shipdale Industries? Perfect. Thin enough to fold with ease, thick enough to splatter Mr. Fly to hell with one sharp, downward blow. *"Yeah,"* he muttered, grinning. *Say your prayers, you little bastard. Old Mortality is on his way. Your guts are mine.*

Pressman drew out the prospectus with extreme slowness. *Take your time,* he told himself. Patience must predominate. Let the prey grow overly secure, slicking up his goddamn hairy little legs. He folded the prospectus once, the long way. Prospectus of Doom. He repressed another grin. *It descended from the Heavens like a Juggernaut of paper-plastic, smashing Mr. F. to that giant Shit Pile in the Sky.*

He kept his gaze fixed on the fly. They have to take off backward, he recalled. Have to snap the Juggernaut Prospectus well behind it, catch that little ass as it was zooming upward to the rear.

Pressman clenched his teeth, grimacing. No. The fly was too close to the glass; he might shatter it and splash milk everywhere, soak the contract. Wouldn't do.

He narrowed his eyes, considered. The hunter must outwile the hunted. And outwait him. Reaching out, he flicked the fingers of his right hand toward the fly. It shot up, vanishing. Pressman felt a pang of anxious disappointment. He shook it off. *He'll be back,* he reassured himself. He leaned back in his chair and waited. *The Great White Hunter hunkered in the long grass, slitted eyes observing, weapon on his lap, primed to fire.* Pressman chuckled at the image.

The fly did not return. Pressman scowled and checked his watch. Jesus Christ. Twelve fucking thirty soon. He should have had Doreen call Masters' office moments prior to noon to make sure he was coming.

Pressman found himself gazing at the standing photographs along the back edge of his desk. Brenda. Laurie. Ken. He reached inside his jacket to withdraw the pack of cigarettes. One left. Nineteen additional nails driven, without hesitation, into his coffin. He lit the cigarette and tossed the crumpled package into the wastebasket. Exhaling smoke, he looked around. Well, damn it, where'd he go? Hiding, is he? Skulking in the brush?

What if it's a female? he thought. Pregnant. With a bellyful of eggs. Jesus. Now he really had to kill it. Prevent those dozens—*hundreds*, maybe—of baby flies from fouling up the office. Leprous maggots wriggling on his drapes and carpeting. The image nauseated him.

He stared, again, at the photographs. When was the last time he did that? Ages. They were backdrop, nothing more. Life props. Decoration. Yet here he was staring at them.

At Brenda: forty-one, red-haired (courtesy of rinses, not of nature), five foot six, a hundred fifty pounds; *un*pleasantly plump, he'd felt an urge to tell her for some time now. Vestiges of that bright face he'd gone ape-shit over eighteen years ago. Now overlaid with that unpleasant "We are not amused" look.

He looked around in irritation. "Well, where the hell *are* you, you little shit?" he asked the unseen fly. "You're not gonna get away from me, so let's stop the horseplay and *land*."

He closed his eyes, wincing. The headache again. "Screw it." Pulling out the top drawer of his desk, he plucked up the aspirin bottle, pried off its cap, and shook the last two tablets from inside. He'd finished the new bottle *already*?

He washed the aspirin down with a sip of milk and set the glass back on the desk. "A-*ha*. Now we've got the means."

He submerged the tip of his right index finger into the milk, then dabbed a smear of it across the top of his desk. *Bait.*

He leaned back in his chair again. *Give up, beast; surrender; there is no escape. With any luck, you'll reincarnate in twenty seconds anyway.*

Pressman took a deep pull on the cigarette and coughed. *Like a goddamn furnace blast inside my mouth and throat.* With sudden anger, he stabbed his cigarette into the ashtray, mashing it to a pulp of paper and tobacco. "Kill you before you kill me," he muttered.

He looked for the fly. No sign of it. *Well, I can wait, you little creep,* he thought. *I have a brain. You have shit flecks on your legs. No contest. You're a goner.*

He looked at Brenda's photograph again. Jesus, what a pointless life this woman led! "Well, hell, she's done her time," he said sardonically. God knew she reminded him of it often enough. "I've done my time, Roy." As though their marriage and her motherhood had been twenty years in stir.

He wondered if she was having an affair. Timewise, highly feasible. Assuming she could steal some Magic Moments from her quest to purchase every goddamn female adornment in the city.

He stared at Laurie's photograph. *Need an update there,* he thought, a sense of cold embitterment twisting at him. This photo was thirteen-year-old Laurie Ann: Daddy's girl, the angel, the delight. Pre-high school, pre-sexual experimentation. Pressman scowled. Pre-abortion. Pre-the moody, withdrawn specter of that former Laurie who now drifted mutely through the house, a look of sour estrangement ingrained on her no-longer-pretty face.

And Ken. He glared at the photograph of his son. Grades in permanent residence in the cellar. Car impounded, insurance canceled, accident trial impending. Drugs? What else? There'd been the short-term bout with marijuana. Now what was it? Cocaine? That angry energy seemed far more chemical than natural. He and Ken had, once, had a relationship as well. No more. *Jesus fucking Christ, did anything work out in life?!* ·

A darting movement crossed his eyeline. The fly was back on the desk. Pressman didn't hesitate this time, slapping at it, backhand, with the folded prospectus. Even as he swung, he knew he'd miss. The fly had sailed up out of sight at least a second before the folded plastic smacked the desk. "God *damn*," he snarled. His head snapped around as he searched for the fly.

There it was, on the back edge of the desk. Pressman pushed up slowly to his feet. *All right, you shit.* He raised the prospectus carefully. *Mr. Fly, your life is at its walloping, squishy end. Right—*

"—now!" he cried, swinging downward, concentrating on putting a hard snap on the folded prospectus. "*Got* ya!" he exulted through clenching teeth.

He looked at the desk, smile fading. *Wait a second,* said a voice inside his head, perplexed, offended. He looked at the prospectus. Nothing.

"How could I miss?" he muttered. "How the fucking hell could I *miss*?"

He winced. Those pains in his gut again, midgets slashing at his stomach walls with razor blades. "God," he said. He closed his eyes. The headache had swelled, too. "God damn it, one thing at a time!" he ordered his body. He drew in a shaking breath and couldn't seem to get enough air into his lungs.

Pressman opened his eyes. The fly was on the desk again, near the dab of milk. With a grimace, he slammed down the prospectus, barely missing the glass, completely missing the fly. It darted upward, out of sight, then, diving down again, was back, perched on the desk once more. "You son of a bitch," Pressman muttered. *You're playing with me, aren't you? This is recreation in your goddamn little world.* Elude the Prospectus. Piss off the Executive. The Sport of Flies.

He held the prospectus tightly. This time he would not be premature. This time, he would be more cunning. He raised the prospectus slowly and with infinite precision. *The hunter raised his weapon,* said his mind. *Fuck off!* he yelled at it. The fly stood motionless. *Does he see what I'm doing?* Pressman wondered. *Is his little bastard fly face grinning with anticipation?*

Pressman swung down as quickly as he could, well behind the standing fly. Too late; it shot up in the air. "Bastard!" Pressman cried. "You miserable, fucking little bastard!" His shoulders jerked around as he searched for the fly's location.

It was on the windowsill again. Pressman lunged, smashing the prospectus downward, missing. The fly swept over to the desk again, descended, landing. Pressman hurled the prospectus, hitting the glass. It skidded across the desk top, spouting milk, then toppled off the edge. "God *damn* it!" Pressman raged.

He had to stop, bend over, both hands on the desk top, bracing himself. His head was pounding. It felt as though it were expanding and contracting like a fire-driven bellows. Pressman groaned. The pains were slashing at his stomach even more. He slumped back in his chair. *Control,* he told himself. He closed his eyes, breath laboring. *That's right, have a fucking heart attack,* he thought. *That's all you need.* That bastard Masters. If he'd only come on time.

Pressman swallowed. *Throat's so dry,* he thought, opening his eyes. He started to reach for the glass of milk. *It's gone, you idiot,* he mocked himself. Lying on the floor. Should he pick it up and dry the carpeting? Fuck it. Let Doreen.

"Oh, shit," he murmured. There were splashes of milk across the Barker contract. He pulled out his handkerchief and laid it, open, on the page, watched spots appear on it. He closed his eyes and rubbed them hard. When they refocused, he saw the fly. It was sitting on his handkerchief. *Sucking up milk spots with his damned proboscis,* he thought.

He looked intently at the fly. He had to kill it; that was certain. Destroy it utterly. His problems would be solved if—

Pressman winced. His problems solved if he could kill the fly? That was insane.

Still, it had a kind of dark charm. Wouldn't it be great if all his problems were encapsulated in that grubby little shit-devouring creep of an insect; that sawed-off, pulsating, hairy, silk-winged, goddamn, crazy-making—!

Whoa, he told himself. *This is a fly, Roy.* Not the Cosmic Nemesis. A fly. A dirty, little fly. Period. Pressman didn't move. He watched the fly. It wasn't much, God knew. Dirty. Stupid. Driven. Insignificant. Still, it had him on the run. He grunted with amusement. *What are flies, anyway?* he wondered. *Why the hell do they exist at all? Did God create them just to plague us? Make us sick?* What was their goddamn raison d'être?

Pressman drew in a quivering breath and shuddered. He felt a tingling underneath his skin as though low-wattage current were being transmitted through his flesh. Odd sensation. Anticipation, was it? Excitement at the prospect of destroying Mr. Fly?

Not with the prospectus, though. He shook his head in disapproval. Too stiff; no flexibility. *My kingdom for a swatter,* Pressman thought. He looked around. "Ah," he said. He pushed up sharply, shoving back his chair against the wall. The fly buzzed off the desk. *Didn't like that, did you, little shit?* Pressman thought.

He picked the newspaper off the sofa and fingered through its sections. World and National News? Local News? Theater? Financial? His laugh was like a seal bark. Sports! How perfect. The sport of kings was not horse racing after all; it was fly splatting. Pressman turned slowly, folding the Sports section with great care so it was broader at the end than at the handle. He hefted it. *A goodly weapon, sirrah,* said his mind. *The lethal smite shall be simplicity itself.* He'd hit the fly so hard the little bastard would have newsprint on his hairy ass.

"Okay, Mr. Fly. Prepare to die," he rhymed. He told himself that it was cool amusement in his voice, not vengeful hatred. Told himself the shaking of his hands was natural; the ongoing tingle of his flesh, a normal sign of keen anticipation; the trembling of his breath, no more than might be expected.

The fly was on the handkerchief again. *Perfect,* Pressman thought. *He cannot resist the milk-soaked landing strip on Barker Field.* His mushy death was nigh.

Pressman's pace diminished to an inching, ministepped advance, his gaze fixed, steady and unblinking, on the fly. *The prey continues feeding,* the PBS narrator in his brain intoned, *unaware of the approaching stalker, so intent on sucking moo juice up its snout that—*

Pressman stopped to contain his snicker. *Cut it out,* he told himself. *This is serious fucking business.* He nodded in agreement. *Right,* he thought. *Advance. Prepare for decimation.*

He moved up slowly on the desk, winced. Surely the fly must see him now with one of those eight thousand goddamn lenses. Pressman clenched his teeth and held his breath, edging closer. *Time to meet your Maker, Fly-boy (girl).*

Pressman lunged, slamming down the folded pages on the handkerchief. *Gotcha!* No sign of escaping flight; the little shit was history. Pressman sang, "Dingdong, the fly is dead!"

The body wasn't on the handkerchief. He stiffened, flipping over the newspaper section. *Oh, now, wait a second.* "*I-did-not-see-him-fly-away,*" he said through gritting teeth.

His eyes moved quickly, an expression of incredulous denial on his face. The fly was standing on the left rear corner of the desk, unharmed, unflustered. *Jesus Christ Almighty,* Pressman thought. He swore to God he didn't see it—

"Wait a second, *wait* a second, let's not—" His agitated voice broke off. He raised the folded newspaper.

The fly shot up and veered away. Amazingly, Pressman's leaping gaze was able to track it to its landing on the drape. Jesus Christ, it looked bigger now. Pressman scowled at the impression. Against the beige drape, it was an optical illusion, nothing more. He started around the desk, gaze fastened on the fly.

He grunted in startled alarm as his right foot stepped on the fallen glass. It rolled beneath his shoe, throwing him off balance, causing him to flail toward the desk. The elbow of his right arm crashed on the desk top. Pressman cried out at the pain, a look of wide-eyed, staring shock contorting his features as he flopped down on the carpeting. "*Jesus Christ Almighty.*" Pressman's voice was breathless and agonized as he clutched the elbow, the newspaper swatter dropping from his fingers. He lay sprawled across the carpeting, eyes closed, face a twisted mask. Jesus, Jesus, *Jesus*! It felt as though his head was near explosion.

It took some minutes for the throbbing ache to fade. Pressman felt tears dribbling down his cheeks, forced out from underneath the lids by pain. *Dear* God, he kept thinking over and over.

Finally, he opened his eycs. Thc first thing hc saw was the fly still on the drape. Pressman felt a welling surge of hatred deep inside himself. *You bastard, you,* he thought. *You lousy, mother-fucking son-of-a-bitch bastard!*

He started to push up, almost setting down his right hand on the fallen glass. *Sure!* his mind exploded. Snatching up the glass, he hurled it to his left, wincing at the streak of pain inside his elbow. He heard the glass break shatteringly against the wall. *Good!* he thought. *Let that bitch pick up the pieces!*

He was balanced on his knees now, wavering slightly, gaze locked on the fly. *Its little claws are buried in the drape,* he thought. Was it happy? Giddy with delight because he'd seen his hunter topple? "Bastard," Pressman muttered. "You are going to *die*." He knew his tone was aberrant. He didn't care. He reached down to grab the folded newspaper, wincing again at the elbow pain. Jesus Christ, did he break it? A half-made smile peeled back his lips. *With my luck, yes.*

He stood up slowly. *Never mind,* he told himself. It didn't matter. Broken elbow, fractured skull, obliterated spine, it wouldn't matter. With his final, dying breath, he'd kill that fucking little bastard.

He edged up toward the window, leaning backward. Gaze unmoving, he raised the folded paper slowly, swung so hard it made him grunt. The fly sailed out, then in, and landed on the drape again. Pressman smacked at it with the newspaper, missed. It skimmed away, buzzing loudly. Pressman slapped the folded paper at it, trying to hit it in the air. It soared up, landing on the drape above his head, beyond his reach.

"*Oh*, no!" Pressman's features contorted with rage. Clutching upward at the drape, he yanked down hard. The rod brace snapped off from the wall; the drape came thrashing down.

"God *damn* you!" Pressman whirled, his look deranged.

The fly was landing on the desk again. Good God, it *did* look bigger. "No!" he snarled. He leaped at the desk and started smashing at the fly in midair as it flew, down on the desk when it landed. He paid no attention to the photographs he knocked across the carpeting. "You bastard, *die!*" he shouted, swinging with maddened rage. He hit the water thermos, and it bounced to the floor, rolled floppingly across the carpeting. The Barker contract and his handkerchief went sailing next. *Fuck 'em!*

The fly had vanished. Pressman stopped and tried to listen for its buzzing flight. But his breathing was too loud, his chest heaving as he sucked in breath. He swallowed dryly. *"Damn,"* he muttered. *"Damn."* This wasn't funny anymore. The fly *did* represent his troubles now. *And I will not go off the fucking edge at forty-seven, driven by a goddamned insect!* His head jerked from side to side as he searched for it. He paid no attention to the shooting pains in his neck, the fiery stabbing in his stomach, the quick expansion and contraction of his head. *Only one thing matters now. One thing—*

The thought broke off; he flashed a death's-head grin. The fly was on the sofa, black against the beige upholstery. *Thank God the decorator talked me out of dark brown,* he thought, advancing.

He closed in on the sofa, pushed aside the coffee table with his right leg. *Got you now,* he thought. He felt his heartbeat getting faster. *Good. Get that damned adrenaline rushing.* He nodded jerkily, the death's-head grin frozen to his lips. *You bastard, you are going to die. To die!*

He flung himself at the sofa, using his entire body as a weapon, snapping the newspaper swatter as he fell. The fly swept upward to his left; he heard it bounce off the shade of the end table lamp, drop downward to the table. He lunged at it, his shredding swatter brandished high. It slapped down loudly on the table. Pressman snarled, elated. *"Yeah!"* He couldn't believe his eyes. The fly was in the air again, settling quickly on the lampshade. Pressman didn't hesitate. Lurching up, he swung the paper swatter sideways, slamming it against the shade. The lamp went crashing to the floor; the

fly went darting off. *"God damn you!"* Pressman screamed.
He slung the newspaper pages at the fly. They opened up and
flapped to the carpeting like a wounded bird. Pressman
twisted around in rabid fury. Where the hell *was* it? *Where?!*
"God damn you." He could barely speak. He felt a dash of
spittle on his chin and slapped it off, eyes wild as he continued searching.

He saw a movement in the mirror hung above the bar and
zeroed in his gaze. For a fraction of a second, he believed
that there were now *two* flies and felt a chill rush up his back
along the spine. Then he scowled in fury at his own stupidity,
realizing that it was only a reflection of the fly, darting
around in tight, concentric circles above the bar, its buzzing
clearly audible. Pressman started toward the bar. *Wait!* a
voice warned in his mind. He had no weapon now. He looked
around in desperate need. No time to waste! Another newspaper section? That was no improvement. A folded magazine?
No better than the prospectus.

"God damn it, I've got to have *something*!" he muttered
frenziedly.

Yes! He virtually dived at the sofa, landing on it with his
left knee, snatching up a pillow. Good! More hitting area! He
shoved up backward to his feet, almost losing balance as he
turned toward the bar. He staggered briefly, then regained
himself and stalked in on the bar, eyes unmoving, gaze narrowed at the circling fly. *Now, you bastard; now.* He winced
at the sobbing noise his indrawn breath made. *Easy,* he ordered. *Don't let it get away now.* The two flies coalesced with
a movement so abrupt he couldn't follow it. The fly was on
the mirror. "Now," he mumbled. "Here I come."

Pressman gripped the pillow corner hard, fingers digging in
like talons. He swung at the mirror, hit it. The fly took off.
He swung again, knocking a bottle of scotch against a stand
of glasses, smashing them. *"You—!"* He couldn't finish,
swinging at the fly again, trying to knock it out of the air.
Another bottle crashed, more glasses. The fly was on the mirror once again. Pressman swung the pillow fiercely in backhand smash that knocked the mirror askew. The fly came out

so swiftly from its surface that it glanced off Pressman's cheek. He howled in sickened fury, swinging the pillow back and forth berserkly in the air, his face a mask of hatred and revulsion. *"Bastard! Stand and fight!"* he shouted.

He saw the fly. The little bastard was back on his desk! Resting. "No, no rest," Pressman muttered, reeling forward. He reached the desk and slammed the pillow down at the fly. He looked at the desk; God damn it, how could he keep *missing*?! He swung the pillow back and forth across the desk, knocking off the penstand set, the paperweight, the cigarette lighter, the lamp and telephone and letter basket—he sent them all tumbling to the floor with vengeful, maniacal cries, lost hold of the pillow so it flew across the office, hitting the door.

Pressman stood immobile, panting, a look of stunned disbelief on his face. The fly was on the window, hanging, motionless. It *wasn't* his imagination; it was bigger. *Bigger.* Jesus Christ in Heaven, *bigger*! It wasn't a fly! It was a—what, a *what*? "Oh, Jesus Christ." Pressman tried but was unable to repress a high-pitched sob. *Good God,* he thought. *It's me.*

It's me.

He slumped down on the chair and pressed his left hand across the eyes. The hand was shaking. *He* was shaking. He'd virtually destroyed his office, all in vain. Just to kill a poor, defenseless—

Pressman's laugh was frightening to him—a choking, demented sound. *Defenseless?* He lowered the hand and looked around his office. Sure, defenseless. As the Antichrist. Lord of the Flies. Wasn't that a nickname for the Devil?

"Shut up," Pressman mumbled to himself. "Shut *up*." He closed his eyes with a feeble moan. His stomach was roiling hotly, burgeoning with acids. His brain was pressing outward at his skull, threatening to crack it open. Every muscle in his neck and shoulders ached with pulsing pain. *I'm going to die. Not the fly. Me.*

He blinked at the buzzing noise, looked down. It wasn't the fly but the telephone. Exhaustedly, he hauled the two parts upward, using the wire, set the cradle on the empty desk, then the receiver down on top of it. The buzzing stopped. He leaned back in the chair. Stiffening as the fly came zooming down and landed on the back of his right hand.

Oh, Jesus, Pressman thought. He couldn't move. His heart was pounding. Couldn't the fly feel it in the veins of his hand? He stared incredulously at it. After all this, on his hand again? His *hand*?

He watched the fly in frozen, breathless silence. It wasn't bigger; it was still the same. That had been a stupid, momentary delusion. Now what, though? There it was in front of him, standing on his hand, for Christ's sake! Did it know? Did it understand that one of them must die? Was it offering itself in sacrifice for the survival of his sanity?

But how? It was blocking his right hand, washing its legs. The prisoner on death row pomading his hair? Or the winner grooming on the giant body of his conquest? Pressman's face distended at the thought. *Don't lose it!* he commanded himself. *This is your last chance. Lose it and you're done.*

Yes, he thought then, smiling. Slowly, he slid his left hand across his lap, gaze fixed on the fly. He mustn't move his right hand, not a tremor's worth. Let him have the right hand. It's his platform, his pulpit. Let him preach his sermon on the fishes and the loaves—in his case, the maggots and the turds. His left hand was the Power and the Glory. Inchingly, he raised his left arm to the level of the chair arm, then slipped its hand across the edge, snaking it down to the left-hand pocket of his suit coat. Thank *God* he didn't have the time to hang it in the closet when he came in this morning.

Pressman reached into the pocket, gaze unmoving on the fly. His fingers gripped the billfold edge and raised it, slowly, from the pocket. Upward—slowly—slowly. Across the arm. *How fitting,* it occurred to him. The weapon: *him.* Ensconced between those leather sides. Driver's license. Social Security. Health and automobile insurance. Membership and credit cards. He even had a reduced Photostat of his birth certificate in there. His life contained within those black walls. Fitting, then, that it should—

Dear God, let it be, he pleaded. He raised the billfold slowly, very slowly. Was it watching him, amused? Was every single goddamn one of those eight thousand lenses focused on his pitiful attempt? After everything he'd tried before, it struck him as beyond belief how truly slow his downward movement was this time. The wallet slapped against his hand, stinging the skin. He saw the fly's dead body tumble off.

Something surged up in him: a cry, a fury, a bestial joy. He shoved back the chair and toppled forward to his knees on the carpeting. The fly lay motionless on its back, legs in the air. With a savage snarl, Pressman reached down, pinching it between the thumb and index finger of his right hand. Lifting it, he laid it on his left palm; then, with a sound he later refused to think about—a lunatic chortling that vibrated in his throat—he pressed down on its body with his right thumb, grinding it to a yellow paste flecked with hair, wing, and leg parts. Even when it was reduced to a smear on his skin, he kept rubbing, teeth clenched, a crazed smile on his lips, the quivering sound in his throat rising steadily in volume. He started, looking up, heartbeat thudding hard. The telephone was ringing. Pressman stared at it as though he didn't understand what it was, as though it was some odd device unknown in his primitive world.

Then he blinked, returning, swallowed, reached up, lifted the receiver, and carried it to his head. "Yes?" he said. Was that his voice? Good God, was that his *voice*? He averted his face and cleared his throat strenuously, then turned back. "Hello?" he said into the mouthpiece.

"That you, Pressman?" asked the voice.

He shuddered. "Yes."

"Masters. Just now noticed, on my calendar, that I was going to stop there on my way to lunch. Too late now; meeting ran on longer than I thought it would. Have to put it off a few days."

Pressman nodded. "Yes."

"No help for it," Masters told him.

"Of course." His voice was back now, its smooth, professional tone. "Listen; these things happen. No point in letting little things disturb us."

"Right," said Masters. "Call you in a day or two."

Pressman kept on nodding. "Yes," he said. "Of course."

He was speaking into a dead receiver; Masters had already hung up. Pressman noticed how his left hand trembled as he set the receiver back in place.

He sat in silence for more than half an hour. Fifteen minutes into it, he noticed the spot on his left palm and wiped it off with a tissue from his desk drawer, threw the tissue into the wastebasket.

At one-sixteen Doreen came back. Pressman tried to tell her not to come in when she knocked, but she opened the door automatically. "I'm back, Mr.—" Pressman felt a biting pain inside his stomach as she looked around the office in astonishment.

He drew in a breath. "A fly," he said. "Drove me nuts before I could kill it."

After she was gone, a coldness gripped at Pressman as he understood her look.

In the seven years they'd rented here, there'd never been a fly inside his office.

"Oh," he murmured. He felt as though he'd just been hollowed out. A fly descended in an arcing plummet, landing on the desk top several inches from the edge of Pressman's right hand.

Somewhere in Time

Theirs was a love that transcended time...

Richard Matheson

A modern man whose love for a woman he has never met leads him back in time to a luxury hotel in 1896 San Diego. There he finds his soul mate in the form of a celebrated actress of the previous century. This classic novel was the winner of the World Fantasy Award for Best Novel, and adapted for the 1979 movie staring Christopher Reeve and Jane Seymour. *Somewhere in Time* remains a classic romance.

"Stylish and gripping, [Richard Matheson's] stories not only entertain but touch the mind and heart." —Dean Koontz

JULY 2008
978-0-7653-6139-4 • 0-7653-6139-6

www.tor-forge.com

TOR

Award-winning authors
Compelling stories

Please join us at the website
below for more information
about this author and other great
Tor selections, and to sign up for
our monthly newsletter!